MARJORIE CELONA

faber and faber

First published in Canada in 2012
by Hamish Hamilton, an imprint of Penguin Canada
First published in the UK in 2013
by Faber and Faber Limited
Bloomsbury House
74–77 Great Russell Street
London WC1B 3DA

Printed and bound by CPI Group (UK) Ltd, Croydon, CR0 4YY

A CIP record for this book
is available from the British Library

ISBN 978–0–571–29495–4

2 4 6 8 10 9 7 5 3 1

For my mom

Y

Y

That perfect letter. The wishbone, fork in the road, empty wineglass. The question we ask over and over. Why? Me with my arms outstretched, feet in first position. The chromosome half of us don't have. Second to last in the alphabet: almost there. Coupled with an L, let's make an adverb. A modest X, legs closed. Y or N? Yes, of course. Upside-downÈpeace sign. Little bird tracks in the sand.

Y, a Greek letter, joined the Latin alphabet after the Romans conquered Greece in the first century—a double agent: consonant and vowel. No one used adverbs before then, and no one was happy.

Part 1

1

My life begins at the Y. I am born and left in front of the glass doors, and even though the sign is flipped "Closed," a man is waiting in the parking lot and he sees it all: my mother, a woman in navy coveralls, emerges from behind Christ Church Cathedral with a bundle wrapped in grey, her body bent in the cold wet wind of the summer morning. Her mouth is open as if she is screaming, but there is no sound here, just the calls of birds. The wind gusts and her coveralls blow back from her body, so that the man can see the outline of her skinny legs and distended belly as she walks toward him, the tops of her brown workman's boots. Her coveralls are stained with motor oil, her boots far too big. She is a small, fine-boned woman, with shoulders so broad that at first the man thinks he is looking at a boy. She has deep brown hair tied back in a bun and wild, moon-grey eyes.

There is a coarse, masculine look to her face, a meanness.

Even in the chill, her brow is beaded with sweat. The man watches her stop at the entrance to the parking lot and wrench back her head to look at the sky. She is thinking. Her eyes are wide with determination and fear. She takes a step forward and looks around her. The street is full of pink and gold light from the sun, and the scream of a seaplane comes fast overhead, and the wet of last night's rain is still present on the street, on the sidewalk, on the buildings' reflective glass. My mother listens to the plane, to the birds. If anyone sees her, she will lose her nerve. She looks up again, and the morning sky is as blue as a peacock feather.

The man searches her face. He has driven here from Langford this morning, left when it was still so dark that he couldn't see the trees. Where he lives, deep in the forest, no sky is visible until he reaches the island highway. On his road, the fir trees stretch for hundreds of feet above him and touch at the tips, like a barrel vault. *This road is like a nave,* he thinks every time he drives it, proud, too proud, of his metaphor, and he looks at the arches, the clerestory, the transept, the choir, the trees. He rolls down his window, feels the rush of wind against his face, in his hair, and pulls onto the highway: finally, the sky, the speed. It opens up ahead of him, and the trees grow shorter and shorter as he gets closer to town; the wide expanse of the highway narrows into Douglas Street, and he passes the bus shelters, through the arc of streetlights, past the car dealership where he used to work, the 7-Eleven, Thompson's Foam Shop, White Spot, Red Hot Video, and then he is downtown, no trees now, but he can finally smell the ocean, and if he had more time he'd drive right to the tip of the island and watch the sun come up over Dallas Road. It is so early but already the women have their thumbs out, in tight, tight jeans, waiting for the men to arrive in their muddy pickups and dented sedans, and he drives past the Dairy Queen, Traveller's Inn, the bright red brick of City Hall, the Eaton Centre. By noon, this street he knows so well will be filled with pale-faced rich kids with dreadlocks down to their knees, drumming and shrieking for change, and a man will blow into a trumpet, an orange toque on his head. Later still, the McDonald's on the corner will fill with teenaged beggars, ripped pant legs held together with safety pins, bandanas, patches, their huge backpacks up against the building outside, skinny, brindle-coated pit bulls and pet rats darting in and out of shirtsleeves, sleeping bags, foam cups, the elderly, so many elderly navigating the mess of these streets, the blind, seagulls, Crystal Gardens, the Helm's Inn, the totem poles as the man drives past the park toward the YMCA, no other cars but his, because it is, for most people, not morning yet but still the middle of the night.

Now, in the parking lot, he is hidden behind the glare from the rising sun in the passenger-side window of his van. He sees my mother kiss my cheek—a furtive peck like a frightened bird—then walk quickly down the ramp to the entrance, put me in front of the glass doors, and dart away. She doesn't look back, not even once, and the man watches her turn the corner onto Quadra Street, her strides fast and light now that her arms are empty. She disappears into the cemetery beside the cathedral. It is August 28th, at five-fifteen a.m. My mother is dead to me, all at once.

The man wishes so badly I weren't there that he could scream it. All his life, he's the one who notices the handkerchief drop from an old woman's purse and has to chase her halfway down the block, waving it like a flag. Every twitch of his eye shows him something he doesn't want to see: a forgotten lunch bag; the daily soup spelled "dialy"; a patent leather shoe about to step in shit. *Wait! Watch out, buster!* All this sloppiness, unfinished business. Me. I'm so small he thinks "minute" when he squats and cocks his head. My young mother has wrapped me in a grey sweatshirt with thumbholes because it's cold this time of day and I'm naked, just a few hours old and jaundiced: a small, yellow thing.

The man unfolds the sweatshirt a bit, searching for a note or signs of damage. There is nothing but a Swiss Army knife folded up beneath my feet. My head is the size of a Yukon Gold potato. The man pauses. He's trying to form the sentences he'll have to say when he pounds on the door and calls for help. "Hey! There's a baby here! A baby left by her mother—I think—I was waiting for the doors to open, she put the baby here and walked away, young girl, not good with ages, late teens, I guess? There's a baby here, right *here*. Oh, I didn't look—" He looks. "It's a girl."

There's a small search. The police mill around and take a description from the man, who tells them his name is

Vaughn and that he likes to be the first in the door at the Y in the morning, that it's like a little game with him.

"Gotta be first at something, guy," he says to the cop. They look at each other and laugh, a little too hard, for a little too long.

Vaughn is wearing his usual garb: navy track pants with a white racing stripe; a T-shirt with a sailboat on the front; new white running shoes. He is still young, in his early thirties, six feet tall with the build of someone who runs marathons. His red hair is thick and wild on top of his head, and he's growing a goatee. It itches his chin. He fiddles with it as he talks to the officer. *What did you see?*

By now Vaughn is used to the way his life works: he is the seer. When the cars collide, he knows it two minutes before it happens. He predicted his parents' divorce by the way his mother's lip curled up once, at a party, when his father told a dirty joke. He was nine. He thought, That's it. That's the sign. It isn't hard, this predicting, if that's what it's called; it's a matter of observation. From the right vantage point—say, overhead—it isn't a matter of psychic ability to see that two people, walking toward each other, heads down, hands in pockets, will eventually collide.

Sir, what did you see?

Vaughn pauses before answering. He feels time slow, and he feels himself float up. From up here, he sees what he needs to: the sequence of events that will befall me if I am raised by my mother. It's all too clear. He wasn't meant to see her. He wasn't meant to intervene. He has seen the look in my mother's eyes; he has seen women like her before. Whatever my fate, he knows I am better off without her.

What exactly did you see?

And so the officer takes down a description of my mother, but he doesn't get it right: Vaughn tells him that her hair was short and blonde, when the truth is that it was swirled into a dark brown bun. (When she takes it out, it falls to her collarbone.) He says she wore red sweatpants and a white tennis sweater—he finds himself describing his own outfit from the day before—and that she didn't look homeless, just scared and young. Maybe a university student, he says. An athletic build, he says.

By now, twenty people have gathered in the parking lot of the Y. Some lady pushes through the crowd of officers and people in track pants. She swirls her arms and her mouth opens like a cave.

"My baby!" she shrieks and sets a bag of empty beer cans in a lump at her feet. Her head jerks. The cops roll their eyes and so does Vaughn. She's the quarter lady—the one who descends when you plug the meter: "Hey, man, got a quarta'?" Her hair is like those wigs at Safeway when you forget to buy a costume for Halloween. If she had wings, she'd look ethereal.

My first baby picture appears in the newspaper. "Abandoned Infant: Police Promise No Charges." Vaughn cuts out the article and sticks it on his fridge. He's embarrassed by one of his quotes—"I believe it's an act of desperation"—and his eyes fill with tears when he reads the passage from Saint Vincent de Paul, which is recited to the press by one of the nurses at the children's hospital: *These children belong*

*to God in a very special way, because they have been
abandoned by their mothers and fathers ... You cannot
have too much affection for them.*

"I believe it's an act of desperation." Vaughn sucks in a
dry breath. The quote makes him cringe and he wishes he
had said nothing at all.

He sits at the foot of his bed, waiting for the phone
to ring. Surely the police have found my mother; it's an
island, after all. There's nowhere to go. Once they find her,
it will only be a matter of time before they get curious and
wonder why his description doesn't match. He sits on the
bed all day and stares at the phone. He stares at it all night.
In the morning, he hoists navy blue sheets over the curtain
rods to block out the light and wedges newspaper under
the door. He sleeps for an hour, dreams that he is hurtling
through four floors of a building on fire.

When he wakes, the room is dark but his eyes are
burning. He closes his eyes and he is falling through the
building again, and when he lands there is blood under his
fingernails.

On his bedside table are a picture of his girlfriend, a
rolled-up magazine for killing spiders, and a triangular
prism. If he opened the curtains, his face would glow a
million colours.

Someone, his neighbour, is playing the piano. Poorly,
absent-mindedly.

He shakes his head.

"I remembered wrong," he tells the room, rehearsing,
but the phone does not ring.

He reaches for the magazine and knocks the prism to

the floor. It doesn't break. He puts the magazine on his lap and spreads its pages in his hands.

"I space out sometimes. Especially in the morning. I must have gotten her mixed up with someone I saw earlier, or the day before."

He watches the phone.

He tries to sleep on his back with a pillow pulled over his eyes. He tries to sleep on his stomach. He buries his head in the bedding like a vole.

"I'm sorry," he says to his empty bedroom, to the image of my mother burned into his mind. "I'm sorry if I did something wrong."

Finally, he tucks the article into one of the scrapbooks he keeps on top of the refrigerator and tries to forget about me, about my mother and his lie. He knows, somehow, that there was an act of love behind the abandonment. He knows, somehow, he wasn't meant to intervene.

A wild card, a ticking time bomb. I could be anyone; I could come from anywhere. I have no hair on my head and there's a vacant look in my eyes, as if I am either unfeeling or stupid.

I weigh a little over four pounds and am placed in a radiant warmer in neonatal intensive care. I test positive for marijuana, negative for amphetamines and methamphetamines. The hospital takes chest X-rays, draws blood from my heel, tests my urine. I do not have pneumonia; I am not infected with HIV. I am put on antibiotics for funisitis, an inflammation of my umbilical cord, and this diagnosis is printed in the newspaper in a final plea for my mother to come forward. She is probably sick, one of the doctors is quoted as saying, and most likely needs treatment. The antibiotics run their course, my mother never appears, and the Ministry of Children and Family Development files for custody.

One of the nurses on the night shift calls me Lily. Her name is Helene, and she is twenty-five years old. She has chestnut-coloured, shoulder-length hair that frizzes when it rains, thick bangs, and a small plump face with a rosebud mouth. She stops by on her breaks and sings me "By a Waterfall."

There's a whippoorwill that's calling you-oo-oo-oo
By a waterfall, he's dreaming, too.

Helene lives alone in an apartment on Esquimalt Road with a view of the ocean. She looks at my tiny face and imagines what her life would be like if she took me home and became my mother. She rearranges her apartment in her mind, puts a bassinet in the small space between her double bed and dresser, replaces one of the foldout chairs at her kitchen table with a high chair. She bakes a Dutch apple pie for me while I watch; all the time she is singing. But Helene meets a man a few weeks later, and her thoughts overflow. She cannot make space for both of us in her mind. She marries the man. They move to Seattle.

I am passed back and forth, cradled in one set of arms and

then another. Once it is safe for me to leave the hospital, I am placed in a foster home.

My new parents don't baptize me because they aren't religious. They name me Shandi and we live in a noisy brown apartment building in a part of the city that has no name. We are on one of two side streets that connect two major streets, which head in and out of downtown. At night we listen to the traffic on one side coming into town, and the traffic on the other side, heading out. There is a corner store a block away, a vacuum repair shop, and a park with a tennis court. City workers come in the morning to clean the public restroom and empty the trash cans, and in the late afternoon, young mothers push strollers down the path, shortcutting to the corner store. At night, the park comes alive. The homeless sleep on the benches or set up tents under the fir trees. The tennis court becomes an open-air market for drugs. In the morning, it is littered with hypodermic needles, buckets of half-eaten KFC, someone's forgotten sleeping bag. Teenagers from the high school down the street play tennis on the weekends, pausing to roll and smoke joints. It is an otherwise beautiful park, with giant rhododendrons, yew hedges in the shape of giant gumdrops, and Pacific dogwoods with dense, bright white flowers. A few long-limbed weeping cedars stand here and there amid a barren grassy field.

My foster father's name is Parez, but he goes by Par. He is satisfied with my meagre medical records but my mother, Raquelle, searches my face and body for abnormalities. The night they bring me home, the neighbours, who have three foster children of their own (*There's good money*

14

in foster care, they'd said), are waiting in their kitchen with a tuna casserole. "This one's got no real father and no real mother," my father, Par, says to them by way of introduction, and sets me on the kitchen table like a whole chicken. "She comes from the moon, from the sky." He spins around, his arms in the air. He is happy and proud.

In the months that follow, Raquelle feeds me shaky spoonfuls of bouillon, mashed carrots with cinnamon, and finally, cubes of cheddar cheese. She sits for hours placing things in my mouth and watching me chew. The kitchen has a sour smell from a gas leak somewhere in the stove, and dark wooden cabinets that reek of turmeric and curry. A few grimy rag rugs line the peeling linoleum floor. I sit in an orange plastic high chair with a dirty white bib around my neck, and take food from Raquelle's delicate hands. She is a tall, lean woman, with straight black hair and an angular face. She is thirty-four. We listen to Lionel Richie on a tiny portable radio. On the weekends, she takes me to the Salvation Army and St. Vincent's, where she tries on huge piles of clothes while I lie in my stroller, smelling the cheap detergent on the clothing and the pungent leather stench from the racks of black, scuffed-up shoes.

As a teenager, Raquelle had a pituitary tumour, and is now infertile. She has wanted a baby for as long as she can remember. She studies her calves, her muscular feet, in the dressing room mirror. We are there for hours.

I don't cry much, and during my first week home Par discovers that I fall asleep if he sings the national anthem, which is all he can think of when Raquelle suggests he sing me lullabies.

"Ohhh, Caaa-na-dah," he croons. He has a face as round as a beach ball, with a thick, almost comical moustache and salt-and-pepper hair that he keeps in a short, tight ponytail. He moved to Canada eight years ago to start a restaurant and marry Raquelle. The restaurant is called, simply, Par's. His English is improving, but he still thinks "true patriot love" is all one word. He sings it fast and doesn't know what it means.

"She's going to be a model," Raquelle decides, because I'm a string-bean baby and a bit longer than average. "Top model. Superstar!"

"Nah," says Par. He is holding me while Raquelle beats the rag rugs over the balcony. He is a decade older than she is, thinks he knows how to raise an industrious, confident girl. For starters, he won't let Raquelle dress me in pink. "I want her to work in trades. That's where the money's at. Plumber, 'lectrician." He dangles my rattle in front of my face, and I grab it expertly in my small hands. "See how good she is with her rattle? Maybe an athlete. Full of sport."

Raquelle sniffs. His English embarrasses her. In her worst moments, she looks at herself in the mirror and thinks that she shouldn't have married him, that she could have done better. "A dancer," she says. "I want her to take ballet. I never got to."

At night, Raquelle and I take the bus downtown and visit Par at the restaurant. He stands behind the host's lectern in a crisp white shirt and red bow tie, his round face beaming. When we walk in he disappears into the kitchen, dries off a small amber snifter, and pours Raquelle a little Turkish raki from a bottle he keeps under the sink. The restaurant has no liquor licence; Par cannot afford it. Raquelle sits at a circular table by the window and feeds me from a jar of maraschino cherries. The restaurant has only one customer, a man in his seventies with deep-set eyes and skin like wax paper. He is hand-rolling a cigarette with loose tobacco and looks over at us.

"Beautiful baby," he says. His voice is low and Raquelle leans in to hear him. "What a lovely family you have."

Par stands behind us, one hand on Raquelle's shoulder, the other holding a mop. "Thank you," he says to the man.

"She looks just like you," the man says back, motioning to my little round face.

Par leans on the mop. The men look at each other for a minute.

Outside, the street is empty. It is ten o'clock. The light from the movie theatre marquee across the street flashes through the glass-block window, brightening the room intermittently. It is a small restaurant, with ten tables. The tables are still perfectly set, except the one where the man with the cigarette is sitting, his napkin in a loose pile on top of his plate. He takes a final sip of water and thanks Par for the meal. On his way out, he nods at Raquelle and me, flips up the collar of his coat and lights his cigarette in the doorway, waiting until the door has closed behind him to blow out the smoke.

"Thank goodness," Par says and makes a big show of wiping his brow. He motions to his one employee, a teenaged girl with a pimple on her forehead. "Go on home now, Liesl. See you tomorrow." We sit there while he mops the floor.

I like to think that if I'd stayed with them, I would have become a ballerina with a pipefitting business on the side, but after a year, Par's restaurant went bankrupt and his brother offered him a job back home.

He is a changed man, angry. He has failed, and now Raquelle and I, too, are a symbol of his failure. After he leaves her, Raquelle starts waiting tables at Scott's downtown, where she worked before she got married. She likes the pink vinyl booths and has missed the handsome cook, who calls her "dearest" and kisses her hand. The restaurant is open twenty-four hours. During her shifts, I am left with the neighbours' foster children, who look after me in exchange for soda pop and comics. We sit on the fire escape and I play with a big tabby cat, who runs his sandpaper tongue over my little hand when I pat him. The children carry me inside and tell me not to make a sound. They view me as a guinea pig or suckerfish—something foreign to be prodded and experimented on—something fascinating, but not at all, not for a second, human.

One day at the restaurant, the cook holds out his hand to Raquelle, a small mound of white powder in the webbing between his thumb and index finger. Pretty soon, that's where her paycheque goes, too.

"I'm real sorry, superstar Shandi," Raquelle says, tapping her nails on the social worker's desk. "But your new parents'll have lots more money than me."

They do. Julian and Moira have me baptized and change my name to Shannon. They are both lawyers. We live on

Olive Street in a periwinkle character house with white trim, in a nice, middle-class neighbourhood two blocks from the ocean. Some of the houses on our block are built to look like ships, porthole windows lining the top floor, curved white walls like windblown sails. Ours is a big, bright house, two storeys, with wainscoting in the living room and an upright piano. A wooden spiral staircase leads upstairs to a master bedroom with cathedral ceilings and an ensuite bathroom with a newly glazed claw-foot tub. My bedroom is across from theirs and is the size of a jail cell. I have a squeaky white crib, a small antique dresser, and a non-working coal-burning fireplace.

It is colder in this part of town, and the air smells of salt and seaweed. The park across from our house is filled with families during the day and empty at night. We have a large front yard and an even bigger backyard; instead of a fence, we have a rock wall. It surrounds the property, save for the entrance, which is marked by an ornate wrought-iron gate, chunks of sea glass wedged between the tracery. A Garry oak takes up most of the front yard, and the back is carefully manicured, a shale stone path leading from the deck to a wooden gazebo with a bench swing.

A week after my new parents bring me home, they have a party to celebrate my arrival. I sleep in Moira's arms while she and Julian share what they know about foundlings. I'm eighteen months old now and although I can walk and say a few words, I still look like a baby. I have yet to grow any hair. To hide my baldness, Moira has knitted me a little cap that looks like a bluebell.

"Some mothers," she is saying, "think their baby is

possessed, and the only way to save it is to kill it." She is tall and stocky with a down-turned mouth. She has curly, chin-length hair and an apple-cheeked face peppered with pale brown freckles. There is something beautiful about Moira—her Scandinavian features, that white translucent skin—but something cagey in her eyes. In photographs, she is often not looking at the camera.

Five of her colleagues are gathered in the living room, all women. Julian mulls wine in the kitchen and talks to a group of men from work with whom he plays racquetball. The soundtrack to the movie *Diva* plays out of large black speakers.

"You know, we looked it up," Julian says and slides a cinnamon stick into the steaming pot. He wears one of Moira's floral aprons. "In the States, twelve thousand babies are abandoned every year—in hospitals. That number doesn't include the trash bins." He snickers, and the men shift their weight.

From the loveseat in the living room, Moira can see her husband stirring the mulled wine. "Don't repeat that awful statistic," she calls.

He isn't a handsome man. Soft in the stomach but skinny everywhere else, and his hair sticks up like a hedgehog's. He looks a bit like a hedgehog, too. Sharp snout, full cheeked. Moira shifts me onto the lap of one of her coworkers and goes into the kitchen to put the cobbler in the oven. Since I arrived, she has rediscovered cooking, and has made molasses cookies and applesauce from a recipe her mother gave her.

The evening drags on too long, and I become fussy.

Julian carries me upstairs and muscles me into my crib, where I wail so loudly that he returns five minutes later and sticks me in the back of the closet.

"Fuck, shut up," he mutters as he comes down the stairs. One of Moira's coworkers hears him and shoots him a look. He takes her hand later, after everyone has had too much to drink, and tells her he has always found her beautiful.

On Sundays, we walk as a family along Dallas Road, down the pebbled beaches, past the world's tallest totem pole, all the way to Ogden Point. If it's not too cold, we walk the length of the breakwater. The salty wind slaps against my face, and the smell of the sea stays on my skin for hours. Sometimes Moira picks me up and I put my little feet on the turquoise guardrail, spread my arms and let the wind blow me back against her.

When my hair finally starts to grow in, it is as soft and white as corn silk. Moira dresses me in her old baby clothes, which are hand-sewn, expensive, and kept in a cedar chest. She takes Polaroid pictures of me in little velvet vests with soft white moons, corduroy overalls, and wide-striped sweaters. My hair glows in the sunlight; I am so well dressed.

When she makes dinner, Moira takes me in her arms, and I press my body into the crook of her hip. It's soft-lit in the kitchen. She likes the lights off. Moira bends and smells the steam and her face glows blue from the gas flame. I touch her cheeks, which are freckled and soft. I twirl her hair in my fingertips. She has such coarse hair; it feels rough in my hands. She puts her face to mine. "Ay-bee-cee-dee-eee-eff-gee. Now what?"

"Aick," I say and she rewards me with a nibble of soft white potato.

On my second birthday, my parents buy me a rocking horse, a marble nightlight shaped like a lighthouse, and the complete set of Beatrix Potter books. While Moira is at work, Julian holds me in one hand and plays the piano with the other. I squirm and fidget. His hands are bony and covered in hair. His fingers hold me too tight.

Sometimes Moira has to work nights, and on these nights Julian insists that I learn how to read. We start with the books *Pat the Bunny* and *Goodnight Moon*, and even though I love petting the fuzzy white bunny and saying "Goodnight, mush" over and over, he grows tired of it and of me. When I see his face loom over mine, the look in his eyes as he points to and sounds out each word, I begin to cry. His teeth are little and coffee stained. The words look like symbols, like hieroglyphics. When he points at the word *the* I stare at him and burst into tears. He forces me into my bed, our evening ruined by my stupidity.

"I can't," he says, when Moira gets home that night, "I can't have her crying all the time."

Moira ties the floral apron around her waist and warms a pot of soup. "Clint said I can have the long weekend off." She scratches the back of her calf with her big toe, and Julian winces—he hates it when she does that. And he hates it when she mentions Clint.

She is called into work at night more and more often. When she gets home I hear her pleading with Julian to calm down while I stare at the glow-in-the-dark stars pasted to the ceiling above my little white bed. Julian has tucked me in so tight I can barely breathe or move my arms.

Is she blind? Is she dumb? I want to tell her how frightened I am of Julian—of being alone with Julian—but I don't yet have the words. I stare into her face. I cry and wail and beat my fists into her soft belly. "What is it, little one?" she says to me. "Why are you so angry?"

One day Julian announces that he is going away for a week, and Moira takes me to Willows Beach. She pushes me on a swing for a few minutes, then stops, stands on her tiptoes, and waves to a man coming toward us. It's her boss, Clint. He's a tall man in a burgundy dress shirt, skinny tie, and black dress pants. He has a sharp face and a long curved neck, like a heron. He's carrying a little girl about my age—two and a half—and we stare at each other from behind the legs of our parents while they talk. She is a confident child, dark-haired and dark-eyed like her father, and I am afraid of her. Moira and Clint walk down the beach together and the girl and I are left to play. We see a garter snake dart in and out of the tall grass, and the dark-haired girl chases it until it disappears somewhere underneath the playground. She begins to cry and Clint reappears, picks her up roughly and puts her in his car. He takes Moira in his arms and kisses her cheek, then bends down and looks at me. I have about an inch of fine white hair on my head and am wearing a little white dress. Clint smiles and says I look like an angel.

When he gets in his car and drives away, Moira gets a look on her face as though she is suddenly in mourning. She stares at me as if I am someone she's seen before but can't quite place. She buys me a root beer–flavoured Popsicle from the concession stand, and I concentrate on eating it before it melts and falls into my lap and ruins the leather seats of her car.

When Julian gets back from his trip, he gives me a stuffed bear wearing a red-and-green-striped scarf. He gives Moira a floor-length camel-hair coat. I hear them yelling one night, then a cold hard slap. After that, we do not see Clint again.

When the weather is nice, Julian rides to work on his bicycle, his briefcase secured to the rattrap with bungee cords. One night he rides home after dark, a ghost on a dimly lit side street. It begins to rain and the temperature drops fast, steaming up the windshield of a car approaching him from behind. The car hesitates at the intersection. Julian is paused at the light. When the car makes a sharp right-hand turn, it catches the wheel of Julian's bicycle and sends him spinning. He hits the curb and is launched off the bike with such force that his back skids along the asphalt before he finally comes to a stop. He stands, curses at the car, which has fled into the night, and pedals the rest of the way home on the sidewalk. The blood on his back sticks to his suit jacket like molasses.

Moira is not home. Between the bars of my little bed, I watch him. I am three years old, my hair a big puff of white cotton, my eyes big and cloudy blue. He strips off his jacket and slowly peels off his shirt, which is caked with deep red blood. He drops it onto the carpet and walks toward me, lifts me into his arms and sets me on his and Moira's bed. He goes into the bathroom and returns with a wet towel and a tub of Vaseline, lies on his stomach and tells me to rub the towel over his back as gently as I can. He finds the remote controls tangled in the sheets and turns on the television, presses Play on the VCR. I play with the blood on his back, running my little fingers down the sides of his spine. He puts a gob of Vaseline in my hands, and I smear it over the blood. I am bored and fidgety and so he makes a game out of it, asks me to draw circles and squares and letters and numbers in the pink gunk. *Cat People* is on the television. We watch it together while I rub his back, and when I wake up it is already morning.

Not long after, Moira finds a deep blue bruise on my thigh. Julian confesses that he has trouble holding me. He says I wiggle out of his arms and drop like a stone. He says he prays for me to be still. At night, he tries to shake off the memory of his father beating his legs with a belt until they buckled and bled. He is a haunted man. He shudders every time I cry.

"Will she ever stop?" he pleads. Moira sits at the edge of their big bed, her head in her hands. The guilt of her affair hangs between them. She will make it up to him, she says. She will make everything okay. What choice does she have? Despite the darkness she sees in him, she cannot imagine her life without him in it, without this solid, beautiful home.

We begin playing a game she calls the Stillness. For every minute I sit still, I am rewarded with a cube of marble cheese. If I sit still for five minutes, I get a square of raspberry-flavoured dark chocolate.

"Concentrate, Shannon," she says to me, tapping my knuckles with a wooden spoon when I break out of the Stillness and begin to move around. "Concentrate and I won't have to hurt your little hand. I don't want to hurt your little hand."

I want to tell her that Julian holds me so tightly that he hurts me, and that is the reason I move around, but I am afraid to say the words. I am not bad, I want to tell her, I am in pain.

"I want you to practise the Stillness for seven minutes now. We're going to work our way up to ten, okay?" She waves her spoon in the air like a magic wand.

At a routine checkup, the family doctor finds purple thumbprints on my limbs. He takes Moira into his office and tells her to make sure she and Julian are gentle with me.

"She's a bit of a Jell-O jiggler," Moira laughs, and the doctor does, too. Moira tells him it's the staircase and my wobbly legs, the way I wrench myself out of Julian's arms.

"She's a very special girl," the doctor says to her. "Take best care of her." He gives me a lion sticker on our way out, and when Moira and I get back in the car she turns to me and says if I can't be still I'll have to go and live with another family.

The longest word in the Oxford English dictionary is *floccinaucinihilipilification*. It means "the action or habit of estimating something as worthless." This is the last thing Julian teaches me before I'm rushed out the door in the arms of a social worker, my little arm in a bright blue cast. One of my fingernails catches on the zipper of the lady's coat, tears, and leaves a bloody trail. Moira stands in the doorway, her face pale. There is nothing in her eyes.

In the backseat of the lady's car is an old video game: Pac-Man. I play it, one-handed, with a boy who is older than me, and he says if I get the keys sticky he'll sock me in the gut. The lady straps me so tightly into the car seat that I can barely breathe. She drives a wood-panelled station wagon and the beige seats are coated in plastic. It smells so strongly of vinyl that I throw up and the boy hits me when he sees what I have done.

I am afraid of the dark. We are led by the hand down a carpeted staircase, and I can't tell whether we're in a church or somebody's basement. Little wooden crosses dot the walls and everywhere I look there's a foam cup with a lipstick smear. The room smells like Hamburger Helper. The man who's holding my hand looks like Raffi, but he speaks in a gruff voice and there's dirt under his nails. There are fifteen cots in rows of five and we each get a blanket and a small pillow. When he lets go of my hand,

I ask him to stay, but my voice is too quiet and the room sucks the sound. *Lights out,* someone says and someone else says, *I don't want to be next to this stinky fucker,* and someone else says, *Shut it,* and that's that. The boy is in the cot next to mine. When my eyes adjust, I can see the whites of his. We watch each other, and when I reach out my hand he whispers, *Baby,* but takes it nonetheless. We fall asleep this way, and all night people come and go.

I am placed in a home the next day, the sixth child in a four-bed home. I share the bottom bunk with a smelly girl who wets the bed. None of us belongs to anyone. The woman who runs the house calls me Samantha, and for a while I think that's my name. I teach the smelly girl to pee in the tub with me before bed, and from then on we are friends. Her mother died while giving birth. The girl plays with my hair at night, and this is what I remember most of all, the feel of her soft nails on my scalp while the other children cry in the bunk above us.

2

The man in the back of the car is my father. His brother is at the wheel and my mother is in the passenger seat, her hand on her belly. Her water has broken and seeps into the seat, moving in ribbons down her thighs and through the thick, rough cotton of her oil-stained coveralls. My father's brother is driving a rusty red '63 Mercury Meteor, white hardtop, with red leather bench seats. The body is so dented it looks like someone beat it with a bat. The heater doesn't work, and my father grabs the Mexican blanket that covers the ripped-up backseat and tucks it around my mother's shaking shoulders. The odometer doesn't work either, and my father's brother judges his speed by feel. He likes to drive fast. He once took a corner so quickly that the passenger door sprung open, loosened from its hinges.

Here they are, in this rattletrap classic car on the night I am born: my father, Harrison; his brother, Dominic; and my mother, Yula. The sun has gone down, and the leather seats are damp and slick from the cold. Yula's belly is so big that for the past month she has been wearing a pair of my father's grimy coveralls. The material is rough on her skin. Her teeth chatter, and she shrieks when Dominic hits a pothole. The car lurches and shakes as they make their way down Mount Finlayson. Yula presses her feet into the floor to keep from falling forward; the road is steep and the car has no seatbelts. She feels warm tears forming in her eyes and fights to stop them. She has to stay focused. There is no time for emotion. Dominic presses the accelerator as far as it will go and the car hiccups into gear, then shoots forward. Yula watches him out of the corner of her eye. The car is dark; the electrical system doesn't illuminate the dash and on this part of the road there are no streetlights. But she can see the outline of his face. Dominic is a hideous man with a shaved head—in all ways larger and uglier than Harrison. He has tried to sleep with her twice. He feels her eyes on his face and turns his head toward her, parts his mouth, and she sees the thick pink of his tongue rolling over his teeth. His breath is as strong and sweet as bourbon.

There is another passenger in this car: my half-brother, Eugene. Swaddled out of sight in the trunk. My mother prays for the car to go faster. She has been able to manage her contractions up until this point but feels a sudden deep pain radiate from within her abdomen and swarm into her belly and around to her back. Her underpants are soaked and she squirms in the seat to get away from the awful cold wetness. My father puts his hands on her shoulders and holds her gently. Her body shakes and she vomits down the front of her coveralls and Dominic, disgusted, floors the accelerator. The wind rushes past them and my mother slams into the passenger door as the car speeds down the treacherous road that runs like a serpent through this cold dark night.

Five days before she gives birth to me, my mother kneels at the edge of a flowerbed, pulling weeds. It is late summer and she is eighteen, seven-and-a-half months pregnant. Her father, Quinn, sits in a deck chair, wearing mirrored sunglasses and smoking a pipe. He has a round, chubby face, a white beard that hugs the lower part of his chin like a stirrup, and a nose that hooks downward. He shouts at Yula's son, Eugene, as the little boy runs back and forth, in and around the flowerbeds. Eugene loves to chase the neighbour's wayward chickens or follow the lawnmower when Harrison snakes and edges it over the grass.

My parents, Yula and Harrison, live together, with my half-brother, Eugene, in a pine cabin on a property adjacent to Goldstream Provincial Park, about twenty minutes up the Malahat, off Finlayson Arm Road. Two homes face each other on the property, Mount Finlayson looming behind them: a flat-roofed, cedar-sided structure with floor-to-ceiling windows, inspired by Frank Lloyd Wright and the hard lines and glass of modernism, the interior walls lined with timber beams to remind them that they were in the woods, *of* the woods—this is the home of my grandfather Quinn, a retired fisherman and amateur cartoonist, his left arm useless and disfigured from a horrific motorcycle crash; and Harrison and Yula's home, about fifty feet toward the stream, a small cabin made of lodge-pole pine, the roof covered on the north side with thick green moss.

Quinn built the cabin for Yula when Eugene was born—she was only sixteen years old—laid sod and a gravel path to connect the two homes, and planted rosebushes and rhododendrons. But everything else that surrounds them is wild: giant black cottonwoods and red alder; the stream rank with dead chum or shimmering with their silver bodies rushing to spawn; six-hundred-year-old Douglas fir. Tourists poke their heads onto the property if they get lost or take a wrong turn on a trail, and the neighbour's dog, Beater, scares the shit out of them with his low growl. Beater's owner runs a grow-op. Their other neighbours, Joel and Edwin, have a scrap yard, and their eleven-acre property is covered in rusted-out tractors and cars. But who can see it. Out here, who can even see the sky.

"Yula." Quinn coughs and shakes his one good arm at my half-brother. "Get the kid out of my roses."

On good days, Quinn and Eugene regard each other as pieces of strange furniture brought in by Yula to add further clutter to the house. Eugene likens his grandfather to a bookshelf put in front of a window, blocking all light, and Quinn thinks the boy is like a footstool pushed carelessly to the centre of the room, a booby trap, something to trip over and skin one's knee. Whirling around them like a dishcloth after dust is Yula, who serves them soup and wonders why her father and son can't see each other as she sees them.

Today, Eugene is collecting sow bugs. He scoops four, five, six of them into a Mason jar with his little hands and shakes them softly. He wears overalls and red gumboots and no shirt. His black hair is slicked behind his ears. While Yula pulls up weeds and throws them into a pile behind her, Eugene runs to the edge of the property, ducks underneath one of the rhododendron bushes, and smears the messy dead flowers into the ground with his feet.

Quinn fiddles with his pipe and looks at the sky. The Snowbirds fly over the two houses, headed toward Dallas Road for some civic celebration. The jets are so loud that he covers his ears. He taps his foot against the metal rail of the chair, raises his good hand, and traces one of the contrails with his finger. A bottle of sleeping pills rests in his pocket, a suicide letter addressed to Yula waiting in an envelope on his desk.

My grandfather, Quinn. How did he get here? In the early sixties, he hopped a freight train west in search of romance and adventure and ended up on a fishing boat, catching shellfish, salmon, and halibut off the coast of Vancouver Island. He lived at the YMCA in Victoria for a few months and then met my grandmother, a woman named Jo, who let him live in an Airstream trailer at the edge of her property, not far from where my parents' pine cabin stands now. Jo and Quinn liked to talk about writing; they both liked James Thurber. Quinn's dream was to publish cartoons in *The New Yorker* one day. They read to each other in the evenings on the porch. They went for long hikes through the forest, and when the trail was wide enough they held hands. Sometimes the view of Mount Finlayson was so stunning that it was impossible to have a proper conversation. One or both of them would become mesmerized by the landscape and whatever point being made was lost. Eventually, Jo sold the Airstream trailer and Quinn moved into the house.

My grandmother, Jo, was a small woman—barely five feet tall—bone thin with a long, elegant neck, her head held slightly forward. She wore her coffee-brown hair cut bluntly at the chin, and her heavy-lidded eyes burned with intelligence. She had inherited the property years ago and lived on it, alone, until Quinn came along. She was a peculiar woman, difficult to classify—Egyptian, people thought, upon first seeing her. In the mornings, she ran a comb through her hair brusquely and walked through the forest in a man's flannel work shirt and corduroy pants, rolled to just above her hiking boots, a travel mug of coffee steaming in her hand. She had one close friend, Luella, but aside from her and Quinn, she seemed to want nothing much to do with the world or its people. "I don't fit in," she said, "except out here."

She was fierce, quick to anger, her temper terrifying and unpredictable, her words deeply damaging when she wanted them to be. Because she had almost no need for people, she had no trouble hurting them. It seemed to enlarge her, to give her strength. Quinn told her she had "poison blood." Sometimes she got so angry she frothed at the mouth.

When Yula was born, Quinn gave up fishing. Every

time a fish looked at him with its silver eyes, he thought of his new beautiful baby. He'd throw the fish back in the ocean and sometimes, he said, they'd lie there, floating like buoys. Too dumb to swim away. When he told this story to Yula, he would get on the floor, roll on his back, and stare at the ceiling like a corpse. "I'm a fish, I'm a fish," he'd say.

Jo hated it when he told the fish story, especially when he pretended to be one.

"Your father is a buffoon," she told her daughter, loud enough for Quinn to hear. "Don't marry someone you love. Love makes you stupid, like his stupid fish."

At night Yula's ears burned with insults and her mother's shrill voice banged around in her head, so loud that she often sat up in bed, expecting Jo to be in the doorway, ready for another one-sided battle. When she saw that her mother wasn't there, that *no one* was there, she rehearsed all the horrible things she could say back. But what could she ever say to hurt this woman as much as this woman hurt her? She did not want to hurt anyone in this awful way.

Her mother wasn't always cruel. After a fight, she showered Yula with gifts, stuffed animals, and expensive clothing, and sometimes, when she was feeling lonely or Quinn was angry with her, she'd climb into bed with Yula, stroke the insides of her ears, tell her she loved her more than anything else in the world. It was these moments that Yula lived for.

When the fights between her parents got violent or threatened to, Yula stood between them, arms outstretched.

She pried Quinn off her mother. She jumped on his back and knocked him to the ground. She ran out of the house and into the woods, and neither Quinn nor Jo noticed until she returned hours later, knees scraped and shivering. She memorized every creak in the stairway, every squeak of the floorboards, until she could float through the house as undetected as a ghost.

One night, when she was fifteen, she snuck out of the house and met a group of her friends down the road; together they drove to a warehouse in the industrial part of town. She wore a pink-and-white mini dress that she'd stolen from Value Village and knee-high lace-up Doc Marten boots. The main room of the warehouse was lit by strobe lights, and a couple of DJs blasted techno on turntables at the back. It was so loud that the bass shook the floor. Behind the bathrooms was a room lit by a single red light bulb. Yula wandered into the room and let herself be kissed by two tall boys, beautiful to her dilated eyes. They ran their hands over her body and she kissed them back, massaged their shoulders, let them put their fingers in her mouth. One stood in front of her and the other behind; she spun between them, let them lick the sweat from her neck. In the morning, when the party was over, she sat in the back of an old Toyota Celica and kissed one of the boys while the other drove them into Chinatown, where he lived above a record store in Fan Tan Alley. She lost her virginity to both of them that morning, and it was a perfect and beautiful act, she remembered thinking at the time, these two young boys adoring her body, taking breaks to pass a joint between them, sips of whisky, long drags off cigarettes, until the late afternoon. Later, they sat in a café and ate won ton soup, egg foo yung, chow mein, and lemon chicken. One of them drove her home. She hid in her bed for the rest of the day, waiting for the drugs to wear off so she could sleep. Her mother came in during the afternoon and brought her a cup of tea. She nibbled at a cookie. Her stomach was as tight as a fist.

The next day, she couldn't remember either of the boys' names. It hurt to pee. She crouched over the toilet and looked at the bruises on her thighs. Her vagina was swollen to almost twice its size. She bit her lip while she peed, grasped the edge of the counter for support, and clenched her pelvic muscles to stop the urine because it burned. She let it trickle out of her for what felt like an hour. She dabbed at her labia and the toilet paper came back dotted with bright flecks of blood. Her ribs ached and it hurt to breathe; her buttocks were red from being slapped. She stared at her naked body in the full-length mirror on the back of the bathroom door. Was this what men did to women? Her breasts were covered in blue bruises where the men had bit her. Her mouth was as dry as ash. She found herself sobbing and hated herself for doing so. No one had forced her to do this, and yet here she was, with a dark and ugly secret to carry around. She shut her eyes and tried to erase the evening from her mind. She wrapped a towel around her body and stuffed her underwear and the pink-and-white dress into the washing machine, everything reeking of sex and cigarette smoke.

She spent so long in the shower that the hot water ran out and she was left standing in the cold. Was she now a whore? It seemed so easy to slip into this new role, this new life. Had one careless act determined her future? Her skin was clean but her mouth tasted like metal and her eyes were heavy in their sockets. She kept pressing between her legs, surprised at how swollen and sore she was. She twisted a towel around her wet hair and rooted in her dresser for the flannel pyjamas her mother had bought her for Valentine's Day. She found them wadded in the back of a drawer and pressed them flat with her hands. They were pale pink with an alternating pattern of red hearts and little white dogs. She put them on, grabbed all her stuffed animals off the floor, and climbed into bed, the creatures surrounding her. This new whore of a woman was not her. She let herself cry then, horribly and hideously. This other woman was not her. Here she was, safe in her bed.

She told her mother about the boys when she couldn't deny anymore that she was pregnant. She winced and waited for her mother's sharp words, but Jo took her hand instead. She rubbed the space where her daughter's pinky finger should have been; it was a birth defect, something that Jo often apologized for, blaming it on the anti-nausea drugs she had taken.

"This is my fault," her mother said when Yula told her she was pregnant. "I haven't looked after you."

She asked her mother about having an abortion but Jo told her that her pregnancy was a sign—she believed in signs. Yula was bringing a new life into the house, and this would solve things, her mother said, this would make everything okay. They would raise the child together. "Let me be a mother to you both," she said.

Yula felt so damaged inside that she etched her mother's words deep into her mind, where she would never forget them.

The two held each other, and Jo sobbed in Yula's arms and apologized for what a shitty mother she'd been.

"You haven't—Mom, please." Yula held her mother and stroked the back of her head.

"In my dreams I am a good mother." Jo stood, wiped her eyes and dried her hands on her jeans. "Your father and I. We have a toxic relationship. I know this. You know this. He knows it, too."

Yula knew that her parents had once loved each other deeply. But now they fought over everything. They fought so hard they forgot they had a daughter. They fought so hard that a month after Yula's son, Eugene, was born, Quinn veered his motorcycle into an oncoming semi truck, just to scare Jo, just to shut her up—and when he pulled back into his lane, the tires slid out on the rain-soaked road and they swerved onto the shoulder of the highway, the motorcycle on its side. Both of them were dragged through the gravel for more than a hundred feet. After three days in the hospital, Jo was dead.

At first, Quinn's grief was visible only in small gestures: a sudden clumsiness, a dropped fork, the way he tripped on the top step as he walked to the front door. He lost thirty pounds in the weeks that followed. The blob of his belly no longer jutted over his pants; his shirts, suddenly, were all too big.

The day they buried her mother, Yula found a suicide note on Quinn's desk. It was just a few paragraphs written in pencil; it wasn't finished. But there it was on his desk—there was the note. *To Yula*, it began. She shoved it into one of the desk drawers; she never read the whole thing. But there it was, always, somewhere, in her mind.

At first, she hated her father. Hated him with a ferocity she had never before felt. She dreamed of killing him, of walking into the house with a shotgun and shooting a hole in his heart. She thought of feeding him rat poison. She thought one day she might walk up behind him with a belt and pull it around his neck. *I'll break every bone in your face*, she said aloud as she did the dishes, and then pictured doing it—crushing his cheekbones with a cold sharp rock.

And yet she found herself looking over at his house multiple times a day, stopping by to give him his mail, ask him if he needed anything, borrow a couple of eggs. Since Jo's death, he'd let the house go, and more and more Yula's anger turned to sadness. She couldn't stand the thought of finding her father dead one day, surrounded by dirty dishes, unopened mail, stinking cartons of milk left on the counter, muddy footprints in and out of every room, the television left on and never turned off—blaring music videos while her father lay open-mouthed and cold to the touch, face up on his bed. No, she wouldn't let this happen. She would take care of her father.

On Sundays, Yula took Eugene to Sooke on one of Quinn's old dirt bikes and they had dipped cones from Dairy

Queen or waffles at Mom's Café, a little diner across from the community centre. They waited in line for an hour sometimes, but it never mattered; it was part of the routine. Yula held Eugene on her hip until he got too big and then she fastened him to her overalls with a dog leash. Sometimes she gave him a bag of marshmallows to keep him occupied while they waited. He loved the big white gummy cubes. They were his favourite thing in the world. And then one day, while she and Eugene stood patiently in line, she saw Harrison, the man who would become my father. He was six feet tall, with deeply tanned skin and long hair a mixture of blond and white, like butterscotch ripple ice cream. He was large and strong looking, but there was a softness—a boyishness—to his face that made him look both naive and kind. He wore a muscle shirt and steel-toed boots into which he had stuffed his mud-caked jeans. His black eyes were shaped like almond slivers, his nose crooked from two ugly bar fights. The hair on his forearms glistened like white silk. My mother could not stop staring. He walked toward her with his eyes on Eugene.

"You've got big bright eyes like your mother, don't you," Harrison said. He crouched and asked the boy if he could join them for breakfast. He was twenty-five; my mother, seventeen. He smelled like horses, like cheap cologne, like mint. He had a raspy voice and some kind of shiny gel in his hair. His arms shone like they'd been oiled.

Over breakfast, Harrison told my mother that he'd moved to town to be closer to his brother, Dominic. Before that, he'd been living in a boarding house in Abbotsford. He didn't need to tell her that he'd been in jail for most of his teens and early twenties; he had a look about him that Yula knew well. She knew the overly muscled forearms. She knew the poorly done tattoos. The way he looked around, guiltily, every time they ran out of things to say.

"I've always been a castaway," Harrison said to her. "Don't know what to do with myself in the world."

Mom's Café was crowded and they had to share their table with two construction workers, who eyed Harrison when they sat down. Yula held Eugene on her lap and fed him bits of waffles with her fingers. The construction workers leered at her breasts when she leaned over to grab the syrup, and when Harrison saw this he pounded his fist on the table, sent the cutlery to the floor. Eugene wailed, but Yula found herself oddly sexually aroused. The men left the café and Harrison followed them outside, told Yula he'd be back in a minute. When he returned, his knuckles were bleeding. He wiped the blood on his napkin and looked at her with sweet eyes.

"You know them?" he said. His face hardened.

"No—never—I don't." She saw it then for the first time: his paranoia, his violence, his possessiveness. She saw other things, too: his sudden loyalty, his need to be loved. She reached for his hand.

Harrison never asked about Eugene's real father, not even when he moved into the cabin with Yula. Somehow Yula knew that whatever Harrison and his brother did for a living wasn't legal, but she knew it was better not to care. He was good to her son. One night she heard him telling Eugene that if they spent enough time together, they'd develop a likeness. He put his face next to Eugene's in the mirror and widened his lips, and Eugene pursed his. Yula took a Polaroid of them this way, and it stayed on their fridge forever.

3

On my fifth birthday, I am adopted by a woman with a daughter of her own. We live on a one-way street in a beige townhouse in Fernwood, within walking distance of downtown and a block from the big stone high school. Hand-painted "Slow Down!" signs are stapled to the telephone poles and a fat woman in a wheelchair sits outside her house all day shrieking at us. The fat woman is called a Block Parent, and we are supposed to run to her if we are ever in danger, but she is terrifying. Our townhouse is mashed together with six other townhouses, all in a row, with a small parking lot in the back. There are no front or backyards here, no sidewalks even. Each floor of the townhouse is small. The rooms are tiny, with low ceilings, and warm. Every room smells like mushroom soup, except for the bathroom, which smells like Ivory soap.

I have arrived with the following possessions: a backpack stuffed with two pairs of pants, two shirts, pyjamas, a toothbrush, and seven pairs of underwear, one for each day of the week. I also have a big shoebox with me, which the social workers call my "treasure chest." Inside, I keep the things I was found with: a Swiss Army knife and a grey sweatshirt with thumbholes. I also have some photographs, taken in my various foster homes. I hide the treasure chest under the bed; I keep my clothes in the backpack, in case I have to leave again.

Miranda, my new mom, is a cinnamon-coloured woman who works as a Molly Maid and was once married to a man named Dell. Her bedroom is on the top floor of the townhouse, and I am prohibited from going up there, as is her daughter, Lydia-Rose. It is "off limits," she says. She "needs her space." Lydia-Rose and I share a bedroom on the second floor, across from the living room, bathroom, and tiny kitchen, a beaded curtain hung in the doorway. A short flight of carpeted stairs leads down to the first-floor laundry room and front door.

There are rules here: no staring, no chewing with my mouth open, no sugar before bed, no wasting food, no talking back. I can handle most of it, but I can't stop staring. I want to stare at Miranda forever. I am fascinated with her. She wears her hair in a tight bun at the top of her head and has a big bright face, as if the moon itself had walked into the room. After work, she pads around the townhouse in Chinese slippers and a plaid housecoat. She makes us lentil soup, then slides an ice cube into each of our bowls until it cools.

Each morning she wakes at five, showers, puts on her Molly Maid outfit (a pale pink polo shirt with "Molly

Maid" stitched over the left breast pocket, khaki pedal pushers, white tennis shoes), fusses with her impossible hair, and then makes breakfast. There is always something different: creamed honey on toast, boiled eggs, Cheerios, jam on toast; on Saturdays, dollar cakes with fake maple syrup. She teaches me her trick: she fills a saucepan with one or two inches of water, brings it to a boil, then adds spoonfuls of brown sugar until it is thick and golden. If we're lucky, she stirs in a little butter at the end. This is something I will grow to despise—this cheapness—but for now I find it ingenious.

Miranda's real daughter, Lydia-Rose, looks just like her, with her big face and honey-brown skin. I'm told that she looks like her father, too: she is a tall, intimidating girl who wears his thin smile, and her lips curl up with every laugh. Her hair, thick and copper-coloured, rests in a messy clump at the nape of her neck, a yellow crayon in the fold of her ear. She is six months older than I. She has long skinny legs and runs as though she were flying. Her face is fierce and determined; her eyes, impatient and keen.

Miranda loves to play dress-up with us, give back-scratches and spend hours French-braiding our hair. She dresses us in shades of pink and purple, always matching, always bright. Although we never go to church, she tries to get me to believe in God. She says I only need to have faith the size of a mustard seed. This seems reasonable, doable, and so, for about an hour, I am a Christian.

But the most exciting thing about this place is that Miranda has three cats and a rangy-looking dog. The cats' names are Scratchie, Midnight, and Flipper. Scratchie and

Flipper are from the same litter; Midnight is a stray. Flipper is a longhaired Siamese. He has ten toes on each paw, which is why he is named Flipper. Scratchie is tortoiseshell-coloured and a fighter. He and Flipper are best friends. Midnight, the stray, is black with a white blaze. She is the only shorthaired cat among the herd.

The dog's name is Winkie and she is part fox terrier and part something else that has given her long, gangly legs that don't work very well. We don't know why. Miranda found her one day, soaking wet and whining, by the side of the road. She is mostly white, with a black saddle and a little brown head. She has big goofy eyes and the longest tongue in the history of tongues. She only harasses the cats if her legs are hurting her, and, for the most part, it's a peaceable kingdom.

Lydia-Rose and I aren't so lucky. I'm not sure what I'm supposed to call Miranda, and so I start calling her Mom. Lydia-Rose drags me around the bedroom by my hair until I promise never to say it again, then she cries so hard that Miranda takes her to the forbidden upstairs bedroom and they don't come down for hours.

Once a month, a social worker comes by for a home visit to make sure I'm okay. Her name is Bobbie, and she's a great big woman who wears long gypsy skirts and has leathery red skin from fake tanning. She and Miranda drink coffee in the kitchen and talk about me while I pretend not to listen. Am I adjusting? Am I sleeping? Am I still crying out in the night? Bobbie talks about the difficulties of raising a child with a "history," one who might be "special needs." She puts her hand on Miranda's shoulder sometimes, as though she needs to be comforted. Later, she pads through the house, checking the smoke alarms and making sure there's nothing poisonous lying around. She asks Miranda to put the Lysol on a higher shelf, "just in case." Lastly, she comes into the living room and eases herself onto the floor, where she stares at me intensely and asks me questions about myself, about Lydia-Rose, about living with Miranda. I whisper that I am fine. I want to tell her that I think I really love Miranda, but I can't yet find the courage.

When Bobbie leaves, Miranda holds my hand and asks if there's anything she can do to make me feel happy. She agrees to paint the bedroom pink when she next gets paid, and when I ask for a neon pink bedspread, she buys dye and throws an old white one in the washing machine. When Lydia-Rose protests and accuses me of getting special treatment, I hear Miranda whisper to her that "at least she wasn't rattled by such a stark beginning." She expects her daughter to be fair, to be kind, to be nice to me.

"Bleeder!" Lydia-Rose shrieks. It is six in the morning, a few weeks after I arrived, and she is in the twin bed across from me. She clutches her bloody nose and falls out of bed onto the floor, hitting her head on the edge of the bed frame. The cats stampede out of the room, outraged. I clutch my new pink bedspread and wait for further violence. But this is just the way Lydia-Rose is: everything with her is physical. When she's angry or sad, she pushes or punches me and then her nose bleeds—huge rushes of blood that last an hour. She holds her head back while Miranda wads the Kleenex and presses it hard against her nose. Miranda tells me that Lydia-Rose has bled everywhere: the mall, the church, the grocery store. Concrete, tile bathrooms, hardwood floor—each surface absorbing the blood in a different way, the carpet in our bedroom forever stained.

Once it stops, Miranda tames her daughter's hair with a bristle brush and forces it into two long braids, the elastics ready to burst. Flipper and Scratchie groom each other on the floor, and Winkie is asleep on my bed, on top of my feet.

At breakfast, Miranda talks and we fidget. The phone is busted and two guys from the phone company are busy ripping up the walls, drilling, pulling phone lines out of little cardboard boxes and then slinging them all over the house, creating a kind of spiderweb of white wires that beep and fizzle and spurt when they walk by. The men have some kind of thing attached to their pants that makes these little lines crazy.

"When we lived on Saltspring," Miranda begins over the noise of staple guns and all the beeping, "we were chased by a white bull. Lydia-Rose's father and I were in our old minivan. We were going to visit friends and the drive was very long."

"What was I doing?" asks Lydia-Rose. Her voice is impatient, a whinny. I push my Froot Loops around, roll the soggy ones into balls with my fingers and stack them like snowmen. Occasionally I reach down and put one into Winkie's mouth.

Miranda folds her hands in her lap. "You were napping in the backseat, sweetie." She tries to salt her eggs but the salt is clumpy from moisture and won't come out. She tries to work the pepper mill but it's stuck, too. "Your father spotted the bull first, coming from the middle of a field—who knows what the bull was thinking, maybe that our white van was a little girl bull, I don't know! His head was the width of this table, Lydia-Rose. No lie."

"There are no 'little girl bulls,' Mom," Lydia-Rose says. "You mean a cow."

Miranda's face reddens. Lydia-Rose kicks me in the shin and I kick back. The table rocks. It's painted orange and flimsy, something found at a garage sale. I put a spoonful of Froot Loops in my mouth and let them sit there. Midnight jumps on the breakfast table and Miranda swoops her off.

"Did Daddy gun it?" Lydia-Rose grins.

"We left the bull in a dust cloud," Miranda replies.

After we've cleared the dishes and the men have fixed our telephone, we spend the morning sorting through bags of clothes. Miranda has a consignment business on the side. Women come around on weekends and look through the dresses, the freshly pressed shirts, the old shoes. Miranda kneels in front of one of the bags and tosses shoes over her shoulder. Lydia-Rose finds a black beret and sets it at a jaunty angle on my head. Then she pinches my earlobe until I wince, but I know by now not to complain to Miranda—if I tell on her, the next time she'll pinch harder. Instead, earlobes hot and ringing, I paw through a pile of clothing as though I were digging a hole. I hold up a leather miniskirt and smirk.

"Someone will want these," Miranda says, and a pair of red heels clatters to the floor.

Lydia-Rose reaches first. "Let me." She slips her feet inside and jerks around the bedroom like a marionette, her cheeks sucked tight in concentration. She pauses in front of the mirror and pulls a face. I laugh and she smiles at me. That night, we pour salt in Miranda's wineglass when her back is turned. Lydia-Rose is spanked and sent to her room, and I am lectured about maturity and sentenced to morning Winkie walks for a week. But I don't care. It is the first time that Lydia-Rose and I have banded together as sisters, and it is great fun.

On the weekends, Miranda takes us to Willows Beach. Lydia-Rose and I catch suckerfish and try to make them mate. We spend all day investigating hermit crabs and plunging our hands into tide pools, making all kinds of sea creatures run for their lives. When Miranda is out of earshot, we run down the beach, screaming *Fuck!* as loud as we can. Lydia-Rose loves to swear. Backlit by the sun, we giggle at our shadows, long and lean. Lydia-Rose wiggles her toes in the wet sand and practises Indian burns on my arm. Winkie flattens out in the surf, her belly coated with sand. We make shadow puppets with our hands.

"Look," says Lydia-Rose. "A rabbit."

I hook my thumbs together and flap my hands. "A dove."

A couple wearing Hawaiian shirts walks past us, kicking up sand with their shoes. They are laughing and talking in another language; it sounds like German. The man reaches into his pocket and takes the lens cap off a small camera. He circles the woman, snapping pictures, moving her by the shoulders to get some part of the beach in, some ocean liner in the background, a bird. Lydia-Rose and I dance behind them, dipping into the shot as the man hits the shutter, making peace signs, sticking out our tongues. Lydia-Rose says, *Hey, look, what's that*, and when I spin to see what she's pointing at, she lobs a piece of bull kelp at the back of my head. My teeth gnash together from the force of the blow but I don't cry. I look across the ocean. When Lydia-Rose hits me again, I think I see the devil in the clouds, but it's only Mount Baker.

At night, I listen to the hiss of the iron, the slosh of water as Miranda lifts it over her shirts, the high whistle of steam. Ashamed, I roll up a pair of soiled underwear and shove them under a loose floorboard in the laundry room, wondering where else I can hide things in this new, foreign house.

After everyone is asleep, I sneak into the kitchen and stick the black beret on my head. The fridge is a mess of phone numbers and Polaroids: Halloween cape-swirling, group shots on the beach, Lydia-Rose's hair in the wind. I wonder how much longer it will be until Miranda puts a photo of me on the fridge. I look up. The ceiling feels too close to my head. Winkie hears me open the fridge and comes running, her little toenails clicking on the linoleum. Winkie thinks the fridge is a small, cold white room. We survey the contents together. A jar of dill pickles, a packet of ground beef. No-name mayonnaise. I hold the refrigerator door open until I am freezing.

Winkie and I pace, open all the cupboards. Nothing is wasted here. A kitchen drawer is devoted to plastic bags and twist-ties, and every doorknob is wound tight with rubber bands from celery and broccoli stalks. A Tupperware container in the pantry overflows with sticky birthday candles, which are only thrown out when they're less than an inch long. We are also supposed to recycle and compost. I hate the fruit flies and find it impossible to peel labels off soup cans, but Miranda says I must persevere. She tells me to put all the fruit and vegetable peelings in a small stinky rubber trash can by the sink, but I hate it, I hate it, I hate it, and when no one is looking, I stuff them into the bottom of the trash or give them to Winkie.

Outside, a man drinks a beer in the parking lot, and the sky is midnight blue. I see my face in the window's reflection. My hair is curlier than it used to be. It's still the whitest of blondes. It looks like a giant cotton ball. My face is pale and slack, some kind of unfinished quality to it. The rest of me: warped from a chink in the glass.

"Go to sleep," I tell the face.

Later, Miranda finds me in the living room, bent over a yellow plastic stereo. It's two in the morning. I'm wearing the red heels; I've scuffed them somehow. Winkie is watching my every move.

"Goodnight now," Miranda says.

I jut my lip and press the Play button. "No sound," I whimper.

"Okay." Miranda turns the stereo on its side. "This isn't a piece of magic. The batteries are in the wrong way." She shivers and pulls her bathrobe tight. I lay my head in her lap while she fiddles with the batteries. I feel so sad and lonely that I wrap my arms around her waist and don't let go.

When I start to cry, she carries me up the stairs to her bedroom and shuts the door. The room is small and square. A queen-sized foam mattress sits on the floor, Lydia-Rose's old Little Mermaid comforter stretched across it. She sets me at the edge of the bed and sits down. Her skin smells like Jergens hand cream.

I look around. One of her pillowcases has a hole in it. A pack of menthol cigarettes lies on the floor beside a coffee tin filled with water. Cigarette butts float at the top like dead men. There's a cardboard box filled with paperbacks in the corner and a chest of drawers with Little Mermaid stickers all over it—must have been Lydia-Rose's at some point, too. A tabletop ironing board is set up on the dresser, along with a stack of her Molly Maid shirts and a pocket-sized Holy Bible. A plastic cosmetics bag sits on the floor, filled with brushes, eye shadow, and tubes of lipstick. There is nothing on the walls except a full-length mirror in the far corner, with a crack at the bottom. The room is lit by a small desk lamp.

"I want you girls to have the nice things," she says when she sees me looking. She takes my little hand and flips it, palm up, in her own. She traces the lines on my palm with her fingertip, something I've seen her do with Lydia-Rose. "You used to beg me to take you up here when you first came to live with us," she says. "Remember how scared you were? The first few days you hardly said a word."

I shake my head. I ask Miranda how long I've been here, and she tells me it's been three months.

"When I was growing up," Miranda says, still stroking my hand, "we lived down the street from a foster family. They had six girls. After I had Lydia-Rose, I thought, I should do this. Someone out there must need a home." She puts my hand down and reaches for the pack of menthol cigarettes, lights one, and blows the smoke into the room. "I was so lucky they let me have you. There weren't any available homes at the time—it just worked out that way, so perfectly. I would have liked to take in more, but I never made enough money to be able to rent a bigger house." She sucks on the cigarette and shakes her head. "I've never been any good at making money. I don't know how people do it. I really don't." She takes one more drag and sinks the half-finished cigarette in the coffee can. "I wanted to have lots of girls," she tells me. "I wanted Lydia-Rose to have lots of sisters. I couldn't have any more children after I had her."

"Oh."

I can tell she is telling me something important, something meaningful, but my eyes are heavy and one of them is twitching.

"Let's go to bed now, honey," she whispers and we pad down the stairs to the bedroom together. Miranda scoots my pillow around, tugs the blanket to my chin. She puts her hand on my forehead for a second. Outside, the neighbour calls for his dog. "Yogi," he cries. "Yo-gi."

Lydia-Rose and I like to lie the same way: on our backs, arms folded across our chests. Lydia-Rose wakes up and shivers. The cold night air blows in from a draft in the window. It smells like wisteria. "Why do we have to share a room?" she asks suddenly.

Miranda leaves my side and pulls the blanket tighter over her daughter. "Go to sleep now, girls."

"But—"

"Just stop."

Lydia-Rose huffs and rolls to her side. "I want my own room."

Miranda kisses my forehead and leaves. I listen as Lydia-Rose's breathing turns deep and slow. I want her to like me.

A few hours later I wake again. Winkie is rooting in the bathroom for mice, and I want only to be asleep. The house is so still. I slide out of bed, then tiptoe to the kitchen. The floor is like ice beneath my feet. I scan the Polaroids on the fridge: Miranda's old house, the park, the time Lydia-Rose dressed as a pixie for Halloween. A brochure for a single mothers' support group, the address circled in red ink.

Lydia-Rose keeps a Polaroid of her father in our sock drawer, and sometimes I stare at it. He looks distinguished, handsome. He looks noble. I never learn where he went. It's not something Miranda ever talks about. Lydia-Rose looks at me with no expression on her face when I ask about him. She tells me she does not remember.

I don't know why I can't stay in my bed. This goes on for years, these secret sojourns to the kitchen. I stand in front of the fridge, yearning for this place to feel like home, Winkie by my side, tongue hanging out of her mouth, hoping for something to eat.

Sometimes, when Lydia-Rose and I have nothing better to do, we practise dying. Lydia-Rose tells me that when her grandma died, they were all listening to a song from *The Big Chill*—that *old* movie, she says—and when it came to a certain part of the song, her grandma died, and Lydia-Rose whispered, *Mom, she died on that note. That's the note she died on.* Lydia-Rose and I take the cassette tape and walk to Clover Point with the yellow stereo, and when it gets to that note, we just kind of let go.

It's very nice dying, we tell Miranda.

The dizziness starts about six months after I move in with Miranda and Lydia-Rose. I am always nauseous, and I keep walking into things. My shins are covered in bruises, my elbows red and raw. Miranda takes me to the doctor and asks him to look at my left eye, which she says has a funny look to it, as if it's not seeing. The doctor isn't nice to her at first, and it's only years later that I realize he was the doctor who used to see me when I lived with Moira and Julian. He puts his hand on the top of my head and asks me, in a quiet voice, to wait outside with the nurse, and then I hear shouting from behind the door. Miranda emerges, red-faced and weeping, and takes me into her arms. She carries me back into the room and pleads with him that she is not hurting me, and would he please look at my eyes. She puts me on the examining table and bangs her fist on the counter. I reach for her hand and tell her not to cry. Something in the doctor's face softens and he obliges. He shines a red light into my eyeball and asks me to follow the light as he moves it around. It is an easy game, and I leave the office bursting with pride because the doctor makes such a fuss about how well I have done, all things considered.

"All things considered, my dear," he says and waves as we walk out the door. On the bus ride home Miranda explains to me what he means. I am going blind in one eye.

Late that night, Miranda crawls into my bed and tells me that people with a sense disability sometimes make up for it by having another heightened sense.

"I know a blind woman," she says, slipping her hand under my pyjama top and rubbing my back, "who can play anything on the accordion or the piano. Anything at all." She speaks so quietly I can hardly hear her. Lydia-Rose is breathing heavily in her bed and Winkie is waiting expectantly at the end of mine, waiting for Miranda to leave so she can resume her place on top of my feet.

I ask Miranda if this blind person is some kind of prodigy and Miranda says no, not really, but that she *really* is a good player. I tell her that I don't think I have any such heightened sense to make up for my bad eye, though I've noticed that my nose is as strong as a bloodhound's. But no one's going to celebrate that: the little blind girl with a snout so keen she can tell you what you had for breakfast. Big deal.

I'm blind because of amblyopia. Lazy eye. My right eye got so good at seeing, it told the other to give up. It takes too much energy to look after a sick thing. The world is flatter; I see in a dimension just under third. Rembrandt had this problem and some scientists think he was a better painter because of it. I think it makes me trip. Where's that stair? How far from my foot? I can't tell. It's all by feel. It's not my mother's fault. I wasn't born blind. Amblyopia comes later, when one eye fails to thrive. I could have worn an eye patch if someone had noticed this earlier, but now, well, why kick a dead horse. In the doctor's office, the eye chart starts with E. For eye, for easy. Everyone can see the E.

While Miranda is at work, Lydia-Rose and I go to Blue Jay School. It is in a nicer neighbourhood than the one we live in, in an old white character house, and is both a daycare and a kindergarten. Blue Jay is run by a woman named Krystal, who has long wild hair and drives a black Pontiac Trans-Am with a yellow firebird on the hood. I decide she is my idol and stare at her whenever possible. Her jeans are high-waisted and very tight, and she looks like a rock star, skinny arms in a muscle shirt, big hairsprayed bangs, and gorgeous almond eyes. "Is she yours, too?" she says to Miranda, her eyes on me, when Miranda drops us off the first day.

"Sure is."

"What a sweet little girl," Krystal says. "And such a pretty girl, too."

"Oh," I say, looking down.

Miranda leaves and we are told to sit cross-legged with the other children. Krystal takes a piece of felt and cuts out little animals and tells us stories using these makeshift puppets. She serves us pieces of oranges and apples, cut into what she calls "boats." We are allowed four each, but I sneak extras into my pockets and eat them in the bathroom, my mouth and hands sticky with juice for the rest of the day.

At lunchtime, I discover that Miranda has slipped a little envelope into my lunchbox. Inside is a piece of paper folded in two, a makeshift card. When I open it, there's a picture of me, asleep on the couch, Winkie curled up beside me. *For your treasure chest*, the back of the picture says, and I hold it close to my body so no one else can see.

When it rains, which is all the time, Krystal helps us into our Muddie Buddies, navy-blue and red waterproof jumpsuits, so that we can still go outside. But despite Krystal's good intentions, kindergarten is a rough place. We are always getting punched. The older kids tell Lydia-Rose and me that we smell bad, that our clothes are secondhand and covered in cat hair. Two girls tell me they want to push me on the swings, and when I climb onto the swing and begin to lift off, they start to laugh and tell me they're going to punch me on the downswing—so I never come down, I swing higher and higher, kick at them with my legs, dodge their fists as I swoop toward the sand.

"You have deformed knees," the popular girl, Peggy, says to me when I show up one day in shorts. She has perfect legs: small knees with calves that round out on both sides, tapering to thin, delicate ankles. Like an hourglass stretched. My knee bones jut, collide with each other, and I have to stand with my feet apart. Peggy can lift her legs behind her head and touch her toes in a V. She has a brown oval the size of a penny on the back of her white thigh. We all gather to see her acrobatics—but mostly to see her underpants. Lydia-Rose steps into the circle, and Peggy points at her forearm. "You're the colour of a baked potato," she says. "Maybe more like dirt."

I begin to sneak off by myself during recess, and finally I find a place at the back of the house where I can hide behind a pile of firewood. It smells so good that I break off a thin splinter of bark and put it in my mouth. Beyond the firewood is a gutted Volkswagen Beetle in the middle of the lawn, the long grass pushing its way into the interior. We are forbidden to go near it, but I can't help myself. I crawl in and grip the steering wheel, which is small and black and won't turn in my hands. The seats smell like mould, and the grass tickles my thighs. But in that car, away from the fists of other children and Lydia-Rose's loud cursing and Krystal's beautiful face, I am at my happiest. I grip the wheel, pretend my legs are long enough to reach the pedals, and shift into first, second, third. I am five and a half and can't imagine having lived anywhere else but Miranda's, having had anyone else's life but this one.

But even though my life is moving forward, Julian starts watching me. He sits in his car outside the daycare while Lydia-Rose and I wait for Miranda to pick us up. The first time I see him we are playing Hunter/Gatherer, a game we've made up about being cave people. I'm busy strangling a pudgy three-year-old underneath the monkey bars and Lydia-Rose is waiting for me to tell her what to do.

"Bad antelope! Bad antelope!" I keep yelling at the kid. "Gonna feed my wife and kids with you." I drag the kid by the ankles and set him in front of Lydia-Rose. "Eat! Eat! Eat!"

Lydia-Rose gets busy fake-eating the kid's foot, and I look up.

"Hey, Shannon." He says it like he's been saying it for years. "You probably don't remember me. Brought you some gummy bears." He is in a suit; maybe he just got off work.

I take the gummy bears from his hand, give half to Lydia-Rose, and watch him wave goodbye.

"Who's that?" she asks.

"My old dad." The words sound funny in my mouth.

He comes again a week later. Always gummy bears, sometimes wine gums, too, but I think they have wine in them, so I decline.

"I don't drink," I tell him. We are sitting in his black Mercedes-Benz. He has asked me to sit with him and eat gummy bears.

"I don't drink either," he says. The radio is on. A husky-voiced woman talking about the prairies. Something about jazz. Julian's car seats are black leather and hot from the sun. He still has a lot of hair on his arms. I look out the window and watch Lydia-Rose swinging on the monkey bars. She lets go and lands in a crouch, stands and does a cartwheel. Julian tells me that Moira left him, moved to another city. He hasn't spoken to her in years.

"There are things I shouldn't have done," Julian says.

I reach for a gummy bear and squish it between my fingers.

He laughs and squishes one, too. "You were my daughter for a while."

"I remember."

"I played Chopin for you at night." He hums a few bars but I don't know what to say. I am suddenly too hot; my feet are baking in my little canvas shoes. "I taught you the alphabet."

"Moira did."

"*Me* actually."

I slip off my shoe and stick my toe in the air vent.

"I love you, Shannon," he says. He passes me another gummy bear and I put it in my mouth, then take it out and put it front of the air conditioner to dry off the spit. Julian asks me not to. He asks me again.

But I can't stop. "Who invented air?"

"No one invented air."

"Can I have an ice cream?"

"Just—please, Shannon—take your toe out of the vent. It's getting dirt all over the—"

"Miranda doesn't let us have ice cream."

"Okay—your toe, Shannon, *now*." He makes a grunting sound and grips the steering wheel. "Stop it. Fucking stop it now." A big vein pops out in his forehead. His hands are taut. He reaches for me and pulls me toward him, roughly, and I hit my shin on the gearshift.

He pushes his mouth against my ear. That's when I remember. Just a little. Just a nudge at first—a small flash in my brain—after all, I was only two. A hand, a fist? Smack of skin on skin, his grip too tight, a lazy kick meant for no one to see, crunchy crack of bone. The whirr of the X-ray machine. White bones on film. My fingers dipped in a pot of hot soup. An eye patch, a cast. His voice thick and weary: What comes after G? Say it backwards, faster now. Jell-O jiggler. Wiggly worm. Did I fall or did he drop me? Thin skull on hard linoleum. Dull thud. Then: no sound.

"I'm not going to hurt you," he is saying, "I'm not going to—I'm not going to hurt you—" and then Miranda is banging on the driver's side window, her big face sweaty and red. She runs from the car with me in her arms and Julian stares after us, his fist in the air. There's no sound coming out of his mouth, but I can tell by his eyes that he is calling her a bitch.

4

After sixty-five million years, the dinosaurs are back. Harrison knocks on the door of the cabin, tells Yula and Eugene to put on their boots, and takes them by the hand. They skirt the edge of the property, through the tall skinny trees that line the cabin for privacy, past the neighbour's chicken coop with its barbed wire to keep the dogs from getting the eggs, past the chickens gathered around a tin dish filled with ears of corn and cantaloupe rinds from someone's discarded breakfast. They walk past all of this until they are standing in waist-high grass. Here and there are pockets of tamped-down grass, and Harrison tells Eugene that this is where the deer have been sleeping. The sky is big over their heads and Mount Finlayson looms, tree-covered and dense with green, in the distance. Most days it is obscured by clouds. To their left is the forest, to their right an endless field that leads to Joel and Edwin's scrap yard. Harrison picks up Eugene and walks into the forest, ducking suddenly under a branch. Yula follows, and then she is no longer under the great expanse of sky; she walks carefully through the trees, for she is seven-and-a-half months pregnant with me, and it is steep and slippery. Harrison and Eugene are headed to the waterfall directly below.

"Be careful," Harrison calls back to her, and she grips the spindly tree trunks for support as she makes her way down, down, down, until she's balancing on a rock in the middle of a stream, the water moving slowly past her because there is a dam below the waterfall to stop it from rushing by. It is so much darker and cooler now that they're in the woods. Eugene crouches and points to a tiny fish, so small it is almost imperceptible. The fish senses his presence and darts under a rock, sending rivulets of mud spiralling into the water so that Yula, Eugene, Harrison— and all the creatures—can no longer see him.

"Now I'll take you to Dinosaur Island," Harrison says and lifts Eugene into the air again. The boy is silent with awe and appreciation. Yula follows them, clambering alongside the waterfall on her hands and knees, amazed at how Harrison scales it effortlessly, her son clinging to his back. They reach a shelf and walk past the waterfall, the rocks covered in mud and moss, and suddenly they are in a stone cave that Harrison says is where the dinosaurs live. Stones balancing on top of stones, something between a cairn and an old chapel. There are frogs, old birds' nests, dragonflies, and fossils of trilobites, which Harrison picks up and shows to Eugene, tracing the little boy's finger over the indentations, describing the creatures' bodies, their time on the earth.

Yula and Harrison have been together for a year now. They are still playful. This is the best part of their relationship; when they are together, it's as if they are children again. They speak in baby voices. They are sweet and full of laughter. When Harrison comes home, he lifts my small mother into his arms and carries her around the cabin, telling Eugene that his mother can fly. In these moments Yula is always slightly outside of herself. She knows it cannot last—everything sours, spoils, eventually. She tries to enjoy it—being carried through the air—but something stops her. The way some of her hair has caught on one of Harrison's buttons, the way his hands grasp her underarms too tightly. There is always some small amount of pain, of wanting it to be over.

He is such a jovial, juvenile, boy of a man. He believes he is destined for greatness. He believes he is special. He believes he is unlike anyone he has ever met before.

"Do you know I used to sing?" he tells Yula one night, his eyes wild. He presents her with a dusty VHS tape, and they watch a shaky recording of him singing in a church choir, then a blurry close-up of his face as he sings the solo in "Once in Royal David's City." He wears a maroon cassock and a white ruff around his neck. As he watches the video, his eyes darken. He walks into the kitchen and returns with a whisky bottle and a mug full of ice clinking around in his shaking hand.

When the video ends, Yula holds him like a baby and lets him weep into her neck. When he drinks, he cries. He and Dominic were sent to a reform school by their parents because they were, in his mother's words, "uncontrollable." He tells Yula about the beatings by the schoolmaster. He talks about his desperate need not to be abandoned. He talks about living with a perpetually broken heart. When he's really drunk—or if he gets too high—he babbles about being raped when he was in jail, but Yula can never get him to talk about this when he's sober. He gets a vacant look in his eye and tells her that he doesn't have any idea what she's saying. He drinks again and tells her about all the people he's known who have died. It seems to Yula an impossibly long list. He cannot have lost so many people. Is he exaggerating? He tells her about being tormented by Dominic, two years older. He is so tender and damaged. Yula longs to minister to him. His self-absorption is, somehow, seductive. She waits for him to be drunk enough, then takes him in her arms and whispers, *Tell me*.

Four days before she gives birth to me, Yula's alarm goes off at seven-thirty and she walks across the lawn and gets her father's coffee brewed and ready, puts *The Globe and Mail* on the kitchen table with a stack of brown toast, three pieces buttered, three pieces with grape jam, and a pear like a giant green raindrop. What Quinn doesn't eat she gives to the neighbour's chickens, which run toward her when she calls for them and take the bits of crust from her hands. The sun is hot on the back of her neck as she bends to feed them, one hand on her belly.

She and Harrison have been fighting lately over how much she looks after her father. When Harrison came into Yula's life she explained her need to look after Quinn, calmly, over coffee the morning after their first night together. Her father was her priority, second only to Eugene. Could he understand this? Would he be okay with it? When he moved into the cabin, they discussed it again. She told him about the suicide letter. She told him not an hour went by when her heart didn't jolt a little, wondering if this was the day when she would find him.

But, more so, she likes it here. She hates to leave—she hates the way people claim her belly when she's in public, asking how far along she is, who is the lucky father, isn't she a bit young to be with child, then telling some anecdote about a teenage pregnancy, a neighbour, a cousin, someone they met once. When she and Harrison fight, he stays out with Dominic. Three, four nights in a row. She can't leave anyway; someone has to make sure her father doesn't get too lonely; someone has to answer the phone when Harrison calls at three in the morning with no way to get home, his hands bloody from a fight, his eyes wild and wet with drugs—cocaine now, she's sure of it; someone has to clean her father's house and make sure he eats. Every month, Quinn slips a small envelope of money (her inheritance) under the welcome mat to the cabin, enough for all the bills, and sometimes a little extra for Yula to take Eugene to the movies or the car for an oil change or to buy Harrison some new Mark's Work Wearhouse boots. It is a terrible, entangled arrangement. They live exclusively off the money from Jo's death. Quinn parcels it out monthly, as stingily as he can, so that there'll be something left over when he goes, too. His pension is gone—eaten by back taxes, which he never paid while he was working. And so they live at the edge of reality, beholden to no one, isolated and strange.

In the late afternoon, she goes back to fix Quinn a plate of pasta and do the morning's dishes. Then she'll dust and vacuum. Tomorrow she'll clean the windows using a special kind of wiper with an extendable handle that Quinn insisted she buy at the hardware store. Sometimes, when she's cleaning Quinn's bedroom, she takes her mother's red satin jewellery box off the dresser and sits on the bed, her arms around it. Inside is her mother's watch, her parents' wedding rings, which Quinn no longer wears, love letters from when they first met, and a Swiss Army knife. She sits on the bed and holds the box to her heart.

She puts a pot of water on the stove for the pasta and waves to Harrison as he rides by the kitchen window on a lawnmower, listening to his Walkman, Eugene on his lap. She rests a minute, her hand on her belly, and notices that the toast she set out for Quinn this morning is still on the table, the coffee untouched. She stands in the doorway of his bedroom and watches him, listens to the soft rattle as he pours the last of his sleeping pills into his hand. She eyes the bedside table—empty bottles of sleeping pills and painkillers and antidepressants, even Eugene's bright pink children's Aspirin. For a moment she is frozen, then suddenly she is standing over him, slapping his face and punching his stomach.

"God fucking damn it," she spits. She punches Quinn's stomach again and he retches, spits the pills down his shirt. She drags him into the shower and straddles his body, grabs his hair in fistfuls, turns on the cold water, and smacks his head against the tiles until he fights back.

"Okay, fuck. Stop." He pushes her off and retches down the drain. They sit in the shower, hugging their knees. His hair hangs in slimy white strands down the sides of his face, the ends dripping. His neck is rippled in little folds beneath his chin; she has never noticed it until now. He looks smaller to Yula somehow, and barrel-chested, as if he is affecting the posture of an old, weathered boxer.

The steam from the shower makes the spray-on dye run out of Yula's hair, and it slides down her shirt in black and purple streaks. Her clothes are waterlogged and cling to her pregnant body like kelp. She leans against the wall of the shower, her back sore from the weight of her belly. She rubs the skin on her swollen feet.

"Yula," Quinn says. He reaches for her with his good hand. "Oh, Yula." He spits into the drain. "I can't do it. I want to, but I can't."

His fingernails are caked with dirt. Yula gets the nail clippers and digs it out, then shampoos his hair. She wraps him in a big blue bathrobe, and after she's changed into dry clothes, they sit on the front porch and share a cigarette.

Harrison waves from the cabin's kitchen window. He has on yellow dishwashing gloves and an orange baseball cap. Yula sits with Quinn until he's sleepy, until she's convinced that he wants to live again. Later, while he eats his dinner, she washes and folds his clothes and turns down his bed.

"Stay with me, Yula," her father says. "Don't ever leave me. I don't know what I would do. Don't ever leave me, Yula."

"I won't, Papa." She watches him eat, then takes his plate, washes it, and puts it back in the cupboard. She puts a smear of toothpaste on his toothbrush and sets it at the edge of the sink along with a glass of water, his antidepressant and anti-anxiety pills.

When she treks back to the cabin, Harrison takes her in his arms. Her body is so tired it feels as though her bones are disintegrating.

"He's all I've got left," she says as Harrison holds her. "I can't lose him, too."

"I'm here with you." Harrison tucks her hair behind her ears. "I'm all you need."

She feels his cold eyes on her suddenly. It's an argument they have weekly and never finish. He is unhappy living under the thumb of her father, but she is too scared to leave. The thought of what might happen if she left—of losing her father—is too horrible.

Besides, she can't imagine her life any other way: listening to her father's troubles, polishing, cleaning, examining his tabletops for dust. She makes him one frozen meal after the other, finds his shit-stained underwear and bleaches them clean, asks him to tell her stories about her mother—why not; what doesn't she want to know. Later, she hears him crying in the shower and, not knowing she's still there, watches him walk into the living room and lie on the rug, weep and clutch his body with his wet hands. Unwillingly, not wanting to, she sees it.

"I need my dad," she says.

Eugene wakes from his nap, runs to her, and wants to know why her hair is wet and her eyes full of tears. He is almost three years old, his hair shiny and black. "You're crying," he says.

She sits at the kitchen table and pulls him onto her lap, but he is fidgety in her arms. His leg kicks out and rocks the table, and Harrison's bottle of beer smashes to the floor.

"Go to sleep, you little shit," she says and carries Eugene roughly into the bedroom. This moment of nastiness is something she will regret forever.

Later, Harrison stands over the garbage can, peeling potatoes, not speaking. He has let his hair grow to the middle of his back and wears it in a thick braid with a twist-tie at the end. He pierced his ears last night (hers, too, a second time) and the lobes are swollen and red. When he gets quiet like this, she assumes he is high. He's been getting high too much, she thinks. He's losing too much weight. His limbs are so spindly these days they look like they've been wrung. He wears ripped jeans and a red bandana, a black T-shirt with a unicorn on the front. He has a French–English dictionary in his back pocket, but my mother doesn't ask him why. Some girl, probably. She runs her eyes over the little scabs covering the inside of his arm and says nothing. When did he start doing this? She tries to remember if he picked at himself when she first met him; the scabs look like they've been there for years.

A few months ago, he lost his job as a mechanic and has been working the night shift at a bakery in town; at least that's what he tells her. What he does after she drops him in front of the bakery she does not know. Their relationship feels so precarious sometimes—this business of living across from Quinn, of Quinn paying the bills, of Quinn *everywhere*—that she dares not challenge Harrison much about anything. She daydreams about standing up to him, demanding to know his whereabouts, who was on the phone just now and what is he high on, but in the moment, face to face with him, it is as if someone plugged up her throat. She imagines her life if he left her, and the thought is unbearable. She wishes, desperately, that he would marry her.

Later, they lie in bed and Harrison reads to her from a little guidebook he's bought about trees, lists off the different layers of the trunk.

"Outer bark, phloem, cambium, sapwood, heartwood," he recites, throwing one of Eugene's stuffed bears against the ceiling, catching it with his feet, then throwing it again. "Heartwood. The dead wood in the centre of the tree that gives it its shape and strength."

"Are you high right now?" Yula says and takes a sip from a mug of milky tea, but he doesn't answer. She looks around the bedroom. Harrison never seems to mind— never seems to *notice*—the clothes on the floor from his mad dash to get dressed in the morning, the knife coated in peanut butter left stuck to the dresser. He takes the mug from her, takes a sip, then sets it on the bed, its contents threatening to spill all over their checkered sheets. She gets up and leans against the doorway, traces a crack in the wall with her finger, flicks away a ladybug that has landed on her arm. She watches Harrison, this mess of a thing.

She takes his arm and pushes into the little scabs with her finger. "You're addicted. I need it to stop."

He moves out of her grasp, annoyed, and picks bits of lint from his long braid. "Everyone has their cross to bear," he says.

After it gets dark, they sit on their porch under a scratchy blanket and look at the stars. Harrison tells her he longs to have money and to live on the Queen Charlotte Islands. There is no sound except Eugene talking in his sleep, no light except from their matches. The air is so damp the blanket feels wet. Their hands are clammy. Harrison pushes three Chips Ahoy cookies into his mouth and tries to chew, does it again once he swallows the big mess. He pushes two cookies into Yula's mouth and makes her swallow. He laughs so hard he roars, and cookie crumbs shoot into the air as though from a whale's spout.

In four days my mother will abandon me, but tonight my parents are childlike and laughing. He lights a joint and they go inside to watch TV. Harrison puts his head on Yula's pregnant lap and roars when a commercial tries to sell them something about sex or pimples. He likes to flop around when he laughs. He likes to roll off the couch. He rolls and crashes into the coffee table and roars so hard he weeps, throws his head to high heaven, and paws the air as if he is drowning.

5

I am a noisy and demanding six-year-old. At dinner, I babble in every direction. Even the saltshaker sets me off. I ask where salt comes from. Then, who built the ocean and do French children think in English and who invented Cheerios. I will not eat peas unless there's sugar on top, and I get angry if Miranda's outfits aren't colour coordinated. She tells me I'm overly sensitive. She says I need to learn the art of conversation.

"Conversation," she says, "is when we all talk about the same thing. Pick a topic, Shannon." A new rule is invented: I have to leave the table if I ask too many questions. Miranda says that if she wanted to be interviewed, it would be by Mike Wallace, not me. I discover that if I pinch the skin on the back of my knee I can stop myself from blurting out. Kicking my ankles together works, too, but then I'm sent to bed without supper so I don't do it again. My nails dig in; I scab and bleed.

While Lydia-Rose does the dishes, I take Winkie for walks in the evening and try to talk it all out with her. Lydia-Rose made her a little raincoat out of an old anorak, and Winkie and I walk with our heads down in the rain. I tell Winkie everything: how hard I have to pinch myself to keep from blurting out; how I hate all the kids at school; how I think I'd be happier if I could live in outer space. I tell her that I stole the Polaroid of Lydia-Rose's father out of our sock drawer and ground it into a puddle with my gumboot. I tell her that I hate myself for having done this. I tell her that the townhouse doesn't feel like home.

We have to walk slowly because of Winkie's back legs. When they're really bad, I hold a towel under her belly and walk with my legs on either side of her while she ambles along. The vet says it's arthritis from badly broken bones. Who knows what happened to her before Miranda found her. Car accident? It makes my stomach hurt to think about it. We only walk on our side of the street, because I refuse to cross the road. It's too frightening. The cars come out of nowhere; they peel around the corner so fast they go up on two wheels. I can't gauge how fast they're moving or how long I have to get across the street. I don't understand how anyone can find the courage to do this sort of thing. Lydia-Rose darts into traffic as if she's parting the Red Sea.

Once a month, Miranda and Lydia-Rose have a special mother–daughter lunch at the Dutch Bakery. They split a turkey sandwich and a vanilla slice. Lydia-Rose sometimes gets a marzipan strawberry to eat on the bus ride home. Miranda puts her hand on my head and tells me that I am her daughter, too, but that she needs to have "alone time" with Lydia-Rose every once in a while. Sometimes she sends me over to the neighbours' house and then I think she and Lydia-Rose watch a movie and make popcorn, Winkie at their feet. At Christmas we each get the same thing, but then I'll find something in our bedroom, later, slid under Lydia-Rose's pillow or tucked into her backpack. A little something extra. A little something to show her that she is number one. At night I am so lonely that my heart aches. I lie in bed, Lydia-Rose already asleep, and listen to her breathing. Miranda spends a few minutes with us every night, but then she's gone, into her private room upstairs, and I'm left alone in my bed.

Lydia-Rose wakes and torments me. *When you were a baby, your mom left you in a closet to die. Your mother was a hooker. We found you in a shoebox outside our door. We found you in a dumpster.*

I lie in my bed until my nose starts to tingle as if it's carbonated, and then I feel the hot sting of tears. No one knows how hard I can make myself cry. I can cry until I'm almost choking. I can cry until I'm gasping for breath. When no one is home, I cry so hard and loud that I am screaming. I tuck myself into a corner of the room and feel the swell of pain in my chest. I squeeze my eyes shut to drain them of their tears, wait for them to refill, do it again. Over and over. Do other people do this? Lydia-Rose cries in the bathroom, talking to herself. She says *I hate my mom. I hate my mom. No. I don't hate her. But. But. But.*

And then she whispers so softly and quickly that I can't keep up. I don't think she cries like me.

The night before we start grade one, Miranda tries to tell us things about herself while we eat corn on the cob. She wipes the butter from her chin and laughs. It's a warm evening in early September. We have our backpacks, notebooks, pens, pencils, and first-day outfits spread out all over our beds. We have new white runners for P.E.

"In the summers, my sisters and I would spend the evenings on the front porch, shucking corn," Miranda says. She is at the head of the table with her back to the open window. Outside, we can see Grant Street. "We hated it." She looks at Lydia-Rose, but her daughter is pushing bits of her cut-up hot dog around on her plate. Lydia-Rose has even more trouble sitting still than I do.

Miranda spreads some more butter on her corn. "We lived in the Interior at the time. It was hot in the summers, not like it is here. We had to be outside; it was too punishing to be indoors. And so many bugs—had to have screens on all the windows." She presses on, keeps talking about the wind and the hot sun and her father calling them in to boil the corn, the awful steam heating up the already hot kitchen. She looks at Lydia-Rose, but her daughter hasn't heard a word. She's wiggling in her seat, desperate for her mother to excuse us and let us play, but I could sit here all night listening to Miranda. I could sit here forever, trying to postpone tomorrow morning. Except there's something else, too—I don't like that I can see how hard Miranda is trying. I don't like that I can tell she's lonely. I don't like that I can see her trying to reach her daughter from across the table. Why should I notice these things when Lydia-Rose doesn't? I try to be more like her, and I stop looking at Miranda's face. Instead, I bang my heel against the chair. And, finally, Miranda says we're excused.

That night I dreamt that I was still living with Moira and Julian, except in some weird wood-panelled motel room, and there was a big spider on the wall, and I asked Julian to kill it, which he was always very good at doing, and just as he was about to hit it with his shoe, its whole body glowed fluorescent green, and I said, *Did you see that, Dada?*, but he had not. At six-forty a.m. I woke from the dream, looked up at the ceiling, and there was a huge spider over my head.

And I thought there should be a word for this sort of thing—when your last dream mimics your first waking moment. Shouldn't there be a beautiful word for that?

The first day of school, Lydia-Rose and I stand side by side, our arms folded across our chests, daring the bigger kids to hit us. We are seasoned fighters from our days at Blue Jay. Lydia-Rose has laced a set of keys between her delicate fingers, but I'm ready to go without armour or adornment. I have toughened my hands. For the past year, I've been punching the wall in the laundry room as hard as I can every time I walk by it. I can't say why I do this, but my hands are calloused and numb.

And I'm ready. I've got on my new pink backpack, pink shorts, and a red V-neck T-shirt. Red flip-flops. Toenails done French-manicure style with Wite-Out. I'm the shortest person in grade one and probably the weirdest looking person, too. My mom or dad must have had really curly hair because I've got white-blonde curls so tight they could hold a pop can. My bum eye is off to the side, sleeping in the corner by my temple, and people don't know where to look when they're talking to me. They stand there, bounce back and forth between my eyes, and try to figure out which is the good one. And I don't know who I inherited it from but I've got a turned-up nose like a little pig. My best feature is my mouth: a perfect puffy pout. I'm not hideous, but I'm definitely a cross between Shirley Temple and a pug.

Lydia-Rose jogs in place and calls the kids who have surrounded us on the playground a bunch of shit-ass losers. She is the skinniest girl I've ever seen, too tall for her age, and knobby kneed. Her hair is pulled into a tight bun at the top of her head and her eyes are full of rage. She is goofy looking now, but I often hear Miranda and her friends tell her that one day she will be a "classic beauty."

"Come on, you fucking fucks." Lydia-Rose has got on white high-tops and pink spandex, a too-big T-shirt with Sonic Youth spray-painted on the front that we found in a cardboard box at the side of the road. She pumps her fist; the other one with the keys is hidden behind her back. The kids look at us like we're aliens, like we're straight-up weirdo freaks.

I wait for the insults. The jokes about being adopted. Shorty shorty dogface. Crazy eyes. Cyclops. Lydia-Rose waits, too. Baked potato skin; brownie. The girls turn away from us, disgusted. The boys stay a little longer, and one throws a handful of woodchips into Lydia-Rose's face. She flinches, throws a punch at the boy, who ducks and darts away. Her nose starts to bleed all over her Sonic Youth shirt and through her hands. She drops the keys and tilts her head back, and I stand on my tiptoes and pinch the bridge of her nose. We stay this way for ten minutes, past the recess bell, while Lydia-Rose chokes on the blood running down her throat and then spits up a big clot. It looks like a chicken liver and we stare at it amongst the woodchips at our feet. It is disgusting and makes her cry, and we sit there for what feels like hours, the woodchips digging into our legs while she occasionally dabs at her nose with the edge of her T-shirt to make sure it has stopped bleeding.

"Do you miss your mom?" She says it quickly, and at first I think I haven't heard her right.

"Miranda?" I pick up a stick and start digging in between the woodchips, trying to make a hole in the dirt underneath.

"*Your* mom, stupid." She laces the keys back through her fingers and rakes them through the woodchips. I look toward the school. I am willing a teacher to notice that we're missing and come walking out of the big double doors, calling our names. I am willing for anything to happen besides this conversation.

"I don't know." It's an honest answer. I've never thought about it before. I don't even know who she is.

"Mom says you were in a bad situation." She looks at me, and I see that her questioning is earnest. She isn't trying to be mean. She dabs at her nose, then spits on her fingertip and rubs the saliva around her nostril. She wipes the goo on her pink spandex tights.

"I lived with some other people before I lived with you." It's all I can think of to say. My face is hot, and I want to go inside and wash Lydia-Rose's sticky blood off my hands. But my heart is pounding, and I'm too scared to move.

"Mom says she loves me in a different way than she loves you." Lydia-Rose stands up carefully, her head still tilted, her hands poised in front of her nose in case the blood starts again.

At three o'clock, the horrible day is finally over. I tap my toe against the concrete steps and bang my backpack against the school's brick side. I am waiting for Lydia-Rose to emerge so that we can walk home.

"Freak," a voice says behind me.

I freeze.

A fat girl wearing a ball cap and three others walk down the steps and form a circle in front of me.

"We heard about you."

I drop my bag and clench my fists.

The girls move closer and the fat girl pokes me in the stomach. "Your mother was a whore." They kick my backpack and I swing at them, knock the cap off the fat girl's head.

"Get away from me," I spit. I see Lydia-Rose at the top of the stairs, and I push past the girls, then grab my bag and use it like a battering ram against the fat girl's chest. "Get out of my way."

Lydia-Rose grabs my hand and we run down the street

together, and even though I know she was the one who told the fat girl that my mother was a whore, I'm grateful to be holding her hand. We run away from the girls, the fat one on the ground, crying now.

When we get back to the townhouse, I stand in the living room, hands on hips. "I'm not going back."

"Everyone says that the first day of school," Miranda says. She looks Lydia-Rose and me up and down. Lydia-Rose's shirt is blood splattered and my shorts are covered in grass stains. "Let's get you girls some better outfits."

She hauls out one of her big bags of consignment clothing and puts her hands on either side of my face. "You'll feel better with something new."

She rifles through the bag, then throws four shirts over her shoulder. She pulls out a little denim jacket with shiny brass buttons. She shifts from foot to foot, holds the jacket up in the window's light. "This one's fit to see the Queen," she says. "All those buttons. And you'll try this skirt on, too." She hands me the heap of clothing, and my arms sink from the weight.

The bathroom is bright and cold, the window left open all day, and I try to slip the skirt over my shorts, but it won't stretch. It's a little plaid thing, and I can tell it's nicer than what I usually wear and fashionable, but I hate it. I tug at the zipper and try to force it up farther, but the fabric hugs my hips and won't budge. I kneel and rest my forehead against the cool of the full-length mirror, wrap my hands around my shoulders, and rock back on my heels.

"Miranda," I say and the word sprays like spit. "Miranda."

"Doesn't fit?"

"No."

"Let me see." She comes into the bathroom and looks down at me and the ball of wadded-up clothing on the floor.

"Stuck," I say, fingering the silk liner under the skirt. I roll my head toward Miranda and blink, droopy-eyed, heavy.

"The littlest things defeat you," she says. "Come on, honey, stand up." Miranda pinches the fabric of the skirt and shakes the zipper and the skirt falls around my ankles. I wrap my arms around her and let myself cry.

"You'll be all right," she says. She takes me by my shoulders and presses her face close to mine. "You'll be all right, little one."

"Who is my mother?" I try to ask her, but no sound is coming out of my mouth.

That night I cannot sleep. The mattress is cold on my back, and I stare into the black ceiling, my legs dangling off the edge of the bed, and wait for my eyes to adjust. Here, there is always something to listen to at night. Slow cars outside my window, the rise and fall of a passing siren, the click of heels on pavement, a lonely dog. Miranda has taken to playing the radio at night; she leaves it on in the kitchen. A low, constant hum. She says it will confuse someone if they try to break in—they'll think someone is awake and talking.

Outside, a car's engine growls, and I snap my head up, wondering what's going on.

"Hi, Shannon," I imagine my real mother saying, one arm outstretched. "Don't tell."

I reach for my jacket off the doorknob and push my arms into the sleeves, blow hot breath on the collar and rub my chin back and forth against the soft fabric. I open the front door of the townhouse, but my mother's not there; there is no one outside.

For my tenth birthday, Miranda gives me a piggy bank in the shape of a cross-legged cow and a French knitting kit. She is a lover of garage sales, of sifting through junk. Lydia-Rose and I now have a whole section of our closet devoted to strange toys from the fifties, Hummel figurines, and Christmas ornaments. I put the cow in the closet and stare at the knitting kit, turn it over in my hands. Miranda has told me my whole life that I need a hobby. She tried to get me to take up kickboxing because lately I'm angry for no reason, storming around the house in a purposeless rage. She caught me punching the wall in the laundry room, something I've been doing for years now, and sat me down at the kitchen table. "Sports, Shannon," she said. "You should get involved in sports."

No. I hate sports. Slap of the ball in my hand in baseball, body checks in basketball, panic attacks during swimming lessons. The gasps for breath, flushed cheeks, the pinch of the swim coach's fingernails as she swam with me in her arms after I, at the halfway point down one length of the pool, started to sink. The ridicule, Lydia-Rose's nosebleeds, the flinching, the bitchy girls, the getting picked last for every team. The hard orange balls, sticks, and cleats of field hockey slamming into my shins. The eye rolling when I tried out for the volleyball team; how every time without fail the dodge ball hit me in the face. Then: the special class I was put into where we rode bikes and did light weight training—I guess to spare me any more emotional and physical trauma. There were four of us: a girl who waxcd everyone at academics and never spoke; a red-haired girl, tall and spindly and more awkward than I; and Charlene, a girl with long blonde hair who was good at sports and had to join our class because of a scheduling conflict. She led us all.

French knitting sounds like something I should do. It's solitary, something for crazy people, weird people, people with too much time on their hands, people who are good with their hands, people who are good with finicky things, people who like finicky things, people who can start something and see it through to completion, take a mess of yarn and make something whole.

Am I supposed to unravel the yarn first?

French knitting is simple to learn: just follow
the instructions and wrap brightly coloured
yarn around the metal guides crowning Madame
Knitting Guide's head.
WARNING — CHOKING HAZARD
Small Parts.
Not for children under 3 yrs.

What instructions? Madame Knitting Guide? Are they kidding?

If I were an archaeologist, I'd photograph the knitting kit, describe it in considerable detail, then liken it to something in modern times.

1. Clump of yarn.
2. Red plastic object the size and shape of a small pen, presumably the knitting needle.
3. Wooden tube with a pink cartoon face and four metal prongs sticking out of her head (Madame Knitting Guide). She is hollow; a hole the size of a Smartie runs through her body. The tube has five grooves and fits in my palm like the handle of an umbrella.
4. Instructions? Nope.

Up until now, I have not been involved in arts and crafts of any kind. Lydia-Rose, on the other hand, makes bunnies out of socks. A ladies' tube sock is best (she says men's socks create Sock Monsters), two black buttons of equal size, white string for stitching, and red or pink string for the embroidered mouth and nose. It takes ten minutes.

She's made one for Miranda, two for friends, and says that when she gets around to it she'll make one for me.

They come with instructions: *Wherever you go, so must your Sock Bunny. Treat him with care. He would like it if you made him a car out of one of your old Kleenex boxes.* A few months ago, she made a Sock Voodoo, which is a voodoo doll made out of a sock. A man's sock works best, she said, because you can stuff it full of cotton balls for pinpricking and other violence. Sock Voodoo lives in the back of our closet on top of the Ouija board. When Lydia-

Rose and I are mad about something, we take him out and stab him with a sewing needle. Sometimes we run him over with Sock Bunny's Kleenex car.

I lug the knitting kit around with me for a few weeks, show it to some kids in my class and to a woman at the bus stop. No one even knows what it is. Lydia-Rose fiddles with it for an hour one afternoon and then throws it at me, exasperated.

"What's with the French, anyway?" she asks. We think for a minute. French toast. French bread. French fry. French vanilla. French braid. French maid. French twist. French kiss.

We ask Miranda how to do it, and she shrugs.

The next day, I show the kit to my teacher, Mrs. Bell. She's a small woman with short dark hair and a face like a fist. I am standing in the low-ceilinged classroom, waiting for lunch to be over. I have no friends this year; everyone is just a hello in the hall. Today I am on probation for writing *Dick* all over the girl's bathroom (I can't explain why I did this), and so I have to spend my lunch hour with Mrs. Bell. Seems like a raw deal for her, too, though we kind of like each other. I can tell she feels sorry for me. I feel sorry for her face.

"Spool knitting!" Mrs. Bell coos. "We used to do this when we were kids." Spool knitting. French knitting. I don't like it when there are more than two names for the same thing.

"So what are you going to make?" Mrs. Bell asks. We look at the box. A multicoloured octopus, snake, ladybug, and circus clown stare up at us with little knit eyes.

"The ladybug looks good." The ladybug kicks ass. Miranda would love it. "Maybe a scarf."

Mrs. Bell points to the snake. "Oh, you must make that."

"Wait," I say, "look at the ladybug."

"No, make the snake. Little knitted reptile. Ooohhh, it's so sweet."

"What do I do?" I put Madame Knitting Guide into Mrs. Bell's hands and stare at her expectantly.

"It's been a long, long time," she laughs and looks at me. I hate it when adults talk about how old they are, how much *time* has gone by in their lives. "If I remember correctly, you first put the yarn through the middle, letting it hang, then wrap the yarn around the prongs. Then with a needle go around again to one stitch and put the needle under the first stitch and put it over the stitch already on and sort of knit it off. I hope that's right." She puts it back into my hands, and the lunch bell rings. I have no idea what the fuck she's talking about.

That night, I lie in bed and stare at the box.

It's after midnight and Lydia-Rose is snoring. Thanks to tweezers, spit, and a flashlight Miranda gave me last Christmas, I've finally gotten one piece of yarn through Madame Knitting Guide's body. Trust me, trying to get something weightless like yarn to "fall" down a hole in the middle of a thing called Madame Knitting Guide is about as easy as it sounds. Oh, fuck it. Fuck the ladybug. No one's getting a ladybug; no one's getting a snake.

That same year, Midnight and Flipper get feline leukemia and have to be quarantined in the laundry room so they don't give it to Scratchie. They have horrible diarrhea, and we take turns each day going in there and petting them and cleaning it all up. Scratchie is so sad without Flipper that he begins sleeping under Lydia-Rose's bed. But soon enough he starts showing symptoms, and then it's into the laundry room with him, too, the three of them trapped in misery. When Miranda tells us that it's time to put them to sleep, I think she means it literally, and so I agree to go with her to the vet, thinking we're taking them for some long, extended nap. Lydia-Rose stays at home, fiddling with Madame Knitting Guide, which she now uses with dexterity. She says she's going to knit three little cats in their honour.

Miranda and I put Midnight, Scratchie, and Flipper into two cat carriers and get on the bus after a long negotiation with the bus driver about having pets on board. Everyone stares at us, cats mewing underneath our feet.

The vet is nice. She's a sunny-faced woman with a gap between her front teeth and a buzz cut. She tells us to go to the 7-Eleven across the street and buy a disposable camera. She says we should take some pictures of these guys; she says it's important. Miranda rubs her temples and says that this is a good idea. And so we buy the camera and I hold Midnight, Scratchie, and Flipper while Miranda snaps pictures. The cats are listless in my arms, like rag dolls. I cradle them like babies. Miranda snaps. I put them on the examining table and push their little heads together, gently, so we can get their faces in the same frame. Snap, snap. The vet lets us do this for a long time.

Finally, she appears in the doorway, her face heavy. "Okay," she says. "Do you want to say goodbye now?"

"They're just going to sleep," I tell her, and she smiles at me like I'm half-stupid. This is fine. I'm used to people thinking I'm retarded because of my eye.

The vet shoots something into their veins and then says I should hold them again. So I do. I cradle them and feel their bodies grow lighter, and only then do I understand, because I've done this down at Clover Point with Lydia-Rose.

I'll probably never get the pictures of them developed. Or not for a while. Someone videotaped Lydia-Rose's grandfather's funeral and it sits on our bookshelf with a handwritten label that says "Grandpa's Funeral." Once, I watched the whole thing on fast forward.

A week later, we return to pick up their ashes. Miranda frowns when she looks into the bag. There are three little white urns, sealed shut, and each has been wrapped in fancy ribbon, two pink and one green, as if they are birthday presents.

"This is distasteful," Miranda says, removing one of the ribbons and dangling it in front of the receptionist's face. "Whoever had such a stupid idea."

The receptionist takes the ribbon from Miranda's hand and looks at her sheepishly. We catch the bus home, Miranda cradling the bag of urns on her lap. When we get back, she stands in the middle of the living room, an urn in each hand. Winkie circles her feet, nose in the air, trying to figure out what she's holding. Lydia-Rose sits slumped on the couch, her feet in fuzzy tiger slippers, dabbing at her bloody nose.

Miranda surveys the room, exasperated. "I don't really want to put these anywhere," she says.

"Let's bury them," I say. "Let's give them a funeral."

There's a little park between our house and the high school that nobody ever hangs out in; it's just this weird vacant stretch of grass with a bench. Lydia-Rose and I go out after dark with a shovel and a flashlight, the urns in my backpack. Miranda has instructed us to tell the police the truth if we're caught doing what we are about to do. She says they'll be sympathetic, and that they'll make us fill up the holes, but that's all. Lydia-Rose and I don't have anything to worry about, though. No police ever come around our neighbourhood.

There are a lot of rocks in the little park, and each time the shovel hits one, sparks shoot out. It makes me feel like a caveperson, discovering fire.

I put the disposable camera in my treasure chest under the bed. It's been a while since I've looked through it. When no one's home, I take it into the bathroom, try on my mother's sweatshirt, slide my thumbs through the worn-out thumbholes, fiddle with the Swiss Army knife, stare at the photographs. In them, I am a strange-looking child, too small, with no hair. Sometimes I imagine that I was abandoned by accident—that my mother set me down for a second and then was kidnapped, for example. But looking at my little bald head and unhappy face, I wonder now if it was my fault. I wonder if she abandoned me because I was so ugly.

Mixed in with the photographs are a couple of newspaper articles written about me the week after I was born. A weird-looking woman at the library photocopied them for me a few years ago. We found the articles together on microfiche, and after she read them, she told me that God had a little bit of extra love in his heart for me. She said she could locate some books for me—books I might like to read.

"*Tom Jones,*" she said, her hand on my shoulder, "is about a foundling."

"So is *Superman.*"

The idea comes to me one morning before school. I pull the covers over my head and breathe hot breath into the tiny space until my face is hot and red. I hold the thermometer under the desk lamp then put it quickly into my mouth, wander into the kitchen and tell Miranda that I'm too sick to go to school.

"Oh, little sweetheart," she says, the back of her hand on my forehead. She studies the thermometer, tells me I don't have much of a fever (why didn't the light-bulb trick work?) but that I'm hot and clammy to the touch. She says I can stay home until lunchtime; she will walk me to school in the afternoon.

She pulls the covers up to my chin, feels my forehead again, and says she'll be back in an hour. She cleans an old woman's studio apartment on Tuesday mornings. "Don't move," she says. "I won't be long."

The minute I hear the click of the front door locking

downstairs I'm on my feet, racing up the stairs to her bedroom. I shut the door behind me and scan the room. Her bed is neatly made, the Little Mermaid comforter stretched tightly across and tucked under the mattress. The coffee can is empty of cigarettes, her shoes are lined up against one wall, the ironing board is against the closet door. The room smells of her skin lotion and the stale, thick scent of old smoke.

I open each dresser drawer and flip past her folded T-shirts like pages of a magazine: her large high-waisted underwear, a different colour for each day; her sensible wide-strapped cotton bras, all the same shade of beige; athletic socks rolled into balls; tiny pouches of potpourri in every drawer, their rose scent mixed with the musty wood of the dresser; folded pairs of old jeans she never wears; flannel and cotton nightshirts; pantyhose. I find nothing.

Hanging in her closet are pressed collared shirts, two belted dresses, and a trench coat. I can reach the shelf but it looks like it's just folded-up sweaters. The floor of the closet is stacked with shoeboxes, and I open each one. Each is empty, save for tissue paper, strips of cardboard, plastic rods, and other things designed to keep the shapes of shoes.

I find the photographs and the letters in a black folder hidden in the space between her mattress and the wall. The photographs are of Dell, her ex-husband, whom I recognize from the Polaroid that I stole from Lydia-Rose. He has the same sharp features as she does. He's in a suit, sitting on a park bench in front of a fountain, his arm raised as if to wave at whoever is taking the picture. On the back of the photograph, Miranda has written *Our Wedding Day* in her delicate, perfect handwriting. Then there's a tiny black-and-white photograph of Miranda and one of her sisters, the two of them kneeling on the grass in front of a tombstone. It isn't difficult to figure out which one is Miranda; she has the biggest and brightest face. I flip quickly through the others. It isn't Miranda's past that interests me—for the first time in my life, it's my own. I skim the letters, searching for any sign of my name, a birth certificate, an adoption record, something about my past. But the letters are all from her sister Sharon. I read them quickly, stopping on a paragraph here and there.

... We're not married. He doesn't believe in it. Spain is too hot. Everyone goes to the casino on Saturday nights, so we do too. I'm sorry it's taken me so long to write. He asks about you, Miranda. It's been so many years. I still love you—I do. I can't wait to meet Lydia-Rose ...

The handwriting is hard to read, chicken scratch, like a boy's.

... She was a real cunt of a woman, she slipped one of my perfumes into her purse and she might have stolen other things too ... and someone brought a little speed over—I know, I know, I feel guilty even writing it, but it was my birthday, for Christ's sake. Anyway, okay, she's hurt real bad ...

A real cunt of a woman. I say the phrase in my head, memorizing it for later use. The next letter is dated three years later, the handwriting bigger and loopier.

... There's one nice thing. When they let you out, they act real happy. Like it's your birthday. They pat you on the

back like you had a rapport. And you know what they say to you? You know what they say to you when you get out? They tell you to go out into the world. They tell you to do great things.

Nothing more except a postcard made out to Miranda's mother, the address in Miranda's writing, but no message and no stamp, never sent.

I ransack her room further for a diary, a notepad, flip through a couple of paperbacks for something slipped inside, but there's nothing in here about me—it's all her past, her secrets, her life before I came into it.

When she gets home I am cross-legged on the couch, feeding bits of Ritz crackers to Winkie. Miranda's hair is tied up in a kerchief. She walks stiffly when she returns from cleaning, especially if she's had to get on her knees to scrub underneath something, or had to walk up and down too many flights of stairs. She stops at the kitchen sink and washes her hands—to get the smell of the latex gloves off, she says—then feels my forehead. She brushes the cracker crumbs off the couch and into her hand. She pats Winkie's head.

"Feeling better?" Miranda puts her hand on my knee. They are the strongest looking hands in the world.

"No."

"You sad today, honey?"

"No."

I push myself off the couch, grab my backpack and run down the stairs, slip my feet into my sneakers, and kick the same little rock all the way until I get to school.

I wish I could think of Miranda as my mom, and I've

tried. I've tried as hard as I can all these years. But I watch her and Lydia-Rose together—the way they twitch their noses when they're thinking—and every time I see something like that, I'm reminded that I don't belong here with them. I'm reminded that something is missing. At night I imagine that my real mother is coming for me, her arms outstretched. I imagine she looks just like me, that we have the same hands.

Sometimes, when I'm in a pettier mood, I like to imagine that she walked into the ocean or disappeared into the woods to be eaten by the elements, so racked with guilt from leaving me. Sometimes I imagine she was an alcoholic. Or a sixteen-year-old girl living in a basement suite with a punk rock band. Free rent if she put out and kept the kitchen clean. My father, I guess, was one of the musicians. I like to wonder—drums, bass, or lead guitar? Maybe saxophone or electronic keyboard. I have no ear for music—the notes clink around in my head when I listen to it and I can't tell what's good or bad. All I know is that one of my parents must have been blond. Maybe my mother hadn't realized she was pregnant until it was too late, and the abortion clinic turned her away. I try not to think about what I know is most likely true—that she was a prostitute—and instead I imagine that she's perfect, and beautiful, and didn't mean to abandon me.

In my head, late at night, I draft letters to my mother and father. I say everything I want to say, everything that needs to be said. In my head, I am so eloquent.

6

It was after midnight when Yula got the call that her parents had been in a motorcycle accident. She ran through the forest, Eugene strapped to her body, a flashlight in her hand, until she got to Joel and Edwin's scrap yard. She tore through the rusted-out cars, the dead tractors, the ancient lawnmowers and disassembled engines, the pyramid of tires, the dilapidated horse barn used as a garage. She ran to their trailer, up the narrow metal steps, and pounded on the door. It was unclear to her whether Joel and Edwin were lovers, or simply two men who didn't fit in anywhere else and didn't want to be alone. She knew that Joel slept on one side of the trailer and Edwin on the other, because they made a big deal of it every time she saw them. She pounded on the door until they opened it, standing side by side, Joel in a plaid flannel jacket and his underwear, Edwin in jeans and a hooded sweatshirt. Joel held a shotgun.

"Yula." Joel put the gun down and beckoned her inside,

but she shook her head. They were burly, unshaven men. Joel had huge hairy calves.

"Can you take me to the hospital?" she said and motioned to one of their old rusty pickups.

Jo had broken six of her ribs, her back, her right arm, and both of her ankles, but it was the road rash that was the ugliest, the most painful. The asphalt dug so deep into her skin in places that the doctors said they couldn't extract it until the swelling went down. Yula stood at the end of the bed and stroked her mother's foot. Jo's face was crusted with blood and there was a bandage around her head. She had skidded so hard on the concrete that her helmet had broken in two and a streak of hair on the back of her head had been ripped off. Her jaw was broken in three places. As she'd lain at the side of the road, her tongue had fallen back into her throat and closed off most of her airway; by the time the paramedics came, both her lungs had collapsed and her throat and nose were filled with blood.

Quinn's left arm was crushed. It had almost been torn off completely. But he'd landed on his side, not on his back like Jo, and though he'd never fully use his hand again, he would make a quick recovery. His leather jacket and pants were thicker than Jo's and had protected him from the gravel. He'd kept his head tucked into his chest; he knew how to fall. He stood at the edge of the bed with Yula and they waited for Jo to wake up. They waited for hours, then days. Yula sat in an armchair in the corner of the room, nursing Eugene, and Quinn knelt beside Jo's bed and told her how sorry he was, how wrong he was, what an awful man he was, and how her life would be different now, better, much better, and that he would leave if she wanted him to, anything she wanted, if she would wake up and be okay.

Sometime near dawn, while Eugene was softly snoring, Quinn took Yula's hand and told her the truth—that the accident was his fault, that he'd purposefully tried to scare her mother. He had willed the accident to happen, and it had. He told her their relationship was full of hate and rage. He told her that they had stopped loving each other not long after she was born.

"Why?" asked Yula, her fingers tracing the soft little groove between Eugene's mouth and nose. Quinn drank coffee from a foam cup, and winced as he spoke, his arm in a sling, too swollen to be set in a cast. His black leather jacket, almost shredded, was draped across his lap, a single gold chain looped around his neck. A thin layer of silver stubble spread out over his jaw. His hair, the colour of white smoke.

"The usual story, Yula," he said. His breath was hot and sour from the coffee. "I had an affair. She had an affair. She forgave me, and I never forgave her. The awful truth is I never will." He sipped his coffee, put the cup down, and played with Eugene's little foot. "Some nights I lie awake and trace the whole history of our relationship—the moment we first met, how she let me live in the trailer when I had nowhere else to go, how goofy all that was. How we bonded because we both liked to read. We took so many long walks together—she was the kind of person I could talk to for twelve, thirteen hours."

Yula readjusted Eugene in her arms, and her father took her hand. He ran his fingers over the space where her pinky finger would have been, something her mother used to do. Jo was going to die, he seemed to be saying with this action, and I need you to forgive me. Yula stared at her father and let him continue.

"I don't know when things went wrong," he said, and enveloped her hand in his. "I found myself jealous if she told a funny story at a dinner party—if she made everyone laugh. Something about it made my stomach ache. It made me angry. See, we're intellectual equals. I am as smart as your mother, and she is as smart as me. This is a problem. There's no pecking order. A relationship is like anything else. It needs a leader and a follower. We could never settle into any kind of routine. We're both too alpha, maybe?"

He cleared his throat and took another sip of coffee. His hand shook when he brought the cup to his lips. "Do you remember all those runs I took you on when you were little, you in the Gerry pack? Later on in the day, your mother would take you out, too. You spent your first five years strapped to our backs while we ran. I blew my knee out first, so your mother won that round."

He stretched out in his chair and tipped his head back, and Yula could see the fillings in the back of his mouth. He spoke to the ceiling. "She forgot my birthday one year, and I didn't speak to her for three weeks. Three weeks, making her feel like a ghost in that house. I wouldn't even look at her. In some ways, I think we tortured each other. Look, these things don't seem like much, but they add up. Your mother has a gimlet eye, that's for sure.

I knew that nothing I did would ever be good enough—professionally, romantically, even when it came to you. We were competitive over parenting, for god's sake."

He sat up and searched Yula's eyes. His voice was suddenly aggressive, and Yula felt herself shrinking back from him, both repulsed and afraid. "I fucking hate hospitals," he said, little bits of froth forming at the corners of his mouth. "We need to get her better, get her out of here. The one thing we could ever agree on is that we didn't belong in the city, in any of its institutions. You were a home birth, like Eugene. I don't believe in any of this. It's all bullshit. We're different, okay? You remember this. Everything we need is at home. This other stuff—" He scanned the room as if someone was listening. "Do not believe anything anyone tells you. You have to evaluate the world with your own eyes."

Yula pushed her chair back and prayed for her father to stop talking. He was motor-mouthing, high on painkillers, slobbering as he spoke.

She tried to stand but he put his hand on her leg and pushed her back down. "What I'm trying to tell you about is your mother. It got sick between us. Things can get sick between two people. I hated it. I hated how much I loved her and how much I wanted her to love me. Look, this is bullshit. I needed to dominate her. She never let me dominate her. She always had to win. But I pinned her down one night and held her throat."

Yula shot the words at his face. "I remember."

"I wanted her to be in love with me. Me. I wasn't trying to kill her. I needed to use my power—she needed to respect me a little." He leaned toward Yula, and she held her breath. He was so high that his pupils were dilated. "Do you see what kind of sickness can develop between two people?"

Yes, she knew. Yula knew her parents loved *and* hated each other. She could also see that they were each convinced they were special—each of them individually, but also the relationship as a whole. She felt the same arrogance from their neighbours on Mount Finlayson, as if living out of the city, in nature, made you different somehow. Apart from the rest. Spiritually, not just geographically. And yet she believed it. Despite herself, she felt it, too—they were all, somehow, different.

"I can't be alone, Yula," her father said suddenly. "I wish I could, but I just can't."

Someone tapped lightly on the door, and Yula and her father looked up. It was Jo's friend, Luella. She was a heavily made-up woman with long, light brown hair and rings on every finger. She wore a turquoise skirt with a black knee-length dress over it, leather riding boots, and a black jacket. Red lipstick. Yula thought she looked like a movie star.

"Hi," Luella said.

Yula was fascinated with Luella. She was a registered nurse, but she painted—she'd even had a show in an art gallery. Yula liked her but couldn't say for certain why. She was tactile—affectionate—and rested her hand on Yula's shoulder when she spoke. She'd once told Yula that she wore mostly black because other colours were too distracting, like bees buzzing around her head.

Yula's mother didn't have any friends other than Luella.

She kept herself so isolated. Occasionally someone would come out to the property and have dinner with them, but it was such a rare occurrence that Yula wasn't sure it had happened more than twice. Luella, though, seemed to be a constant in her mother's life. They spoke on the phone every other night. Yula remembers the three of them walking through the park to Beacon Drive-In to get soft-serve ice cream, then sitting in the bleachers by the soccer field and eating the cones. Luella's long brown hair had white-blonde highlights back then. She wore a lot of powdery foundation, which sparkled when the sun hit her face. Unlike Jo, she covered herself in jewellery— ten or fifteen beaded necklaces circled her neck, her ears were lined with silver hoops, her fingers heavily ringed. She wore striped pedal pushers that day, a thick elastic belt cinched around her waist, a sleeveless black silk blouse and red peep-toe heels. She looked like something out of a French fashion magazine, Jo had said. Jo sat between Luella and Yula in corduroys and a plaid shirt. She never wore makeup. Sometimes, when the women talked, they would reach across and hold hands.

Quinn made a sound and shook his head, then padded out of the room. He seemed to disapprove of Luella; Yula didn't understand why.

"Honey." Luella walked toward Jo and gently took her hand. She wasn't the type to cry. She stood beside the bed, holding Jo's hand. Quinn didn't come back in again.

They sat in the hospital room for the next two days, not waiting for Jo to wake up anymore but waiting for her to die. She went, finally, on the third day.

Three days before I am born, Yula and Harrison work in the garden while Eugene is sleeping. The leaves are crowding the flowerbeds and they scoop them into black garbage bags before they turn acidic. Harrison works away in a pair of suede gardening gloves; a cigarette in his mouth slinks smoke into the corner of his eye. He wears navy coveralls and his orange ball cap, his white-blond braid running the length of his back.

When they get tired, they drive into town and order egg sandwiches and French fries from Mom's Café and read the *Goldstream Gazette*. Another swimmer has drowned in the Potholes and a grow-op down the road, though not the one next to Joel and Edwin's place, has been raided.

"What's the difference between an island and an archipelago?" Yula says to Harrison, pointing to the word in one of the articles. She cuts up bits of her sandwich for Eugene, fiddles with his ears, wipes the crumbs from the corners of his mouth. He is docile today, still sleepy from his nap, and Yula keeps bending over to kiss his forehead. She is always surprised by how much she loves the way he smells.

"I don't know, Yula." Harrison laughs and dips his sandwich in a smear of ketchup. "Island is easier to spell." He watches a man at a neighbouring table take out a cigarette machine and roll two cigarettes; he puts one behind his ear and one in the pocket of his shirt. Harrison asks the man to roll him one and tosses him a couple of quarters in return.

Harrison's skin is deep brown from working in the sun, and the space around his eyes is covered in fine lines, moist from sweat. His hair needs to be washed; one piece hangs down in a little dreadlock under his cap. His face these days has a tired, pinched look.

He smiles at Yula and takes out his wallet, puts a couple of tens on the table. Mom's has been remodelled; they've added a new section in the back and a jukebox. "We could go somewhere, you know," Harrison says. He reaches over and ruffles Eugene's hair. "We could move."

"Like where."

"Nothing fancy. Drive up north. You, me, Eugene." He gestures at her stomach. "The baby." When Yula doesn't respond, he shakes his head and nods toward the door. "Need a smoke."

Outside, Harrison leans on the hood of the car and lights his cigarette with a cupped hand. Across the street a few people walk up the steps to the Holy Trinity Church, and he watches some kids playing in the empty lot beside it. He wonders if the old car will start. He stands there and watches the kids kick a rock around on the pavement. He drums his fingers on the roof of the car until Yula is ready to go.

That night, he doesn't come home. Yula makes her dinner alone, and eats it alone, and forgets to turn off the water after the broccoli is done so that it boils and boils as she eats on the porch with Eugene, and when she goes inside to wash her one plate, the pot has blackened and is smouldering at the edge of the stove.

And she starts to whimper, because she doesn't know what else to do—the handle of the pot too hot to touch and the smoke-filled room and the minutes that feel like whole years as she stands there weeping, for so long that she feels herself grow into an old woman, alone in her kitchen with a smouldering pot, alone with her little boy, as if all her lifetime has passed in that kitchen, her wrinkled skin, her aging hands, waiting and waiting, for Harrison to come home.

7

A couple of days after she turns thirteen, Lydia-Rose gets her period. I do not have mine yet and am horrified and embarrassed—*mortified*—by the idea. Miranda buys her a big pack of pads and Lydia-Rose bursts into tears and says she feels like she's wearing a diaper. And so they disappear into the bathroom for an hour while Miranda shows her how to use a tampon. When they come out of the bathroom, Lydia-Rose is still crying.

"I can't do it," she says to me. Her hands are shaking.

I shrug at her. I don't know what to say.

Miranda kisses us goodnight and tells Lydia-Rose that they'll discuss it tomorrow. For now, she says, try to survive with the pads.

Lydia-Rose sits on my bed and holds her head back for fear of a nosebleed. "I hate this," she says. "I hate this. I hate this."

I put my hand on her shoulder, but she shrugs it off.

"I'm such a baby," she says. "I hate this." She stabs a pushpin into Sock Voodoo's crotch. She stands up and makes me look at her butt. "You can tell, can't you. You can see the goddamn pad."

"I can't see it." This isn't entirely true. At thirteen, Lydia-Rose is five-foot-ten. She stands in an arc over the dresser, her back slightly hunched from being so tall. Her ballet flats are as long and thin as skis. I am barely five feet. When we walk to school in the mornings, some of the kids yell that we look like Bert and Ernie.

Our bedroom is a disaster. Lydia-Rose has a faux zebra-skin bedspread and I still have my old pink comforter, which is covered in dog hair. Her balls of yarn compete for space with my mix CDs on a tipsy wooden desk. A teetering bookshelf and tower of banker's boxes filled with photo albums threaten to crash down. Lydia-Rose's ukulele and paint-by-number attempts crowd the top of our dresser, and our stint at making Fimo animals has left crooked dinosaurs and red hedgehog-like things balanced on all available surfaces. Lydia-Rose tried to knit a stuffed giraffe with Madame Knitting Guide this morning, and little giraffe parts, some half-eaten by Winkie, litter the room. Last year, Lydia-Rose painted the ceiling black and stencilled yellow stars and then hung maroon curtains over the window that she made herself. A wayward bird smashed a hole the size of a baseball in the upper right-hand corner of our window the other day, but we're in no rush to get it fixed. Pencil crayons, tubes of oil paint, paper maché masks, berets, scarves, ironic posters, buttons, a baby carriage filled with CDs, rows of shoes, a pile of screws and washers, a stack of stuffed animals shoved in one corner, an outstanding collection of sea glass, sixteen paperbacks, and a full-length mirror reflecting it all, giving us the mess twice.

A Post-it Note is pressed to the wall. *Go big or go home*, it says.

Our bedroom is never beautiful except at six-thirty in the morning, when it looks like the sun is rising right into the room. The mirror reflects the light and shoots it everywhere. I tell Lydia-Rose that we should get up at dawn more often, but she is never game.

That night, we don't sleep. We shove a towel under the door to block the noise and put on a Nirvana album that I secretly hate but don't want to admit it.

Lydia-Rose stands in front of the mirror in her bra and flattens her breasts with a scarf. She tells me to wrap packing tape around the scarf while she holds up her arms. She shines the desk lamp on her face and draws stubble on her chin with a smoky eyebrow pencil, then shoves her hair under an AC/DC ball cap, leaves the bedroom, and comes back with two pairs of men's corduroy pants, a denim shirt, shoulder pads, and two pairs of huge black army boots, three sizes too big, from Miranda's consignment pile. She pulls on the shirt, pushes the shoulder pads in, slips her legs into the big pants and her feet into the boots. She turns to me and then gives herself a moustache with the smoky pencil and colours in her eyebrows. Winkie sits at the end of my bed, looking at her as if she's insane.

"Now you," she says, and throws a boot in my direction. I slip my foot into it and then reach for the big pants. I don't have to do much to my upper body; Lydia-Rose tosses me a sweatshirt because we know it'll suffice. She picks up the pencil and gives me a huge moustache, then pulls a Canucks toque over my huge and ridiculous blonde hair.

We stand in front of the mirror, heads cocked.

Boys stare at Lydia-Rose. When her arms are full of textbooks and she's about to kick her locker door shut, they come running. *Let me get that for you,* they say. They give her the window seat on the bus. They let her move to first in line. They offer to pay. She is, at thirteen, a knockout.

"You're hideous," I say. "I'm sorry, but you're a really ugly man."

Lydia-Rose laughs and examines her face. She moves her legs apart and tries to stand like a guy.

I can't stop laughing. "You're fine from the neck down. It's your face—sorry—it's your face that's the problem."

I am right. The boots, baggy khakis, and facial hair have made her look like a gangsta-rapper. But her face frightens us both. She is a weasel-faced, heavy-browed, dark-skinned man; *America's Most Wanted* material; the guy staggering out of his trailer in white underpants on *Cops*; a crack dealer; someone who digs kiddie porn; Kokanee-out-of-a-can.

"Holy shit-fuck," I say. "Maybe it's the hat?"

She puts it on backwards and we consider the new look. I am laughing so hard that no sound is coming out of my mouth.

We stagger out of the bedroom in our boots. Lydia-Rose tosses me a pair of gloves and then I understand what's happening—she wants to sneak out. "Don't take off the gloves—your hands look *so* stupid," she whispers.

She creeps into the kitchen, takes a sausage out of the fridge, and gives it to Winkie to keep her occupied. And then we open the front door in increments, until it's wide enough for us to slip through, and once we're outside we break into a run, baggy pants flapping, boots pounding, all the way to the McDonald's down the street. Lydia-Rose holds the door for a couple of ladies. I have to pee but I don't dare. We sit, slouch-shouldered, with our legs apart, elbows on the table. We let our stomachs sag. At one point, I burp.

"I hope we don't run into anyone we know," Lydia-Rose whispers.

"How the fuck are we going to order?"

"I'll do it." She stands and grins like a prizefighter, marches right over to the counter. I watch, horrified. I study the face of the boy taking her order. He looks scared.

But in the green vinyl booth of McDonald's that night, no one bothered us. There were a couple of girls about our age in the next booth over, with trendy parkas and striped mittens, earmuffs, and bright pink cheeks. I smiled at them and they looked away quickly, then looked back again. Lydia-Rose looked legitimately like a man. A creepy man. I don't know what the hell I looked like. Ronald McDonald?

Behind me, I heard a splash. One of the girls in the booth bent over to pick up a fallen cup of root beer, the brown liquid on her shoes and fingertips. Lydia-Rose and I locked eyes. We looked at her ass, her pants pulled taut, the faint edge of her panty line. Lydia-Rose's lips curled upward and she nodded at me, as if we both knew something now—something that the bent-over girl would never know.

When we stood in line to get more French fries, no one said *Excuse me* to us when they needed to get by. In an ugly man's shoes, it was all pushes and dark stares.

Back at the townhouse, Miranda is waiting for us in the living room. Her face is screwed up in a tight little knot. She looks at us and I can tell that she wants to laugh but knows she can't. Someone's got to be in charge. And so we are lectured—at length and it goes too far—until Lydia-Rose's nose begins to leak blood.

As punishment, when we get home from school the next afternoon it's Spring Cleaning Day with Miranda, except that it's not spring. We clean the bathroom, walk and bathe Winkie (who for some reason smells like duck poo), clip her toenails (hell), prune the dead parts off plants, pick up every single leaf that Winkie has tracked into the house, vacuum all the animal fur off the carpet (at first we tried to lint-brush it in an attempt to avoid lugging the heavy vacuum out of the closet, but this proved futile), beat the rag rugs, disinfect the kitchen, launder every machine-washable thing in the house, water and fertilize the newly pruned plants, and then clean something we've never cleaned before, just for the sake of cleaning. For example, the paper towel dispenser. Which I wasn't aware could get dirty. Miranda calls our activities a "blitz." After dinner we iron the pillowcases and the cloth napkins, which we use once a year.

The only thing that makes this ordeal bearable is that Miranda puts on the *Edward Scissorhands* soundtrack—to promote speed and efficiency and to create a sense of whimsy, she says, somewhat lightheartedly, dishcloth in hand.

The next morning I take the dog for a poo, then pretend I'm walking to school but turn back once I'm sure that Miranda has gone to work. I've decided to take naked pictures of myself with Lydia-Rose's fancy digital camera.

I'm hoping to angle the camera so that the mirror won't capture the flash, but I'm scared Miranda or Lydia-Rose will come home, so it ends up being a series of haphazard snapshots—amateur angles, ill-thought-out poses, poor facial expressions. It is a cliché thing to do, but I have no choice. I want to know what my future lovers will see when I undress for them. And I can't tell from looking in the mirror because a mirror reflection is actually your reflection backwards, i.e., your left hand becomes your right hand; therefore, it isn't accurate. I need accuracy. So I take eight fast clicks, throw on my bathrobe, jam the USB cable into the back of the computer, wait for the icon to appear on the desktop, and double-click on the first image.

We have an old Apple ColorSync monitor, which is only a good thing if it's working. It's not. The RGB settings are all fucked up, and instead of "Millions of Colors," I get green. So I read the Help files, which suggest I recalibrate my monitor. So I do it, and all that happens is I get an error message that says "Error. Factory settings have been restored," and then everything turns a brighter shade of green. I feel like taking a big Jiffy marker and writing GreenSync on the bottom of the monitor just to clear things up around here.

The point is that thanks to the ColorSync monitor, my mission to spend the day deconstructing an accurate rendition of my naked body is left unfulfilled. My skin is a kind of pasty chartreuse mixed with putty, and my nipples are outlined in a deep emerald. Not what I am looking for. Plus, the flash has indeed been caught by the mirror and my head looks like a big ball of pale green cotton on fire. Again, inaccurate. But that's not the ColorSync monitor's fault. It's the digital camera's, for having its Flash selection menu be a series of ambiguous icons instead of words like "Flash On" and "Flash Off." How am I supposed to know the difference between a lightning bolt and an eyeball?

When I am fifteen and Lydia-Rose is sixteen, she goes to a party with a boy she has a crush on and tells no one about it, not even me. She walks into our bedroom, face pale, a little after midnight and climbs into my bed. This is something she hasn't done in years. My feet are instantly hot and uncomfortable. I am drinking NeoCitran (*three* packets) and wearing flannel penguin pyjamas because it gets cold here at night, even in the summer. I've been reading bits of Judy Blume books to Winkie for hours, waiting for Lydia-Rose to come home, and feeling like I've spent my whole life with a head cold.

We lock eyes. She has become the classic beauty that everyone predicted. But there's a pimple on her cheek that looks like a tapioca bead. It is swollen and red from her picking at it.

"Put some toothpaste on that thing," I tell her. "It'll shrink by morning." I push her out of the bed and worm off my socks. Sometimes I think I have the sweatiest feet in the world. There's no way other people's feet sweat as much as mine.

Lydia-Rose sits at the end of my bed and kicks off her sneakers. She is wearing a sleeveless wrap-around sweater with a little belt around the waist and flared jeans. Her socks are bubblegum pink. She lifts up the sweater and shows me her purple satin bra.

"I bought this for tonight. I feel like such a fucking idiot."

I stare at the bra. It is lined in black lace and exposes the tops of her breasts. It is an amazing looking thing. But what catches my eye is the long red welt that runs down the length of her stomach, puffy and raw.

"What the fuck happened?" I reach up and trace the welt with my finger.

She flinches and drops her sweater. "Don't ever have sex, Shannon. Just fucking don't." She unbuckles her jeans and lets them drop. Her thighs are covered in red welts, too. She stands in front of me in her underwear.

"He said it would be fun," she says and looks at her feet, still in the pink socks.

"What?"

"If we did it rough."

"Jeremy?"

"He said we should have filthy sex. I don't know. Fuck. What the fuck is wrong with me."

"There's nothing wrong with you."

"Do you know what he said to me after he finished? He said, 'You're due, soon. I can smell it.'"

I pull back the covers and pat the mattress. She climbs in. I feel a rush of sympathy for her, but there's something stronger—more selfish—and it's my own shame and jealousy. I've never gotten a period. I don't radiate sexual. I could stand on the corner in a nightie and spike heels and men would walk on by. Miranda says I'll get my period soon, but I just don't think I have it in me.

Lydia-Rose picks up a book about Marina Abramovic and starts reading out sentences from it. Lately I am so sick of her I could scream. She spends all day browsing art books, then delivers mini lectures to me when I try to use paper towels for dinner napkins or wash our whites with colours or don't say *Excuse me* before I answer the phone. I find it nauseating. I want to eat with my hands.

And then I have this funny thought as we're lying in bed. It kind of bursts into my head, like a bright flash. I want to carve a little star into my calf. Where did this thought come from? Regardless, here it is, ping-ponging around in my head, restless until I do something about it.

"This woman lets people do whatever they want to her," Lydia-Rose says and points to a picture of Marina Abramovic in crotch-less leather chaps. I fling the covers off, rescue Winkie from the comforter burrito I've turned her into, grab my Swiss Army knife, and lock myself in the bathroom. *She let someone hold a gun to her head!* I turn on the water so I don't have to hear any more of this crap and roll up my pyjamas to study the hideous white flesh of my calf. I have such ugly legs. I've made a habit of studying women's legs, and no one's legs are as ugly as mine. My knees are so fleshy that I can grab handfuls of fat. No one else's legs look like this, I'm sure of it. When I have money, I'm going to get liposuction. Suck the fat right out of these things.

My calf is so white that it looks blue. My shins are covered in bruises because I'm still so clumsy. I must hit my shin five times a day. I flip open the Swiss Army knife and drag it down over my lower calf, about an inch. It seems right, somehow, to do this—to carve this star. But the knife doesn't break the skin. It leaves a white line and that's it. Is the blade too dull? I close my eyes, push as hard as possible. The skin is red but there's still no blood. I think about the knives we have in the kitchen. A serrated knife is what I need. My heart pounds. I like having secrets, doing weird stuff. I like being stealthy. I open the door to the bathroom. "Gonna trim my hair," I say to Lydia-Rose. "I need the good scissors." Lydia-Rose doesn't look up. *This woman took pills for catatonia and had a seizure!*

I push past our beaded curtain and stumble into the kitchen. Part of our kitchen wall is mirrored, a white lattice dividing the large pane into a checkerboard. It gives me nine different faces. I balance a steak knife in the elastic of my pyjama pants and walk stiffly past the bedroom, past Lydia-Rose and her stupid book, and into the bathroom. I take her blue shirt out of the laundry basket and rip it a bit.

The steak knife does its job efficiently. I don't even have to press that hard. I'm surprised at how well I handle the pain. My hand is shaking but I make one clean cut, about an inch long, on my lower calf. Tiny beads of blood bubble out and I mop them up with my finger and swirl them around in my mouth. The blood tastes dark, like molasses. I make two more cuts until I have a triangle. The next part is more difficult—the next triangle. For some reason, I am making a Star of David. It's difficult because I have to cut over the parts I've already cut. I hold my breath and press down with the knife. I get a weird sensation in my stomach, something like guilt or shame, like how I felt when Lydia-Rose and I threw rocks at a suckerfish until it died. An evil feeling. I put the knife under the bathroom sink; I'll deal with it in the morning.

I blow my nose and walk into the bedroom, catch a stack of *YM*s with the side of my foot. "Damn." They fan out on the floor.

"Filthy sex," Lydia-Rose says. "What is wrong with me?"

"Nothing's the matter with you," I say to her. "Do you want to go to sleep?"

"No. Do you?"

"No."

Lydia-Rose flips onto her stomach and fights with the covers for a second. She spits out some of Winkie's fur that has found its way into her mouth. "He didn't know it was my first time. I never want him to know."

I stare at her and want to slap the back of her head. My calf is burning but it's a pleasant, warm burn.

I climb into bed and wince when my pyjamas rub the cuts. "Why'd you fuck him if you didn't want to?"

"Don't lecture me." She pushes herself out of my bed and climbs into her own. "You're a stupid freak sometimes. Grow up."

A week later, I have to break the news to her.

"He has another girlfriend. I'm sorry." I've seen them at the Vietnamese restaurant downtown. The new girlfriend wears a pink coat and has long black hair. She is short and buck-toothed and hangs off Jeremy's arm as casually as a rag. I sit at the bus stop and watch them in the picture window of the restaurant, where they huddle like chipmunks over their food. The girlfriend slurps her noodles and wipes the end of her nose with her hand. Jeremy doesn't notice because she has wiggled her toe into the corner of his shoe. He looks smug, and high, and happy.

I tell Lydia-Rose this, and she does not speak to me for days.

Now that I am older, I am a better spy. I've snuck into Miranda's room countless times, read all her letters from her sister Sharon, determined that Sharon was in rehab for a while and that this was the cause of a lengthy falling out (discovered via more letters, in a manila envelope underneath the mattress). I've also discovered that Miranda doesn't seem to notice if I slip a five- or ten-dollar bill out of her purse every once in a while, and so I do it every few weeks and buy myself a pair of shoes from the Sally Ann or some cigarettes so I can finally learn to smoke. I have a summer job in the mailroom at the Maritime Museum, but it's volunteer work—for experience, Miranda says. That's fine, but I need something on the side every now and again. Because Lydia-Rose is already sixteen, she has a job bagging groceries after school. That's where she met Jeremy.

Lydia-Rose keeps a Moleskine diary stuffed in the toe of her giant tiger slippers, and I have read every page. She writes about everyone except me. Pages and pages about Miranda, about her teachers, her friends, some woman she met on the bus, the old Chinese man who stands outside the corner store, about Jeremy. Sometimes I'll do something strange—or, if I catch myself saying something profound, I'll say it again—in an effort to affect her, but nothing makes its way onto the diary's pages. Even when we fight. I must not be in her head as much as she is in mine. I would never keep a diary, lest someone like me discovered it. There are too many ugly thoughts in my head. Who wants to write this stuff down? Who wants to remember it? *Today I thought about stepping in front of a bus. Today I wondered whether it would hurt more to slit my wrists or hang myself in the closet. Today I prayed to God because my stomach hurt so bad I thought I was dying.*

Miranda starts having me see a counsellor. He is a short man named Leo, with a bald head and a thick, dark brown beard. We sit cross-legged on the floor, on little blue mats. He throws his hands around when he talks, has me chart my moods on a piece of graph paper. He tries to talk me out of things, gets me to punch a pillow. But my problem, I tell Leo, is the way I was born.

Leo considers this for a minute, then asks me what I know about my birth parents, and so at our next appointment I bring in my shoebox with the sweatshirt, the Swiss Army knife, the newspaper articles. But I don't say a word. I sit on my little blue mat and keep it all inside my head.

"Do you think about her often?" Leo asks. "Your birth mother?"

I take the Swiss Army knife out, flip open the little blades and the ice pick, shove them back inside. "Dunno."

Leo's eyes follow my hands, and something darkens in his expression.

"Do you—" he starts, leaning in slightly, "ever think about hurting yourself?"

I know how this goes so I don't answer this one either. The girls in my class have been dropping like flies. First they get this weird, faraway look in their eyes, then they start wearing long-sleeved shirts, even in summer, then they disappear for a while and come back with big white bandages wrapped around their wrists. Then they lose twenty pounds, transfer to the fucked-up school, and no one ever sees them again. That is *not* what's going to happen to me.

"No, Leo," I tell him finally. "I don't."

After my appointment, I'm supposed to go home, but instead I tug on my mother's sweatshirt and take the bus downtown. I whine and make a big fuss about forgetting my bus fare at home, and the driver lets me on for free. I spend ten of the twenty dollars I stole from Miranda's wallet this morning on two used CDs from Lyle's Place, then head to Market Square. A bunch of guys are sitting around banging on bongo drums, so I sit by them and nod my head in time until one of them passes me his drum and I get to bang along. But it's pointless and boring and there's too much pot smoke, so I walk to the Johnson Street Bridge and look out over the water. The wind is cold and rips through the sweatshirt, through my jeans. I clutch the shoebox to my chest. I want to know who my mother is. I want to know who my real family is, who I really belong to, why I look this way, why I feel this way. I want to know these things more than anything in the world.

The sun comes out behind me, and I turn to face it. It's late in the afternoon and the temperature is dropping. The wind gusts and rattles the masts of the boats below. I walk over the bridge and onto one of the docks, where a man is unloading crabs off an aluminum boat. He's a small guy with a big moustache. He wears a ball cap, overalls, and gumboots. I watch him hoist a plastic crate off the boat and set it on the dock, reach into it with bare hands, pick up a protesting crab, and then toss it into a keeper cage that has been tied to the dock with rope. When the cage is full he throws it over the side, and it sinks with a dull splash into the ocean.

"Ever get pinched?" I ask.

He laughs. "Sometimes. Not too often. It's usually not the one you're picking up, it's the one underneath him."

He tells me the crabs were caught off Esquimalt Lagoon. They'll be shipped to Vancouver and then to Hong Kong.

A man with a ratty beard and a toque pulled low over his forehead walks by and nods to us. He has smooth, pale skin and looks about twenty-five; his cheeks are flushed from the wind. As he passes the crab boat, he stops and says, "How's it goin'? How'd it go out there?"

The crab man nods and says it's all right.

"Got a light?" The crab man's friend is tall and skinny, his toque pulled down so low that I can barely see his eyes. He twitches an unlit cigarette up and down in his mouth.

"No."

"Party tonight." He hands me a flyer and tells me how many deejays there are going to be, that it goes all night. "You want to go?"

I look at the flyer. "Doesn't say where it is."

The guy twitches his cigarette. "Call the number after ten," he says and points to the fluorescent green numbers scattered all over the flyer in a weird robot font. "Then come find me."

"Okay."

He tugs his hat even lower over his eyes and spins around, heads back toward downtown. A seagull slaps its feet along the dock, and I follow it to the edge where we both stare into the foamy green water.

"Don't jump," the guy calls out.

I watch him disappear up Johnson Street and shove the flyer in my pocket. I guess I could go to the party. Why not? My heart pounds at the thought of not going home.

I still have ten bucks so I walk up to McDonald's and

get a chicken sandwich and fries and swivel around on a plastic seat under the big chandeliers. It is six o'clock. What am I supposed to do for four hours?

At seven, the manager asks me to leave, so I walk up Douglas and talk to some lady at the bus stop with a huge backpack and a couple of dogs. She has chin-length black hair and a nose ring and says she's going to the mainland tomorrow.

"You been off the island before?" she says.

I shake my head. She is almost crazed to hear this.

"No, no, no," she says. "You can't become one of those people who never leave. Don't do that."

I laugh. "Okay, okay." I like her already.

"Your folks ever take you on a holiday?"

"My folks are dead."

"Oh," she says. She pats one of her dogs, this big slobbery looking thing, and then looks at me like she doesn't have anything left to say.

It's getting cold and my desire to go to the party is waning. I kind of just want to hang out with Winkie and then get in my bed.

When the bus comes, I finger the change in my pocket and instead tell the same sob story as last time but the bus driver looks at me cold and hard and then asks me in a loud voice to get off his bus.

The lady with the dogs looks at me and smiles. "You need to work on your act," she says. "You gotta act like this is the first time anything like this has happened to you, like you just can't believe you don't have enough for a lift home."

When I get back to the townhouse, I open the front door as quietly as possible and stand at the bottom of the stairs, holding my breath. I can hear Miranda and Lydia-Rose talking in the kitchen. I close my eyes and strain to listen.

"Is she?" Miranda is saying.

"What?"

"Is she using drugs?"

"I don't know." Lydia-Rose sounds annoyed. "Probably. What do you expect? You're too easy on her."

I hear Miranda curse, something she never does. "Are you on my side or not right now?" she says.

"I wish it was just us."

"Oh, no, you don't," Miranda says. "Don't start that."

I hear one of them rattling around in the cupboards, then the sound of Miranda going upstairs. "Twenty more minutes. Then I'm calling the police."

"I'm making something to eat. You want to eat?" Lydia-Rose calls out, but Miranda doesn't answer.

I wait a few minutes, then open and close the front door again and walk up the stairs. Lydia-Rose is sitting at the kitchen table, pale-faced, scribbling in her diary.

"Mom was going to file a police report," she says without looking at me. "I talked her out of it."

I put the shoebox on the table. "Thanks." I crouch and pat Winkie, let her lick the salt off my fingertips from the McDonald's fries.

"Where were you?" she says.

"Nowhere."

"You better go talk to her."

The hallway is black except for a small stream of light filtering in from the kitchen. Miranda stands at the top of the stairs, backlit by her bedroom light. I stop on the landing and lean into the newel post.

Lydia-Rose stands behind me, and we look up at Miranda. Here I am: dorky thing with wild white-blonde hair, bum-eyed Smurf. Miranda stares down at Lydia-Rose, her nearly six-foot-tall daughter, this striking young woman, and me.

"I don't know who you are tonight," Miranda says to me.

I shrug. I tell her I got wrapped up in looking at CDs at the record store. I tell her I got upset after my appointment with Leo and needed to walk around. I tell her about the crab fisherman but not about the guy with the flyer. "I can't believe I lost track of the time," I tell her. I look at Lydia-Rose, and she rolls her eyes.

Miranda stares at me. "It's me or nothing, Shannon," she says. "I'm all you've got."

When I don't respond, she goes back into her bedroom, leaving me in darkness. I grope for the banister and slide my feet down each stair. If Lydia-Rose were in a better mood she'd joke with me that I need night-vision goggles. But tonight all she has to offer is a cold dead stare. She looks at me like she hates the very core of my being.

"Not much of an apology," she says.

We walk into the kitchen, and I watch her take a salad bowl out of the cupboard. Two globs of olive oil, one blip of balsamic vinegar. Pinch of salt. Grated lemon peel. She works in silence, in the light of a street lamp streaming through the window. The sound of Miranda's radio travels down through the floor vents, and then the gurgle of her turning on the shower.

Later, we sit in silence, eyes glued to the flickering TV screen in the blackness of the living room. We sit on opposite sides of the couch, Lydia-Rose underneath her zebra-skin bedspread, and I wait for her to stop being so mad.

"I'm sorry," I say to the television, to the couch, to my empty bowl of salad, to my sock with a hole in the toe, to sleeping Winkie.

Finally, Lydia-Rose looks at me. "Hey, it's all right," she says. "It's all right."

And so I climb underneath the bedspread with her, Sock Voodoo at our feet, pins sticking out of its head. After a while Lydia-Rose complains she's too warm and opens the window. She falls asleep before I do.

The curtains stretch out in the wind like thin white arms. So often we fall asleep together this way, in front of the TV in the living room, her head on my shoulder.

But after an hour I jolt awake, my neck throbbing with pain. Somehow, during my long and unfulfilling day, I've pulled a muscle. I ransack the bathroom for Lydia-Rose's old Tylenol 3s, left over from when she had her wisdom teeth removed. I take a heating pad and two tea towels, wrap them around my neck, and fasten them with packing tape. I look like I'm about to be shipped somewhere.

While Lydia-Rose sleeps, I tiptoe into the kitchen and search her diary for something about my disappearance tonight. *I hate myself for still being in love with Jeremy,* tonight's entry reads. *I thought I could have a few drinks, that it wouldn't be …* And then there's a list of all the things she wants to achieve before she turns twenty. *Start a magazine. Travel Europe by train. Lose fifteen pounds.*

There's nothing about me. Not a word. The absence of anything—the indifference—hits me harder than I want it to.

In the back of her diary, she writes terrible poetry, and the latest one is about her breasts. I sneak into the bedroom to tear one of the pages out—I might need to blackmail her someday, for instance—when I feel Miranda's eyes on me. Even through the codeine haze, I feel her bristle with anger.

She is holding her wallet so that it gapes open, empty of cash. It's after midnight, and her eyes are tired. She looks at me, the towels around my neck, then down at the diary. In an instant she knows what it is and what I'm doing. I feel the patience drain right out of her.

"Do I need to buy a bigger house?" she says, and points to the diary. "You can't respectfully share a room?"

I close the diary and push it toward her, my cheeks hot with shame. "Please don't tell her."

"What do you want?" she says, gesturing to the diary, the empty wallet, the diary, the wallet.

My heart swells with guilt and I stab my fingernails into my palms.

She waves the wallet at me. *Where are you? Where are you right now?* "You're acting like a criminal, Shannon. Skulking around. You won't even meet my eyes."

I try to pay attention to what she's saying, but I don't want her to hurt me.

"When you steal," she says, "when you invade our privacy, it makes me feel like I'm at risk. I can't," she says, "I *won't* be made to feel at risk in my own home."

I stare into my pink bedspread, examine the little threads, the places where the dye is fading, and then the little hairs on my arm, bright white, my little chubby hands. In the time it takes my eyes to travel the length of my arm, I've removed myself from her words completely.

Somewhere, in the distance, I can hear firecrackers. Miranda hears them, too, and pauses her lecture for a second. *Kah-boom, bang, boom.* "Why tonight?" she asks. "What's going on that we don't know about?" Her arms hang limp at her sides.

"I'm worried," she starts to say, though now that I've started to dissociate, her voice is rising above me, thinning out into the atmosphere, "that you spend too much time alone."

I hear Lydia-Rose wake and go into the bathroom, then the sound of her rummaging for something.

"Shannon," Miranda says. "I can't talk to you if you won't look at me."

I stare at my fingernails and wring my hands. "I'll pay you back."

"When you love someone," she says. I watch her move closer to me, her exhausted face exaggerated in the dim light, and wait for the rest of the sentence.

I lift my heavy head, the tea towels threatening to come

loose, the heating pad about to slip out of place, and slide Lydia-Rose's diary into the toe of her slipper.

"I'm sorry," I say to Miranda, but her anger has shifted to a more unreachable place; it has moved past me, onto other disappointments in her life, to Dell.

"Go live somewhere else if you don't like it here," Miranda says and spins around, headed upstairs.

8

"Harrison, please."

Two days before Yula gives birth to me, she watches as Harrison sits at Quinn's kitchen table, rolls a ten-dollar bill into a tube, and carves out a little line of cocaine with one of Quinn's credit cards. It's the first time he has done this in front of her, though she's suspected for months. She stands in his old coveralls and rubs her belly as she watches him. It isn't enough to get him addicted, he says to her, it never is.

"Where were you last night?" she says, but he does not answer.

He drops his head when the cocaine hits his bloodstream, and she thinks about how the last time he made love to her he couldn't come. He had punched the mattress and she had been frightened, for the first time, that she could no longer please him.

"You've got work in an hour," she says and goes back

to loading the dishwasher. They're in the big house, Quinn asleep in the back bedroom. It is the last week of August, and the air inside the house is still and hot. She looks out the window to the cabin, where Eugene is taking a nap. She hopes he won't wake soon and need something from her.

Quinn has dark blue Fiestaware, giant clayey mugs and saucers, plates the size of pizza platters. Yula crowds the dishwasher, balances cut crystal on top of egg cups, but none of it ever breaks. She bangs the coffee pot into the porcelain sink and whaps the milk saucer against the steel faucet. "Come on. Fuck. Get ready."

"Can you make me some toast first?" my father asks. He licks what's left of the line off the table and picks at a scab on the inside of his arm until it bleeds. "With peanut butter. I like peanut butter."

He holds his arm to his body like a broken-winged bird and gropes in Quinn's cupboards. He kisses her face, his mood suddenly jubilant, and farts.

"Well, hello there!" he says and waves his hand back and forth behind his butt. "Chocolate chips. With chocolate chips."

She makes him peanut butter toast with chocolate chips on top, then peers in at Quinn, lying in the back bedroom with his arms over his face.

"Can I take the car?" she whispers when she sees he's awake.

Quinn's voice is thin and tired. He mumbles feebly. It is good enough to be a yes. Yula walks back into the kitchen, takes out a frozen lasagna for him, and sticks it in the oven. She sets the table as though she were throwing dice, and the plate, knife, and fork bounce and clang their way perfectly into place: another high score.

"We leave in five minutes," she says to Harrison, dropping the keys to the Meteor on the kitchen table. He puts a chocolate chip into his mouth, picks up a knife coated in peanut butter and waves it in front of her face as though he were conducting a miniature orchestra.

"Where to?" he says.

"To work."

She walks back into Quinn's room to change the sheets on his bed while Quinn paces groggily, waiting. She checks the roll of toilet paper, Windexes the bathroom mirror, pushes some dust off his bedside table with her hand and wipes it on her pant leg. She spits into her hand and shines the doorknob. Her mother's red satin jewellery box rests on the chest of drawers. She opens it, holds the Swiss Army knife in her palm, feels the heavy, pleasant weight of it, and slips it into her pocket. It will be her knife now.

The last time she went to the cemetery was last Christmas. Yula drove and Quinn sat in the front seat, holding a little bouquet of lavender. He had on a wool coat, a navy blue V-necked sweater, and freshly ironed pants. He looked dignified. Eugene and Harrison sat in the backseat, not speaking. Harrison wore a checked shirt, a tie, and a jean jacket; Yula wore a parka over her skirt.

Quinn told Yula to stop at Safeway, and they all went in and milled around the produce aisle, sneaking grapes into their mouths, until Quinn found what he needed. A little tree, a gift card hanging off its branches, for $7.99.

The cemetery was by the highway and looked like a

miniature golf course. There were no headstones, only flat stone markers under a row of cherry trees. They found Jo's grave and stood in a semicircle around it. Quinn pushed the tree into a little thing in the ground that was supposed to hold flowers.

"I'm sorry it took me so long to visit you this time," he said. Eugene moved away from them and began to study the graves, running his hands over the inscribed names, looking back at his mom and Harrison every now and again.

Yula fished a pen out of her parka and handed it to Quinn, and the two of them signed the red-and-gold card attached to the tree.

"Come and sign the card with me, Eugene," she said. The wind felt cold and wet on her legs, and the damp of the grass had settled into the soles of her shoes. Her fingertips were bright red. She signed Eugene's name, balancing the card on her knee, then showed it to her son. Harrison bent down and signed his name, his handwriting as shaky as a child's.

"Every car is filled with a family. Everyone's going home for dinner," Quinn said suddenly, looking out at the highway.

"Yula, I love you." Harrison stands in the doorway of Quinn's back bedroom, his shirt around his waist now, his chest bare.

Harrison and Quinn lock eyes. Quinn gets into the bed and rolls over, his back to them. Yula and Harrison step into the hallway, and Harrison takes her arm. His eyes are suddenly full of anger. "I'm not the biggest fan of your father, Yula," he whispers. "Of any of this." He steps toward her. "I told you, I want us to move."

"I have to stay," she says. She looks at Harrison's body, and she looks at his hands. He is a beautiful, dangerous thing, and she puts her hand on his chest. "My father is sick."

It gets so cold here at night, even in August. Yula tucks Eugene into her and Harrison's bed and turns off the space heater for fear of a fire. She tells her son she won't be gone long. She'll take Harrison to work and be back in less than forty-five minutes. She'll climb into bed with Eugene and in the morning Harrison will be home, flour on his jeans and little bits of dough under his fingernails, with stories for both of them about the people he saw on the bus.

It takes three tries to start Quinn's old car, but she gets it going and down the road. She drives with one hand on the wheel, the other on her belly. Harrison sits with his legs on the dash and watches himself light a joint in the vanity mirror.

"Me, too." She holds out her hand and takes it from him. He pulls the Mexican blanket from the backseat and throws it over his lap. She drives down the narrow road slowly, overly worried about deer or Joel and Edwin gunning it up the hill. She waits for the pot to kick in so she can relax.

"You're not taking me to work," Harrison says and

takes the joint from her hand. "I quit. Look—I'm going to tell you the story, and you're going to see that I did the right thing."

Yula feels her stomach lurch. "I'm sick of this shit," she says. "I'm sick of looking after you."

"Shut up, shut up." Harrison rolls down his window and puts out his head. "Drive to the water. Let's talk for a while." Yula obeys and pulls onto the highway: finally, the sky, the speed. Eugene will be okay, she tells herself, he's sound asleep and she'll be gone only a little over an hour. She's left him alone before for short periods of time, careful to lock the cabin so that he can't get out, surrounding him with his favourite stuffed animals, swaddling him in the goosedown duvet in case he gets cold.

She drives all the way to Mile Zero, and by the time they get out of the car and walk down the long staircase to the beach, it's almost dark. They sit on the biggest log they can find and look out to Port Angeles. The log is wet from the spray and soaks through my mother's coveralls. Harrison gets that look in his eye, and she takes him in her arms and lets him talk.

"When I was a teenager I used to suck off guys in the bathroom for drugs," he says, and pretends he's giving head. His lips are dry and cracked, and Yula runs her finger over them. He gets in these moods more and more frequently, needing to confess his past to her, needing to be babied. She tries to listen but her thoughts are with Eugene. She needs to get back.

My mother picks up a big smooth rock and lobs it into the ocean. Her belly aches and she rubs it, slips her hand inside her coveralls and feels the incredible warmth radiating from inside her. "Tell me why you quit the bakery."

But Harrison is irritated by her questioning—he's so *fucking* damaged, she thinks—and doesn't want to talk. She prods anyway. "Tell me what happened this time."

The waves are quiet. It isn't too windy to talk. When he doesn't respond, she looks at my father and yells in his ear, "I'm bothering you, aren't I."

"Don't be mean to me," he says, digging his finger into his sneaker. "Listen. My brother gave me this incredible shit, not like the stuff you get in the city. It's at the house."

"What do you know about the city?" She feels him warming back up to her, and so she runs her fingers down the back of his neck and fiddles around in his hair. He likes this. He closes his eyes.

"It feels like bugs are crawling in and out of my bones," he says. "When I do this shit, it ends like that." He snaps his fingers and then gestures to Yula's pregnant belly. "After—you should try some with me." She leans in to him, lets him cradle her. He takes another joint out of his pocket and waves it in front of her face.

"I can't," she says. "I have to get back to Eugene."

Harrison lets go of her and she watches him walk down the beach, balancing on logs with his arms outstretched, his cheap sneakers slipping every couple of steps, his ankle threatening to twist, the sound of his footsteps on the rocks and sand. She climbs the long staircase that leads to the car, slowly, holding the wet metal rail in the dark. It is frightening here; my mother has forgotten how dark it gets, that this is a place where homeless men live. She can see their fires farther along the beach; if she kept walking she would meet one, or a group of them, all of them high. They think they're psychic here; if you grow up in the woods you think you're some kind of visionary, and now in the parking lot, where Quinn's car waits, there are four men in a Volkswagen camper, bearded men, looking at her, waiting for her to leave so they can claim her spot, the best part of the beach on Dallas Road at night, right under the lookout. The men run their eyes over her belly. She looks behind her for Harrison and holds her breath.

When he finally appears at the top of the stairs, his eyes are bloodshot, the joint in his hand smoked down to a roach. He waves to one of the men in recognition.

"That's Darryl," he says to Yula. "Let's stay a little longer. Ten minutes, that's all."

It's hard to say what happened next, or why so many hours later my mother was asleep in the back of the Volkswagen camper, peacefully high on weed. At eighteen, she still sleeps like a child: deeply and happily. Her hand rests on her pregnant belly, and her eyelids flutter as she dreams. My father is on the beach with the men. They pass around a bottle of Irish whisky. It is three in the morning and their campfire is smouldering, but they're all too drunk to be cold.

"I hate my life. I hate life," my father is saying, letting the waves slop up underneath his boots. He leaves the group of men, walks to the pay phone at the top of Clover

Point, and calls his brother, Dominic, who lives a couple of blocks away. He is so high that at first he holds the phone away from his body, unsure for a second what it is.

"You up?" he says into the phone. "Can you drive us home?"

9

By sixteen, it is clear what I am and what I am not. I'm not going to be a supermodel—Vaughn didn't tell the police that my mother was only five feet tall and that her shoulders were almost twice as wide as her hips, giving her the build of a miniature linebacker. This becomes my build. It also becomes clear that I am completely blind in my left eye now, though we still don't know what or whom to attribute that to. I get headaches; I can't see in 3-D. I've gotten used to it. I don't like fickle men (are they all fickle?), and I don't like Baptists or people who can't make up their minds about people being gay.

Miranda and I are still tense with each other. There's a kind of desperation that comes from having a small family, a palpable strain between her and me, especially when Lydia-Rose isn't around. Each of us tries too hard—each must encompass, for the other, an entire family combined. When I can't take it anymore, I go down to Dallas Road

and watch the tide come in. I try to be grateful that I live in
this beautiful place. I try not to be so restless. But I feel like
I grew up on the moon. When you live on an island, all you
can think is, "How am I going to get off it?"

Some of the kids at school get cars for their birthdays.
Miranda gives me a bus pass and a five-dollar bill. She says
if I fold it a certain way I can make Sir Wilfrid Laurier's
head look like a mushroom, but I've got other plans.

"Ticket to Tsssshhwassen," I say, my right eye focused
hard on the queer spelling under Destinations. "That's
Vancouver, right?"

"Yeah. Well, almost. You get the bus, little missus.
Travelling alone?" He pushes the ticket under the glass but
keeps it under his thumb. "Nine dollars."

I start counting.

Here's a trick: mind over matter. When you're counting
five bucks in change but it's got to add up to nine, say
"twenty-five" instead of "five" when you throw down a
nickel. They're almost the same size.

"Safe trip."

"Yup. Thanks."

The ferry's engine rumbles to a start and so does my
stomach. I stand on the deck and watch the water move
in big white sprays. Most people have cameras. The wind
picks up, rattling the tarps slung over the safety boats, and
I watch the island move farther and farther away. My hair
is in my face, in my mouth. The air is salty and cold but the
sun is hot on my back. When the ship's whistle sounds, it is

so loud that I jump. Someone behind me says "Let's get a hot dog" and I dig in my pocket for more change but find one lousy paperclip instead.

The inside of the ferry is warm and smells like vinegar. After one safety announcement ends, another begins. This goes on for what feels like an hour. I wonder what everyone's so worried about.

Here's another trick: walk up to the vending machine, slide in a paperclip, press A5 or B6, or whatever.

"What? Hey! *Hey!* This thing ate my loonie! Give me my chips! Aw, c'mon, I don't have another loonie—"

"'Scuse me? Honey? Here's a loonie." It's a nice mom or grandma, and I hope she buys me a root beer, too. "What's your name, sweetie?"

"Shannon."

"You travelling by yourself?"

"Yeah. I have to take the bus into town. I'm pretty hungry, too."

The woman looks behind her, searching for her husband. "Maybe we could give you a ride. Why don't you come over to where we're sitting and we'll see if we can work something out."

Here's the thing: I'm not trying to be a user, but people are curious about me. They stand and stare and try to figure out if I'm mentally slow or what it is exactly that makes me so odd looking—I'm saying I pique their interest. I'm saying they're very happy to give up a dollar or a seat in their car to find out what's wrong with me.

"Hugh, this is Shannon. She has to take the bus all the way into town by herself, so I thought we—"

"Sure we could! Hi, Shannon. I see you've met my wife—"

"My name's Belle, dear. I forgot to tell you my name."

I smile at her and admire her little outfit, which is colour coordinated, right down to her clip-on earrings and ankle socks. Everything is the same magenta shade. Her husband taps her leg with a shaky hand. He's wearing a Rotary Club vest and blue jeans with an elastic waist. They look like the nicest and most naive people in the world.

"Plenty of room in the car, Shan," he says. "Our kids grew up years ago—where you going all by yourself?"

I have to stop and think about this because I don't know the answer. I want to get off the island; I want to get away from Miranda and Lydia-Rose for a while. I want to see what it feels like to be alone. Miles and miles of alone, big empty stretches of alone, endless trails through dark green woods alone, pebbled beaches and nights spent with only driftwood for a pillow—alone, alone, alone. "Vancouver?"

"Yes, dear, but where do you want us to drop you? Is someone meeting you at the bus station? I hope they won't find us odd to be giving you a ride. Will they find that odd?"

"No, I don't think so. The bus station is fine, thank you so much."

"Belle, why don't you offer the girl a piece of your Toblerone."

By the time we've rounded Active Pass, Belle and Hugh have bought me a tuna sandwich and another bag of potato chips. It's my sixteenth birthday, but I've told them I'm twelve, and Hugh says that when he was twelve he was independent also.

"Had a job at the shoe store," he says. I can tell he's a nice man, that he's been good to Belle. I guess they're in their sixties, but I can't really tell. Neither of their children has married, and that makes them sad. They want grandchildren. Belle, I bet, wishes she had a granddaughter like me, only not so funny looking.

"What do you want to be when you grow up?" Belle asks.

"A firefighter. Or dog trainer."

The police find me the next day at a homeless shelter on Burrard Street, just around the corner from the Y. Vancouver has a bigger Y than Victoria does; I think, actually, it has more than one. Miranda called the police after I'd been missing for twelve hours, and my description got faxed to every station in B.C. Short, stocky, frizzy blonde Afro, lazy eye. I'm hard to miss.

"You're Shannon, I bet," one of the officers said and held my arm tight.

I had an okay time. Vancouver smelled like rain and pizza. The Skytrain was like this big white snake that darted all over and into parts of town where no one spoke English. Everywhere I went, someone wanted my money for drugs. It's a grey city, mostly because the buildings are made of glass and the sky is grey. Someone should have thought this through a bit.

I met a lot of people in fur coats. Some were homeless; some were rich. Everyone gave me a dollar or two. One lady paid me three bucks to hold her poodle while she went for lunch, and I met a guy who hadn't slept or eaten in six days. He said it was the crystal meth. He told me about the homeless shelter, and we walked together and talked about hot dogs.

"You can get six dogs for a dollar at the Mustard Seed and they throw out perfectly good bread at this bakery on Robson," he told me. "The dumpster's got a lock, but a small hand can fit inside." He stared at my hands as he said this. We bought the pack of hot dogs, then walked to Robson.

"Get as much as you can, don't let anyone see," the guy said and tossed me his backpack. His name was Matthew, and he had curly hair that reached his shoulders. He wore a black trench coat with a hole in the armpit and a silver pentagram around his neck. He smelled like cigarettes and sweat and something I couldn't put my finger on, something like a wet carpet. He said he was twenty. I liked his boots, which he said were from the army surplus store. They were two sizes too big but he said he liked them that way, 'cause then he could wear four pairs of warm socks. He took long strides when he walked and kept his head down and his arms by his sides. I'd never met anyone who walked like that before, as though they were out to avenge something. He told me that if the dumpster wasn't locked I should climb inside, and then he disappeared into an electronics store.

I stood in front of the bakery. Two Asian women were working behind the counter, putting together sandwiches and toasting bagels for businessmen and women in jogging suits with big strollers. I slung Matthew's backpack over my shoulder and walked down the alley. His backpack reeked of beer and the wet carpet smell. I wanted to take him and the backpack to the laundromat and soak them for hours in soap. I tried to imagine him with shorter hair and wearing a nice sweater. He'd be attractive if he were clean, I decided. But who was I to insist that someone look better? I stared down at my chubby legs in the tight jeans I'd chosen for the occasion, my white Adidas shell-toes with fat pink laces, white tank top, and suspenders from the Gap, the brand name cut out so no one would know. I'd combed out my curls, and my hair stood straight up all around my head like a big bright halo. A couple of weird-looking guys walked by and gave me the eye, but I stared at them so hard and fierce that they scooted away.

The dumpster was locked. I dragged a pallet over and then another and stood on them, finding my balance, until I could reach inside. The bread slid right into my hands; it was all there, right there, filled to the brim. I wormed it out, using my elbow to prop open the dumpster lid as best as I could and got out five loaves—flattened and squished—before I heard someone coming. I crammed the bread into Matthew's backpack and ran back onto Robson, where I was quickly sucked into the crowd. My tank top was covered in sweat and grime, and my sports bra was showing through. With Matthew's big canvas backpack on, I studied my reflection in the glass window of the electronics store. I didn't look like anyone I'd ever seen before.

Inside, Matthew was trying to sell a watch to the clerk, but it was a fake and the clerk knew it. He asked us to leave. We walked up Burrard, and it started to rain so we walked faster. There were cops outside the shelter, and when Matthew saw them he grabbed my hand and we bolted.

I've never run so fast in my life. Matthew's trench coat flew out behind him like a cape, and the straps of his backpack whipped against my back so hard I thought I might start crying. He had my hand tight in his. We ran all the way down Nelson Street until we reached Granville. The blood was pounding in my temples and it hurt every time my feet landed on the concrete.

Matthew pumped his fist in the air and hooted, then ducked into the doorway of a liquor store to light a cigarette. He offered me a puff and I breathed it in deeply, surprising us both when I didn't cough. It tasted good, like warm rye bread. He told me he'd teach me how to blow smoke rings. We stood on the corner of Granville and Drake, across from the 7-Eleven. I looked at the White Spot across the street with envy; I wanted a hamburger and French fries more than God. Matthew pointed down the street to the Cecil—a strip club, he said.

"You're like a little Marilyn Monroe." He cupped my cheek in his hand, ran his fingers through my hair. His nails were caked with dirt, the skin on his hands rough. He opened the backpack, hooted again when he saw how much bread I'd taken. I waited outside while he went into the liquor store, then he emerged minutes later with a mickey of Jim Beam in his hand.

"Come on," he said. "Got a buddy who lives upstairs."

He held open a door that I hadn't even noticed; it was the same colour as the wall we'd been leaning on. We walked up a stinky flight of stairs covered in cigarette butts and junk mail, then stopped in front of a door with *FAG* spray-painted across it in big sloppy letters. The hallway reeked of pot smoke. It was dark except for a flickering black light at one end. Matthew kicked the door, his hands full with the mickey of Jim Beam and a loaf of what looked like cinnamon raisin bread. The pack of hot dogs stuck out of his front pocket. I hoped he couldn't hear my heart, which was pounding so fast and loud that I thought it might rip out of my chest and dribble down the hallway like a basketball.

A tall skinny man with long hair and wire-rimmed glasses opened the door and looked at us, the bread, the Jim Beam, the hot dogs. "Let's do it," he said, and held the door open.

Matthew walked ahead of me and plopped down, wide-legged, on a couch in the middle of the room. There was an old television on top of a milk crate in the corner and a chest of drawers across from it with empty bottles of booze, some with candles shoved into their necks, the wax spilling down the sides. Two sleeping bags were splayed out on the floor beside a hot plate. Aside from that, the room was empty. The only window looked out onto Granville Street and I walked to it, stared across to the 7-Eleven. I turned around and studied the room again. There was no bathroom, no kitchen. I rolled my shoulders back, tried to hide the look on my face. I looked at the cigarette butts on the floor, the ragged hole punched into the wall, the single burnt-out bulb swinging from the ceiling, as if none of it surprised me. As if I'd been in rooms like this all my life.

I found my voice. "We got bread." The man in the glasses looked at me and nodded. "I'm Shannon," I said.

"Gregor." He opened the chest of drawers and took out three plastic glasses. Matthew poured the Jim Beam, and we each took a sip. I drank it as though it were apple juice. Gregor took a little cassette player out of one of the drawers, unplugged the hot plate, and plugged it into the wall. He pressed Play, and the Ramones shot out through the speakers. I felt proud that I knew who it was. I tapped my foot in time. This was all going to be okay. The Jim Beam was sweet and Matthew passed me his cigarette and I sucked on it then blew the smoke out into the room. He ripped open the pack of hot dogs with his teeth, tore off a hunk of bread, and pushed two dogs into the centre. He handed this to me and grinned. It was getting dark out, and I was starving. I crouched and ate the cold hot dogs like a wild animal. One of my suspender straps slipped off my shoulder and I let it drag on the ground while I ate my dinner. Gregor and Matthew sat on the couch across from me, passing the whisky back and forth. They were drinking out of the bottle now, using the cups as ashtrays. I could hear people on the street. Girls screaming and crazy men shouting back. The buses clanked along and blew exhaust and their brakes squealed and whined. There was no air in the room and I struggled to breathe. I hoped we would go for a walk or something. I wanted to see more of the city. I looked out the window and saw a woman lift up her skirt for some guys in a beat-up sedan. She wasn't wearing any underwear, and the guys honked the horn and one of them threw something at her that looked like a crumpled-up paper bag. I tried to pretend I didn't find it shocking, the dark swatch of pubic hair, her skinny thighs, her birdlike hands as she awkwardly caught the bag then threw it at the car, screaming "Fuck you, too!" as they sped away. I tried to pretend I hadn't seen anything at all.

Someone knocked and Gregor leapt up, peered out the peephole. He opened the door and a tall, bone-thin woman walked in, covered head-to-toe in tattoos. Her lip was pierced, plug-like earrings stretched out her earlobes, and her long black hair was shaved on either side of her head so that it fell to the side like a horse's mane.

"*Sexuelle Monstrositaten* was number one this week at the store," she said to Gregor. Her voice was as deep as a man's—guttural and raspy. She held up a videocassette. Women with four-inch-long nipples and men with more than one penis dominated the cover. He kissed her cheek, took the video, and tossed it to Matthew, who studied it for a minute and then put it aside as though it weren't the least bit interesting.

The woman walked over to me and stretched out her hand. "Cole," she said. "Pleased to meet you." She was beautiful, though she had the same wet carpet smell. She wore an ankle-length leather coat and tight red pants with a snakeskin pattern.

"Shannon." I tried to make it sound edgier. I wished I were wearing black boots and some eyeliner. I wanted to find a way to tell her about the star on my calf.

"You Matt's girl?" She didn't wait for my response, spun around, and punched Matthew in the arm. "She looks a bit like Kurt Cobain's kid, huh?" she said, and they both looked over at me. I could tell Matthew didn't like her. He shrugged her off, took another swig of Jim Beam. Gregor was rooting around in the chest of drawers again. He walked over to the couch, grabbed Cole and pulled her down on his lap. He stuck out his tongue and made a big show of wagging it around. "Ahhhhhhhhhhhhhhhhhhhhh," he said, wagging it at us. A little square of white paper was stuck to the end. He motioned for Cole and Matthew to open their mouths and placed one of the little squares on their tongues, too. Matthew came over to me, a little section of foil on his finger.

"You'll never forget your first time," he said, and knelt in front of me. "Time goes by so slowly." He raised his finger to my mouth, and I opened it hesitantly. He leaned in and kissed me gently, and I smelled the wet carpet smell so deeply that I felt as though my entire nose was stuffed with it. His breath was smoky and sweet from the booze. "I like you," he said.

"I like you, too." And, to some extent, it was true. I looked at his eyes, a pale vibrant blue flecked with little black lines, like a piece of broken turquoise. He had high cheekbones and a strong jaw lined with stubble. I understood that he was a good-looking man. I understood that I was not the kind of girl he would usually be with. He placed the white square on my tongue and kissed me again, even more gently this time, as though he were scared to. He pulsated to the music, slid his trench coat back from his shoulders and took off his sweat-stained shirt. His chest was smooth and almost hairless, deeply muscled and taut, with huge blue veins running across his stomach and arms like vines. I told him I had to go to the bathroom.

"Down the hall," he said, unbuckling his pants.

Cole was straddling Gregor. He held her butt in his hands. She had taken off her shirt, and I could see the back of her black satin bra. It rode high on her back, like it didn't fit right. Her skin was pocked with acne scars and looked greasy and pale. I shut the door behind me and spat the white square of paper into my hand. I hoped it wouldn't already be in my bloodstream. I could hear the music through the door and then the sound of someone walking toward it, likely Matthew coming to look for me, and I ran. I ran as fast as I could, down the stinky hallway and the filthy staircase and out into the horrible dark street. The temperature had dropped and I hugged myself, rubbed my bare shoulders and wished I'd brought a sweatshirt—it had been so warm when I'd left home. My shoelaces were untied but I didn't want to stop. I ran past a tattoo parlour and a hash bar and a Chinese takeout joint and a smelly little grocery store and a Pita Pit, until I was in front of the huge blinking marquee of a movie theatre, a long line of people waiting to see the shows. I had a bus pass in my pocket but I didn't think it would work on the buses here and I didn't want to ask. I thought about Winkie, probably waiting up for me, and felt a deep pang of shame. I looked at the people in line for the movie and I hated them. I could tell they had never been unhappy.

To kill time, I rode the train. I climbed up onto the platform and pushed through the crowd of bodies until I found a seat. My hands settled in my lap, and the train shot out of the station like a mad dog unleashed.

I took the ferry back with two policemen, who bought me French fries with gravy. They let me browse in the gift shop for a couple of minutes, and I pocketed one of those pens where the whale floats back and forth when you tilt it the right way. The ferry ride lasted a year. Everyone stared at the cops, then at me, and then looked away.

I sat between them, wrapped in a wool blanket. I was still cold from the night before. Matthew hadn't told me that the Burrard Street shelter would only take you if you were over eighteen. I pleaded with the guy who seemed to be in charge of the operation, but he said I'd have to go to the youth shelter downtown. He wrote the address on the back of a brochure about HIV and drew a crude little map. He was gruff, unfriendly. He wore faded jeans and white running shoes, a little silver cross around his neck.

I tried to find the youth shelter. I did try.

I walked down Nelson, past a group of First Nations teenagers standing outside a supermarket, undeterred by this awful classical music blaring from speakers in the awning. They all wore red jackets and bandanas. Two of the boys held each other at arm's length by the collars of their coats—*I'm gonna fuckin', I'm gonna fuckin', don't you push me, man, don't you fuckin'*—and two of the girls tried to break it up by kicking the boys' shins. I knew they were just punks, but they frightened me all the same. It was all over the news: there had been a hundred and twenty-eight shootings in the city since January. The shootings didn't happen downtown very often, but still, I kept looking behind me, ready to run.

Granville Street was packed with people. All with that wet carpet smell. The closer I got to Hastings, the more people there were. I pushed them off when they stumbled into me. I stopped and bummed a smoke off a couple of tourists who were staring dumbly at a man sitting on a wooden pallet in the doorway of a twenty-four-hour café, a river of piss streaming out under his feet.

I walked up Hastings, past the Royal Bank and Birks. The sidewalks were all torn up by construction, and so I walked on the road. It didn't feel as dangerous anymore. There were fewer people around. Everything was made out of concrete. I'd never seen a cityscape so grey. It was colder and damper down here—closer to the water. A Blenz Coffee; a Mr. Big & Tall. And then I was past the skyscrapers and it was just little old buildings, an art college, a record store. The offices of the B.C. Marijuana Party. The New Amsterdam Café, a big pot leaf over the awning; a war memorial. And then I made it past Cambie Street and the city came alive. It was midnight, but there were almost as many people on the street as there'd been on Robson. Victory Food Market; Asia Imports. Pawnshop after pawnshop. Everything was boarded up except for an all-night grocery store with bars on the windows. About thirty people were gathered in front of it, shuffling around, taking turns going inside. I watched a man, scrawny, tall, and hunchbacked, with a bearded face and eyes buried deep in their sockets. I watched two women, one short and First Nations, a scraggly ponytail clinging to her back like seaweed, the other pink-skinned with terrible dope sores, her stringy hair pulled taut from her face and yanked into a mean little bun. I stared at the women but they did not look at me. I'd never seen people like them before. The street smelled like piss, and I marched forward, one foot in front of the other, trying to walk with purpose. Trying not to look scared. I could do this. I was as much a freak as anyone else. In some ways I felt good walking down this street of broken faces. I stood at the edge of a park and watched a man shoot heroin into his neck. I let myself have the thought that I might find my mother on a street like this one day. I let myself have the thought that I might be on a street like this one day. And then it was all hotels, their lobbies stuffed with men, and abandoned shopping carts filled high with empty bottles and rough wool blankets and plastic bags, and a laundromat, and a cheque-cashing business, and after that everything was just empty, just blocks of boarded-up and painted-over storefronts, the windows barred or covered with flyers or broken. I shivered and looked around. A few people—men or women I couldn't tell—were asleep in doorways. There was pigeon shit everywhere, and when I looked down I saw a hypodermic needle at my feet and a bright pink condom wrapper, a bloody handkerchief and someone's old tennis shoe.

It started to rain, and I walked under the awnings as much as possible to avoid the rain and the splash of the city buses as they shot by. I thought about Matthew in that shitty room with no bathroom and no bed, the square of paper on his tongue, him wagging it at me.

"Weed?" A man motioned to me from an alleyway. A group of men had gathered under a fire escape, taking turns getting head from a woman in white jeans. I stood and watched for a minute. One of the men slipped a bill into the woman's hand and she limped down the alley, away from the group. I had walked all the way to Chinatown.

What's to say? I walked as fast as I could back to the Burrard Street shelter and crouched in the doorway until it was morning.

One cop was a stubby guy with a shiny bald head. He introduced himself as Officer Lucchi. The other guy had a silver goatee and hair the colour of cigarette ash. His hairy wrists peeked out from the sleeves of his uniform and he wore a gold chain around his neck. His name was Officer Hoffman.

They sat on either side of me, drinking coffee out of paper cups. I pretended to be asleep. The door to the outside deck blew open, and Officer Hoffman took a breath of the crisp ocean air.

"Good day for a cigar," he said.

Officer Lucchi fiddled with an elastic band, stretching and snapping it between his fingers. They talked about their kids. Lucchi said he had three boys, all in their teens.

"And I looked at him and said, Don't pretend like I don't remember where you said you were going tonight," he was saying. "You telling me I have amnesia?"

Hoffman shook his head. "I've got easy kids."

A mosquito was buzzing around Lucchi's leg and his

hand swooped down on it, triumphant. "Fucker," he said. He put the elastic band in his pocket. An announcement came on that we were nearing Swartz Bay. It was time to go.

I curled up in the back of the police car and listened to them talk. Lucchi said he was going to Ottawa for a week to visit an old girlfriend.

"Want me to look after your wife while you're gone?" Hoffman said.

"Fuck you," said Lucchi.

"Wrap it up, all right?" Hoffman said, and the two men laughed. "Seriously, man, wrap it up. You don't know what's going around these days."

When we turned onto Grant Street, Miranda and Lydia-Rose were waiting in front of the townhouse, hands on hips. Lydia-Rose looked at me with hate in her eyes. Her hair was wild, uncombed. She put her arm around her mother, as though she were protecting her from me.

For the first time, Miranda looked old. Her eyes were dark and heavy, the skin on her face slightly grey. She swayed a bit as she stood there, as if it was taking every muscle in her body to keep her upright.

The police took one last gloomy glimpse at us and disappeared around the corner. I watched their tail lights; I watched a squirrel run up a big tree. When there was nothing left to look at, I faced Miranda. I had never seen her look so tired.

"Go inside," she told Lydia-Rose, pushing her toward the townhouse.

I fiddled with the strap of my suspenders, looked at my sneakers, and waited for her to speak.

Instead she stepped toward me and put her hands on my shoulders, then pulled me into her. She held me like this for a long time, my head on her shoulder.

"Are you hurt?" she said.

"No."

"I don't want you in the house right now," she whispered. "I don't want you to come inside."

I tried to pull away, but she held me tight.

"I think," she said, "it's time we found alternative living arrangements."

"But—"

"I'm too angry," she said, "to have you in my house."

I struggled against her, but she didn't budge. I felt the strength of her arms for the first time, the result of years of physical labour.

"Do you know that I had everyone on the block out looking for you? I had to call every one of them just now and tell them you were fine. Tell them you were being brought home by the police."

"Where do you want me to go?"

I heard her swallow, and then her words came out slowly and precisely, as if this was something she'd been rehearsing for a long time. She told me that one of our neighbours had offered to let me stay with her for a little while, a woman who used to babysit me. She's a nice woman, Miranda said, and could use some help around the house. "She'll be nicer to you than I'd be right now."

"How long do I have to stay with her?"

"Until you're ready to be a part of our family again."

"But I never—"

She took a laboured breath and kissed my cheek. "A few days. That's all. Just let me cool off."

She released me finally, and we stood eye to eye. I said the cruelest thing I could think of to say. "You're not my mother."

She told me to wait on the sidewalk while she got my things.

"We're at a real fork in the road here, Shannon," she said.

Part 2

10

Eugene is curled in a ball in the middle of Yula and Harrison's bed when they finally get back from Dallas Road. He is wearing Harrison's Cowichan sweater and silver oven mitts on his hands. It has been hours and hours since they left, and the cabin is dark and damp with cold. Yula switches on the lamp by the side of the bed and puts her hand on the child's forehead. It is hot and dry to the touch. Dominic stands in the doorway, smoking a cigarette. He is a huge man with a shaved head and white-blond eyebrows, eyelashes, and patchy facial hair, which make him look as though his face has been dusted with glitter. He has tiny eyes, one blue, one brown, and leathery hands with bitten fingernails. My mother feels his eyes on her and finds him to be repulsive.

Harrison is on his knees in the living room, sifting through the cigar box he keeps under the couch for the little baggie of cocaine that his brother gave him the day before. The boy was hungry. One of the kitchen chairs is pushed up against the counter and his dirty footprints are on the countertop, his handprints on the cupboards. An empty bag of marshmallows is on the floor and the fridge is open, a couple of mouldy oranges in the bottom of the crisper. There are cans of soup and tuna fish, but the boy is too young to know how to use a can opener. He has found and eaten the crumbs from a bag of potato chips in the trash. The medicine cabinet in the bathroom is open, two empty bottles of grape- and cherry-flavoured cough syrup on the floor.

Yula runs her hand down Eugene's cheek and sees the cold pool of vomit under his chin that has seeped through the sheets and onto the mattress. She hears my father emptying the contents of the cigar box onto the floor and then cursing, the soft crackle of Dominic's cigarette burning down. The bedsprings creak under her weight. In another few hours it will be dawn. She can hear the rush of the creek below the cabin, a raccoon rummaging through their trash can. Dominic pinches out his cigarette and puts the butt in his shirt pocket. He stands in the doorway and wrings his big hands. "He'll be fine. He'll be all right," he says.

When the boy begins to vomit again, each of them takes a turn cradling him in the bathtub. The vomit bubbles out of Eugene's mouth like sea foam. Later, the bedroom fills with blue light and the morning arrives. Yula holds her son in the corner of the bedroom, the Cowichan sweater over both of them like a blanket, the oven mitts hours ago thrown on the floor. She sits with her legs straight out in front of her, repositions her son so his weight isn't on her belly. She cradles him as best she can. She is furious with Harrison for getting her high—furious with herself for leaving her son for so long—and has shut the door. Eugene is breathing in little gasps. His heart pounds against her body as she holds him. She wants to call the hospital, but she is too stoned. She will give herself an hour to come down, and then she will call. She is tired, but she knows she cannot let herself fall asleep. He'll be okay, won't he? Yes, she thinks, he's just sick from the cough syrup.

Outside, in the living room, Dominic and Harrison sit on the couch and watch the sunrise out the window. They pass a bottle of beer between them. Dominic has switched on the space heater and it glows red in the middle of the room, filling the air with a high-pitched buzz. Other than the bedroom, the cabin is one big room, living room bleeding into kitchen. The furniture is cheap, found one weekend at the Sally Ann, dragged down the narrow gravel pathway, set down and kicked across the scuffed wood floors. For a long time the cabin has had a ladybug infestation. It started with one, three, sixteen, twenty per windowsill, thirty in one corner. For a while, Yula scooped them into Tupperware containers and ushered them into the yard. Harrison puts his finger next to a cluster of them on the windowsill. They startle; their little metal bodies break apart and fly. He traces over an outline of a heart on the fogged-up kitchen window and stares at the dented, rusty classic car in the driveway.

11

Back on the island, I stand in Caffè Fantastico on King Street and admire a poorly done watercolour of a fishing boat at dawn. I have skipped school and spent the better part of the morning leering at things I don't like about this city: the narrow sidewalks, ceaselessly beeping traffic lights for the blind, bronze plaques everywhere blabbing about some historical event, some site made important once by a man whose name I ought to know. The playground across from the café is for disabled children but only half finished: I watch a few construction workers hammer down the wide ramps and railings for wheelchair navigation and fasten giant plastic geometric shapes in bright colours with giant plastic screws.

I order a coffee, and the girl behind the counter starts telling me about the date she went on last week. She hasn't heard from the guy since. "And that was Sunday," she's saying. "Now it's Wednesday."

"Yep," I say, and I take my mug to a worn-out looking couch at the back of the café and slip off my raggy old duffle coat—it's September, but it's already freezing.

I am waiting for Lydia-Rose. It's been a week since I ran away and neither she nor Miranda has spoken to me since. I've been sleeping on the neighbour's couch like an unwanted houseguest, until, as Miranda put it, we can "reach an agreement."

"Hey, you!" Lydia-Rose says, too gaily, and I understand instantly that although she's agreed to meet here she hasn't even begun to forgive me. She stamps her sneakers on the café's welcome mat and undoes the top two buttons of her coat. She has on a fedora and jeans with a patch on the knee. I want to tell her about Matthew and Gregor and Cole but I pinch my lips together instead—*Shut up, shut up!*—and take her in my arms. She smells like Miranda's pumpkin bread, her breath like gummy sours.

"Shannon." She says it dark, deeply, and puts her cold face on mine. She is almost a foot taller than me, and we hug awkwardly. She pulls away and snaps one of my suspenders. "You wear these every day or what?"

"Sure."

I sit on the beat-up couch and wait while she gets herself a hot chocolate. Her backpack is half open. I peer at the neat stack of notebooks and paperback novels inside, their dust jackets covered in parcel paper so they don't get ruined. After a brief infatuation with performance art, she has decided she wants to study literature.

"I'm reading this book right now that you'd love," she says to me politely, as if we've only just met. The mug of hot chocolate steams in her hand. She takes a sip and a big gob of whipping cream clings to her lip. "About a locksmith who breaks into people's houses."

"Sounds great."

Lydia-Rose leans back into the couch and crosses her legs. She looks goofy in the hat, with her long, narrow nose and dark, deep-set eyes. Now if she'd only learn to pluck her eyebrows. They're big and unruly. She takes off the hat and puts it on my head, and her hair sticks up in tufts. "You skipped today."

"I know."

"I'm just saying."

"I can't go to school anymore."

"Why not?"

"I don't know." I point at her lip, and she wipes off the foam with her forearm. "I don't want to hear any more about Trotsky, and I don't want to speak French."

I try to explain to her that I am anti-intellectual. Every time anyone wants to "analyze" anything, I feel a kind of rage. I detest abstract discussion of any kind and find my eyes rolling around in my head when anyone wants to talk about why we exist, or what is art, or life's meaning, which people often do. It seems to me as if people want to talk about this sort of thing all the time.

I wait for Lydia-Rose to smile but she doesn't.

"No, listen, I'm serious. I'm not like you. It's hard to read with my eye the way it is, the words go all blurry after a couple of lines. If I could see, I'd get my pilot's licence, and then I'd learn to shoot a gun and drive an eighteen-wheeler. All I want is to be able to tell one tree from another, and if a bird flies by, I want to know what kind of bird it is. That's all I want to know. There's no point in me going to school."

"Okay, Shannon." Her face falls a bit, and she fiddles with her cuticles. "You need to apologize to Mom."

"I will."

"Not on your time. On her time. Now." She takes a big sip of hot chocolate and winces when it burns her mouth. "You can't just run away and expect everything to be all right."

"I don't expect that."

She puts her mug between her knees and stares into it as she talks. "We stayed up all night waiting for you. We even took the bus downtown and walked around, asking people if they'd seen you. We walked around so long we missed the last bus home and Mom said, To hell with it, we'll walk home, maybe we'll run into you that way. She was so scared she was shaking. Do you know that?"

"I'm sorry."

"You're not sorry is the point. I can see it. We walked home and it took forever and I have blisters on the bottoms of my feet, and Mom called the police again when we got home and at some point I fell asleep in the living room and when I woke up Mom was gone and I waited up for her and she got in at dawn, she'd gone downtown again, she spent the fucking middle of the night asking fucking drug dealers and fuck-offs if they'd seen you, my fucking mom, all right?"

"All right."

"She got home and we made coffee and she was fucking shaking from being out all night in the cold—and then she went right back out again and knocked on all the neighbours' doors—"

"It wasn't exactly a picnic for me either—I just mean—I didn't run away and then have some kind of amazing time—"

"We went through your things to see if there was anything—I don't know—a note, something that would help us find you," she says. "Mom couldn't stop crying. It was awful to see."

My stomach lurches. My shoebox. My mother's sweatshirt. It horrifies me to think of them unfolding it, their eyes moving over my photographs, the weight of my Swiss Army knife in their hands.

"Don't go through my stuff," I whisper, but Lydia-Rose acts like she doesn't hear me.

"Do you know what it was like," she is saying, "to finally get a call from the police and have them tell us that you were on the mainland? Mom just started screaming. And then suddenly there you are, stepping out of a cop car, reeking of cigarettes. Looking like absolute shit."

"I don't know. I'm sorry I made you guys so worried. Sometimes I don't want to be cooped up in that townhouse."

"Okay. Be a fuck-up then." Lydia-Rose buttons up her coat and takes the fedora off my head. "And don't bother coming home if you're going to be this new fuck-up version of yourself."

"I'm not a fuck-up."

"Then come home and apologize to Mom. Everything we've done for you."

"I didn't ask to be a part of your family."

"I didn't ask for you to be a part of our family either. You ever stop and think about what it's been like for me? I lost my mom to you."

"That's not true."

"We were happier when it was just us. I know this. I begged—I fucking begged her—to take you back."

"That isn't my fault."

"Just come home and apologize to Mom."

"But I'm not sorry."

"What are you so angry about?"

"I don't know."

"Figure it out. Figure it out and let us know. I'll be at home."

Through the glass window of the café, I watch her walk down the street. She has her head down as if she's crying. But I don't want to think about her and her feelings. I've got enough swirling around inside me. She'll be fine. She and Miranda. I want to hate them. I do. It would be easier. I want to hate them so much that the earth will open up and they'll sink down into its fiery centre. I want to hate them so much that they'll die. But they're not bad people and never have been. How do you become a part of someone else's family? You don't, and you never do.

The Ministry of Children and Family Development is right beside the highway. I'm tired and grouchy from being on the bus to get here. In the waiting room are two worn-in couches, a coffee table with the *Times-Colonist* strewn over it, and a plastic rack filled with pamphlets on methadone, depression, and trauma. The walls are lined with posters advertising upcoming counselling seminars and support-group meetings. There's a shelf in one corner stacked high with loaves of bread. A sign reads, *Help yourself: but please, two bags per person. Thanx*. In another corner is a box of children's clothing. *Only one bag of clothing per person from this donation box*.

"I want to tell you something, honey." The social worker's name is Madeleine. She has a pale pink complexion and blonde hair that's been dyed dark brown. She wears a sleeveless navy blue dress with a white bow on the front and cheap white pumps. Her upper arms have a lazy, bloated quality to them that I associate with upper-middle-class women who do things like eat cake batter right out of the mixing bowl. Her office is right off the waiting room and is the size of a bathroom stall. A half-eaten tuna fish sandwich sits on a square of wax paper on her desk. Her trash bin is full of protein bar wrappers. "A low percentage of abandoned children have successful reunions."

I stare at her, hard. She peers into my bad eye like she's searching for something.

"I want to find my mother."

She types for a minute on an old piece-of-shit IBM desktop. "I remember reading about you. I was just a teenager at the time."

Her eyes darken as she reads whatever is on the screen. She swivels a bit in her chair, and I stare at her feet. A ratty-looking Band-Aid is stretched across her heel. She's barelegged and her legs are thick and covered in tiny varicose veins. I can't decide whether she's attractive.

Her face is pleasant enough, boring, but there's nothing inherently wrong with it. I wonder why she's so dressed up. The office is dingy and lit by flickering fluorescents. Her keyboard is covered in a thin film of grime.

"I want to be honest and realistic with you." She puts out her hand as if I'm supposed to take it. "Abandoned children don't have the same hope for a reunion as those whose parents have put them up for adoption. Often"—her voice wavers, and she takes a sip from a bottle of flavoured mineral water—"the place they were found becomes their only contact with who they are."

I stare at the tuna fish. The air in the office is hot and stale. There's a report on her desk, and I stare at its first line. *If you crack open the shell of the Ministry of Children and Family Development, 10,000 foster children will spill out, each child requiring a specific type of care.*

"Shannon," she says, in a voice more forceful than before, "it's likely your mother was homeless. On drugs. Sick with AIDS. A victim of incest or rape. In an abusive relationship or mentally ill." She coughs into her elbow and pushes her hair behind her ears. "Sometimes, Shannon, it's better not to know."

I hear someone enter the waiting room and moments later the high-pitched ding of a desk bell.

"What I can do," she says, "is make a photocopy of the newspaper article for you—about when and where you were first found." She waits for my reaction but there isn't one. I'm so disappointed that I feel almost dead. "Okay, then," she says. "Give me a second."

She leaves the office, her heels somehow squeaking like

tennis shoes every time she takes a step. And only then do I understand what is possible. The computer's screen is tilted in my direction, displaying my file.

My full name appears at the top of the screen, my date of birth, social insurance number, my designation as "special needs." *Complications from being born prematurely,* the file reads. *Vision impairment. Evidence of a learning disability. Emotional and behavioural problems.* "Developmental delays" in growth and speech. It says I tested positive for drugs at birth and spent the first few months of my life in neonatal intensive care. It says I didn't have any hair on my head until I was two.

When I scroll down, I see a list of all the foster homes I have lived in. A woman named Anna in a six-bed house in Royal Oak, her status listed as level three, whatever that means; Julian and Moira; Par and Raquelle. Another name is listed, too, after Anna's—someone named Linda McIntosh. I do not remember this. When I click on Julian and Moira's name, the screen takes me to a page that requires a password. I search the perimeter of Madeleine's desk but don't find one. The same thing happens when I click on Par and Raquelle. I write down everyone's full names on a couple of pink Post-it Notes and stuff them into my backpack.

At the bottom of the page is a postscript. *Letter from H.C., William Head.*

Nothing happens when I click on it.

I look up, and Madeleine is standing in the doorway. She holds the photocopied newspaper article in her hand. In her navy blue dress and white heels, she looks as if she's stepped right out of the fifties. She looks as if she's waiting for a sailor to debark from a ship.

Another social worker walks out of her office and peers in at us. Madeleine shakes her head at me, motions gently for me to return to my chair. "I'm afraid this is all I can do for you right now, Shannon."

I take the newspaper article. It's nothing I haven't seen before.

"The act of abandoning a child changes everything," she says. "There's nothing more I can do to help you."

"Okay. Thanks." I wave to Madeleine as I walk out the door and stand for what feels like forever at the bus stop. I feel bad about making fun of her. Am I a bad person? I think about this almost every day. Would I know if I was?

Outside of the Mac's on Cook and Pandora, I flip through the phone book until I find Julian's name. There it is. He still lives on Olive Street. Raquelle's name is listed, too. She's still in the same apartment. I barely remember her. I remember being left alone a lot. I remember watching a little boy stick a penny up his bum. I don't think I'll call her. Anna—I don't remember her at all. There was that girl who wet the bed. I'd like to see her again. But who knows what her name was? Anyway, Anna's not listed. And neither is this Linda McIntosh. Who the hell was she? It's like there's a black curtain hung over a part of my brain and it's too heavy to slip off and see what's underneath. Fuck it, who cares.

Letter from H.C., William Head.

This, though, is interesting. William Head is a prison in Metchosin. I know this because my drama teacher took us to see a play out there one time. The prisoners have a little theatre. We watched their performance of *Endgame*. The guy who shuttled us from the prison entrance to the theatre told us he was in for murder. He was in his eighties.

I walk into Mac's and get a hot chocolate, which is syrupy and gross, so I give it to a man playing the trumpet outside and we talk for a while. I like him. He's always around, playing that crappy old trumpet. He has curly hair, lots of it, piled on his head like a wig, but today he's wearing an orange toque. He tells me his name is Mickey.

"Mickey," I say. "Got a cigarette?"

He looks at me like I'm nuts. The guys around here have *not* seen this new side of me. He rolls me one, lights it with a dog-eared pack of matches, takes a big long puff and hands it to me.

"Tastes weird."

"Might be some hash mixed in there," he says and winks. He's got watery eyes and a deeply lined face and he's short, five-four max. I like short people, short men. So, fine, I'll smoke this cigarette. I'll smoke this hash. We lean up against the big glass window of Mac's, and he picks up his trumpet and blows into it some more.

"I went to the mainland," I tell him. I tell him my trip did nothing to curb my restlessness. I tell him I am still so curious. I want to feel to the fullest extent.

He rests his trumpet against his thigh and turns to me. "With eyes like those, you need to be outdoors. Maybe you ride horses? Yes? No? You should be at the ocean definitely."

"Okay, Mickey." My way of dealing with people who make no sense is just to agree. Works every time.

Some dudes drive up blasting hip-hop, and I bob my head to the music for a minute. They say hey to Mickey and come out of Mac's a minute later with bags of potato chips and Slurpees, then peel away.

A shitty-looking car pulls up and parks so close to our feet that Mickey calls out, "Hey, man." The car is red with a white top, but it's so rusted out that there are holes in the chassis. The engine sounds like it's dying when it kicks off. The driver's door squeals when it opens and a shrivelled little man steps out and pushes it shut with his hip. He's got a puffy face and a white beard. He looks a hundred years old, and it takes him forever to get to the entrance. When he comes back out, there are two packs of cigarettes in his hands. He tosses one into Mickey's trumpet case. It takes the old guy a couple of tries to start the car.

"Mickey, Mickey, give me a real smoke." The hash joint is gross, and I've let Mickey smoke most of it anyway. I don't feel anything except my heart beating too fast and too loud.

"I can hear your heart," he says to me, and we look at each other for a minute. My chest thumps up and down. My hands have started to sweat. "Close your eyes for a second, Shannon. Say goodbye to yourself for a day."

I close my eyes. The concrete feels like it's tipping. I'm worried I'll slide into the street. With my eyes open, I can control the feeling. It's easy to describe: it's like a minute ago I was living in the world, and now I'm watching a movie of it. The frame rate has slowed. I'm at twenty-four frames per second while everyone else is seeing life flicker-free. That's all. That's all there is to being high.

Mickey rests his head against the window and shuts his eyes. His fingers are working the pistons of the trumpet. He puts it to his lips and then rests it on his thigh, as if he's forgotten he was going to play. I don't know how much time goes by. An hour? Three? I watch the street. I wish I could float through the city, in between the lampposts and curving under ledges. I want to reach with an outstretched hand. I want to open all the windows. I think there are angels in this city. They are in the windows with the lights left on.

There's a poster for a band shellacked to a telephone pole. *Blue City*, it says, and I wonder which city is blue. Little children, little dogs, little bicycles go racing by as we sit outside Mac's. I close my eyes and dream of my father. He is a man who stands eye to eye with me. He is barrel-chested and his skin looks weird, as though he's suddenly developed acne. In the dream he answers the door in a pair of cargo shorts, a muscle shirt that gapes below his underarms, and worn-out tube socks that have slipped beyond his feet and gathered in front of his toes so that they look like giant, half-on condoms.

My mother's hair is matted and cut just above her shoulders, which she says she had to do because it is so damaged. It is a weird colour, a botched dye job. She is sunburned from swimming, her skin all broken out, and she is wearing a Harley-Davidson tank top and army fatigues, a bunch of her tattoos visible. She has a little white dog that spends the whole dream running around with a stuffed snake in its mouth.

My father makes chicken and then dumps a can of mushroom soup over it. We eat dinner on an old couch, which is so old that when I sit down I sink to the floor. Half of one of the arms is torn off, like some animal has recently been in the apartment and gnawed it.

I take my plate into the kitchen. The counters are covered in flour and broken eggshells. There are eggs just sitting out, sweating in the heat, a box of ice cream bars melting on the counter, and something that looks like vomited-up macaroni salad. A baby wails from one of the back bedrooms, and I discover it, bald and grey-eyed, in the middle of an unmade bed.

Then I am a little boy who travels to Europe with his older brother, mother, and father, and shoots his father on a deserted beach. The gun is light in my hands and my heart is bursting. My father lies half-submerged in the sea.

"Wake up," Mickey says and takes my hand. Somehow we are on the roof of a building across from Beacon Hill Park. The art deco one that looks like a wedding cake. I shift my weight. I wiggle my toes. I run my tongue over my teeth.

I look at Mickey. He is talking to himself in a low sad voice. We are both in some kind of tragic mood, a hundred feet off the ground, looking down.

"Take the vulnerable, sweet, and secret things in life very seriously," he says when he sees me staring at him, "if you want to be true to yourself."

I show Mickey the piece of paper with *H.C.* written on it, and then all the addresses. I unwad the photocopied article about my abandonment and show it to him. My story is nothing new to Mickey. Everyone in this town, it seems, knows about me. But he takes the article and reads it nonetheless. His eyes are clearer. We're both coming down.

"Why don't you go find him," he says. "This Vaughn guy." He points at Vaughn's name, his quote. *I believe it's an act of desperation.* "He saw your mother."

Mickey wraps his scarf tighter around his neck and picks up his trumpet case. He signals to me that our afternoon is over and disappears down the narrow set of steps that somehow got us up on this roof in the first place.

This part of the city has no name. I close my eyes and hear the rush of traffic heading into town on my left side, out of town on my right. I can feel the hash pulsing around in my head like a little hyper snake, trying to find its way out of one of my ears. The corner store is boarded up, graffitied, a For Lease sign swinging. The vacuum repair shop is open, four dusty vacuums on display in the window, little ancient-looking price tags wrapped around the hoses. *Go, little snake.* I walk inside and look around, but no one is behind the desk. I plug in one of the uprights and take it for a spin, and still no one comes. I file this information in my head should I ever need to steal a vacuum.

The city park has been landscaped further, the yew hedges shaped into perfect spheres. The tennis court is

surrounded by a barbed wire fence. It's unclear how a
person enters it to play tennis. Maybe no one does. I find all
kinds of trash among the flowerbeds, beer cans and stacks
of cigarette butts, greasy newspapers that once held fish
and chips. It is a rare, perfect day, the sky Michelangelo-
blue above my head, cumulus clouds unmoving. The buzz
of lawnmowers, the traffic, the stupid, stupid sun.

Raquelle's apartment is two minutes from the park,
sandwiched between two identical apartment buildings,
three storeys high, white stucco with brown trim, brown
wooden balconies, the windows unadorned. Shangri-La,
it says on the door. Did it always say that? Who names
these depressing buildings, I want to know. I scan the list
of names, find hers, and press the buzzer. My reflection
warbles in the glass door in front of me.

I press it again after a few minutes, then I press them
all. "Pizza's here!" I shout into the intercom, and finally
someone buzzes me in.

The lobby smells like old carpet and mildew. The walls
are mirrored and the floor is covered in pale pink tile, a
burgundy runner shooting out in front of me and around
the corner to the elevator. There's a royal blue armchair, a
stack of *Pennysaver*s beside it. Metal mailboxes built into
the wall. The hallway is lit by fluorescents, and I wonder
if everyone feels as sad as I do when they stand in front of
the elevator, hands full of grocery bags, struggling to push
the little black button that says Up. The elevator opens so
slowly it's like something out of a horror film, a hideous
man waiting to leap out at the last minute and rip me
apart with terrible claws, but it's empty, the floor covered

in peeling linoleum, the walls made of fake dark wood. I press the button and wait for the interminable doors to close, and the thing clunks into life, and we wearily ascend.

Raquelle's floor smells like soup and Chef Boyardee, and it hits me hard because I remember it. I stand, eyes closed, willing some specific memory to come into focus. The little snake in my brain is flicking its tail. Flick, flick. I breathe in deeply, imagine myself being pushed in a stroller or carried down the hall in someone's warm arms, but no memory comes.

Raquelle's door is the same fake wooden brown as the others. One of the digits of the apartment number is tilted and slightly farther apart from the rest. I want to fix it, but the little gold sticker won't budge. I peer into the peephole, wishing I could see her before she sees me, and knock.

A skinny boy with glasses and an Iron Maiden T-shirt answers the door, and when I ask for Raquelle, he tells me to skip off. It looks dark in the apartment, beer bottles on the floor. A cat meows in the back. He slams the door before I can explain myself.

I take the bus downtown, walk to the Inner Harbour and through the heavy doors of the Empress Hotel. Everyone is having high tea under the cut-glass chandeliers. I watch an old woman struggle with a tiny sandwich, the roast beef caught in her teeth. A little boy, her grandson, I guess, globs Devonshire cream onto a raisin scone. I sit on a bench and eavesdrop, listen to the woman's phony British accent. She is the type of person who comments on everyone's movements and then speculates on their motives, i.e., "Oh, she's getting up. She must be going back to her room. Nope, she's just going to the bathroom. Oh, look, here. Now she's coming back." It is nauseating to listen to.

The little snake has almost disappeared completely from my brain and I'm tired and starving. I try to put it in perspective—the fight with Miranda, Madeleine not being able to help me, getting high, not finding Raquelle—but I feel doomed. My whole life seems doomed.

I slip into an elevator and get off on the sixth floor, behind two reed-thin people wearing bucket hats, khakis, and those hideous sandals that look like harnesses for feet. I follow them until they get to their room and then slip down another hallway, trawling for room-service trays. The Empress uses beautiful silver cutlery and it occurs to me suddenly that I could steal it. I could amass an outstanding collection of forks, teaspoons, and butter knives under my bed.

There is murmuring behind the doors, someone's television. At the end of the hallway I find a tray, lift the huge salver, wipe a fork on my pant leg and slip it into my pocket. When I see a man coming down the hall in neatly pressed black pants, patent shoes, maroon vest, white shirt, and black bow tie, I make a run for it, slamming my body against the heavy door of the emergency exit stairwell, down the concrete steps, down down down, my body flying around each curve in the stairwell, my backpack pounding against my back, such momentum built up that when I get to the last storey, I just kind of let go and lift off and sail down the last flight of steps and land on all fours. I can hear the man shouting down the stairwell as the door clinks shut behind me but I'm off, off down the pathway that leads back to the harbour, past the buskers, the cartoonists, a man wearing a gas mask as he paints neon landscapes with something that looks like a gun, the First Nations people selling their turquoise jewellery and little jade animal things, then down onto the causeway with its mess of tourists swarming the docks. A seaplane flies over my head, kicking up huge ribbons of water as its big white feet make contact with the sea, and I push through the crowd, past the hot dog stand and the stinky public restrooms and all the way to the parking lot until I've reached the park beside the Johnson Street Bridge, a group of men huddled around a huge burning spliff. They holler at me but I run past the orca mural and up Store Street, all the way to the homeless shelter and Value Village and then up through Chinatown, down Fan Tan Alley onto Pandora so that I can run through Centennial Square, see if anyone I know is hanging around, but they're not, so I run all the way down Quadra Street until I'm spitting huge gobs of phlegm into the drain in front of the YMCA, sides aching, so nauseous I could vomit.

The YMCA is in a brick building and I like it immediately. Miranda used to take us swimming at Crystal Pool or Oak Bay Rec but never here. It's kind of hard to get to by bus. The towers of Christ Church Cathedral rise up behind the Y like huge stone rabbit ears.

The Y is small. A royal blue awning covers the entrance,

and I can see people lifting weights and using machines through the windows and people eating in the little café. Something like a hundred bicycles are parked underneath the awning. Between the cafeteria and the glass doors of the entrance is a stretch of stone wall. Birds are chirping their little bird heads off and the traffic on Quadra is busy. In the cemetery beside the cathedral, a group of young men sit in a circle, banging on drums. One of them is playing hacky sack. They pass around a joint, and I can smell it all the way from over here. Please no more dope. Not ever again. There are dogs, too, dogs tied up in front of the building and dogs in the cemetery, skinny homeless dogs with bandanas or studded leather collars. They're circling the drummers. One of the guys stops drumming to reach out and swat the dog for some offence I can't discern. The dog yelps and runs to the guy with the hacky sack. There are other men around, men on benches in trench coats, men huddled in the parking lot across the street, men on the corner. One is throwing a pair of dice into the air. I can see all the way to View Towers from here, but I'm not close enough to see if anyone's about to jump off.

A woman is standing in front of the cathedral with a basket in her hands. She looks up and down Quadra as if she's waiting for someone. But she's not all that interesting, so I run my hands over a yew hedge, kick a couple of dead rhododendron flowers off the bottom of my shoes—rhododendrons are the ugliest flowers in the world; when they die, it looks like a bunch of dirty toilet paper lying on the ground—and stare at the Y. It always sounded kind of virtuous to me, abandoning a baby at the YMCA, but this place is a goddamn shithole. Sure, there are a hundred yuppies milling in and out and getting on their bicycles in their gross head-to-toe spandex, as if you need to dress up like Spider-Man to ride a bike, but they're not going to be here at quarter to five in the morning. These homeless guys, though, they'd be here. There'd be even more of them than there are right now. They'd be all over.

"What would you do if you found a baby?" I'm standing beside the drum circle, yelling over the bongos. "What would you do if you came here one day and there was a baby here? What would you do?"

The guy who slapped his dog rests his palms on the bongo drum and looks up at me. He's short-lipped—I can see all his teeth even though he's not saying anything. Big yellow smoker's teeth. He looks young but he's got huge lines around his eyes like someone carved up his face. His head is shaved and he's wearing a green army jacket that looks a little too small. "What's up, little honey?" he says. His friends keep drumming. He digs in his pocket, pulls out a baggie. "Weed, little honey? Huh, little baby?"

The men on the bench are more interesting to talk to. One of them, Vincent, I've seen before. He wears a white tennis shoe on one foot and a black Nike sneaker on the other, a green nylon jacket, a purple scarf, and ill-fitting black pants. He's a mumbler. He has short black hair cut awkwardly around his face, which is dark-skinned and heavily creased, like a Cree's. I like this man. I run into him every time I go downtown.

"Shannon," he says, and takes my hand in his.

The man beside him tells me his name is Dean. He

talks about himself for a while, and Vincent doesn't say anything. He smells his fingers and plays with his scarf, the ends of which are covered in cigarette burns.

I look at Vincent. "If you came here one day and you saw a baby lying on the ground, what would you do?"

"Dead baby?" Dean squeezes the tobacco out of a bunch of cigarette butts and rolls a cigarette with the half-burnt tobacco. He licks it shut, takes a big long drag, and passes it to Vincent, who sucks on it like it's helping him breathe.

They hold it out to me, but I'm not that hardcore yet. "Just a little baby," I say to Dean. "Alive. Wrapped in a sweatshirt."

Dean shrugs, and Vincent takes another deep hit of the cigarette. His fingertips are dark yellow, dirt caked and encrusted in every groove of his nail. I'm not sure I like this Dean guy, but I press on. "I was found here. Right over there, in front of the Y. When I was a baby."

"Oh yeah?" Dean makes eye contact with me for a second and then goes back to the cigarette. "Vince, finish it."

I can see they have no interest in me, so I cross the street and stand in front of the entrance to the Y. I take the fork out of my pocket and carry it inside with me like a spear.

People are accommodating to someone so small. The woman behind the front desk is named Chloe. She's got a high forehead, made even higher by her ponytail, which is pulled so tight it stretches back the skin on her head, making her look like a Siamese cat.

The Y is a noisy place. It smells like chlorine. There's terrible country rock playing and people going in and out of a turnstile, like at the entrance to a subway. Some of the people make lame jokes with Chloe on their way out.

"Another day, another dollar," a fat guy says to her, shaking his head as he waddles past. Chloe does this sort of half-laugh and widens her eyes at me. She is lonely; I can tell from her big eyes.

I pretend at first that I want to buy a membership, and she tells me there's a special rate if I pay in advance for a whole year.

"I don't think I can get my hands on that kind of money," I tell her, and she hands me another brochure.

Chloe's veins bulge out of her forearms, and I try not to stare at her but fail. Besides, she's staring at me. We can't get enough of each other. Short weirdo with a bum eye; android fitness freak.

"We have financial assistance interviews," she says. "I'm sure we can work something out for you."

"Even if I don't make any money at all?"

"Even then." Chloe goes into salesman mode and starts telling me about the yoga classes, swimming, aerobics classes, the state-of-the-art machines, the dance classes, Pilates, and all the opportunities for volunteer work, something I've always hated. "We rely a lot on the generosity of our volunteers," she says, and I give her a big bright phony smile. Then she gets a funny look on her face as if she's seeing me for the first time—the entirety of me, bum eye and all—and she asks me if I have a home.

"A home?"

"We have youth programs, too, community outreach programs. We facilitate a supported independent living program for young people. We offer counselling services, employment training, that kind of thing. We also have a program where we set you up with your own bachelor apartment, help you get on your feet. You want a brochure?"

I feel the planets aligning, the puzzle pieces sliding into place. I'll get my own apartment. The Y will help me. It will be that easy. I look around. I could get used to this place. I could live on my own. Sure. Why not?

"We can set up a meeting with one of our social workers. Would you like me to do that?"

But then I feel the sting of tears in my eyes because I'm thinking about Miranda, and about Winkie, and Lydia-Rose. Goddamn it. I wish I could just be happy with what I have. Either that or cold-hearted enough to leave.

"No, thank you," I tell Chloe. She waits for me to compose myself. Finally, I do. I say, "I have a favour to ask."

She leans toward me and, like someone has cracked me open, I start to tell her the story of my birth. I point at the entrance. I tell her the date and the year. I take out the article about me and smooth it out in front of her. She looks at the baby in the picture, then up at me. I'm so little that I don't even look human.

"He's the one who found me." I point at Vaughn's name in the middle of the article and then stare at her face.

"I never knew about this," she says finally. She shakes her head and then looks around as if to see if anyone is paying attention. "Vaughn's basically a fixture here. He's worked here for years."

"What's he like?"

She does another one of her half-laughs. "He's great. He's really great," she says and I see something behind her eyes—is she in love with him? I can't tell, but there's something there. "Look," she says. "I'll give you his address. He's not in today." She writes it on the back of a business card and holds it out to me. One of her coworkers sidles up to her and asks if I'm a new member. He's a stringy guy, skinny as hell, his hair spiked up like a cockatoo's. He puts his skinny hand on Chloe's shoulder. Clearly he's interested in her.

"She was found here," she says to the guy, then looks at me quickly, as if maybe this is a big secret she's not supposed to give away. I grin at her. "She was abandoned here as a baby," Chloe continues, like a little engine gaining speed, "right out front. Vaughn found her. *Vaughn*. Can you imagine?"

The coworker leans over the counter to get a look at the article, skims it, then rears his cockatoo head at me. "This is you, huh?"

"Yeah."

"Shit, man." He looks at the article again. "Oh, yeah, look at that. Vaughn." Both he and Chloe look at each other and then at me. And then we have nothing to say to each other, so I tap my foot against the metal bar of one of the turnstiles for a second and thank them for their time. On my way out Chloe hands me a sticker that says This Is a Drug-Free Zone, and I press it onto my backpack.

12

My mother comes out of the bedroom sometime in the late afternoon, Eugene slumped over her shoulder. The living room is empty, the car gone. She lays Eugene on the couch, tucks a coffee-stained pillow under his head. She gave birth to him in the back bedroom of her parents' big house. Her mother, Jo, wiped her brow and later, after he was born, taught her how to nurse. Yula was sixteen. Quinn was outside, pouring concrete into a hole in the soil. The pine cabin took thirty days to build. A month after it was done, Jo was dead.

Harrison and Dominic have left the space heater on, and the room is too warm. Yula flicks off the heater and examines her son's face. He was not a tactile child. He did not like to be touched. It seems to her now that this is the most intimate she has ever been with the boy. She runs her fingers over his face and studies the way the bridge of his nose rises up and forms a deep ridge between his eyes. His eyelashes are thick and black. His lips are full, the insides stained red from the cough syrup.

How could she have let herself fall asleep? Yula places her hand on the top of her son's head. He is as cool as a harbour seal. When her mother died, Yula held her hand over her mother's head and felt her mother's soul shoot out and away. The back of her son's head is cold. There is no energy there, no heat. He has died alone, without anyone to witness it. This is the greatest tragedy of all, Yula thinks, that she did not bear witness to her son's death. This is worse than the death itself.

Moments later she hears the screaming. It seems to be coming from a place outside of her—somewhere within the cabin but not from her own mouth. She crouches on the floor in the middle of the cabin and hears the scream all around her, from every surface and every wall. Whose voice is this? She does not recognize it. The shadows are too black, and the wind makes a horrible hollow sound. It rushes right through her. And then there is no floor beneath her and no walls. She feels herself falling, but when she puts out her hands she can still feel the hardwood floor. The house must be falling. A sinkhole has opened up in the earth and she is plummeting toward its centre. Her hair rushes past her face and streams out above her. She reaches for Eugene but he is still on the couch, balanced at the edge of the sinkhole, and she puts out her hands, and she waits for it to tip. She will catch him. She will catch her boy when he falls.

Harrison finds her on the floor of the cabin, unconscious, and Eugene, his skin almost blue, on the couch. He rushes outside, where Dominic is waiting in the old car, the engine idling. In a panic they discuss things, and the decision is final: they will give the boy a private funeral and a proper burial. They will do it now. He was born in the woods; he will be buried in the woods. They will do this before Yula wakes, and they will wait awhile before they tell her. There are too many factors at stake. The boy might have drunk the two bottles of cough syrup, choked on his vomit, and died—he might have. But Harrison's bag of cocaine is missing and this is the greater concern. Harrison can't—won't—go back to jail. He just won't. And then there's the baby. A mother who lets her child die will not be allowed to raise another. The baby will be taken away. No, and this is final—Harrison and Dominic will bury Eugene, and they will do it out of respect and love for Yula, for the new baby, for their family. They're not "covering up" anything. This is not a sinister act. This is a father who wants to continue down the righteous path he suddenly sees himself on; this is a father who wants to leave this isolated compound, leave the drugs behind, take Yula and the baby and start a new life, far away from here. Leave the old man, Quinn, to fend for himself. Yula has given up too much of her life to him and his suffering anyway. And he is a miserable man. He killed Yula's mother. He is the murderer here. Let him die alone in his big house. Harrison will tell Yula the plan in the next couple of days, when she's out of shock. He will sit her down, kiss her, tell her that this is a sign. They will set out together, take the ferry off the island, find a new life somewhere on the mainland. They will stay with one of Harrison's friends in Abbotsford, then drive to the Interior in somebody's borrowed van. He will work construction again. Yula can clean motel rooms. Dominic will sell most of his stash and lend them some start-up money; he'll stay on the island and keep an eye on the miserable old man. This will be Harrison's promise to Yula; this will be the thing that will let her leave. What is the alternative? Jail for them all? A baby born to murderers? No. They will bury Eugene and flee. No one will know. Everyone will assume, when they leave, that they've taken Eugene with them. Why wouldn't they? A family starting again. A new beginning. They'll bounce back from this. The human heart is resilient. It can bust apart; it can heal.

Harrison bundles Eugene in Yula's grey sweatshirt and carries him out to the car. Dominic opens the trunk and watches his brother lower the boy in. It isn't as if it's easy— it isn't as if Harrison isn't broken inside, some part of him crying out and bleeding as he adjusts the boy's head so that it rests at a more natural angle. He tucks his little hands by his sides. The boy's feet are bare, and Harrison thinks this is wrong somehow.

"Wait," he tells Dominic and goes into the cabin for Eugene's little red boots and socks.

The cabin is dark and Yula is still on the floor. Her hands are curled like claws. He walks into the bedroom and opens the top drawer of the dresser, where they keep their underwear and Eugene's clothes. His little socks are rolled into balls at the back of the drawer, and he takes one out and puts it in his pocket. One of Eugene's rubber boots is on the floor, but he can't find the other one and it isn't under the bed. He searches the cabin quickly and gives up, walks back outside with the one boot in his hands.

"Can't find the other one," he says to Dominic, as if to make up for it somehow. He slides the socks over Eugene's cold feet and puts the boot on. Dominic has put a flashlight and a shovel in the trunk, too, and Harrison stands over the boy, looking at the awful scene for a minute before he closes the trunk and gets into the car, his brother at the wheel.

"'Preciate all this," Harrison says out the side of his mouth. He flips up the collar of his jacket and blows hot breath on his hands. Just as Dominic starts down the gravel driveway that leads to the long stretch of Finlayson Arm Road, Harrison sees Yula in the side mirror, running after them. It is early in the evening, and the sun is setting fast behind her. Harrison squints in the golden light and puts his hand on his brother's arm.

"Stop," he yells to Dominic, and Dominic hits the brakes. Harrison leaves the passenger door open and jogs toward her, takes her in his arms. "Baby, baby. Baby, it's going to be okay now, I promise you." He pulls away from her and cups her face in his hands. She is sweaty and her skin is cold, clammy to the touch.

"We have to go to the hospital," she says, her voice shaking. Her face is pale. She can barely say the words. "Harrison, it's too early. It's too early."

Harrison looks at his brother, tapping his hand on the steering wheel, chewing his lip. The sun falls rapidly past the forest's edge, and the temperature plunges.

"My water broke." She says it as softly as a frightened child.

What should he do? "Okay," Harrison says. "Okay. We're going to go. Come on, get in the car."

"I can't find Eugene." She grabs his jacket, but her fingers are numb from the cold and it slips from her hands. She pounds her fists against his chest. "Where's Eugene? Where's Eugene?"

Dominic gets out of the car and stands between them. "We took him to your dad's. He's over there. He's fine."

It's such a bold lie that Harrison almost stumbles. He braces himself on his brother's arm.

"He's fine, Yula," Dominic says again. "He was just sleeping. He's fine now."

Yula looks back and forth between Harrison and his brother. His words are so beautiful that she wants to swallow them whole. Is this true? Did she dream this? Is Eugene with her father, in the big warm house? She wants to run back toward the house but a pain swells in her back.

"He's there, baby," Harrison says. He takes her hand and pulls her against his body, lets her put her whole weight on him. "He's with your dad, in the house."

Yula spits and then wipes her mouth. "I want to go see him." She walks as if through mud, holding her belly with one hand. "I want my baby."

And then Dominic is behind her, grabbing her, his hands on her shoulders, pulling her toward the car. She fights him, but she is no match for his strength. She slumps in his arms and the men lead her to the car.

"Get in the car, baby. Get in the car." She lets Harrison

muscle her inside. He kisses her forehead, shuts the passenger door and nods to Dominic.

"Let's do this," Dominic whispers to Harrison. "Let's go."

Harrison thinks a minute, drums his fingers on his thigh. "I don't know what to do about Eugene."

"I'll get out at the bottom of the hill and then you can carry on to the hospital. I'll bury him myself. Just don't let her see me take him out of the trunk."

The brothers look at each other for a minute. In another few minutes, it will be dark.

"This is going to work out," Dominic says. "This is going to have a happy ending. Just take her to the hospital. Stay with her while the baby is born."

13

Sometimes Vaughn pictures time as being a long stretch of satin, all the events of the past and future laid out and shimmering before him, a tiny shifting line where the present moment keeps inching forward. His father shared his gift of prescience, but the two men never spoke of it. Still, by the time Vaughn was three, he could sense his father's actions moments before they occurred. He could see his father so much more clearly than other people. He concluded, eventually, that it was because his father was like him: two men so aware of their own placement in time—of their place in history—that the future was never surprising, only inevitable.

At some point when he was very young, Vaughn discovered, too, that he could manipulate the future in small, inconsequential ways (he never wanted to disturb anything until he saw my mother). It was a matter of visualization—he'd be walking hand in hand with his father after a day of running errands, and in his head he'd picture a giant ice cream cone and send the message to his father. Sure enough, moments later, his father would suggest they go for ice cream, a bright smile on his face as if he'd come up with such a generous idea on his own. Vaughn misses these moments of connection now that his father is gone. There is no one else he can communicate with in this way, though they must be out there. They must exist.

After his father died, Vaughn lived in Langford, on the backside of Mount Finlayson, with his mother. She, too, was predictable. She smoked and died of lung cancer. Nothing mysterious there. Is he himself predictable? It's obvious to him that he'll never marry again—that he had one shot at love early in his life, and now it's gone. It's obvious he'll never have children. It's obvious that this is his life: weight training every day and taking three weeks off every summer to go whitewater rafting. This is it, and that's okay. He knows he isn't supposed to amount to much. Some people he meets, though, burn a little brighter. Some people burn as bright and fierce as stars. He tries to find a way to tell a person this when he sees it in them. They're meant to do something; they *will* do something. Usually, he can't find the words.

But he knows people. He *knows* people. That is all. He doesn't think he has special powers, and he doesn't believe in psychics. But his eyes are wide, wide open—they always have been—and he sees everything. He takes in the whole world at once.

"If you stand back a bit," he says to me, "that leaf won't hit your face when it falls." The little stuff, too, is important.

"Oh, thanks," I say. We watch it tip off the edge of the eave and fall between us.

I am standing on Vaughn's front porch. Hillside Avenue, just up from the mall. There are a few blocks where every house is one storey and has lots of crap lying around in the yard—like the houses that line the highway long after you've left the city behind. Yellow lawns like hay fields; cracked paint; homemade For Sale signs on the cars; dead spider plants in the windows. This would be a good neighbourhood if it weren't for this stretch of houses. What happened here? Vaughn's kept his house a little neater, I'm pleased to see. He's put down stepping stones in the middle of the yard, and his front door is painted burgundy. The curtains are drawn and the eaves are full of twigs and dead leaves. The traffic on Hillside makes a constant buzz. There's a guy on the corner who looks like he's waiting to make a buck.

"You want something or what?" Vaughn looks past me at the guy on the corner and tries to gauge the odds of us being some kind of criminal operation.

I don't give him a minute to think. I've rehearsed this a thousand times. "You might be the reason I'm alive, sir. I'd just like ten minutes of your time."

Vaughn steps back and rests his weight on the doorframe. "I'm just starting dinner," he says. "But come on in."

I had hoped for a nice, fatherly type, or a handsome man in a suit, but Vaughn is neither. His shirt says *Don't Mess with This Texan*. He's a red-haired guy with a week-old beard and a deep oily tan. Every muscle in his body is ready; his calves look like they've been stuffed with rocks.

Faded jean shorts and bare feet. He wears square stylish glasses, and behind them his eyes are soft. There are bits of burgundy paint in the corners of his fingernails.

"Come on in," he says again. "Mind the step up, and when you take your shoes off, put them to the left of mine on the floor—if you put them on the right side we won't be able to open the door again without moving them."

I slide my sneakers next to his running shoes and he shuts the door behind me. His house smells like fried chicken and salt-and-vinegar potato chips. Photographs of the Grand Canyon hang in Ikea frames on the wall behind him.

"Forgive me if I don't know who you are immediately," he says, and cleans his glasses with his T-shirt. "But I've done more than a few things that might prompt a person to knock on my door and thank me for saving their life. Maybe if we sit down and have a soda first you can tell me the story until I remember it again."

He gestures toward the kitchen. His house is warm from the afternoon sun. I take a seat at his kitchen table while he pours ginger ale into two tall, frosted mugs, setting one in front of me so nervously that the foam bubbles up and over the edge. I catch it with my finger.

He sits across from me and we stare at each other. His kitchen is tidy, except for one stretch of counter stacked high with newspapers. A photograph of him and a border collie is stuck to the fridge with a wooden magnet in the shape of a frog. The fridge and stove are the same dull olive green.

I fiddle with one of my suspenders and watch him watching me. And when I can't take it anymore—him searching my face, trying to place me, pausing on my lazy eye and wondering if maybe he's got something to do with it—I tell him what I know:

Cold morning, just after five a.m., the glass doors of the Y on Broughton Street, a young woman. A small fresh version of myself wrapped in a grey sweatshirt with thumbholes, a Swiss Army knife tucked under my little cold feet.

"Well, you wouldn't have died, Shannon—" Vaughn's phone starts to ring and he rushes out of his chair, rifles through the slippery magazines and newspapers on his counter until he finds the handset, and pushes a few buttons to shut it off. "Sorry—sorry. My brother Blaze might pop over," he says, shrugging at me. "Teaches tango at this little joint on Herald Street. Nice guy. Won't stay long."

He takes the bottle of ginger ale out of the fridge and refills my glass, hand still trembling. "You wouldn't have died, Shannon. The doors were right about to open—your mom would have known that. She left you there so that someone would see you. I just happened to see you first." He grabs a scrapbook off the top of the fridge, flips through its pages until he finds the newspaper article. "Do you want this?" He holds out the yellow page, and the corners, flimsy from age, curl up like flower petals in his hands.

Abandoned Infant: Police Promise No Charges Will Be Laid.

I take the article and rub the thin newsprint between my fingers. I've read it hundreds of times. I've studied my little potato-sized face. Someone is holding me in the photo, but his or her face has been cropped out. *Baby Jane.*

"Was she crying or anything?"

Vaughn considers this a moment and sits back down. "Your mother? That was sixteen years ago—sheesh—you don't look a day over—yeah. She bent down and kissed your cheek, I think. I'm pretty sure she was crying real hard."

"Was I hurt at all?"

"Nah." He blinks. "You know, I thought it was you the minute I saw you through my curtains. Jesus. You a meat eater? I'm making beef stew; there's plenty for both of us."

"I would love to stay."

Vaughn puts his hands together and makes a face like he's being squeezed. "I really don't remember anything other than what's in the papers. It was real early and the whole thing happened pretty fast. I was more interested in you than I was in her, if you know what I mean."

He takes out a stack of napkins and folds two into triangles, and I wish I could fold napkins the way they do in restaurants, but it never works out. I can tell he wants to ask me questions, but he's not sure what's appropriate. He doesn't want me to cry.

"I'm fine, you know," I tell him. "I'm okay."

Vaughn smiles at me. "I'm glad," he says. "I mean, I've wondered."

He hands me a peeler, and I peel potatoes and carrots while he cubes and flours the meat.

"Slice them thin, then halve the onions," Vaughn tells me. He says he does Shake 'n Bake when it's just him. "But this is more of a special occasion."

We watch the timer on the stove while the stew simmers, and he tells me bits of his life: a retired decathlete, a brief marriage to a kayak instructor, his days now filled teaching weight training at the Y. "I'm there every morning anyway," he says and picks at his beard. "You know, it's still weird. Every morning when I pull up, I think of you being there." I let him talk on and on. I can tell he doesn't have kids. If he did he'd say a lot of nonsense about love and hardship and the troubled girls of the world.

He tears up pieces of iceberg lettuce into a plastic bowl and slices a tomato, sets a bottle of ranch dressing on the table. A few years after I was born, he says, he moved into town and has been here ever since. He puts a little bowl of plain potato chips in front of me and tells me to eat.

"When I was sixteen," he says, "I thought I'd like to play in the pro leagues. You a sports fan?"

"My eye's not so good."

"Well then." He starts to bend down to inspect my face, then thinks better of it and scans the countertop. "I swear I put that oven mitt down here just a second ago."

"It's in your hand."

"Thanks."

He stirs the stew with a wooden spoon and offers me another glass of ginger ale, but I have to go to the bathroom and wander out of the kitchen and down the hallway. It's a small house with a living room in the front and bedroom to the side. The bathroom is at the back of the bedroom, separated by a sliding door. It's tiny, with a plastic shower stall. I stand for a minute in Vaughn's bedroom and inspect. His bed has maroon sheets and a navy blue comforter balled up at the end of it. A paperback copy of *Neuromancer* lies on one of the pillows, along with a tiny headlamp, and the bedside table is stacked with some outdoor magazine called *Explore*. He has a cheap-looking lamp in the corner with no light bulb in it, and there are cobwebs hanging from the ceiling. He must not notice this. There's a thin coat of dust on the white venetian blinds. I separate the blinds and look out the window. A small stretch of wild lawn separates Vaughn's house from his neighbour's, a yellow stucco number with boarded-up windows. A couple of rusty-looking bicycles lean against the side of the neighbour's house, along with the innards of an old lawnmower, a couple of wooden doors, and a splintered mirror in a mouldy gilt frame. A stack of planter boxes tower precariously beside the mirror, one of them sprouting some kind of wild-looking, ivy-like plant. I close the blinds and look under Vaughn's bed. A DVD of *Trainspotting*, a couple of dust bunnies, the hardwood floor attachment for a vacuum. Nothing weird, thank God. He has a little TV across from the bed, balanced on top of a dresser. It, too, needs to be dusted. The ceiling is low, the walls the colour of putty. In most ways, it is a depressing room and doesn't give much away about its occupant.

The bathroom is livelier. Vaughn shaves with a Mach-3 disposable razor and uses Barbasol Beard Buster shaving cream. He washes his hair with Head & Shoulders and there's a little tube of some gross-looking anti-itch cream that I don't wish to inspect further. The walls are covered in workout routines cut out of magazines and secured with Scotch tape.

Vaughn's hand towels smell like Tide, and there's a brand-new bar of Ivory soap resting on the side of the sink. I'm so hungry I could eat it. I wish it were a piece of white cake. Balancing in a glass beside the soap is a toothbrush so big that I can't imagine cramming it into my mouth. The bristles are splayed from months—years?—of use. The floor needs to be mopped I guess, but it isn't too bad. The mirror needs a good Windexing, and I search under the sink for some but there's only toilet paper, a crank flashlight, and a stick of Old Spice deodorant. I think after dinner I'm going to ask Vaughn if I can stay with him for a while. I'll clean the house and mow the little strip of lawn. I can sleep in a sleeping bag on the couch, and we'll just work out some kind of schedule for the bathroom—shouldn't be hard, especially if he's out of the house and at the Y every morning. I could probably get a job at the mall. I took a food safety course at school, so I could work at the souvlaki place or Mrs. Vanelli's pizza. There's so much fast food around here. There's a good Chinese place around the corner, too. East Garden or something. Wonder if Vaughn likes Chinese. I bet he does. There are two gas stations down the street and the new Thrifty Foods and a Zellers, and it's a little noisy being right here on Hillside but I can buy some earplugs tomorrow, and I'll buy some for Vaughn as well. His brother can teach us the tango.

When I walk back into the kitchen, Vaughn is doing calf raises and flipping through a cookbook. "Looking at my biceps routine, I bet." He smirks at me and I blush; obviously I've been gone a little too long. The stew is bubbling in the pot, and there's a big part of me that wants to stop time and just eat the whole thing myself.

"I always wanted to be a dancer," I say.

"Nothin' to it."

Vaughn sets a bowl in front of me filled to the brim with beef stew, a pile of potatoes and carrots heaped on top. We put huge amounts of salad on our plates. His cutlery is flimsy and the plates are chipped. We toast our mugs of ginger ale and I wonder why he doesn't drink. Recovered alcoholic? I look at the deep lines around his eyes and decide there's something there—in his past. Something hasn't gone the way it was supposed to. Halfway through dinner he gets up to answer the phone, and when he hangs up he tells me that Blaze isn't coming—got held up at work.

"It's this woman he's seeing." He nods at me. "Can I ask where you live?"

"On Grant Street."

"In Fernwood?"

"Yeah."

"And who you living with?"

"It's not the greatest situation anymore." I tell him all about Miranda. About Lydia-Rose. I tell him about the Ministry of Children and Family Development, about the initials H.C. I tell him the story of my running away. I tell him that Miranda is the best person I've ever known, the most selfless, the most loving. But I want to find my real parents. I tell Vaughn that this business of placing kids in other people's homes is a nice idea and all, but I think we'd all be better off with our own families in the end.

"Don't know that I agree with you there. You don't know anything about your real family."

"That's why I'm here—to find out."

Vaughn puts down his fork. "Now I need to tell you something and I want you to not freak out until I'm done." He gets up from his chair and, hands shaking again, leans against the kitchen counter. "I want to tell you something about people." He takes off his glasses and rubs his eyes. "Not everybody makes it. Life doesn't work out for everybody, despite what your teachers and such might tell you. People want to encourage you at your age, and there's some dignity to that, but there's a falsehood to it, too, Shannon. Most things are, in some sense, predetermined."

"Okay." I feel like I'm back with Mickey. Please don't be insane. Why does everybody have to be insane?

"I'm not about to say that what she did was right. But you look okay. You look healthy, and if you'll pardon my language, you don't look all effed up. I see what girls look like around here. Your mother, Shannon—"

The neighbours' wind chimes are clanking in the wind, and we both pause a minute and listen to the sound.

"I've seen things," he says finally, "I wasn't supposed to see."

"I don't have anywhere to go," I say, my eyes betraying me. They fill with tears and I fight them, wipe them furiously from my eyes.

"Easy now," he says. He pulls his chair around the side of the table and puts his hand tentatively on mine. "Most people have good and bad in them. Like yin and yang, all right?"

"All right." I look at his earnest face, his scraggly red beard, his goofy T-shirt. "If you saw my mom again— would you know it was her?"

He puts a giant forkful of stew in his mouth, and I watch him chew. "I didn't really see your mom's face," he says finally. The light is fading, and he checks his watch. "Shouldn't you be getting home?"

"Dunno. Do you have a car?"

"Not anymore."

"Are you busy tomorrow?"

"Work until three."

"Would you go to the Ministry with me? Maybe if you come with me—maybe if we explain the whole situation—Madeleine will help me a little more. We can take the bus."

"Shannon, I want to go back to something I was saying earlier—"

"About it not working out for everyone. I remember. I don't need her to be a good person. But I have to know."

"Grant Street's not that far. You can borrow my bike—I've got two anyway—it's getting late now."

"Is that the right thing to do?"

"It is. Listen, things get clearer as you get older. Hop on my bike. I'll get you my helmet. Tomorrow we'll go the Ministry together. Okay? Come by the Y around three."

"Okay."

"Hey, I'm grateful for the dinner company. And I'm happy to help you find your mom. Listen, I'm over the moon that you're okay. All right? You have no idea what this is like for me, you showing up at my door. Do you know that? Huh? Look at you. You turned out great, I can see it. You're great. And there's something else, too—you've got some kind of crazed animal inside you. I can see it. Am I right? I know it's there. But just take my bike, go back to your family—they are your family, Shannon—and I'll help you out. But tell Miranda what you're up to. Do you want to hurt her like this? You said yourself she's the nicest person you know. Don't hurt the nicest person you know."

When I get to the townhouse, Lydia-Rose is taking notes while she watches an art-house film for a project she's doing on video art. There are a lot of penises. She doesn't say anything to me when I first walk in. We sit on the couch together, looking at the penises. She's eating Wasa bread, Winkie begging at her feet, and her pyjama pants are covered in crumbs. *Penises*, she writes in her notebook. She looks at me.

"You're back," she says. She turns the mute on, and we watch a man who looks like an albino, the film sped up so his eyes flicker.

I start to tell her about Vaughn and stop. I don't want her to know. I want to keep certain things a secret. "Is Miranda upstairs?"

Lydia-Rose nods. "What's with the helmet?" she says.

"Found it." I look at myself in the hall mirror. In Vaughn's white helmet, I look like a storm trooper.

I pad up the stairs to Miranda's room and knock on her door. This is something we're still not supposed to do—even now, her room is off limits. But I stand there anyway and knock.

"Shannon." She's wearing a pale pink housecoat. Some kind of thick cream is smeared under her eyes. She looks at me, looks at the helmet. "I was really angry before," she says. "I was just so angry."

"I want to apologize." I look at her face and she blinks softly.

"You should," she says. She steps back and lets me into the room, and we sit on the Little Mermaid comforter together, which is by now so faded and threadbare that I find it embarrassing. I want to buy her a new one—and I will. As soon as I have enough money, I will.

She reaches into the pocket of her housecoat, takes out a cigarette, and lights it. "Don't tell Lydia-Rose I'm smoking again."

"I'm sorry for running away."

She inhales deeply and ashes into a coffee tin. Minty cigarette smoke fills the room, and she stands up and opens the window.

"Shannon," she says. "I want you to know that you'll always be my daughter."

And so I start to tell her everything—I don't leave out one bit. I tell her about the nice old couple, Belle and Hugh, who dropped me off at the bus station; about Matthew and his smelly trench coat, his long curly hair; about getting the bread out of the dumpster; and Gregor's apartment; and Cole; about how I was too scared to go to the youth shelter and stayed up all night in the doorway of the homeless shelter on Burrard; about spitting the little square of acid into my hand.

What I don't tell her about is my visit to the Ministry of Children and Family Development, about Madeleine, about Vaughn. About wanting to find my mother. Already it seems to me that to survive you have to keep a part of yourself hidden from everyone you know. Something has to be yours and yours alone.

"I wonder," she says. "I wonder if you remember this at all." She picks up her cigarette pack as if she's going to light another one, but then sets it down. "When you were five years old, that horrible man you used to live with—"

"Julian."

"Julian. He waited for you one day outside of your daycare. He made you get in his car."

"I remember."

"Your sister ran and told one of the women who worked there. I still remember her name. Krystal. Lydia-Rose ran to her and told her you'd gotten in the car of some strange man. Krystal didn't even stop to call the police; she just took off running until she got to Julian's car and tried to open the door to get to you, but he drove off. The police found the car by Gonzales Beach. You were hurt pretty bad, sweetheart. It was so awful."

"I don't remember it that way," I say. "I remember being in his car and then you coming and picking me up and carrying me away."

Miranda pauses a minute, and we look at each other. "I don't think so. I didn't see you until later, at the hospital. It would have been a police officer who would have carried you out of the car."

I search my thoughts for this, but I can't find it. I still see Miranda's face, all sweaty, crying, lifting me out of the car. The feel of her soft sweater. Looking back at Julian's face. That's all I can see.

"This is important," she says. "Maybe not right now, but in your lifetime. There are men in this world who are so damaged that they become evil." She looks at me. "I just don't want you to ever encounter another man like him again." She finally tilts the pack of cigarettes and slides one out, taps it against her leg, and lights it. "Damaged men are dangerous," she says to me.

"Where is Lydia-Rose's father?" I ask, and she searches the air in front of her, seeing something from her past.

"Gone," she says, and puts her hand over mine. She looks tired suddenly, and I know not to ask her any more questions about it. I suppose she'll sit down with Lydia-Rose one day and tell her everything there is to know.

"Why don't your sisters ever visit?"

She unclips the bicycle helmet and takes it off my head, and I let her comb out my hair. It is snarled and greasy, and I let my head drop to my chest while she untangles it, her fingers endlessly patient, one hand grasping the snarl and the other tugging through it with the comb so that it doesn't hurt as much. She combs, then takes a puff of her cigarette, combs again.

"They used to," she says. "We used to see each other all the time."

"What happened?"

"One of my sisters died, honey. Years ago."

"How old were you?"

She puts the comb down. "Twenty or so."

"And Sharon?"

"Sharon and I don't speak anymore."

I think about the letters I found under her bed. *A real*

cunt of a woman. "What happened between you and Sharon?"

"She's mentally ill. She's not right in the head. Some people think that should excuse her behaviour, but I don't think so. I think we're accountable for what we do, no matter what."

"What did she do?"

"She hurt me."

"Hurt you how?"

"I don't want to talk about it. It would take forever to explain."

"Okay."

"Let's just not talk about it."

Crows are screaming outside, and I remember when Miranda and I once went to the library and researched what their different calls meant. The crows outside are doing our favourite call—it's as if they're laughing madly. Before we knew that crows were making this sound, Lydia-Rose and I called them the Jackass Birds. We pictured them as maniacal beasts, roaring their heads off.

"It's the Jackass Bird," I say to Miranda.

"Always."

I sit up and face her. "Can I still live here?"

The skin around her eyes is shiny from the eye cream. She dabs at it and then wipes her finger on her housecoat. "I want you to go to school," she says. "You think I don't know you tear up your attendance reports?" She fixes me with a look as if she's about to slap me, but then her whole face softens. "You're not as sneaky as you think you are. Go to school. This is my only condition."

We shake hands. I feel bad about not telling her about Vaughn, but it's fleeting, and when I go back downstairs and Lydia-Rose is already asleep, I climb into my bed and think about how after school tomorrow I'm going to jump on his bike, ride to the Y, and then we're going to go to the Ministry together, and at that moment I feel so excited about my life I can hardly stand it.

14

Quinn watches the tail lights from his bedroom window, two red dots disappearing into the night. He can't sleep. He's been up for hours. He is still awake when Yula, Dominic, and Harrison pull back into the driveway and stumble out, drunk and stoned and shouting. The motion lights flick on as they make their way down the gravel path to the cabin. The two men have to hold Yula up, her feet dragging on the ground. He watches them open the door, and Harrison slips and falls to his knees before wrenching himself up and inside. He watches them struggle to get his pregnant daughter through the door. What a horrible mess. He realizes his grandson has been alone all this time. He shakes his head, feels a sudden anger rise in his chest. He takes two sleeping pills and lies in his bed, awake, until the sun comes up. He watches the sun rise, fingers his pill bottle, wonders if he should take two more and sleep through the day.

When he wakes again, it is late afternoon. Why hasn't Yula woken him with his lunch? He gets out of bed and moves to the window, angry, his head heavy with sedatives and sleep, his left hand tingling with numbness. The Meteor is gone again. He tries to recall his dream—something about a train? He searches for the ending in his mind but can only see the colours, the red and blue of the subway station, and then they, too, fade away. He holds his arm to his chest, rubbing it against his pyjama top. Each day he prays for his hand to come back to life. Sometimes he thinks it's just a matter of thinking hard enough about it, of willing it to rejoin the nervous system of his body. As he stands by the window, he visualizes the hand opening and closing. He stares at the hand and wills it to move, but it hangs limply off his useless arm. Some days he wants to go outside and chop it off with an axe. He hates having something dead hanging off his body. Today maybe. Today maybe he will chop off his hand. Make his daughter take him to the hospital in her hungover and repulsive state. What was she thinking? Was this all his doing? Is she weak, or has he broken her? The blame shifts around inside of him like sand.

He is still at the window when the Meteor comes back down the driveway. He watches Harrison get out the passenger side and go into the cabin. Dominic is smoking a cigarette in the driver's seat. These are bad men, anyone can see it. Quinn wonders what makes women so blind. Why would a woman want to be around these two? Ex-cons are what they are. Half the time he expects to wake up with them over his bed, a butcher knife in one of their hands. They'd gut the house, turn the land into a grow-op. It's only a matter of time, Quinn thinks. So be it. He's ready for the next thing. He's ready to die.

Through the window, Quinn watches Harrison rush outside and get back into the Meteor. The men talk for a few minutes and then Harrison disappears into the cabin again. Dominic gets out of the car, walks around the side of the cabin, and emerges with a shovel and a flashlight, which he puts in the trunk. He lights another cigarette and leans up against the car, his body slightly concave in an effort to keep warm.

And then Harrison comes out of the cabin with Eugene in his arms. The little boy's face is so blue that Quinn gasps. God, what have these monsters done? Quinn fears for the boy's life. He has never seen a child look this way. The little boy's body hangs in Harrison's arms. He is wrapped in one of Yula's old sweatshirts and his legs and feet are bare. Quinn watches Harrison carry him to the back of the car, where Dominic meets him and opens up the trunk again. What in God's name is going on? What are they doing? Harrison lays the boy inside, then disappears inside the cabin. When he returns he has one of Eugene's little red boots in his hand. Dominic and Harrison stand over the trunk, talking, and then Harrison reaches up and slams the trunk shut, gets in the car and the men begin to drive away.

The door to the cabin opens, and Quinn sees his daughter break into an awkward sprint after the car, her hand underneath her belly. Her face is white. Her eyes are wild. She chases the car until it slows and Harrison jumps out, runs to her, throws his arms around her. What is going on? They are talking but he can't make out the words, even though they are right in front of his house. When Yula starts to walk away from them, Dominic lunges for her, and the two men drag her back to the car. She wrenches forward, grasping her belly, and Harrison pushes her into the car.

A second later Quinn is on the phone with Joel and Edwin. They'll be right over, they say. Just hold on. We'll be right there.

15

At three o'clock the next day, I am on Vaughn's bike, pedalling down Cook Street as fast as I can, my backpack thumping against my back, my sneakers occasionally slipping off the pedals and shooting forward so that the pedal catches the back of my calf. I am a terrible cyclist, plus the seat is too high and I have no idea how to lower it. I pray I won't have to make any left turns. I fly down the street, going too widely around parked cars so that I veer into traffic. I am constantly honked at. But I'm so scared that someone will open their driver's side door and hit me, and then that will be my life. Over and out. The end.

By the time I get to the Y my armpits are wet and my hands and legs are shaking. I lock up the bike and walk inside, try to get my heart to pound a little more slowly, try not to look so jazzed up. But I can feel my eyes are wild.

Chloe and the cockatoo are behind the counter. Chloe is filling out a form and the cockatoo is folding towels. They nod at me when I come in. I feel like a small alien wearing this bike helmet. I push through the turnstile and scan the weight room for Vaughn. He's standing by the leg press, holding a clipboard in one hand and ticking things off while an older woman with white hair works the machine. Vaughn is wearing a pair of red running shorts with a white stripe and a white polo shirt. His runners look huge. His feet are splayed slightly, I notice for the first time. He looks a bit like a giant duck. The Isley Brothers are playing. Kind of a weird choice. Vaughn nods in time to the music. Then I notice that everyone in here has white hair. Oldies' hour. I get it now.

"Just a sec?" He gives me a big smile but I see something in his eyes—fear? Irritation? I can't tell, but my stomach starts to hurt.

"Hey, kiddo." The cockatoo sidles up to me. "Seniors' hour is over. What should I put on?"

"Punk."

"'K."

I approach one of the weight machines and fiddle with it but have no idea how to make it go. I climb on a recumbent bike, but the seat's too far back and my feet won't reach the pedals, and I don't want to stand up and fix it because I don't know how.

Vaughn puts his hand on top of my bike helmet. "There's a lever under the seat."

"It's okay. I already cycled a bunch today."

"How're things?" He stares down at me.

"Good. Okay. You?"

"Yup. Let me get my things."

Vaughn pushes his bike up Quadra Street toward View Towers—still no one jumping off—and I walk beside him, still wearing the bike helmet. We're going to take the bus to the Ministry. We're going to talk to Madeleine.

"You ever eaten," Vaughn is saying, "at the German schnitzel house?"

"I've always wanted to." We look into the dark windows for a second. The waitress—a big, matronly woman—is sitting at one of the tables, scratching a lotto card with a penny. There's no one else in the restaurant.

Up the street we stop at the 7-Eleven to get a Slurpee for me and a Powerade for Vaughn. I look around for Mickey, but he must be playing at one of the other convenience stores today.

"You know the trumpet player, the one who wears the orange hat?"

Vaughn hands the store clerk a couple of toonies and we exit the store. "'Course."

"He's the one who told me I should contact you."

"Oh yeah? He some kind of friend of yours?"

"Guess so." I shoot Vaughn a look. "Why?"

"Nothing. I'm not your dad. Not going to get a lecture from me."

We wait at the bus stop and watch people drive by, blowing smoke out their car windows, blasting bass. A man pushes a shopping cart filled with bottles and cans by us, and Vaughn tosses his Powerade bottle into the mix.

It takes forever for the bus to come. It always does.

Vaughn leans his bike against the shelter, and we share the bench with a man holding a baby. The man has a black eye and Vaughn and I look at each other. There's something about holding a baby and having a black eye—simultaneously—that seems incongruent with the world, or how I think the world should be, but I've got too much on my mind to think about it.

"Not everybody is who they pretend to be." Vaughn picks at a hangnail on his index finger and doesn't look at me. "It's a small town, but that doesn't mean it's a safe one."

"What's wrong with hanging out with Mickey?"

Vaughn lets out a heavy sigh. "You got a boyfriend, Shannon?"

"Nope."

"It might do you good to spend time with boys your own age."

I rattle my bus fare around in my hand. "I'm too old for people my age."

The man with the shopping cart comes clattering back down the street and stops in front of Vaughn and me. "Got a smoke?" he says.

"Gave it up years ago, man," Vaughn says, and the men nod at each other.

Two guys on choppers come around the corner and stop at the light, engines revving. "Check it out," I say to Vaughn and the shopping cart guy. They blow through the intersection with a noise so loud that the black-eyed man's baby starts wailing.

"Used to live on the other side of Finlayson," Vaughn is

saying. "Those guys rule out there. You know, one day I was out walking and it got quiet all of a sudden, too quiet, and I realized I was standing in the middle of a grow-op. Not two minutes later, two guys with beards are pointing rifles at me, coupl'a pit bulls behind them."

The man with the baby is rocking her, and she quiets down. He turns to us with his big swollen eye. "I got a story like that. Cops busted a big operation a few years ago up-island. Found a couple of black bears guarding the property. Imagine that, huh?"

"Good security system," says Vaughn, and the men laugh.

"I was living in Ladysmith at the time," the man says. "Some people said the bears even came into the house."

"Nuts." Vaughn shakes his head and holds his hand out to the man. "Vaughn."

"Earl."

When the number six comes, Vaughn fastens his bike to the front of the bus. We say hello to the bus driver and sit in the raised section at the back. We read the graffiti and the ads. The bus isn't too crowded this time of day, and I'm grateful for it. I hate standing for miles. It hurts my knees.

Vaughn stretches his legs out in the aisle. They are so muscular that they frighten me. "Thinking about getting your licence any time soon?" he says.

"Nah."

"Why not?"

"Can't see."

"Right. Sorry."

"It's okay."

"Were you born with a bad eye?"

"It got that way."

Vaughn smiles at me like the sun has just risen over my head. "Sorry. Sorry," he says. "Sometimes I look at you and think about how little you were. Makes me happy, that's all. To see you okay."

"Yeah, I'm fine."

We head up Quadra Street, past the cop shop and the curling rink and the swimming pool and the Roxy and the pawnshop and the cheque-cashing joint. Vaughn is looking at the ads that line the top of the bus.

"Did you talk to Miranda?" he says.

"Yeah. We're okay now."

"She know you're with me?"

I pause. "Nah."

"Shannon."

"I know. I know."

He shifts uncomfortably in his seat and flexes his calves. "I want you to tell her what's what. Don't feel comfortable with her not knowing."

Vaughn takes off his glasses and cleans them on his gym shirt. The bus is headed up the highway now, and we both lean back and enjoy the speed. I can hear the tinny bass from some guy's headphones and the murmur of two women talking in the handicapped section up front.

So much silence on a bus trip. All these miles, all these minutes, nothing to say. That incessant hum in my ears as the wind whips past—the *pshoo, pshoo, pshoo* of cars going the other way. Right now it feels like it would be a sin to speak. I know Vaughn is as lost in the shadows of his life as I am.

I sit on this bus, and every bad thing I've ever done comes flooding back to me. I am lost in guilt. I am a liar. I am a cheat. I steal things. I use people. I have no friends. I have five stars carved into my leg now. There is something wrong with me. Sometimes I just really want to go off the deep end. Get myself addicted to heroin and check out. I want an off switch. I don't want to be me every day. When I wake up and look in the mirror, all I can think is *You again*. Again and again.

"Listen," Vaughn says. "I have to be honest with you about something."

"What."

"When I saw your mother that day." He pauses, searches my face. "She left you there so that someone else would find you, and love you, and raise you. I don't believe this was something she decided to do—I believe this is something she *had* to do."

"Okay."

"Shannon, I think there's something deeply wrong with her, but also fundamentally right. I saw her intention for you—she left you there because you were better off that way. It was an act of generosity. An act of love."

"I don't need my mother to be a good person. I just want to know who she is."

"I understand." He closes his eyes. "She kissed your cheek when she put you down. She was wearing men's coveralls, with motor oil all over them. She had on these huge workmen's boots. This is not someone who lived in

Y

the city, the way I see it. She put you down, kissed you, and she walked into the cemetery beside Christ Church. Dark hair. Little woman, I think. Our eyes have the hardest time at dawn or twilight, you know—it's the hardest light for our eyes to process—"

I frown. "In the article, you said—"

"Shannon, not a day goes by when I don't think about it."

"Red sweatpants? White tennis sweater?"

And then he's telling me all kinds of things: how the inside of his van smelled like diesel fuel that morning and he thought he might have a leak—that he was living in Langford at the time, took him over an hour to drive in—that my mother took short steps, not long strides. In the last sixteen years, he says, it was the one day he didn't get a proper workout. The night before, he'd watched *Uncle Buck*.

"You have to understand something," he says. "I wasn't supposed to be there yet; I was early. I was living so far out of town, I left early thinking there'd be traffic, and there wasn't. Shannon, it was an error—my presence. Or, at least, my intervening would have made it so. Your mother wasn't crying. No. She was beyond that. When you're truly hurt, you don't have enough left inside of you to cry. Listen, I didn't *want* to intervene with what was happening. It seemed important not to trouble the waters of fate like that. There was a look in your mother's eyes—"

"So you *would* recognize her?"

"Pretty sure, yeah."

"Okay."

"I'm sorry, Shannon. I'm sorry if I did the wrong thing."

I look at his big sad eyes. I shrug at him. What am I supposed to say? "This is it." I pull the cord, and we jostle into position by the back exit.

I hate being out here. Suburbia. It's hideous. How can people live like this? Row after row of the same-looking house. I'd kill myself for sure.

Vaughn unloads his bike and we walk up the street toward the Ministry.

"Strange location," Vaughn says. "I never come out here."

"It's weird out here."

"It is."

"Only robots live out here. Robot people."

"There are a lot of robot people," Vaughn laughs.

"It's this building, here."

Vaughn holds the door for me, and we walk into the waiting room. He inspects the loaves of bread, picks out a whole wheat one, and pushes two slices into his mouth. I start reading a pamphlet about methadone. Vaughn taps the front-desk bell and we pace around the room. The door to Madeleine's office is shut, as are the other doors. I can hear people talking behind them.

"Guess we should have called ahead?" Vaughn shrugs at me, and for a moment I miss the organization and efficiency of Miranda.

But then the door to Madeleine's office opens and a man spills out, red-faced and dishevelled, tugging a little girl behind him by the hand. She has to run to keep up with his strides so that he won't drag her to the floor.

Madeleine steps out in a white cotton sundress and open-toe white wedges. Her hair is pulled back by a headband covered in daisies. Her blonde roots are showing even more than last time.

"Oh," she says and looks back and forth between me and Vaughn. "We're about to close."

"Spare five minutes?" Vaughn steps forward and offers his hand.

She smiles weakly and takes it. "Come on in," she says and gestures to her little office.

Surprisingly, Vaughn does most of the talking. He tells her who he is, how I found him. His voice gets really quiet when he leans in and tells her he may have misremembered what my mother looked like, that the description he gave the police wasn't as accurate, say, as it could have been. "I'd know her if I saw her again, though. I want to help Shannon find her. I understand there's something in her file about William Head, something about the initials H.C."

"I'm afraid," Madeleine says, running her long fingernails over her forearm, "that information is confidential." She looks tired. She is not charmed by Vaughn, and whatever door that had opened between her and me seems to be closed now. She looks at her computer for a second and taps her nail on the mouse. "We never became aware of your birth parents' identity. There's nothing I can do to help you."

"Why did you leave my file up for me to see?" I look at her and try to burn a hole in her forehead with my eyes.

"A mistake. I'm sorry." She purses her lips, gets up from her desk, and opens her office door. "What you can do,

Shannon, is request a copy of your file through Freedom of Information. I can help you do that."

Vaughn puts his hand on my shoulder and thanks Madeleine for her time, then shimmies past her. "Shan, I'll be outside," he calls. Madeleine and I stare at each other until he leaves.

"Shannon, you keep in touch, if you want," she says. "You come back and see me any time."

I don't want to cry; I don't want to feel bad. I dig my nails into my knees and press my calves together until I feel the scabs from my stars. It burns and stings, and I focus on the pain, which is manageable and small.

I remember her words from our last visit. *Sometimes it's better not to know.* I feel so heavy with disappointment that the weight of me could crash through the floor. "I don't care if they're monsters," I tell her. "I just want to know who they are."

She looks down at me and closes her office door. She leans against it for a minute and closes her eyes, as if she's willing the day to come to an end. She reaches to straighten out her headband and exposes the inside of her wrist, which is so white it's almost blinding. A long-ago stitched-up scar runs the length of her arm.

"I want to know who I am," I say.

She looks at me, and her eyes sparkle. "There is one thing," she says. "But you need to keep this between us." She walks to her desk, scribbles something, then takes my hand and cups it around a little slip of paper. "I think this man might be your father."

Harrison Church, the little piece of paper says. *H.C.*

16

The man in the back of the car is my father. Dominic is at the wheel and Yula is in the passenger seat, clutching her belly. Her water has broken and is seeping through the thick rough cotton of her oil-stained coveralls. My father rubs her shoulders, tells her everything will be okay.

My grandfather, Quinn, is five minutes behind them, sitting between Joel and Edwin in one of their dented pickups. Joel is driving. Edwin has a shotgun and a flood lamp at his feet. Joel guns it down Finlayson Arm Road. His truck is infinitely faster than the Meteor, and it is only a matter of time before they catch up with Harrison, Dominic, and Yula.

"They've hurt my grandson," Quinn says as they speed down the road. "They've done something to him."

"We'll catch up to them." Joel nods at Quinn and presses the accelerator down as far as it will go.

The truck smells of manure and marijuana. Quinn

clenches his teeth and focuses on the road ahead of him. With each bend, he careens into Joel or Edwin. He braces himself with his legs, but it's been so long since he's exerted effort of any kind that his muscles are limp, useless. His legs are like twigs. His dead arm hangs between him and Joel, and he wills it to life so that he can shoot the men who have hurt his grandson.

Up ahead, the Meteor's tail lights glow. Quinn watches it slow and make a hard right before it reaches the highway. They're headed into Goldstream Park, on one of the service roads. He points at the car and nudges Joel with his shoulder. "That's them. Go."

"Stay in the car." Dominic puts his hand on Yula's leg. "Stay here."

Harrison rubs her shoulders. "Listen to my brother. We'll get you to the hospital in no time. But I need you to stay here for just a second."

"Where's Eugene?" Her words come out weakly, a whimper. She shrugs off the Mexican blanket that Harrison wrapped around her and turns to face him. "Where is he?"

"At your father's."

"He's alive?"

"We'll talk about this later. Just stay here." Harrison gets out of the car and meets his brother around the back.

Dominic opens the trunk. He fumbles in the dark for the flashlight and shovel, then rests them at his feet. "I'm going to lift him out and lay him over there." He points to a huge redwood by the side of the road with the flashlight. "Don't turn on the headlights until after you turn back onto Finlayson."

The blackness around them is thick as molasses. Then, suddenly, the headlights of a truck approaching. "Fuck. Get the fuck out of here," Dominic says. "We'll talk later."

Harrison nods at his brother and hears him groping in the trunk. He grunts. "Got him." And then Harrison hears him walk into the woods, then the soft sound of him setting the little boy, his son, on the ground.

Did they turn off? Joel slows down and the truck bumps along the service road, Quinn searching left and right for signs of the car, but the truck's headlights are weak and they can only see what's right in front of them.

Quinn puts his hand on the dash. "Stop a second. Kill the engine. They have to be right around here. This road doesn't go all the way up."

The men sit in silence for a minute, the windows rolled down. They hear voices, the sound of a trunk closing, someone's footfalls on the forest floor.

"Get out. Get out." Quinn pushes into Edwin, and the men get out of the car. Edwin switches on the flood lamp and the forest jumps into life, suddenly visible. The Meteor is about a hundred yards up the road. Harrison stands by the driver's side door. Edwin swings the lamp to the left, and then the right, and Dominic comes into focus. Eugene's body lies at his feet.

Joel raises the shotgun to his shoulder and walks toward Harrison, who fumbles to get back into the car, his hands shaking so badly that he can only paw at the cold steel handle of the door.

"Stay right where you are," Quinn says. "Don't move. Neither one of you move."

But Dominic has broken into a run; they hear it before Edwin swings the flood lamp to the right and sees Dominic disappear into the black of the forest.

"Damn it." Edwin swings the lamp around to Harrison, who squints in the horrible brightness.

"I'll shoot if you run." Joel points the shotgun at his chest. "I'll chase you all night. And I'll shoot you when I find you."

Harrison puts his hands over his heart, as if to shield it. "I won't. Okay. Please."

"You tell me," Quinn starts. "You tell me what's going on here."

The light sweeps over the forest, and Quinn looks at Edwin. "Keep that light on him."

And then there is the sound of the passenger door opening and Yula's footfalls as she rounds the car and approaches Harrison from behind. When she enters into the light of the flood lamp, Quinn sees that her face is crazed.

She reaches out for her father's hand. "Tell me you have Eugene."

"Eugene." He stares at his daughter. In his mind, he sees the boy being lowered into the trunk, his little bare feet.

"I need to know where Eugene is."

"The little boy?" Edwin swings the lamp around and walks past the car to the other side of the service road, where Eugene lies, Yula's grey sweatshirt around his shoulders like a cape.

17

Lydia-Rose and I are friends again, and I've quit cutting classes. The weather has turned and every week bleeds into the next—the same endless *fitz fitz* of drizzle on the windows all day, all night, the same low-hanging stratus clouds, like a ceiling too close to my head. The winds have started, too. Every year here is the same: one minute we're outside in our hoodies until midnight, the next we're racing home at ten o'clock, the wind whipping our heels and blowing all the leaves off the trees with one big fatal breath. It happens so fast. Then everything is dead. I hate this time of year. My winter depression settles in like a heavy blanket.

I found an address in Ontario for a man named Harrison Church. I wrote a letter. I still haven't sent it. I carry it around in my heart like a rock. It isn't anything I feel capable of facing, and so it sits inside of me, ignored, festering. What if I send it and then never hear back?

What if he's a horrible man? What if he isn't even my father?

Lydia-Rose has a new boyfriend, a guy a year older than us named Jude. I do not like Jude, but I don't fault him for that. He lives down the street from us in a little white single-storey house, a big untamed front yard separating it from the street. The grass is over a foot long and has been stamped down in a makeshift path that leads to the front door. He lives with his father and older sister, though she's never around. His father is a sweet man, that much I can tell. Miranda says he drives a Handi-Dart, the bus for disabled people. As I said, it is not Jude's fault that I don't like him. He's a good person. But now that he's in our lives, he's always around: we eat our meals with him; we watch movies with him; every weekend is spent with him. If I want to see Lydia-Rose, which I do, I have to see him, too.

Jude is handsome; I'll give him that. He is thin but muscular and wears the same outfit every day—a short-sleeved checked shirt buttoned up all the way, baggy dark blue jeans, Converse sneakers. He dyes his brown hair a bright yellow-blond and Lydia-Rose cornrows it for him, which makes him look a lot cooler than he actually is.

Miranda seems fine with this arrangement—happy to have this young handsome man in our lives. She even lets Lydia-Rose sleep over at his house sometimes. I'd thought she would have been stricter. She has been so protective of us until now. I suppose she knows that Jude is nothing to be feared. I know she marched Lydia-Rose down to the clinic to get her on birth control, but beyond that she seems content to let the relationship be. Unlike so many other mothers we know, she treats Lydia-Rose and me with respect. She's respectful of our personal space, our privacy. So many girls in our class have stories about their mothers ransacking their rooms, finding their journals and poring through them, making them empty out their backpacks when they get home from school, interrogating them if a boy calls. Miranda never does anything like that. She expects us to be decent, that's all. And we don't want to disappoint her. I already have. I am eager not to do it again.

It rains all the time, and there is nothing to do. My feet are always wet and I don't feel like wandering downtown by myself to go find Mickey because if I don't find him I'll just be soaking wet and standing at a bus stop by myself, waiting for no one to come along and take me back home.

"Shannon," Mickey said to me one of the last times I ran into him, "something keeps us connected."

Yes, Mickey. But what?

Vaughn and I haven't seen each other since we went to the Ministry. I feel weirdly protective of myself since Madeleine told me the name of my father. I feel like I don't want anyone to get to know me too well. I feel like I carry around a big heavy secret. I don't know why, exactly, but I feel ashamed.

There is nothing to do but watch television or go downtown and sit in a coffee shop until the manager kicks us out for asking for too many refills. Or go to McDonald's, order a large fries, eat half of it, pluck one of Lydia-Rose's hairs off her head and slide it into the fries, go up to the counter, demand new fries because of the hair, get those fries, eat them. Walk to another McDonald's, repeat. I'm just trying to find some way to spend the time. People talk about when you're young as being full of possibilities, but the uncertainty of it all makes me feel lost and insane. I try to be cheerful. I try to live in the present. But it's hard.

Sometimes we go to this coffee shop downtown that has pool tables. It's in the basement so we have to walk down a little black metal staircase to get there. We can play chess there, too. I don't know why we like it so much, but we always gravitate to it when there's nowhere else to go, no more fries to be eaten. By now we know the regulars and the staff. The regulars are guys with long grey hair and skinny Goth girls in their twenties. On Fridays they have an open-mic night that we go to sometimes, but the real appeal of the place is that the tables are covered in broken shards of glass set into tar so that you can look down and see hundreds of versions of your face—we never get sick of doing this—and it's one of the last places in town that lets you smoke indoors. In this pitiful weather, it's a necessity.

So Lydia-Rose, Jude, and I are there drinking coffee with one of Jude's friends, this guy named Nicky. Jude and Lydia-Rose are always trying to set me up, and Nicky is their favourite candidate. He's okay. He's a little less cool than Jude—a little lower on the social ladder. He wears the same uniform as Jude, the checked shirt and baggy jeans, but his sneakers are all wrong—cross-trainers. Does he not notice the difference between sneakers and running shoes? He has dark brown hair and a dark complexion—I think he's half-Hawaiian, though we never ask him and he never talks about it—and little scars all over his face from a battle with acne that is, thankfully, now over. He's short, like me, just over five feet. I like him for this but am hard-pressed to say much more. He seems to lack a personality. Or he seems to be perpetually trying to copy Jude. But, whatever, he's harmless. He is a guy I can handle.

So here we are. I look great—I've got on a white tuxedo shirt, jean jacket, black dress pants and my suspenders. I've pulled my hair back with bobby pins so I don't look so much like a lion, and Lydia-Rose has traced black eyeliner over both my top and bottom lids. We both wear the same pale pink lipstick. Lydia-Rose, as usual, looks stunning. She has on a black lacy slip over a long white cotton dress and knee-high army boots. Her hair is pulled back in a severe bun and she has finally—at my insistence—plucked her eyebrows.

I can feel Nicky's eyes on me. And I can feel Jude's and Lydia-Rose's eyes on him, watching me. My face is hot. Everything I do seems suddenly unnatural—the way I pick up my coffee, the way I cross my legs. I suddenly don't know what to do with my hands. What did I used to do with my hands? I try to act like however I remember myself acting. I'm the kind of person who might shove her hands in her pockets, so I do that.

And then this woman comes over. I've seen her in here plenty of times. She's always trawling for guys and always disappointed when it's just the same pack of long-haired men in leather jackets, full of dumb jokes, playing pool. She's maybe around twenty. She isn't bad looking—long curly auburn hair, big bright green eyes, wide hips, and dark eyebrows. She wears tight red jeans and an oversized sweatshirt that slips off one shoulder and exposes a black bra strap. It's kind of a sexy look, in a desperate way. I can tell she's drunk. She looks like someone who's just run away from home and now doesn't know what to do.

"Got a smoke?" She stands over our table and tells us her name is Bess. Up close she's even more attractive. Her face is covered in pale freckles, and she has big plump glossy lips.

Jude runs his eyes over her, and Lydia-Rose gets a wild look. She's been in a strange mood all day. When he sees her eyes, he reaches for her hand and she leans into him. He's good about things like that.

Bess picks up my coffee and takes an uninvited sip. "I love your face," she says to me, then spins around to survey the room. She's slurring her words a little. "How about that smoke then," she says, and Jude hands her a cigarette.

I look at Nicky. He's shifting around in his seat as though he's either uncomfortable or has to use the bathroom. I try to picture him as someone's husband. I can't. I look at him and think that whatever people mean when they say "So-and-so's got personality," it isn't this.

"You ever been in love, Nicky?" I prod his foot with mine. I don't know why I'm provoking him. Something about his meekness makes me angry.

He reddens and shakes his head, and Jude and Lydia-Rose burst out laughing.

I light a cigarette, and Nicky and I share it without speaking. Lydia-Rose and Jude start to kiss, and Bess stares into the million little pieces of her face in the table. It's dark outside now, and the coffee shop is dim and full of smoke. Two guys in the back are setting up the mic stand.

"Let's go sit on the top of the parkade and look at the city," Bess says. "I'll get us some beer."

We stand outside the liquor store, shifting from foot to foot to keep warm. Bess emerges with two six-packs in a plastic bag, and we walk to the Yates Street Parkade then up the eight flights of stairs, huffing and wheezing and practically dead by the time we reach the top. We walk to the edge of the lot, spread our jackets on the concrete, and face the harbour. The boats sit in the water like big ducks. We drape our legs over the railing and Nicky spits out his gum. We watch it fall to the sidewalk. Bess passes us each a warm can of beer, and Jude and Nicky have a contest to see who can drink theirs first. It's cold out so we smoke constantly, our fingers kept warm by the embers. Lydia-Rose drums her boots on the concrete and leans against Jude. And suddenly the air is as warm as July, though the sun went down long ago and the sky is a deep purple blue with no moon. I am half drunk. I lie back and feel the cold concrete on my shoulders and the back of my neck. Bess does the same, and we watch each other in the bright white light of the lot. Her lips are full and red and wet with gloss. She has little wrinkles starting to form at the corners of her eyes. Her chest heaves up and down as she breathes. I examine her hands. Her nails are bitten down and ragged, a single silver ring on her index finger but no other jewellery. I move closer to her, the pull of her body like a magnetic field. But she's looking past me at Nicky, who is sharing a smoke with Jude and Lydia-Rose.

He's put on a toque and is suddenly more handsome in his black knit hat, a cigarette hanging from his mouth. He's grinning wildly—Jude is making fun of him for some stupid remark he made in class—and Bess reaches up and puts her hand underneath his shirt and starts to stroke his back. He flinches at first—her hand must be cold—but then shuts his eyes and lets his head drop. Lydia-Rose and I lock eyes. She nudges Nicky with her boot, and then he opens his eyes and looks at me. It is a peculiar look. He seems to be asking me if it's okay. I reach for another sip of beer.

"Shannon," Bess says, "feel how warm Nicky's back is." She smiles and reaches for my hand, and I let her put my hand against his back, which is so warm against the night air that it feels hot to the touch. I understand her immediately. She is an instigator, a fire starter, an accelerant of a human being, throwing herself into the middle of a crowd and lighting it up. She is fucking lighter fluid.

"Let's go to my apartment," she says, and then we're all stumbling down the eight flights of stairs and out onto the street. I follow her in her tight red jeans as she leads us out of downtown, over the Johnson Street Bridge, past the rail yard, and into Esquimalt. We walk for over an hour.

When we get to her apartment we're sober and freezing. We stand in front of the refrigerator and drink from a big cold bottle of vodka. We drink it as fast as we can, eager to get back to that feeling where sex seemed possible. Jude and Lydia-Rose disappear in the dark of the living room, and Bess leads Nicky and me into her bedroom. She lights a few candles jammed into liquor bottles, and I examine the room. She has a double bed, the sheets sloppily pulled over the mattress, a ratty wool blanket wadded at the bottom. The floor is covered in clothes, papers, textbooks, and packs of cigarettes. Her closet door is open and full of cardboard boxes, a few pieces of clothing draped over the edges.

Bess lifts her sweatshirt over her head. Her stomach is soft and sags over the front of her red jeans, but her breasts are full and gorgeous in her black bra. I shrug off my jean jacket, let it drop to the floor, then unbutton my tuxedo shirt. I'm wearing a grey sports bra, which I struggle to get over my head. I have never shown my breasts to anyone, not even Lydia-Rose, who changes unabashedly in our small bedroom as if it were the most natural thing in the world. I feel fierce and strong standing in Bess's bedroom with my shirt off. My breasts are small—hardly breasts at all. Just two soft protuberances from my chest, the nipples inverted and hidden somewhere inside. I know my stomach is nothing to admire. I have no waist. It is stunning the way Bess's breasts round at the top, gently pushing against the lace of her bra. I hear Nicky behind me and feel suddenly horrified that he might touch me, but when I turn, I see that he has settled into a chair in the corner of the room. He puts his hands behind his head and leans back. He is so drunk I'm not sure he knows what's happening.

"You look like a child," Bess says to me, her eyes running over my body. "You have such a child body. Look at you!" She walks over to Nicky and pulls him to his feet. "Look at her little body!" she says, and they stand there staring at me.

"She's lovely," Nicky says. "I love the way she looks."

"Can I ask you something?" Bess says to me, and I nod my head. She holds my face in her hands. "What's it like to have a lazy eye?"

I take a big breath and try to will my eye into alignment with the other one. "It's not lazy. It's dead." I stare at her as best as I can.

"She only sees out of the one eye," says Nicky.

"Oh, wow," says Bess. "A Cyclops."

"Yeah, I'm a Cyclops."

"What's it like?"

"I trip a lot. I can't see in 3-D."

I stand there and let them stare at me. Bess asks if she can touch my breasts, and I let her, and I let Nicky touch them, too. They run their hands over my breasts and stomach and my earlobes and into the thick curls of my hair. I do not feel sexy anymore. I feel like crying. I struggle against the feeling and try to grasp onto what I felt before—the longing to be touched by another person. Now that it's happening, all I can think of is how I can get it to stop.

Nicky cups my face and kisses me. His breath is hot and tastes sour and of vodka. He's a gentle kisser, and I let him hold my face and kiss my lips softly, the top lip, then the bottom. I try to enjoy the feeling. I try to be present, instead of how I feel, which is like some wild helium-filled balloon floating around the room, knocking into things, searching for an exit out into the sky.

Nicky asks why I'm not kissing him back, and I say I don't want to. I have sucked all the sexual energy out of the room. Bess sits cross-legged on the bed. She fiddles with the ends of her hair, her stomach big and heavy over her tight red jeans. We can hear the sound of Lydia-Rose and Jude in the other room. It is a strange, haunted sound, and I do not like to listen to it.

"You fucked before?" she says.

Her words startle me and I fight to hide it. "No."

"That's cool," she says. We avoid each other's eyes. I want to be home in my bed, with Winkie at my feet.

Lydia-Rose gasps in the other room, and I wish I had something that wild and unbridled caught up inside me. But all I feel right now is a horrible emptiness, a sense that I'm watching things happen to me and will never fully take part.

"My cousin has breasts like you," Bess says.

"They barely seem like breasts."

"They're not so bad." She climbs under the covers and closes her eyes, and I understand that the night is over and this is as far as it will go.

"I'm taking off," Nicky says.

After Bess falls asleep, I hold her. I lie there with my arms around her. I breathe in the stale air of her small messy bedroom, and I listen. There are people walking by outside. I hear the smash of a thrown bottle. The candles burn out and the wax oozes down the sides and onto Bess's dresser. The room fills with their smoke. Bess rolls onto her back, and I slip my arms out from under her. She snores softly, her mouth slightly open. A grey haze creeps in through the blinds as the sky starts to lighten, casting the room in a muted, depressing light. It is the most horrible light in the world, the light from an overcast dawn. I creep out of Bess's bed and paw around on the floor for something—anything—of interest. Old receipts from Mac's for cigarettes, magazines, gum. I find an expired driver's licence in her red jeans. Her name is Elizabeth. She is twenty-six years old. I flip through a nursing textbook and an old issue of *Vogue*, some of the pages torn out and taped to her walls. They are of alabaster-skinned women, freckled faces, long red hair. They are who Bess wants to be, what she wants to look like. The perfume ads unleash their scent into the room when I flip past them. So much to do this week. Apply for an after-school job. Lydia-Rose is going to be a cosmetics girl at The Bay. I don't know what I want to do yet. Sell hot dogs, maybe, at the Inner Harbour. Work at the movie theatre. A few of our friends work at McDonald's, but I don't want the grease in my face, in my hair. Slinging popcorn and tearing people's tickets seems okay. I get great pleasure from tearing off perforated ticket stubs for some reason. It's like popping bubble wrap. If I could get a summer job doing just that, I would.

In the morning we trudge home. Lydia-Rose tells me she called Miranda last night and told her we were safe but too tired to walk back, and she assures me that Miranda was okay with this. I am sweaty and panicky. Lydia-Rose is cold; I can tell by the way she's holding onto Jude. We cross the Johnson Street Bridge and head toward Fernwood.

"What happened to Nicky?" Jude says. I can't believe he's only now noticed his friend is gone. His blond cornrows are coming undone, and his eyes are thick with sleep.

"Left last night," I say.

Lydia-Rose shoots me a disappointed look. She wants me to lose my virginity. She loves the idea that the four of us could pal around. She shrugs at me to elaborate, but I walk ahead. I stare at my feet. I wish I were able to get along with people my own age, but I just hate them. The sky drizzles rain, and I walk faster. Lydia-Rose and Jude catch up and she takes my arm and the three of us walk side by side, back to the neighbourhood. Her hair has fallen out of its bun and is springing out crazily from all sides of her head. I can't bear to think about how I must look. At the corner, before we turn onto our block, Jude gives Lydia-Rose a long kiss goodbye and I stand there watching them. He's at least a head taller than she and stoops awkwardly, his legs apart for balance.

He watches us as we walk up the pathway to our townhouse without him. I give him a half-hearted wave and push Lydia-Rose inside before she can run back and kiss him again. Someone has to curb this grossness a little bit. No one has patience for love except their own.

The first thing I do when I get inside is pet Winkie and take her for a pee. It's early, not even eight a.m. Winkie trots ahead of me, her back legs bowed and awkward, and is swarmed by a group of small children walking to school. They place their hands on her body, gently, and one of them gets down on his knees to hold her.

A city truck pulls up, and a couple of men jump out and block off a section of the pavement with road cones. They draw lines in the street with chalk. Winkie and I spin around at the corner and walk back to the townhouse. I'm not supposed to take her farther than a block—her legs have been giving out lately, and Miranda doesn't want her to get any worse than she already is. When one of the men starts up a jackhammer, I cover my ears and Winkie runs.

Lydia-Rose is in the shower when I come back inside, and Miranda is at the kitchen table, drinking coffee. She taps the table as I walk past, and I sit down.

"Want some coffee?"

I smile at her. She wants to have a morning ritual with somebody. "Sure."

She pours me a cup and loads it up with milk and sugar. Her face is bright but I can see that she's tired, that there is something on her mind.

"You two were okay last night?" she says and her voice comes out strained, brittle.

"Yeah."

"You've got school in an hour."

"I know."

She taps the table again, and I see that the tapping wasn't meant as an invitation to sit down but rather to show me something. She is tapping a piece of paper, folded in three.

"This was in the pocket of one of your pants," she says. "You forgot to take it out when you stuck them in the hamper."

I look at it. It is the brochure for young adult housing from the YMCA.

She waits for me to say something. I reach for my coffee, but my hand is too shaky and I know I'll never be able to bring it to my mouth. I press the soles of my feet into the floor and pray for the moment to be over.

"I don't want there to be secrets in this house." Miranda gets up and puts on a pot of oatmeal, sprinkles in raisins and cinnamon as it boils. I watch her back as she stirs. She's wearing her pink Molly Maid polo shirt. She's either gained weight or the shirt has shrunk in the wash, the back of her bra visible through the fabric. I've seen pictures of her when she was our age and she looked just like Lydia-Rose, long and lean.

It's like there's a fissure growing inside me. The part that wants so strongly to show Miranda the letter I wrote to my father and to tell her about Vaughn. And then the part that wants to keep all this information to myself, to keep it sacred, safe, and hidden. I can't reconcile the two.

Miranda spins around, wooden spoon in one hand, a little glob of cooked oatmeal about to fall off the end. I look at her then, in the bright morning light of the kitchen. Her face is wet. The men are still jackhammering outside.

"Are they going to do that all day?" she says suddenly, and her tone is so accusatory it's as if everything that is wrong in the world is my fault.

I shake my head and push the brochure aside. "I have to tell you something," I say.

18

My mother sees her son lying by the side of the road, one little red boot on, the other foot in a white sock. Her sweatshirt is wrapped around his shoulders. She feels something fall down inside of her, like a guillotine. The men are talking: Joel, Edwin, Quinn, and Harrison. She sees Joel push Harrison into the Meteor and slam the door. Edwin lifts Eugene off the ground and walks toward her. She feels her face twist into ugliness, like the gnarled stump of a tree. She has the overwhelming desire to pick up a rock and pound it against her mouth until her teeth break. She wants to break every bone in her face. She wants to take out her jawbone and bury it in the ground.

Instead, she hears the sound of Joel's fist hitting Harrison's face. The car rocks back and forth. And then Quinn has her by the shoulders and is guiding her into the truck. He helps her into the cab, then pushes her legs in, tucks her arms into her lap, pulls the seatbelt over her belly, just like he used to do when she was a child.

Joel gets out of the car and jogs toward Quinn, tells him, quickly, gasping for breath, about the cocaine, about Harrison's plan to bury Eugene. He has blood on his knuckles. Yula looks at the Meteor, where she can see the outline of Harrison slumped over in the front seat. Quinn closes her door, and the cold of the truck seeps through her clothes and into her skin.

She watches Quinn and Joel walk to the Meteor and get in on either side of Harrison. Are they going to kill him?

Edwin drives her and Eugene to the hospital. The weight of her son rests against her body, and then against Edwin's, as they curve around the Malahat. It is a fifteen-minute drive.

When they pull up underneath the bright red awning of the emergency entrance, Edwin tells her he's going to take Eugene in first, then send a nurse out for her with a wheelchair.

"Be right back," he says. "Hold tight, honey. They're going to take care of you." His voice is soft and gravelly. He leaves the truck running, feeble heat coming out of the vent like soft breath. Edwin flips up the collar of his flannel jacket and reaches into the cab for Eugene. Her grey sweatshirt falls away from his body as Edwin lifts him. He cradles the boy and walks toward the entrance. His pants are half tucked into his boots, the laces untied. The pneumatic doors slide open and Edwin disappears, obscured by the fogged-up glass.

I could be born here, into this life. My mother could wait for the nurse to emerge, pushing a wheelchair with a slippery leather seat. My mother could allow herself to be wheeled through the doors, to check in, to be pushed past the patients in the waiting room who have just seen a man carrying her dead son. A short labour, like her first, the baby born without incident, despite being premature. The police outside the door, waiting for it to be over. She'll give her statement. Maybe she'll get to nurse me. She will be charged with her son's death. She'll plead guilty. She is, after all. And what will become of Harrison? Will he survive Quinn and Joel's beating? What if he doesn't? Quinn will go to jail, another life taken. If Harrison survives, the police will charge him, and he will spend the next decade at William Head. Quinn will not file for custody of me, being too old. I'll be taken away, this harrowing beginning to my life forever stamped down upon me. The birth certificate cursed with my mother's name.

Or, there is a better alternative. She will take Edwin's truck and drive away from this place. On an island, there isn't really anywhere to go, but she can get out of the woods and into the city. Her mother's friend Luella lives near Beacon Hill Park. She is a registered nurse; she can help Yula deliver the baby. Luella will let her stay until the baby can travel. She will take me to the mainland and start a new life. Years later, my mother will balk at how similar her fantasy was to Harrison's. Years later, she will feel a dark twinge of regret that they couldn't have made this happen somehow.

Yes, this is better. Yula begins to talk to me. She tells me we're going to drive into town. She says she needs me to wait a little while. Just let her drive into town. That's all she needs from me now.

She slides into the driver's seat, and the truck hiccups when she shifts into drive. It lurches forward and she doesn't even need to press on the gas. The truck slides through the parking lot, toward the street, as if by sheer will alone.

And here we go together, down the Trans-Canada Highway. At first there's nothing to see. It's dark out, just the arc of streetlights as we go under each overpass. The highway narrows into Douglas Street, and she drives past the car dealerships, the A&W. A memory—driving one night with Harrison and Eugene. Harrison saying, "Hold on, I want to run in, just pull into the parking lot for a sec." Moments later him coming out with a stuffed A&W Root Bear in his arms for Eugene. Her heart lifting. Everything momentarily okay.

"I don't want this to be happening," Yula says to me. "I don't want this to be my life."

The street lights on Douglas are blue, each with five frosted globes. They light the sidewalks like little white moons. The Ukrainian Dance Association. Fitness World. Money Mart. She has never been in any of these places. There is hardly anyone on the road but she's a nervous driver in Edwin's truck. The engine, a V8, feels alive under the hood. At each stoplight she hesitates, then presses the gas pedal too hard, and the truck shoots forward as if propelled by a rocket. The engine makes a terrible low growl. She notices the smell then, after all this time. It is a horrible mix of chicken manure and skunkweed. Bile rises into her mouth.

Swiss Chalet. Mayfair Lanes. The bowling alley's huge parking lot is empty save for one white sedan. Two women stand at one of the bus stops, eyeing the truck as she drives past. Luella worked as a nurse in a women's prison for a few years, that's what her mother had said. *It's no good being a woman, Yula. They drag you by your hair.* Jo told Yula once, If you're ever in trouble, any kind at all, go to Luella. She'll help you.

The Esso station. Mayfair Mall. Mount Tolmie to her left. KFC. Denny's and more car dealerships. Past the Traveller's Inn where she and Harrison once stayed for two nights when they first met. They bought a case of beer and a two-six of Jack Daniel's, got hungry and ate breakfast at Denny's at three in the morning. Yula remembers throwing a French fry at the waitress's back. Why did she do something so immature? What was wrong with her? She hoped Harrison didn't think ill of her because of it. He had laughed, then walked over to the waitress and apologized, as though Yula were his child.

More strip malls. Canadian Tire. The street lined with oak trees. Getting closer and closer to Rock Bay. Slightly safer now than it used to be. But still so awful at night.

The Ford dealership. The liquor store. Finally, Hillside Avenue. The little motels. The strip club. Bay Street and the Dairy Queen. Thompson's Foam Shop, Red Hot Video, another Traveller's Inn. A few cars are on the road with her now, and she grips the wheel, suddenly aware of how much pain she's in.

A contraction forces her to lurch forward and she takes her foot off the gas, rests her head against the steering wheel. She lifts her head and the truck is pointed toward Herald Street, stopped in the road. A dark-haired woman with huge hoop earrings is leaning up against a building, a can of beer in her hand. Yula presses down on the gas again and carries on. The bright red brick of City Hall, and then she is downtown and the streets are littered with men in sleeping bags. This is where she'll end up, she thinks. This has always been the logical place for her, hasn't it? There's something missing inside of her—something that makes her unable to get by in the world like a regular person. Without Harrison and her father and the cabin on the side of Mount Finlayson, she's not sure she can survive. She does not feel strong. She cannot think about Eugene now. She lets her thoughts go numb. There is nothing in her mind.

Down Douglas Street past the Eaton Centre and the Strathcona Hotel, the Conference Centre and the back of the Empress, the street curves and rises and the truck works harder to take her up past the totem poles, then left on Southgate and into the park. She's been in the park late at night. It isn't dangerous like everyone says. She's always thought it was the safest place in the world. Aside from her home, there isn't a single place she feels as safe as in Beacon Hill Park.

Her contractions are closer, and the pain is too much now. She stops the car on Heywood Avenue and looks into the dark windows of Luella's first-floor apartment. It is late August, but on this cold evening she can see her breath in the dim light from a street lamp overhead.

She knocks sharply on the front door and digs her nails into her palms. And then Luella opens the door in a blue terrycloth bathrobe and little black moccasins. She is in her mid-fifties now, with long grey hair almost to her waist and long wispy bangs. Her face seems to glow from within. Her eyes are heavily lined with kohl, even at this hour. They are bright blue. Her pale skin is the colour of a pearl. She pulls Yula into her apartment and cups her face in her hands. The girl has never looked so ugly and fierce. Her eyes are hard, her jaw tense. Her face is twisted.

"My mom said I should come to you if I was ever in trouble," Yula says.

Luella and my mother lie in the bed together, waiting for the labour to progress. My mother tells her what happened: they left the boy for a few hours while they took a drive to the beach. She was too stoned. She fell asleep. When they got home, he was sick. So sick. He'd drunk two bottles of flavoured cough syrup. She thought he would be okay. He died while she was sleeping. Then: Dominic standing by the side of road, Eugene's body at his feet. Her father.

"Harrison and his brother were trying to hide him from me," she tells Luella. She tells her about the plot to bury her son in the woods. Harrison's bag of cocaine. "They killed my son," she says. "I just thought he drank the cough syrup. I thought he'd be okay. He'd already vomited it up." If she'd known about the cocaine, she says. If she'd only known. She never would have gone back to sleep. "How could they have let me go back to sleep?"

My mother blinks, and the room comes into focus. It is a small bedroom, the walls painted purple with white trim and crowded with art. Luella's bed has a wrought-iron frame. A mahogany bedside table holds an elegant silver lamp and a fancy clock. The door to the bedroom is closed, and a pale blue nightgown hangs from a hook on the back. It is such a civilized bedroom compared to her own. The floors are swept, the little Persian rug still bears the track marks of a vacuum. One of Luella's oil paintings hangs on the wall, a portrait of a woman in a white dress and red scarf, her arms around a little girl. My mother wishes she could stay in the safety and stillness of this small tidy bedroom forever.

She stares at the ceiling. Her legs are cramping and she stretches them out, arches her feet. "Why did they let me fall asleep? If I'd known, if I'd known, I never would have let myself fall asleep."

Luella strokes my mother's forehead. "Let's go to the hospital. Make sure the baby's okay."

"I'll go to jail. They'll take her away from me."

Luella sits up and fiddles with one of the rings on her hands. She looks at my mother's face and imagines this small sweet girl, her best friend's daughter, in prison for killing her son.

My mother reaches for Luella's hand. "I don't want this baby to ever know who I am," she says. The words come out of my mother's mouth unwittingly, and then it begins.

19

"Lift it by the little handles there—yeah, that's it—and, one, two, three," Vaughn says, and we lift the dinghy into the air and walk, grapevine-stepping, down the pebbled beach toward the water. It is the first sunny day in what feels like months, the water and sand so bright that we scrunch up our faces, hair blown back in the vicious wind. When you're this close to the sea, everyone walks with his or her head down and a kind of pained look, as though their lips were being pulled back toward their ears via invisible wire. It's almost a sinister smile. The cyclists wear it, too, as they whip around the coast on their spindly bicycles built for speed. I've come to think of it as Island Face.

Vaughn and I have been hanging out every once in a while, weekends mostly, for the past few months. I finally told Miranda about the Ministry and Madeleine, and about writing a letter to my father. Every morning she and

I check the mailbox together, hopeful. We finally have a morning routine.

The oars shift on the floor of the dinghy as Vaughn and I jostle it toward the ocean, his side at least a foot higher than mine because he is so much taller. The sea sparkles and dazzles as bright as a thousand suns. Whenever I can close my eyes, I do. We both wear bright orange life jackets and ball caps, our pant legs rolled, our sneakers shooting around in the dinghy, banging into the oars, into my backpack where we've put the sandwiches and cans of 7-Up. It is almost too cold and windy to be doing this. The sun on my skin feels healing, and necessary, and I raise my face to the sky and let it burn into my cheeks. Vaughn's face, of course, is slathered with zinc oxide, his nose completely white. He's wearing mirrored wraparound sunglasses, and I look at him and see the beach behind me, the trees beyond it, then the sky.

"You gonna rub that in?" I point at his white nose.

He laughs. "I know this is hard to believe," he says, "but I really don't care what I look like."

There is a group of children on the beach, pails dangling from their little hands, and gulls, and the smell of salt and seaweed is at times—when the wind blows the right way—overwhelming. Sand fleas bite our ankles and hermit crabs scatter when disturbed. The dinghy is army green, the words *Fish Hunter* printed in black block letters on the side. It is Blaze's boat, and we have borrowed it. We're not going to fish, just bob around in the water for a while. Vaughn says that someday we'll put an outboard motor on the thing and take it all the way to Discovery or Chatham

Island. He says there's a rope swing on one of them, but he can't remember which.

People describe the sea as looking like glass, but I think it looks like metal, and I still don't understand why people think the sea is blue. It's green. At the shoreline, we stand at the edge of the world. As the tide comes in, the whole world pushes into itself, and when the tide goes out, we all stretch toward the sea. It looks like someone has spread a huge piece of tinfoil right in front of me and is shaking it from some invisible point.

A seagull is floating in the water a few feet away, and we eye each other for a moment. He coasts to shore and I follow his tracks in the sand as he walks toward the group of children, who are eating French fries spread out on a piece of newsprint. The gull's little feet slap the wet sand and he walks right up to the children, dips his head quickly, and then lifts himself into the sky, fries dangling out of his mouth like worms. The children scream but are delighted.

We lower the dinghy into the water, and Vaughn holds it steady while I climb in. I tuck myself into the bow and spread my arms over the sides while Vaughn hoists one leg and then the other over the side and flops down. He hooks the oars into place and swings the dinghy around so my back is to the shore and rows us out into the water. The waves slap against the rubber sides, and Vaughn's oars slice through the water like blades. The muscles in his upper arms ripple when he rows.

All the windsurfers are out, their sails stretched taut. I lean over the side and watch for jellyfish. Their circular bodies ooze by, pulsing in and out like beating hearts.

Deadheads; kelp. A beer bottle, but there isn't much trash in the water. Finally we catch up to a seal, which follows us for a while, his head bobbing. Then he disappears, only to appear moments later, improbably far away.

Vaughn rests the oars against the side of the boat and unwraps a sandwich, hands it to me. We made them earlier in his kitchen: turkey and slivered iceberg lettuce, mayonnaise. Vaughn eats his in three large bites, then glugs his 7-Up. He wipes his mouth with the back of his hand. At dinner with Miranda and Lydia-Rose, I have to be careful to take small bites and to chew everything and not to slurp. I hate it. I don't want to eat at all if I can't eat like a wild animal.

We unwrap our second sandwiches and eat those like beasts, too. We are silent, our cheeks as full as chipmunks'. A seagull lands near us and watches us chew. Vaughn rips off a bit of crust and tosses it into the waves.

He picks up the oars again and rows a little farther out. A windsurfer loses his balance and falls backwards into a wave. I watch Vaughn row. Even the muscles in his wrists respond to the pull of the oars. I look at my own wrists, my soft white arms. It doesn't seem as though he and I are even of the same species.

Vaughn rubs at the zinc on his nose. His arms are already a shade darker. He says, "Did you ever hear back from your father?"

"No."

Before I got the courage to send the letter, I read it so many times that I memorized it. When I close my eyes at night, I hear it. Whenever there is silence, or any kind of pause, the words creep into my head. Did he even get the letter? If so, did I offend him? What if I never hear back? What if he isn't my father after all? The possibilities skip around in my head.

"When you're in the thick of your life, Shannon," Vaughn says suddenly, "it feels like a mess—one surprise after the next. But later, when you look back on things, it seems like a plot. One thing leads to another. Et cetera. You start to see the causal relationships between things." He pauses and lets the oars drop. We let the wind push us back toward the shore, the waves lapping against the thin vinyl floor of the dinghy. "But you know, I suppose if you have enough time on your hands, you can make connections about anything."

I drum the floor of the dinghy with my feet, feel the waves push back against it. "Just feels like a big mess to me."

We drift closer to the marina, and the wind dies down but I can hear it whistling through the masts. I should get a sailboat. I should live on a sailboat. Everything is better when you're on the water.

After a while I say, "Miranda wants to meet you."

"Happy to."

"She says she wishes I would have told her about all this earlier."

"I'm sure."

"She says she'll give me as much space as I need. She says she'll do whatever I need, even if it's to stay completely out of it."

Vaughn shakes his head at me. "You're one of those people, aren't you. So unlucky in some ways, so lucky in others."

The seal re-emerges about five feet away from us with his shiny, bowling-ball head.

"I wish I were a seal," I say.

"A bird," says Vaughn.

"A fish."

"A whale."

"A porpoise."

"A manatee."

"An anteater."

"An aardvark."

"Tortoise."

"Wombat."

"Great white shark."

"Woolly mammoth."

"Elephant seal."

"Back to seals then."

"Back to seals." The seal dunks his head and shoots back down.

"You know there's a monster in the bay," says Vaughn.

"I know. The Cadborosaurus."

"Like the Loch Ness monster."

"The Canadian version."

Vaughn laughs and stretches out his legs, lets them dangle over the edge of the boat. I stare at the soles of his feet, which are calloused and dry.

"You should ask Chloe out on a date," I say to him. I think about her high forehead and ponytail, her amazing android body. The look in her eyes when she talked about him. Yes, this should happen.

"Chloe? She's too young for me, don't you think?"

"Nah. Ask her out. I promise you she'll say yes."

Vaughn tilts his head, considering this. "If you say so. Okay. But we work together. That could get weird, no?"

"Who cares. Life is weird. You're weird."

He laughs again. "You're weird."

"You're weirder."

Vaughn dips the oars into the water again, rows us around some more. He says he can't believe I've never been out on the ocean before. He says there's no excuse, living where we do.

The tide has pushed us almost all the way back to shore. Vaughn dips the oars into the water, rows us one stroke forward, and then I feel the rocky sand beneath me. The waves nudge us farther and farther up the beach while we sit lazily in the boat, letting the tide do all the work.

The sun beats down, and I feel my shoulders burning. I could stay in this boat all day. Time is suspended in a boat. I take a deep breath and try to remember this moment, the heat on my face, the grit under my feet, the strength of the waves. I run my hands through the pebbles and sand, searching for sea glass. One thing leads to another. There are tide pools between the larger rocks, tiny rivers connecting them to the sea.

After we've deflated the dinghy, washed the sand from between our toes, and rubbed our shoulders with aloe vera, I stand in front of the mirror of Vaughn's bathroom and wash my hands with his little cake of Ivory soap, which is now as curved and thin as a seashell. He's up the street, getting takeout from the Chinese joint. We're having hot-and-sour soup and egg rolls. I can't wait. I'm starving. I lift my shirt in the mirror and stare at my belly. I look like a seal pup. Planet Big Stomach over here. I want to eat until I burst.

In Vaughn's living room, I kneel on the couch and stare out the window. The traffic shoots by, tailed by an endless stream of people on bicycles. I try to picture what my life will be like, but it all seems impossible. It seems impossible that I'll graduate from high school, get a job beyond dishwashing in the summertime, have a home one day, a partner, children of my own. It seems impossible that I'll ever hear back from my father. Or that I'll ever travel, see Europe or Asia, take a road trip all the way to New Orleans. Life seems full of *impossibility*. I don't know how anyone gets through it.

This is what the inside of my mind looks like today: it's a skinny white room with wide-planked floors and four windows, one on each wall. In the middle of the room is an elaborately carved nineteenth-century double-pedestal desk, stained black. It's a real eyesore. The room is in an old farmhouse, and the farmhouse sits in the middle of a great green field. It's so quiet there. Inside the farmhouse, I stay so still I forget I exist. I barely make a ripple.

I find a pack of matches in Vaughn's kitchen and burn the lint off my socks, then I hold the flame under my heel until it hurts. Vaughn's house smells like potato chips. It always smells like potato chips. He must eat them in secret and then stuff the bags in the bottom of the trash. There is evidence everywhere—salt and crumbs on every surface, illuminated in the window light. One of his cupboards—the one where he keeps his spices and cooking oil—is filled with diet pills, fibre pills, weight-loss supplements, and vitamins. But the spices and the oil are lined up in front, so I have to peer over them to see the pills. There is a bottle of Milk of Magnesia and then a huge tub of protein powder behind the canola oil. I unscrew the lid and smell it. It's made with kelp and smells like the sea. In another cupboard he has a huge stack of cookbooks, the pages dog-eared and marked with Post-it Notes. His freezer is bursting with leftover food. I take out a chocolate Popsicle, which claims to have only one hundred calories, and finish it in two bites. I can relate to this hunger Vaughn must feel, this need to cram the kitchen with food. Lately I've been feeling so hungry that I buy a bag of potatoes on my way back from school and then boil the whole bag and eat it with huge melting slabs of butter before Miranda or Lydia-Rose gets home. I do not feel sick after. I feel like I could eat an entire cake.

Miranda doesn't like to have leftovers. We have to eat everything in the house before she'll go grocery shopping again. She can't bear the thought of wasted food. She also can't bear the idea of us eating for the sake of eating—mindless eating, she calls it. At dinner, she tells me to slow down and chew. To chew everything twenty times. I can't do this. I want to eat everything in the world, and I want to eat it very quickly.

Vaughn is taking forever so I ransack further. I lift the couch cushions and find nickels and pennies and a receipt for a bicycle pump. The front hall closet is crammed with anoraks and fleeces, the floor crowded with rain boots, flip-flops, and five worn-out pairs of running shoes, some more worn out than others. He has a great CD collection, lots of reggae. And then I find a photo album of his wedding. His hair is shoulder-length and an even brighter red than it is now. He's softer looking somehow, not as sinewy or strong. He wears a blue suit and tie, a corsage on the lapel. He's standing with his arms around half of a large redwood tree. His ex-wife encircles the other half, their hands barely touching. She is a small thin woman with dark hair pulled back into a ponytail. She has a plain face. She looks no-nonsense to me. She looks like someone who never farts. She's wearing a three-quarter-length emerald green dress and a pair of Birkenstocks. There are only six more photographs. The rest have been taken out. One is of Vaughn standing with three people, two of whom I guess are his parents, and Blaze, his brother—they're all shorter than Vaughn and grinning—and the rest are photos of his ex-wife. Cross-legged, eating a piece of cake. In the crook of a tree. Against the trunk of another. The last is a close-up. Her smile is a little half-moon, her skin stretched taut. She looks more like an athlete in this photo than in the others, even though it is just of her face. Her eyes are small and she's squinting—the sky is overcast but bright. And then there's a letter folded in thirds, and I take it out.

Though I can't prove this with any kind of certainty, I do not believe I fulfilled you, and I found you radiated a peculiar kind of sadness and resistance, particularly when making love. As I came to know and love you, I accepted that your true heart was elsewhere. Be it with a former lover or an imagined one to come, I do not know. I mustn't feel second rate, you'll understand. And now that I know about Sylvie, I know I was in fact second rate, and that you were searching for more.

I can't be your friend, Vaughn. I don't know how. I might have loved you the most of all; either that or the sum of our heartbreaks never diminishes, only keeps silent until we're ripped open again. Whatever the case, the idea of laughing with you seems foreign and cursed. If we can't laugh, we can't be.

I trust your life will bring you plenty of magic.

The rest of the album is empty. I slide it back into the bookshelf and wait for Vaughn. What is it like to marry someone and then have it not work out? What is it like for him to live alone? I wonder if he thinks about these things much, or at all. I can never tell if other people are dissecting themselves and the world the way I do.

I watch him cycle up the street, the bag of Chinese takeout dangling from his handlebars, then dismount and walk toward the house. He's wearing navy blue rain pants, a faded red sweatshirt with a hole in the elbow, white tennis shoes, and a ball cap. He knocks on the front door, then opens it and says, "Anybody home?"

Part 3

20

If you ask me what I remember about Julian, I'll tell you that his lower lip jutted when he spoke, exposing his bottom teeth. I used to study the way he talked, watching his lip shoot down if he said a word that started with G, J, U, or Y. He had tiny, coffee-stained teeth. He had a gummy smile. His lower lip was plump, topped by a skinny upper lip that seemed to fall down upon the bottom one like a lid when he closed his mouth. He had a deep groove between his top lip and his nose—this little thing is called the philtrum, I've since discovered. His eyes darkened when he drank. He was always going to the bathroom, especially at night. Up, up, and up again, five six seven eight times before finally settling in to sleep. Anywhere we went, he had to find the bathroom. He wore a blue windbreaker when it was cold out, and underneath, a mustard-coloured fleece. His skin was perpetually flushed. His hands rough and cracked. He slept in striped pyjama bottoms. His stomach sagged over the waistband of his pants. Hideous but odourless feet. On Sundays, he didn't shave and padded around the house in gym shorts and a ripped T-shirt a couple of sizes too big. His socks pulled to the knee, and little black slippers. He liked to read. He read everything—novels, magazines, menus, flyers, instructions. The bathroom, stacked high with newspapers.

I think of my memories as being card-catalogued and neatly put away in drawers in the big black desk inside my head. I can open most of the drawers, take out a card, look at it, consider it, put it away. I have drawers for Lydia-Rose, for Miranda, for our pets, for Vaughn, for Blue Jay School, for Matthew. I can search through them and find almost anything if I need to. I can't remember Par and Raquelle—though I swear I can remember the smell of the little bags of cumin and turmeric that had spilled in the cupboard, wafting out with a stale mustiness each time Raquelle reached in to find a certain spice. I'm certain I can remember that smell.

When I want to store something in my memory—when I want to make sure it ends up in the card catalogue—I burn it into my brain. This isn't hard to do. I never want to forget that moment in Gregor's apartment when Matthew was across from me, whispering, *You'll never forget your first time*, a little dot of acid on his finger. I framed him with my eyes. I took a picture. I filed it. Done. It's there now, and I'll never forget it. This mindfulness has a flipside: when I want to forget, I can do that, too.

Easy. I take another picture. But then I take a huge black Jiffy marker—the fattest one you can buy—and I colour over the picture in my mind. It doesn't take long, and the picture is covered with black ink forever. If I look really hard I might be able to see the outline of whatever lies beneath, and if I can see too much, I reach for the marker again. If it refuses to disappear, if the image keeps bubbling to the surface, I encase it within a brick wall. This takes more time. I have to get the bricks and the mortar. I have to start from the ground up: lay the bricks, the mortar, the bricks, the mortar, until I have a wall in front of me, the memory entombed behind it. This might take a few hours, but it works.

But we are naturally self-destructive. If I press myself against the brick wall, I can find a tiny pinhole where the mortar didn't settle and left a little space for me to look through. I can see the blood on Julian's back and the jar of Vaseline. I can see what's on the television, the silvery green eyes of the panther, the naked body of Nastassja Kinski. I can see the fear on my little face.

It is six in the morning, and I have left Miranda's under the guise of going for a run before school but instead I am standing outside of Julian's periwinkle house on Olive Street. Things have changed: there are huge, unruly rhododendron bushes lining the sidewalk now, obscuring the house from the road. The lawn is neatly mowed and edged. He must have a gardener. A Price's Alarms sign is jammed into the dirt beside one of the bushes. The park across from their house has a new playground—it's made of big brightly coloured plastic, like all the playgrounds are now, instead of the splintery wood and chains and metal bars that I used to play on with Lydia-Rose. It's still dark out, though the horizon is lit by a faint orange haze. I hear seagulls and the crash of the surf down the block and the occasional car speeding along Dallas Road. The lights in the house are off. The lights in all the houses are off.

There are a few ways to go about doing this. I can be petty if I want to. I can destroy the rhododendrons, which I hate anyway, or I can graffiti his door. I can do little things to his house, once a week, until he's forced to put up security cameras. I can knock on the door, introduce myself, pretend I have no memories, and accept the invitation inside. I can sit in the living room, run my fingers over the piano keys, and ask to go to the bathroom. I can squirt some ipecac into his big bottle of mouthwash. If I find myself in the kitchen, I can put a shot or two into the milk, the plastic jug of pulpy orange juice. I can prank-call him at night, but after a while he'll turn off the phone. How many times will he vomit until he throws out the milk and the juice? Would it even work if he only swirled the mouthwash around and then spat it out?

Through the tiny window in the front door, I peer in and can see a distorted image of the foyer, warped by the bevelled glass. Muddy boots lie in a heap on the floor. The stairs leading to the second floor are covered with magazines and newspapers, and I wonder how anyone could go up or down. I try to see into the living room, but my view is obscured. The mailbox is nearly full. I take out the mail and sift through it. *Julian Marchand. Julian B. Marchand. Mr. J. Marchand. J.B. Marchand.* There are a few pieces for a Karl Marchand and the rest is junk.

I look through the window again and that's when I see the wheelchair at the very end of the foyer, near the entrance to the kitchen. Was it there a minute ago?

Thirty seconds later I'm on the back deck, looking through the French doors that lead into the kitchen. My footprints leave marks in the dew. The wooden deck is slippery and I brace myself on the railing and peer in. The eucalyptus tree is moulting in the backyard and I'm sure that any minute now a strip of bark will fall on my head. I stand underneath it on Julian's porch, look up at the thick drops of dew plunking down from the wet leaves, and smirk at my stumpy reflection in the French doors. There's a cigarette in my hand and a pack of Camels stuffed in my pocket. I've got on a well-worn pair of jeans and a striped turtleneck sweater. The nicotine makes me reel, and I crush the remainder of the smoke under my shoe.

It looks like no one has mopped the kitchen floor in years. The white linoleum is stained brown, sections of it covered in what looks like tar. The kitchen table is swaybacked from the weight of buckets filled with water or paint, I can't tell. It looks like its legs are going to buckle. The refrigerator door is ajar, the light out. Nothing is on the fridge except a few muddy handprints.

I can't see the sink, but under the kitchen table is a mountain of vegetable peelings, which ants have surrounded and are in the process of carrying away to some other location.

Who has such an immaculate lawn and such a disastrous kitchen? Also resting on the kitchen table are issues of *Reader's Digest* and a bunch of dog-eared paperbacks. I can't make out the titles, except for one—*Slaughterhouse Five*.

Do I leave? Do I ring the doorbell? Do I break the glass panes of the French doors and walk in? The sun rises behind me, and I can see my reflection now in the golden light. I would give the whole world not to be so small. I look like a midget standing out here. A midget with a golden Afro, backlit by the sun. The weirdest cherub around.

And then I'm doing it. I'm breaking the window with a rock, my sweater wrapped around my arm. It isn't easy. It takes three tries. I take a deep breath and visualize the rock, and my hand around it, sailing through the glass. The glass breaks and I shake off the shards, reach in and turn the deadbolt, open the door.

The smell of rotten vegetables, whatever tar-like substance is on the floor, and the buckets, which, I can see now, are full of pickling vinegar, surrounds me when I step into the kitchen. It's a big kitchen, with high ceilings broken up by tracks of halogen lights. I flick them on, but the bulbs are burnt out. Either no one has heard me or no one is home. It's cold. The heat is off. I pull on my sweater and hug my shoulders, try to figure out what to do.

The sunlight rushes through the windows and fills the room. I can see my breath. The ants continue to carry away little bits of carrot peel. I push the fridge door closed and examine the sink, which is full of Mason jars. The counter is covered in cucumbers. I've never seen so many cucumbers in my life.

The walls are still painted a pale yellow, although the paint is cracked and bubbled near the ceiling. The gas stove is covered in grime, little coils of hair pressed into the stickiness. A cast-iron pan sits, unwashed and rusting, on one of the burners. There is a rag rug at my feet, which once was red but is soaked through with so much mud that it might as well be brown. A car dealership calendar is on the wall, still flipped open to February, displaying a picture of a blue Model T Ford.

I don't know what accounts for the delay, but when the alarm goes off I'm poking my finger into the soft green flesh of a cucumber. It's a horrible piercing sound and I'm immediately furious at myself for ignoring the Price's sign, for not taking it seriously. Will it turn off at some point? Will the police come? I press my back into the countertop and push my chin into my chest, willing the sound to stop. My heart pounds and my armpits bead with sweat.

And then Julian is in the doorway, in a plaid flannel bathrobe and bare feet, his hair pushed flat against his head, his eyes small from sleep. "Jesus. Get the fuck, the fuck out of here."

He doesn't have his glasses on, and he squints at me, sees how small I am and makes a kind of disappointed grunting sound, as though he's bored. He lets his body slump against the doorframe.

"Do you remember me?" I step toward him.

"Get out." He barely raises his voice. He spins and disappears into the foyer, where I hear the beep of little buttons being pushed on the alarm's console. And then it's over. The sound stops, and the silence fills my ears. The smell of the vinegar and vegetables comes rushing back, too, and I brace myself on the countertop.

"Hello?" I call out when he doesn't reappear. "Hello?"

I walk into the foyer and then through the living room, but he's not there either. The piano is where it was when I last saw it, a coating of dust like icing sugar over its black keys.

When he finally walks into the room, he is dressed in corduroy trousers and a button-down shirt. His hair wet and combed back, his face washed.

"Hi, Shannon," he says, and we make eye contact for the first time that morning. He motions to the couch, pushes a pile of junk mail to the floor. "Sit down?"

He looks lumpier but mostly the same. Doesn't look like age has really hit him hard yet. He fiddles with his watch strap, then reaches for one of the half-dead plants, a foxtail fern. He pets it the way someone would pet a dog's tail: long, pulling strokes. Finally, he sits across from me on the piano bench. He still looks, incredibly, like a hedgehog. I wait for him to speak, to see that lower lip pull down and reveal those hideous little teeth.

"You want coffee?" he says and I see them, I see the teeth. "Cup of coffee? I'm going to put some on."

I shake my head and watch him stand up shakily and disappear into the kitchen. I hear the tap and the freezer open and the whirr of a grinder and the kettle boiling, and then he comes back into the room with a French press in one hand and a tall silver travel mug in the other.

"There's plenty if you change your mind."

I scoot closer to the coffee table and put my feet up on it. I suppose I'm trying to be irritating.

"Next time, knock," he says and we both start to laugh. It *is* funny after all.

He pushes the filter down and pours himself a cup of dark, sludgy-looking coffee.

All my plans of breaking every bone in his face, smashing a vase over his head until both split open, kicking his shins until they bleed. All my plans disappear. I can't even find the strength to straighten out my sweater, which is caught underneath me and is pulling on the back of my neck.

"My dad lives with me now. I know it's a mess." Julian laughs softly and shakes his head. "It's not always this bad. We've been making pickles. We get tired. We forget to put stuff away." He takes a loud slurp of coffee. "Who cares anyway. Who cares what this place looks like."

The sunlight filters in through the back of the house, but the living room is still dark. Julian coughs into his hand and reaches for the lamp.

"Suppose you've come to raise the dead," he says.

"I'm just here to ask why," I mutter. I say it so quietly that I barely hear myself.

"Why."

"Why."

"Why what?" He gives a kind of hideous-sounding chuckle and runs his hand through his hair.

I wish I were taller. I wish I could do the splits. I wish I were good at sports. I wish I were a ballerina. I wish I didn't feel like a small, weird-looking dwarf sitting in a crazy man's house at dawn.

"You're pretty bold, you know. Breaking into my house. Do you know what you've put me through?"

The sound of horrible phlegmy coughing comes from upstairs and Julian shifts uncomfortably on the piano bench. "Shit," he says. "Shit." He puts both hands on his knees and straightens his legs, then walks stiffly toward the staircase. I watch him ascend and then listen as he opens and shuts a door, and then the sound of more coughing and Julian's voice.

Next to the couch is an old desk with cubby-style drawers. I slide them open quietly and peek inside each one. Receipts, chequebooks, a paperback copy of *Gift from the Sea*, a spilled box of ballpoint pens, gross-looking erasers, graph paper. One of the drawers is empty, save for a wedding ring. I put it on my finger. If Julian notices, I'll give it back. That's my bargain.

When he returns, I am flipping through the little paperback, one leg up on the piano bench. "Why is your garden so neat and your house such a mess?"

"Neighbours complained," he says. He walks to his French press, swishes the coffee around for a second, and pours the rest into his travel mug. "So we hired Juan." He takes a sip and then spits it into the mug. "God knows I don't give a damn what it looks like out there. Be right back."

He goes into the kitchen, and I hear him filling the kettle again.

And then Julian's father appears at the bottom of the stairs in grey sweatpants with elastic ankles and a faded turquoise sweatshirt. His slippers look homemade. He's a short man with a long face—wide-eyed, stout—with pearl-grey hair cut in short bangs. His eyes are bathwater green. We look at each other. What feels like ten minutes goes by.

"Shannon?" Julian calls.

I leave Julian's father standing on the stairs and walk into the kitchen. Julian's got both hands on the kitchen table and is half bent over, grimacing, bracing himself.

"I ate this huge omelette before bed last night," he says, clearing his throat. "Bad idea." He shakes his head like a dog coming out of water, blinks a few times and stares into one of the pots of vinegar.

I put my hand under my nose to stop the vinegar smell from reaching me, but it's too late, and I have to clench my jaw to keep from gagging.

Julian taps his foot on the floor, turns to the fridge, and opens a can of diet ginger ale.

"Can I have some ginger ale?"

Julian nods and passes me a cold can.

He looks so ugly in the harsh light of the morning. That lip, those teeth. He grimaces again and pushes a handful of antacids into his mouth. I can hear his father coughing, and the sun has risen, and the heater has come on and is blowing hot air up through the floor vents. There's nothing I need to do or say to him. It's been done. He's done.

"You're always welcome here." He holds out his hand, but I don't take it. He shrugs, drops his hand to his side, and takes out a broom and dustpan from the closet and starts sweeping up the broken glass. I watch him for a second. He bends down and slides the glass into the dustpan and shakes it into the trash. He moves jerkily, as if someone is directing his movements with a remote control. I leave him and walk into the living room.

There are no photographs, nothing on the walls. No art. The hardwood is covered with a threadbare Persian rug, half of it faded from the sun. Sometimes I feel so weak, as if nothing has ever really happened to me. I feel as weak as a sponge. I walk to the window and set my can of ginger ale on the sill. I put my hand on the glass, leave a handprint. The glass is cold under my palm, and my hand is damp when I take it away. This mark is all I'll leave Julian with. This is the last he'll ever see of me. But I'll always be here in this house, like a ghost.

21

I am an easy birth, as was Eugene. My mother pants, like Jo taught her to do, and Luella tries to get her to relax.

My head appears, then retracts, and Luella makes space with her fingers to prevent my mother from tearing. Each contraction brings me closer and closer to being born. The air in the bedroom is cool and sharp on Yula's legs and somehow soothing.

When Luella sees me start to crown, she puts her hand on either side of my head to guide me out. She pushes down, freeing one of my shoulders, then pulls up to free the other. Yula pants and pushes hard, and in an instant I am in Luella's arms, slippery as a fish, my eyes clenched shut. Luella strokes my nose to release the mucus and amniotic fluid, then rests me between Yula's breasts, my head slightly below my body to help drain out the fluid. My arms and legs reach out aimlessly, quiver and paw the air, then curl back in again. My mother's hands are trembling. I am half the size of Eugene when he was born and covered in soft, dark downy fur. Luella rubs me clean with a towel, wipes the vernix from my tiny face and body until I start to cry. I have skinny little limbs and my skin is red and wrinkled. My mother listens for my breath in the dark, silent morning. Luella dries me off as best she can and places me back on my mother's chest, then covers us both in a flannel bedsheet.

Yula feels her womb begin to contract again and then the pressure as the placenta moves down. There is a small gush of blood, and Luella guides the placenta out until she is holding the entire thing in her hands. She inspects it to make sure it is all in one piece, that there are no ragged edges, nothing left behind. She feels Yula's abdomen to make sure her uterus is properly contracted and tells her that she is okay, that everything is going to be okay.

My mother hadn't expected me to be this small. Her heart pounds. She is holding such a small, delicate thing. I frighten her. I am too small to seem human. My eyes are still shut tight, and I've gone silent. Everything she should not have done rushes at her—stayed out that night, left Eugene by himself, gotten high, taken me into the city to be born. The weight of her decisions settles into her heart like rocks. She has killed her child. Will she kill another? I look so small and helpless that she's not sure how I'm even alive.

She feels my breath on her skin and looks into my little potato-sized face. I am brand new. I know nothing. I know no one. The thought comes to her in a bright flash. I must never know her. I must never know what a monster she is. I deserve better. Someone will raise me here, in the city. Someone will raise me right. A real family.

As she lies in Luella's bed, she plans her death. She could walk to Dallas Road and drown herself in the ocean. She wants it to be painful. She wants to suffer. She searches her mind for options. She could probably get into the lobby of View Towers if she waited long enough for someone to walk outside, hold open the door. Oh, hey, let me in, okay? It would be that easy. Then it would be a matter of getting into someone's apartment on the top floor. Take the elevator. Wait. Could she just knock on all the doors until someone answered, then push her way through and out onto the balcony? Could she do that? One of Harrison's dealers used to live there. If only she could remember his name. Maybe in a little while she'll remember. In her mind she sees herself falling toward the ground. It pleases her. I will never know her. I will never know about any of this.

Luella rests her hand on Yula's arm. Her fingers are covered in delicate silver rings, the nails neatly manicured and painted peach. Yula stares at her own hands, the cuticles overgrown and haggard, the nails deeply ridged and caked with dirt. They are still the hands of a girl.

"I miss your mother," Luella says. "Strange as she was."

"Me too."

"She named you after me. Did you know that?"

Yula shakes her head. "Why doesn't my father like you?"

Luella pauses. "Your mother and father—"

"Had a toxic relationship. I know."

"At its simplest," Luella says, "it was jealousy. She loved

me more than she loved him. He wanted her to be in love with him, and only him, not someone else, too."

Yula shuts her eyes. The thought of Eugene overwhelms her, and she can't bear to hear any more about anyone else's pain, anyone else's history.

"Please," she says. "Please take her." She hands me to Luella, who cradles me while my mother struggles to get up. She sits on the toilet and lets the blood drain out of her. She hears Luella stripping the bed.

She could take me to the hospital. She could go to jail. Every choice seems feeble somehow. Every choice feels wrong. She searches her mind for the name of Harrison's dealer. She likes the idea of jumping off the balcony of View Towers. It seems so easy, so quick. If she goes to the ocean she'll have to wade in, then let herself be carried away by the tide. There is a chance she'll fight it; there is a chance she'll fight to stay alive. But if she jumps? She likes the finality of this choice. This is what she will do.

"Luella?" she calls from the doorway to the bathroom.

Luella appears in the dim light of the hallway, holding me in her arms.

"I need," my mother begins, her words slow and careful because she is lying, "I need to be alone with my baby for a while. I'd just like to rest for a bit and think things over. I need to do this before we go to the hospital."

Luella looks at my little face. I am breathing; I seem to be okay. And Yula is right—I will likely be taken away, and she will be arrested. Luella nods. She will give my mother as long as she wants before they decide what to do.

In the dark of the bedroom, my mother waits. It is three in the morning. She nurses me, and I fall asleep. My mother waits another hour, then pulls herself from the bed, leaving me momentarily, and peeks into the living room. Luella has fallen asleep on the couch, the television on mute, the screen displaying hundreds of small birds gathered at the shoreline in search of food. She goes back into the bedroom and swaddles me in her grey sweatshirt as tightly as she can. She pulls her coveralls over her body and finds a pad of paper and a pencil on the bedside table.

This is the most important thing I've ever asked of anyone in my life. I need you to forget that I was here and that this baby was born. I'm going to leave her at the hospital and then be on my way. I do not ever want her to know about me or Harrison. Please do not tell anyone. Please. I will take her to the hospital, and then I'm going to disappear. Please—whatever you do—don't tell anyone about this. I want her to grow up free from the burden of all this. I want her to have a wonderful life. Such a wonderful life. This will not happen if she knows anything about me or how her brother died. I never want her to know these things. Please do this for me. It is the right thing to do, I think.

Together we creep past Luella's sleeping form. My mother unhooks the chain and opens the front door inch by inch, holding her breath, until the door is shut behind her and she is standing in the cold night air. She rests me on the bench seat of Joel and Edwin's truck and tries to start the vehicle but the ignition won't catch. She curses them and their fleet of old shitty cars, wrenches the door open and slides out of the truck. She lifts me out and holds me tight to her body. She looks toward Park Boulevard and the big white apartment building that looks like a wedding cake. It is too far to walk to the hospital. She'll never make it. It would take hours and too many people would see her. She presses her face against mine and listens to my breathing. I am okay. I am okay. I am so small, but I am okay.

She could rest me on the doorstep of one of the apartments but it is so early, and it is so cold, and what if no one walks by? She could ring the doorbell but she'd never get away in time. She walks down Heywood Avenue, toward downtown. It is four-thirty a.m.

High above the trees of Beacon Hill Park, my mother sees the towers of Christ Church Cathedral. She thinks of the old video Harrison showed her once of him singing "Once in Royal David's City" as a choirboy. How he stood stiffly in his maroon cassock and white ruff, hands clasped, and sang the solo part while the rest of the choir stood behind him. How sweet and innocent his face was; how sweet and innocent all the boys' faces were.

She decides she will take me to the cathedral. She will give me the most majestic start to my life. She will set me beneath the blue front doors, beneath the tympanum. She heads up Quadra Street, and a few cars pass but no one stops and no one slows down. I am so small that it looks as if she's carrying a loaf of bread or a little stuffed animal. The cathedral rises up ahead of her, and she shifts her weight. She is so tired that she is limping. She wills the heat of her body to transfer into mine. If she can just get me to the cathedral. If I can just survive.

She crosses Burdett, carries me up the wheelchair ramp that leads to the cathedral's entrance. The cathedral looms cold and grey in front of her. As she kneels to set me down, the hideous thought enters her mind that I will not be discovered here either. It is too early. She sees my face grow grey in her mind, my little body cease to move. She thought it would feel sacred, but instead the long shadows from the spires drag over my face and she fears that I will be taken away by demons. She looks down at me. I lie motionless on the concrete. It is too much, and she snatches me up into her arms.

The possibility exists, too, that she could end it for us both. She sits on the steps and rocks me in her arms. We could die together. Not everyone was meant to survive. Not everyone was meant for this earth. But there is such a sweetness coming from me that she cannot bear this thought either.

She traces my features with her finger, explores the divot between my lips and nose. It is Eugene's face; it is mine. My cheeks are full and heavy. My lips gummy and malleable. My brow is furrowed, as though I sense something is wrong. Still, I have yet to open my eyes.

Across the street, the fluorescent lights of the YMCA flicker on. The Y opens early, my mother recalls. The sky is getting lighter, an eerie purple blue. She will wait a few minutes, then she will leave me in front of the glass doors. I will be found immediately, she thinks. I will survive this. She wishes she could leave me with something beautiful—a conch shell, a gemstone, something to be cherished. She fingers the Swiss Army knife in her pocket. It's all she has, and she tucks it between my feet: a parting gift.

And so my mother, a girl in navy coveralls, walks down the steps of Christ Church Cathedral with a bundle wrapped in grey, her body bent in the cold wet wind of the summer morning. She opens her mouth as if to scream, but there is no sound here, just the calls of birds. The wind gusts and her coveralls blow against her body, framing her belly as she walks toward the YMCA, exposing the tops of her brown workman's boots. Her coveralls are stained with motor oil, her shoes far too big. She is a small, fine-boned woman, with deep brown hair tied back in a bun and a pale, startled face with wild, moon-grey eyes. There is a coarse, masculine look to her, a meanness. Even in the chill, her brow is beaded with sweat. She stops at the entrance to the parking lot, then takes a step forward and looks around her. The street is full of pink and gold light from the sun. The wet of last night's rain is still present on the street, on the sidewalk, on the buildings' reflective glass. Everything shines pink and gold and blue. If anyone sees her, she will lose her nerve. She looks up again, and the morning sky is as blue as a peacock feather.

22

Dear Shannon,

I guess first of all thank you for writing. Yes, I am your father. Sorry it took me so long to get back to you. Never imagined I would hear from you and it took me a bit to figure out what to say.

Well, hi there. I live twenty minutes north of Niagara Falls with my wife Nancy and our two sons Kip and Arthur. I work as a mechanic and Nancy stays at home with the boys but she's got a little eBay business on the side. The boys are six and two. I am forty-two years old. I was born in Powell River, left when I was fifteen and never went back. I have an older brother, Dominic, who I haven't seen or spoken to in years, though last I heard he's moved back home. Our parents died a couple of years ago. Long-time smokers, both of them. My father worked at the mill. We weren't close. Speaking of parents, my wife's mother is living with us right now. She had a stroke last year and has dementia. Twice this morning she asked if I was here to deliver a pizza!

Yeah, I've got blond hair.

I don't think there's anything unusual about my sense of smell. Nothing that I've ever noticed anyway. Does your blindness bother you? You write about it as if it doesn't.

I keep writing things and then erasing them. It sounds like you're a lot like me—you've got the wandering spirit. You're restless. I always had a hard time staying in one place for too long. Your mother is the opposite way.

Your mother was real sick right after you were born—I mean, sick as in beyond upset, as in changed. She didn't abandon you because she didn't love you. I just want you to know that. I need to tell you a few things. I hope I can explain this well.

Our son died the day before you were born. Eugene was almost three years old. It was my fault. I was having a lot of problems—okay, look, I'm just going to be honest with you and not candy coat anything. With the help of my brother, I'd gotten myself addicted to drugs pretty bad and your mother and I were fighting about it non-stop. The night it happened I was supposed to go in for work but all I wanted was to drive into town and get a fix.

There's a kind of superiority you feel when you're high sometimes, like nothing can go wrong. That's why I used to get high. I used to love that feeling. I longed for it. Your mom and I left Eugene alone for a bit so we could take a drive and sort some things out. We drove to the water and talked and I hate to admit this, even to myself, but I was just waiting for these guys to show up who I knew would have some stuff. The other thing I want to tell you is that your mom was only eighteen. She was just a kid. We were both kids. Kids on the beach. And all I really cared about was getting high. It's in your blood—your poison blood, your mother used to say to me—so keep that in mind. Drugs grab hold of you like you wouldn't believe.

The guys showed up and I got your mom a little stoned so I could enjoy myself without her yelling at me. Well, I got too high. I didn't mean to get that high. I don't even know how many hours went by, but I had to call my brother to come and drive us home.

When we got back, Eugene was sick, really sick. He'd managed to get the tops off a couple of bottles of cough syrup—knowing us, they probably weren't even on properly—and he drank the whole thing. We just thought he was sick from it, you know? He threw up and your mom took him into the bedroom and they went to sleep.

The whole time I was itching for another fix and at some point I realized that the cigar box where I kept my stuff was on the floor of the living room and that Eugene had gone through that, too. And god knows how much of it he ate. This is hard for me to say. Once, when he walked in on me, I told him I was eating powdered sugar—do you see? Do you see how horribly I fucked up here? Our boy just thought he was eating sugar. I keep saying our boy but he was your mother's son—I mean, I wasn't his real father— somehow this makes me feel like more of a monster. He died in his sleep, in your mother's arms. As I said, this was the day before you were born. I don't know if you've ever seen someone lose the one thing that's really keeping them connected to this earth, but all the life just shot out of her when she realized Eugene was dead.

I did sixty days in Kent and three years in William Head for killing our son.

I was charged with Failure to Provide the Necessities of Life to a Child, and Criminal Negligence Causing Death. I pled guilty to the first charge, and the Crown did not prosecute me on the second. I was lucky, Shannon, though I'm not sure why.

I want you to know how much of an accident this was. We loved Eugene. I loved him like he was my own son. We were in such a fog that night. I can't tell you how many times I've gone back into my mind and tried to search for the part of myself that let us leave him alone that night. Whatever part of myself let me make that choice is a part of myself I want to destroy. I go hunting for it late at night. I want to find it and make sure it never takes over me again.

Your mother didn't do any time. I told the police that she had nothing to do with our leaving Eugene alone. I mean, it was my fault but I didn't want anyone to think for a second that she had anything to do with it.

Your mother's name is Yula. I can't tell you enough good things about her. She's a small person with a heart so big she doesn't know what to do with it. I've never met someone who feels so much. No one will ever love you like Yula loves you—her own father said that to me one time.

Gee, what else. She was born without her left pinky finger. On her right ankle she has a little tattoo of a peace sign. She likes chocolate doughnuts. She had it pretty rough growing up. Her mom died in a motorcycle accident when she was sixteen and her dad was a peculiar and moody man. He was always threatening to kill himself.

We lived in a little pine cabin across from her parents' house on Mount Finlayson. I am not in touch with her anymore, but I'm going to tell you where we used to live and there's some chance that if you go out there, that's where she'll be. Her kind doesn't leave. It's 2317 Finlayson Arm Road. It's right past the entrance to Goldstream Provincial Park, up the Malahat. She has had nothing but a horrible dark time since Eugene's death, and I know that meeting you would be like the sun coming up.

I don't want you to think that I left your mother because I didn't love her anymore. It's just that—well, first of all, I was in prison for almost three years and that's such a long time to be away from someone. But also she didn't want to see me anyway after Eugene died. She tried to kill herself right after she left you. While she was still in the hospital she wrote me a letter saying she needed to never hear from me again. I gave her that. I figured it was the least I could do.

I'm not sure that I am a bad person at my core. But I have done such bad things. I don't know where one starts and the other stops.

I was not there when she left you. But I know for certain she did it because she wanted to give you a better life. She didn't want you to know that you were born to people who had fucked up their lives so bad. She thought you would be better off without her.

Your mother is not the bad person. I am. None of this would have happened if it weren't for me.

I don't know what it is like for you to read this letter. Or how any of this sounds.

Your mother chose to give you a fresh start in this world. I hope that's what you got. She thought the least she could do for you was to give you some relief from us, your parents.

Well, what is there to say?

When you're up, you're really up, you know? When low, really low. You sound like you're in one of the low places. Despite my initial surprise, I am glad you got in touch, though it is breaking my heart to have to tell you these things. I thought about lying or not writing back, but I don't want to do the wrong thing anymore.

I guess the only other thing to tell you is that your mother wanted to name you Jo, after her mom.

Send a picture of yourself, okay? Here's one of me. I used to look a lot younger, I promise you that.

I want to keep writing to you but I fear I've run out of things to say. My wife's mother is driving me crazy. Every time she walks into the kitchen, she washes her hands three times and then takes a sip of water and spits it into the sink like it's mouthwash. It's been kind of a weird day. For instance I woke up and looked out our kitchen window and Kip's soccer ball, which had been in the very back of the yard (in the long grass, impossible for it to roll), was now around the other side of the shed, on the patio, by the patio furniture. Impossible for it to have gotten there on its own. How did it get there? This has been bothering me for hours. My wife is upstairs watching a movie with the sound on loud and the only place to escape the noise is in the basement, where I've set up a little office space for myself. I like to read down here. Never was much of a reader but I've gotten into it a bit lately, nonfiction mostly, biographies and history books and the like.

I think about you every day, do you know that? How would you know that. Well, you know that now.

I'm going to give you a P.O. box number should you wish to write me again. My wife doesn't know about you—and, for reasons that are too complicated to get into, I don't wish to spring this on her right now. Maybe at some point in the future I will come out to B.C. and I can meet you. I miss the ocean. Do you love it as much as I do?

Because you ended your letter with a joke, I feel compelled to respond in kind, but I don't know any jokes, except for one about a snail.

So a snail buys a new VW Beetle but he decides that it's missing something. So he takes it to an auto body shop and he says to the guy, "Hey, guy, I got a question. Could you paint a bunch of S's all over my car?"

And the guy says, "Well, sure, Snail, I guess we can do that. Come back tomorrow and it'll be ready for you." So the snail goes home and makes himself a bowl of chicken noodle soup and falls asleep watching a rerun of *Cheers*. And the next day he goes to the auto body shop and there's his VW Beetle, all ready for him in the lot, and he goes up to the counter to pay, and the guy behind the counter says,

"Hey, Snail, glad to see you again. But I got a question—why do you want a bunch of S's all over your car?"

And the snail leans in to the guy and he says, "Well, guy, so that when all the pretty girls see me driving by, they'll say, 'Hey, look at that ESCARGOT!'"

With love,
Harrison

23

There's no wind and it's hot this morning, even though it's barely nine o'clock. I've got on Lydia-Rose's old Sonic Youth shirt and my penguin pyjama bottoms, and Miranda walks beside me in her bathrobe, a mug of coffee steaming in her hand. Lydia-Rose stands on the sidewalk, wipes the sleep out of her eyes, and watches Winkie noodle around, looking for somewhere to pee. It's the end of August. All summer we've started our days like this—first coffee, then oatmeal, and after Winkie starts barking (though we never hear anything), we walk outside to check the mail. You'd think we'd have given up by now, quietly abandoned the ritual and never spoken of it again, but this is what has brought us together as a family once more: this slow walk from our front door to the row of mailboxes on the sidewalk, the little key in my hand, our mailbox, day after day, stuffed with junk mail, bills, pleas for charity donations, credit card applications, the local newspaper, Lydia-Rose's glossy new driver's licence, the latest issue of *Rolling Stone,* Miranda's paycheques, but never, until today, a letter from my father.

Miranda opens the mailbox and we stare at the single envelope inside, our address written in small shaky letters, my name underlined above it. She puts her hand on my shoulder but does not speak.

"What's going on?" says Lydia-Rose. Winkie trundles over to where we're standing, her tongue hanging out the side of her mouth from the heat.

"Should we go in?" Miranda asks, but I shake my head. I hold the envelope and weigh it in my hands. I'm trying to gauge the odds of it saying, *Dear Shannon, Thanks for the letter but I'm not your father. Good luck to you.*

"Open it, honey," Miranda says. "You can handle whatever is inside."

We stand in a herd on the sidewalk in the hot sun. I fold and unfold the letter, stare at his shaky handwriting, which is even messier and more unruly than my own. It looks like someone was shaking him while he wrote it; it looks like there was an earthquake going on. It looks like he wrote it on his knee while being jostled side to side on a city bus.

I read the letter to myself at first, my back to them, my shoulders hunched. I study the little black and white photograph, attached to the letter with a paperclip. My father.

In the photo, a man sits in a white plastic patio chair on someone's back deck. He's wearing a baseball cap and has a big bushy beard. His white-blond hair pokes out from under the cap, and the curls frame his face. He looks too thin. He is wearing jeans and a plaid flannel shirt, his feet bare. He holds a can of diet 7-Up. There's an ashtray by his foot, a cigarette balanced at the edge of it, the smoke drifting toward his pant leg. The sky behind him is overcast. There are no trees, just a large barren field. He isn't looking at whoever is taking the photograph. He's looking up. Whatever he's looking at holds his full attention. Maybe a bird. He has big, strong-looking hands. He looks tired.

I stare at the photograph for a long time, then turn and read the letter out loud to Miranda and Lydia-Rose. Miranda's face pales when I get to the part about Eugene. As I read, she looks up at the sky, as though she is searching for him.

"Vaughn. Vaughn. You awake?"

I am tapping on his bedroom window, on my tiptoes, praying none of his weird neighbours emerge and ask me what the hell I'm doing. But it's urgent, and he isn't answering his front door. So: I'm in the weeds, tapping. I'm still in the penguin pyjama bottoms, and I'm wearing Vaughn's big white bike helmet. I'm so full of emotion that I could catch on fire.

I hear Vaughn's big laugh before I see him, and then he's standing in the small space between his house and the neighbour's, in gym shorts and flip-flops, his denim shirt buttoned up wrong so that the left side hangs down farther than the right. Behind him, Chloe appears in a pair of sunglasses, car keys jangling in her hand. She waves, her hair twisted into a bun on top of her head. She's wearing a nylon tracksuit, black with a pink stripe, and bright red running shoes.

I take in the whole scene: his shirt, the time of day, her.

"Oh, jeez, I'm sorry," I say to Vaughn and blush.

"Hey, it's no problem." He waves goodbye to her, and we watch her get into her car and drive away. She drives a brand-new silver Mini, and I wonder where she gets her money.

"Oops," I say to Vaughn, but he shakes his head, tells me not to worry.

He looks at me, then at the envelope in my hands. "Should we get some breakfast?"

"Yeah."

Vaughn gets his bike, and we ride together to the greasy spoon across from the hospital. I ride on the sidewalk while he rides alongside me on the road. If anyone yells at me, which they frequently do, Vaughn tells them to mind their own beans. He tells me when to change gears, and when he sees how tightly I grip the handlebars, he says I need to loosen up or I'll damage my wrists. He tells me to roll my pyjama bottoms up a bit or tuck them into my socks. He cycles slowly beside me, one hand on his knee. He can tell I don't want to ride on the street or go very fast. I tell him it's because of my eye, but the truth of the matter is that I'm scared. He says I'll get better at it—one day, he says, I won't notice the speed at all. The cars slow behind him on Shelbourne Street; there isn't enough room to go around. He rides ahead of me on the sidewalk for a while, glancing back every now and again to make sure I'm okay. He stretches his arms out like a bird, as if to show me how easy and effortless all of this could be.

When we get to the café, we lock up our bikes and spend a few minutes wandering up and down the block, considering the old art deco building. There used to be a magazine stand attached to the café, but it's been boarded up and is covered in graffiti. A blue marquee above our heads, the bulbs burned out years ago, says *Magazines*.

"They'll bulldoze this place soon," Vaughn says. "After a while no one will remember it."

Inside, we sit at the counter on squeaky metal stools. The walls are decorated with old photographs of famous people, mostly baseball players, in crooked gilt-edged frames and there's a handwritten sign in the window advertising homemade doughnuts. From our seats we can see through to the kitchen, where a tall, skinny guy wearing a bandana is frying eggs on the grill.

The old guy who runs this place fills our coffee cups with his big shaky hand, hollering at his daughter to put on a fresh pot. Vaughn has a rapport with both of them—he seems to have a rapport with everybody in this town. The old guy's daughter tells Vaughn he's goofed up the buttons on his shirt. She is a husky woman with olive skin and frizzy black hair. She has a little tattoo of a heart on the back of her hand.

I run my fingers over the laminated menu and try to figure out what to have, what will be the biggest plate of food for the least amount of money. Vaughn always pays when we're together, but I don't want him to think

I don't notice or appreciate it. I rip open a pink packet of sugar and pour it into my hand, and Vaughn eats a little personalized container of peanut butter with his teaspoon. We are starving.

"This your daughter, Vaughn?" the waitress says to him and gestures at me with an empty coffee carafe.

"I wish," he says, and then we're telling her the story while she stands there shaking her big frizzy head. She's the kind of woman who would stand there forever if we kept on talking. She beams at us, in no rush for the story to be over. The sunlight pours through the windows and dazzles all the silver things: the salt and pepper shakers, the cutlery, the metal sides of the napkin holder, the rim of the counter, the edge of the stools, the woman's little wedding ring.

"You hearing this, Dad?" she says to her father, and he nods while he refills our cups again. His white hair is pulled back into a little ponytail, his nose spiderwebbed with hundreds of broken blood vessels, his cheeks bright pink. The two of them don't look related at all. The old guy asks us what we'd like and we both say pancakes.

When he's gone, I take out Harrison's letter and hand it to Vaughn. He reads it, one hand cupped over the page. The paper is blindingly white.

After he's done, he hands it back to me. "Escargot," he says.

"I know." We laugh a bit.

"Well?" he says.

"I'd given up," I say. "So much time passed. I figured I'd never hear from him." But the thing I find most shocking, I tell Vaughn, is how much has happened to my father in sixteen years. He has gone to jail; he has gotten over my mother; he has married and had children. He has suffered and come out on the other end of it. He lives thousands of miles away.

"It takes a while to understand this," Vaughn says to me, "but there's enough room in a life for failure and loss." He picks up his coffee and takes a big sip, swivels in his stool. "You can really fuck up in your life. You can fuck up and then have things be okay.

"You learn something else, too, after a while," Vaughn says. "Everyone's happy when someone fails."

"I wonder if he'll come out here," I say.

Vaughn scans the letter again. "He will."

"I hope he tells his wife about me."

"He'll do that, too."

"How do you know?"

"Just do." Vaughn holds the photo of my father up to my face. "It's hard to say," he says. "Hard to tell, really, what he looks like."

I study my father's face again. His eyes are small and dark. His nose is crooked. His hair falls around his face like white silk. It's his eyes that make him attractive. They are soft, almost feminine. They are terribly sad.

I try to get a sense of what kind of person my father is from the photograph. He doesn't look like a bad person. He doesn't look like he has any money. He looks a little rough around the edges, I guess, but not as bad as I'd imagined. The thinness is troubling. I wonder if he's sick. Still on drugs? That seems impossible, after what he said in his letter. I don't know what I wanted him to look like, but now that I can see him, I know I didn't want him to look like this. I wonder what his children look like, if they look like me. I wonder about his wife. I wonder about Eugene.

"Escargot," Vaughn says again.

"Will you come to Finlayson Arm Road with me?" I ask.

"Yep."

"Soon?"

Vaughn nods. We pause for a minute while the old guy sets two stacks of pancakes in front of us. Vaughn unwraps a little foil-covered packet of butter and drowns his cakes in hot syrup. He cuts through the stack with the side of his fork, shovels a huge bite into his mouth. "How we getting there?" he asks between chews.

"Know anyone with a car?"

"Sure, sure."

I stare at my pancakes. For the first time in my life, I don't feel like devouring them all on the spot. "Do you think you'll recognize her?"

"Your mother?" Vaughn sets down his fork and looks at me. "Maybe. Maybe not."

"What if she's not there?"

"Then she's not there."

"Then what?"

"Someone will be there. We'll talk to them. We'll make a new plan."

"But what if no one is there."

He takes another bite. "You never take the road back empty-handed, Shannon. You return to the place you left and see it for the first time."

I fiddle with my pancakes, spread butter and syrup over and underneath them, but I still don't take a bite. They look weird suddenly. Eating seems weird. The old guy fills Vaughn's coffee cup again, and his daughter starts talking to a couple who have just come in. Her laugh is suddenly loud and grating. The light in here is too bright.

"I saw Julian," I tell him.

His body stiffens, and he turns to me. "What? When?"

"It was my choice. I went to see him."

"Shannon. What on earth for?"

I furrow my eyebrows at Vaughn. I'm in no mood to be interrogated. "Don't get all worked up."

"Okay."

I keep glaring at him.

"Okay," he says, throwing up his hands. "I'm sorry."

"I wanted to see what happened to him, to see what he'd be like."

"And?"

"He's a disgusting little man."

"Are you glad you went?"

"No. Not really. I don't know."

"Well, you survived it—all of it. The past, I mean. That's what matters."

I pause a minute, staring at my uneaten pancakes. "Do you get along with your family?"

"I saw my brother yesterday," he says. "I hadn't seen him in weeks."

"Okay."

"He's shrinking, for one thing. Used to tower over me. Now we stand eye to eye."

"Where does he live?"

"Not far." He pushes his plate away, tosses his napkin over it.

"You like each other?"

"He thinks I'm okay," he says. "I like him more than he likes me."

"What's with you and Chloe?"

"I asked her out a couple of months ago," he says, "like you told me to."

"Told you it'd work out."

"Well. We'll see."

"But you like her?"

"Jeez," he says. "What's with all the questions?"

I look at him. "I'm a snoop."

The old guy comes over and clears our plates, and Vaughn says he'll take my pancakes and a powdered doughnut to go. He puts a twenty-dollar bill on the counter, tells the guy to keep the change. We leave the café together, his right hand on top of my head, his left holding a Styrofoam container with my pancakes and the doughnut. The hot morning sun is obscured by a cloud and the air cools. The hair on my arms stands up in protest.

"You going to send Harrison a picture of yourself?" Vaughn asks. He unlocks our bicycles, fastens his helmet and hands me mine.

"Maybe." I study my reflection in the picture window of the café. "Definitely wearing this bike helmet."

"Suits you."

"I know."

Vaughn swings his leg over his bike and pushes off, and

I watch him cycle up the street. He has said nothing about giving him back his bike or extra helmet, and I wonder, suddenly, how much of a burden I have become over this past year—how much of an obligation. I hope he needs my company as much as I need his.

At some point he senses I'm not following him. He swivels the bike around and coasts back down to where I'm standing.

"What if she's not there?" I say to him.

"Then she's not there."

"What if I never find her?"

"Then you never will."

"What if she isn't happy to see me?"

"Then we'll leave right away."

"What if she doesn't like me?"

"Not possible."

"When's the soonest we can go?"

"We'll go this weekend," he says.

24

It is five in the morning and my mother is walking as fast as her tired body will let her, down Quadra Street, away from me, away from my little face. Her boots pound the pavement, and her whole body shudders with each reverberation. She feels as though the ground will shoot right through her. The sky is clear overhead, and the city is waking up. She crosses Fort Street, makes a right at View, and heads toward the entrance to the Towers. The front doors are locked, but she bangs on them anyway. She wills someone to come down. A man is passed out on the long ramp that leads to the entrance and she tries to kick him awake. When he doesn't stir, she searches his pockets for keys. But there is just a bottle cap and a couple of pennies.

When the police find her, she is slumped against the side of the building. She is in shock from giving birth and being cold. Her blood pressure is dangerously low. The paramedics think she is just another drunk. She is hauled into the ambulance roughly and taken to Jubilee Hospital. She could be anyone. She could come from anywhere. There is no ID in her pockets, and she stays in the intensive care ward, nameless, until she wakes.

Harrison has been arrested. He tells the police everything there is to tell, save for one important detail: he says my mother had nothing to do with Eugene's death. He tells them that she was visiting a friend when it happened, and that she'd left Eugene in his care. It was all his fault. He was the one who left the boy alone. The cocaine was his. He says the words quickly and quietly, then writes them down.

He says nothing about his brother; he has pleaded with Quinn. "I will say that Yula wasn't there, if you let me leave my brother out of it, too." In the woods that night, the men stared at each other. They shook hands; they made a deal.

My mother will not speak. She stares blankly. When she regains consciousness she tries to slice up her wrists, but she is already in the hospital and they discover her immediately, and she is bandaged and restrained.

My father is sentenced to three years. For a while, he calls Yula every day. He tells himself that some part of her must still be in love with him, even though when she hears it is him, she hangs up the phone.

Halfway through his sentence, he makes a phone call to the Ministry. He wants to know the fate of the abandoned baby: where I live, who my new parents are. The social worker says she cannot tell him that. When he says he is my father, she says she'll have to refer him to the police. The years go by, and I continue to haunt him. Before he gets out of prison, he writes a letter to the Ministry, hoping someone has met me, hoping someone will write back and tell him something. He hears nothing.

Eugene is buried in a small plot beside Jo. There is no funeral, and Quinn is the only one who attends the burial. Quinn brings a potted plant for his grandson and his wife, and reads to them both from *The Wonderful O* by James Thurber, his favourite book when he was a child.

> "It's all the vowels except the O," Black said.
> "I've had a hatred of that letter ever since the
> night my mother became wedged in a porthole.
> We couldn't pull her in and so we had to push
> her out." He shuddered and his eyes turned hard.
> "What is the name of this island?" he asked,
> shaking off the thought of O.
>
> "Ooroo," said Littlejack, and once more the
> other shuddered.
>
> "I hate the name," he said at last. "It sounds
> like the eyes of a couple of ghosts leaning against
> an R."

Quinn returns to the big house. He reshelves the book. Luella calls and leaves messages, but he doesn't call back. He feels the grief in his heart as sharp and black as ever.

25

Vaughn rents a car—a bright blue Chevy Cavalier—
from a cheap lot downtown and begins the drive past the
totem poles, the YMCA, the Crystal Gardens, the homeless
kids in front of McDonald's, past Mickey blowing into his
horn, the Eaton Centre, the red brick of City Hall. He turns
up Caledonia, past the Szechuan restaurant and the pink
police station, and winds his way down the skinny one-
way streets that lead to our townhouse, where Miranda,
Lydia-Rose, Winkie, and I wait for him in the warm bright
light of this early afternoon, this day, August 28th, the day
I turn seventeen years old.

We have been up since six o'clock, rooting through bags
of consignment clothes, picking out our outfits. Miranda
wears a denim shirt, the sleeves rolled to her elbows, a pair
of wide-legged linen pants, and white canvas espadrilles.
She let Lydia-Rose dust her face with bronzing powder and
line her eyes with kohl. She has never looked so elegant.

Lydia-Rose towers over us in a pair of heeled gladiator sandals, a black pencil skirt, a black-and-white-striped short-sleeved top, a red bandana framing her face.

They are dressed up and made up and I love them for it.

But I am who I am, how I always am and will always be. Hair shooting out from all sides of my head, big and white-blonde from the sun, still as fine and dense as a ball of cotton. It's hot, but I've got on my baggiest jeans, held up with suspenders, a white tank top, and a man's black blazer. I found a pair of checkered Vans in one of the consignment bags, one size too big, and wadded a bunch of Kleenex in the toe so they'd fit. Winkie stands beside me, a red bandana around her neck to match Lydia-Rose.

We have talked about the possibilities. We have talked about how there could be no one home; no one living out there anymore; no house. We have talked about how my visit could be unwelcome. We have talked about how poorly this could all turn out. Miranda and I have made a chart, listing as many possibilities as we could think of, so that I will be as prepared as I can possibly be. We have discussed how it might be better to write a letter first, to wait for a reply. And finally, at my insistence, Miranda has conceded that I can't wait any longer than I already have. And that it is my style, after all, to show up unannounced.

Vaughn steps out of the blue car and walks toward us. He has slicked back his red hair with gel. He wears a white button-down shirt tucked into black jeans and cowboy boots. He shakes Miranda's and Lydia-Rose's hands, tells them how great it is to finally meet them, then crouches and gives Winkie a kiss on her little head.

"Packed a cooler full of sandwiches, potato chips," he says to us, "in case, well, I figured at the very least we can spend the afternoon at Goldstream. Miranda, why don't you ride up front with me? We'll put the girls and Wink in the back."

He opens the door for Miranda and she slides inside, then he opens the back door for Lydia-Rose, Winkie, and me. We pile in and the car is as hot and stuffy as a microwave.

"I've never been in a new car before," says Lydia-Rose, and I realize I haven't either. It smells so strongly of vinyl and new carpet that I almost gag. We examine the cup holders, the arm rests, the space to slip a magazine behind the passenger seat. Vaughn tells us to roll down our windows until the air conditioning kicks in. Lydia-Rose sits on the driver's side and Winkie sits between us. She has never been in a car in her whole life. She sniffs the seat furiously, then slides onto the floor and tries to wedge herself under Miranda's seat, her little tail wagging frantically. In my backpack I have a Tupperware full of ice water for her and a marrowbone, which I fish out and give to her so she'll calm down.

Lydia-Rose and I take forever fastening and then adjusting our seatbelts, which are hot to the touch and seem to pin us too tightly to our seats. Finally, after what feels like an eternity, we are ready to go.

Vaughn takes us to Douglas Street, and we drive past one Traveller's Inn and then another, and we talk about stopping at Dairy Queen for cones but I am too nervous. Red Hot Video, White Spot, Thompson's Foam Shop, the 7-Eleven, all the car dealerships, Mayfair Mall, and Lydia-

Rose sticks her head out the window to get away, she says, from Winkie's hot stale breath. The highway widens and we go by the big-box stores that are everywhere now—this part of town used to be just barren fields, parking lots—and Vaughn hits the gas and we shoot up toward the Malahat, the wind whipping through the car until our ears can't take the pressure anymore and we have to put up the windows. Winkie is heavy on my lap, staring dumbfounded at all the trees as the city falls away. The winding road leads us north, toward the forest. For a long time, no one says a word.

Jo. Jo-Jo. Jojoba oil. Jo. I don't look much like a Jo. When I think of the name Jo, I see a woman much taller and more beautiful than I, dark hair cut in a dramatic bob above her shoulders. She is an angular woman. She is my grandmother. I am not sure I have the body or the spirit with which to fill out her name.

Finally, the sky disappears, and Vaughn turns down the air conditioning as the car plunges into the shade of the forest. When we reach Goldstream Park, Vaughn slows and makes a hard right at the park's entrance. I careen into Lydia-Rose and Miranda makes a little sound, and Vaughn says, "Oopsy daisy. Sorry about that." The parking lot is full of cars, families piling out with children. We drive over the old wooden bridge that leads up the mountain, the trees now stretching hundreds of feet into the sky, denser and denser, and start the ascent up Finlayson Arm Road, flanked on each side by the majestic and spindly Douglas firs. Past these, here and there, are Western red cedars, their bases wider than automobiles, their trunks like red ropey cords of muscle, like giant pieces of red licorice smashed together and then petrified. They shoot up into the sky for what looks like miles.

"Look up," Vaughn says to us, "look at how the trees touch at the top of this road and form an arch—like a barrel vault—like a nave."

"Like an Emily Carr painting," says Lydia-Rose.

"She lived out here, you know," says Vaughn.

"I know."

"You do?"

"I used to study art," she says to him. "She lived in a caravan."

"With a monkey." Vaughn smiles at her in the rearview, and I can tell they are growing on each other.

"I'd like to live in a caravan," I say and shift Winkie onto the seat beside me. I hold out my hand, and she licks the sweat off my palm. "Or a trailer."

"You're an alien," Lydia-Rose says and lets Winkie lick her hand, too.

"Winkie is an alien."

"Alien dog."

Here we come: me, Miranda, Lydia-Rose, Winkie, and Vaughn, up a deserted road the width of a double bed. The hot hot sun, no one. Pasture. Fence. Little wooden house. The sound of the river in the distance. Lydia-Rose sees an eagle, and we go around in a circle, each naming our favourite bird. I like owls, I say. I like their faces. We agree we will all dress up as birds next Halloween.

We start reading the numbers on the mailboxes, 2210, 2253. A scruffy-looking German shepherd races to the edge of one of the properties and barks wildly as we drive by. A man barrels past in a pickup and waves. We drive by a girl on horseback, cantering in a riding ring. When we get to the mailbox marked 2317, Vaughn slows the car and pulls into a narrow gravel driveway. It winds upward for about a hundred feet, deeper and deeper into the woods, until we finally come to a field of overgrown wild grass. The driveway ends, and Vaughn parks behind the oldest, most rust-covered car I've ever seen.

"A Meteor," says Vaughn. "Classic." Whatever it is, it looks like junk. There are holes in the chassis, and the passenger door has come unhinged and is lying in a rusty heap on the ground. We get out of the rental car and stretch our legs. I hear dogs barking in the distance and the hum of the traffic from the Malahat, but other than that, it is a completely silent world.

Vaughn leads us, single-file, through the waist-high grass. The field is dotted with bluebells and lots of wild broom— the yellow startling in the light. I carry Winkie in my arms for fear of losing her. Lydia-Rose steps gingerly forward in her heeled sandals and glances back at me with a worried look. Miranda is behind me, her hand on my shoulder.

At the end of the field, obscured by a wall of evergreen trees but visible to us now, is a flat-roofed cedar-sided house with floor-to-ceiling windows separated by giant timber beams. The house is fancier than the others we passed on the way up here, but the yard is so filthy and overgrown that I wonder if anyone lives here at all.

Past the house is a moss-covered wood cabin, which has sunk on one side and sits in the earth at a dramatic angle. Wild grass grows between and around the homes, and there is a tamped-down path between them. Beyond the homes is the forest.

As we get closer to the big house, I see that some twinkling icicle lights have been strung around the windows from some Christmas past. Someone has left them on, but only half of them work. Another bald eagle circles overhead, and we watch him for a few minutes before he disappears into the trees.

"Ready?" Vaughn asks when we reach the front steps. I nod and he knocks twice.

Miranda and Lydia-Rose stand behind us, holding hands. I bury my nose in Winkie's fur and kiss the top of her head. She smells like popcorn.

Through the little window of the front door, I watch a small man walk toward us in a blue, coffee-stained bathrobe with a torn sleeve. He is wearing mirrored sunglasses and walks with a cane. He holds his left arm to his chest as if it hurts him.

He opens the door. His white hair sticks up in little tufts around his head and his skin is deeply tanned. He has a sunken face and a patchy white beard that hugs the lower part of his chin. He is barrel-chested and husky and reminds me of a small bear.

I peer into the house. The hardwood floor gleams behind him, catching the light.

The small bear and I consider each other. We are the same height. I look at myself in the reflection of his sunglasses. My hair is full of sunlight and glows around my head. I look like a dandelion.

"Car break down?" he says. His voice is ancient and raspy.

I put Winkie down and hold out my hand. "I'm Jo," I say. "I'm Yula's daughter."

The bear parts his lips but doesn't speak. We stare at each other for a minute. Winkie sits on my foot, and I hear Vaughn clear his throat. I can feel Miranda behind me. I can feel her desire to put her hand on my shoulder. I can feel her so strongly behind me that it hurts.

The bear leans his cane against the doorframe and takes my hand in his. His hand is warm and dry. "Did—did your car break down, honey?" He speaks with the slow, careful elocution of someone deeply humbled by his life.

I look at Vaughn. "No." I shake my head at the bear and drop his hand.

"We're sorry to bother you," Vaughn says, "but does a woman named Yula live here?" He taps his cowboy boot against the porch. For the first time, he looks unsure to me.

The bear takes off his sunglasses. He has piercing grey eyes. They startle me they're so bright and fierce. He doesn't seem so feeble now that I can see his eyes. He looks past me and nods his head at the moss-covered cabin. "Come and see me before you leave, Jo," he says. "I'll leave the door open."

We step off the porch, and the door to the big house closes. Lydia-Rose picks up Winkie, and Miranda puts her arm around me and squeezes.

"Do you want us to wait here or come with you?" Miranda says. She smoothes the lapel of my blazer and runs her hand down my arm until she's holding my hand.

It's hotter out here than it is in the city. The buzz of insects is suddenly loud in my ears, and I feel the sweat start to gather on my forehead and under my arms. I shrug off my blazer. "Hold this?" I say to Miranda.

She takes it, and I motion to Lydia-Rose to hand me Winkie, who is panting from the heat. I'll get her some water when I meet my mom. That'll be the first thing I'll ask.

To the left, Mount Finlayson looms over my head. To the right, the traffic buzzes along the Malahat. It's barely audible through the trees. I walk with my head down to avoid sunstroke.

Miranda, Lydia-Rose, and Vaughn stand together in the grass, watching me. I carry Winkie down the path, toward the cabin. It has a steep pitched roof covered in bright green moss and is unpainted, the wood faded to a dull grey. It is the size of a shed, or a garage. There can't be more than two rooms inside. The front door has a tiny window with a blue curtain, and there are a couple of rocking chairs on the porch, a Mexican blanket slung over one of them, heavy with water from last night's rain. A coal bucket filled with cigarette butts sits beside one of the rocking chairs. A spider plant hangs from a metal hook. It's hot outside but the house looks cold, water-stained, and damp. I take a step onto the porch, shift Winkie to one arm. Whatever's going to happen is going to happen, so I knock.

My mother is shorter than I am by about an inch. Her shoulders are broad—too broad, really, for such a small woman—and with her feet together, she is the shape of a triangle. She is thin, too thin, with no hips. She has a long neck, an angular, muscular face, and eyes as grey and marbled as the moon. The skin on her face is taut and deeply lined. Her deep brown hair is flecked with grey at the temples. She wears it in a tight braid that hangs over her shoulder and tapers to a fine point. Her eyes are as piercing as the bear's, and I understand immediately that she is his daughter.

My mother is small, so very small. She fiddles with the end of her braid, and I see that she has the tiniest, most delicate hands. Her expression is as blunt as a cliff's edge.

She cocks her head and considers me, this other tiny person standing across from her. I can tell she doesn't have any idea who I am.

The sun is burning my shoulders, and my feet are sweaty in my shoes. I reach into my pocket and pull out the Swiss Army knife. It's an old thing now, the blades dull and rusty. It rests in the palm of my hand, and we stare at it, and we don't say anything at all. The sun blazes down and the knife heats up in my hand. She takes it from me and examines it, pulls out the little blades and scissors and the tiny ice pick, then snaps them back in. She hands it back.

"It's you?" My mother stutters out the words, her hand covering her mouth as if to muffle them.

"It's me."

We stand eye to eye, and she searches my face. "Your eye?"

"Blind."

"Did something happen?"

"Born that way." I turn my head to the left and then the

right and my mother does the same. We study each other's faces as though this is the last time we will ever see each other. I commit her face to memory; she does the same. From afar, we likely don't look that similar—her long, straight brown hair; my wild white-blonde curls. Her bony, delicate frame; my wrestler's build. She wears maroon-and-white knitted mukluks pulled to the knee over pale blue jeans, a navy button-up sweater that stops at her waist, the buttons done all the way up to her neck, even in this heat. It looks as though she is holding herself together with her tightly buttoned sweater. Her clothing hugs her body as if it is keeping her safe. Her eyes are deeply creased but she is only eighteen years older than I am, hardly old at all.

Up close—this close—I can see that she and I have the same face shape. The same small forehead, heart-shaped face, deep-set eyes. We are cut from the same pattern; we are set from the same mould. Her hand is still covering her mouth, and I look at the way her fingers taper slightly, the pronounced half moon on her thumbnail, the big knuckles, the blank space where her left pinky finger should be. These are my hands, just thinner, older. Neither one of us takes much care with them—both of us have dirt under our nails, the cuticles overgrown. Our skin is so different. Mine is so pale and puffy, soft against my bones, a layer of icing. Hers is drawn so tight it looks stretched. Her knuckles are deeply grooved and dry.

I wonder what she sees in me. This shock of blonde hair, the colour of butterscotch ripple ice cream just like my father's, standing up every which way, curls so tight they're practically clenched, these bullish shoulders, this chubby frame. The baggy jeans, old suspenders, my white tank top, sports bra showing through. My little round face, which seems to me to morph every day, so that every time I look in the mirror I feel as though I'm looking at someone new, someone else. I wonder when it will settle into itself. Other people look the same every day; I don't know why I always look so different. Today I'm a bit puffy from lack of sleep. I can feel it in my eyelids and in my cheeks. It's a pleasant, swollen feeling, and it also makes me look a lot younger than I am. What are you supposed to look like when you're seventeen? The thought flickers in my mind as my mother considers me, this weird little stranger on her front porch in the heat of the afternoon. Weird little dog in my arms, her nose twitching, taking us both in.

"This is Winkie," I tell my mother.

My mother looks past me at Miranda, Lydia-Rose, and Vaughn, standing in the tall grass in front of the big house. "And is that your family?"

I turn around and look at the three of them. "Yes."

I take a step toward her. My mother. She smells just like me.

She reaches for my hand suddenly, and it startles us both. "I don't know what your name is," she says. "I'm looking at you and I don't know your name."

"It was Shandi at first. Then Samantha. It's Shannon now. I'm thinking of changing it though."

"I'm Yula."

"I know. Could my dog have some water?"

My mother's face softens, and she spins into the dark of the cabin, comes back moments later with a yellow plastic bowl filled with water, a single ice cube floating in its centre.

"Winkie loves ice. Thanks." I lower her to the ground and we watch her lap up the cold water, her head tilted to the side in concentration. Her little white tail twitches as she drinks.

Winkie finishes her water and looks up at us, and we both crouch and pat her head. Her tail wags and she smooshes her body against us, wiggles through my legs and then flops to the ground so we can rub her tummy.

"Hi, Winkie," she says. She pats Winkie's belly, fiddles with her ears. "She's very geometric, isn't she," my mother says and points to Winkie's square face, rectangular body, isosceles-triangle ears. "And bow-legged."

"She's old. She has trouble walking."

"You've had her a long time?"

"Since I was five." Winkie wiggles out from underneath our hands and sticks her paw in her water dish, something she does when it's really hot.

"It's your birthday today," my mother says. Her eyes are watering, and I can see that it is taking everything she has to fight it.

"I'm not mad at you," I say.

She looks past me, toward the mountain behind us, and covers her mouth with her hand again. For a while, there really isn't anything to do but cry.

"Will you come and meet everyone?" I say to her. I pick up Winkie and start walking up the path toward Vaughn, Miranda, and Lydia-Rose. When I look back, Yula is sitting on the porch of the cabin. She pulls off her mukluks and slips on a pair of dark green gumboots. She walks toward us stiffly, and I can see how nervous she is. Her hand trembles as she holds it out to Miranda, who, bless her heart, takes it in both of her hands and doesn't let go.

Quinn leads us through the great hall of his big windowed house and into the bright kitchen, where he hands me an elaborate silver frame with a picture of my mother in profile. She wears a red plaid shirt and a pair of baggy sweatpants, and her hair is dark brown and goes all the way down her back. She's sitting in one of the rocking chairs on the porch of the cabin. She holds a pair of silver scissors and is pulling the strands of hair in front of her face, about to snip off the ends. She's wearing slippers with smiling polar bear faces. Her stomach is round beneath the plaid shirt; she is pregnant.

"A month or so before you were born," he says in his raspy voice. "She cut off all her hair." I hand him back the picture. He has changed out of his bathrobe and wears a pair of paint-splattered khakis and a black T-shirt and has slicked his hair back with water. He smells like expensive cologne and mint. His cane wobbles in his feeble hands.

A suit wrapped in dry cleaner's cellophane is hanging over one of the kitchen chairs, and a half empty glass of Scotch sits on the counter. He picks it up and takes a loud sip.

The kitchen is immaculate, the granite countertops gleaming. There's a dishwasher and a silver washing machine that looks like it could beam me into space. Yula pulls out the chairs from the kitchen table and invites us all to sit down. The house is cool and pleasant to be in, and so, so clean. There isn't a speck of dust on anything. A huge ceiling fan whirs above our heads. I look at Miranda, who is slightly wide-eyed. None of us has ever been in a house as sophisticated as this before. Miranda and I sit on one side, Yula and Lydia-Rose on the other, facing the windows. Quinn and Vaughn sit at either end. Winkie, as usual, sits on my feet. There is a huge peace lily on the table, and we all struggle for a minute, trying to figure out where to place ourselves so that we can see one another over the bright green leaves. Finally, Yula lets out a little laugh and moves it to the counter behind her.

"How did you find us?" Quinn says suddenly, and I pause a moment, wondering how much to say.

"Harrison."

"I wasn't the biggest fan of your father," Quinn says, and Yula grips his arm with a startling ferocity.

"For God sakes." She looks at me and Miranda apologetically, pleadingly. "He's been drinking," she says. "He's sick."

I look at his body and I look at his hands. He is an old, angry, dangerous thing, and I put my hand on his. "It's okay. It doesn't matter to me if you liked him or not."

Quinn takes my hand and studies my fingers, measures the thickness of my wrists. "Your arms look a little like your mother's," he says.

"I know that."

"You're short but long limbed," he says. He swirls his Scotch around and takes a long drink.

"It's beautiful here," says Vaughn. "I forgot how beautiful. I used to live around here."

"We don't forget. We've never been away." Quinn lets my hand go and points at Yula's face with his pinky finger. "She's looked after me all these years. Have you seen my drawings of her? I used to draw all of us, all of us with thought-bubbles coming out of our heads, thinking silly things." He points to the walls. There are drawings tacked up everywhere; I don't know why I didn't notice them before. The walls are covered in pen-and-ink. My favourite one is of a pointy-toed dress shoe, the laces spilling out over the sides. I look for a drawing of a person, but they're all just things: shoes, a saltshaker, a pitcher of milk, a baseball, a peacock feather, a lawn chair, a rake.

Quinn looks at me with his wild grey eyes. He looks tired. "You've got bright eyes like your mother."

"Like yours, too."

Yula gets up from the table and slings a dishtowel over her shoulder. "Will you stay awhile?" she says. "I'd like to make you something to eat." She says she's been to the farmers' market recently and has two fresh chickens, which she'll roast with carrots, red potatoes, fennel, and parsnips. She'll even make me a birthday cake—yellow cake with chocolate frosting.

Vaughn looks at me, and Miranda reaches over and squeezes my hand. Do I want to do this? I do. I do.

But it's early still, and Yula puts the kettle on, takes down some mugs, roots around until she finds some tea. The kitchen is warm from the sun streaming through the windows. Lydia-Rose squints in the sunlight. Yula has taken off her blue cardigan and wears a ribbed grey undershirt, her arms ropey and muscular. I hope I'll have muscles in my arms someday.

None of us has any idea what to say to each other.

After the kettle boils and the tea has steeped, Yula puts a mug down in front of Miranda. She bends close to her and says, "Thank you for bringing her to me."

We do, though—we find something to say. Quinn tells us the history of the property—it was Jo's parents' originally, passed down to her, inherited by Quinn when she died. Eventually it will be Yula's. The strangeness of the house is Quinn's. He put in the wooden beams, took out the exterior walls and replaced them with the huge floor-to-ceiling windows. We admire his handiwork, and then he and Vaughn disappear outside for a while to look at the exterior. Both have the good sense to leave me with Yula and my family.

Once they're gone we reposition ourselves: Yula sits beside me, Miranda and Lydia-Rose across from us. We drink hot cups of bush tea with honey, and Yula puts out a plate of shortbread cookies. I take a bite of one and then give the rest to Winkie.

Miranda spends a long time telling Yula about me. She can tell I'm too nervous and in shock to speak clearly about myself. She tells her about the homes I lived in before she adopted me—stopping a minute when she gets to the part about Julian to check in with me that it's okay to go on.

"You can tell her," I say.

Yula's face pales and she bites her cheek while Miranda speaks. There is a horrible moment when Yula starts apologizing and can't stop and just looks at me and says I'm sorry I'm sorry I'm sorry over and over again. But we get past it, and she recovers, and Miranda tells her about our first few years together, how I wouldn't sleep, how she'd find me at all hours, wandering the house. Lydia-Rose talks for a time about what it was like at first to share her mom. It's amazing to me that we can speak so frankly. None of these things has ever been said. But once they are, I realize I'm not holding on to any pain from the past anymore. I can hear Lydia-Rose talk about her initial jealousy and all I feel is grateful that I have a sister, no matter what it took to get us to this point.

"We had three cats, too," Lydia-Rose says, and we tell my mother about Scratchie, Flipper, and Midnight, about burying them in the park. I have never developed the photographs from the day we took them to the vet's. I tell Yula that I will now. I'll develop them and bring them to her. I'll show her our wonderful cats.

Miranda is honest about how I do in school—not well. She says I'm a drifter. And I'm still not a good sleeper, and I still fidget. I talk a lot sometimes or sometimes I say nothing at all. She says I have trouble staying in the same place or doing the same thing for very long. This is why, she thinks, my attendance is so bad. She says the school has called her countless times. I hang around downtown too much. I don't have any close friends. But I know everybody. And everybody knows me and my hair.

"I like my life," I say, a little defensively, while Miranda narrates. "It's been a good life. I like my life!"

She tells Yula that I never said anything, not even once, about wanting to find my birth parents, even when she asked. She says I keep secrets, but she's realized over the years that it's a way of protecting myself from being hurt, that it's not malicious, that I carry the special things in my heart, wrap them up deep inside so they're never discovered, never taken. Physically, am I healthy? Yes. My arm hurts at night from Julian breaking it when I was a little kid. Tendonitis. Miranda says I've never said anything about the pain, but she sees me worrying my wrist at the dinner table, rubbing it when it rains. The blindness seems not to be a problem at all. It was at first; I walked into everything. Miranda was so scared they'd take me away from her because of all the bruises on my arms and shins. But now I seem to navigate the world just fine. She thinks I can probably even get my driver's licence, though I have no interest in it. I'm a bus person through and through. I haven't menstruated yet. She's worried about that. She's not sure if it means anything. She tells Yula that she thinks I'm a special person, put on the earth for a reason. She says she's never met anyone like me. She says she feels honoured that she was given the opportunity to shepherd me through my life. I suppose it isn't surprising that she thinks about me so much and with such depth and sensitivity, but it startles me all the same to hear it. I blush. I feel my legs start to kick together, that old familiar pattern of nervousness. Winkie unearths herself and begs to be lifted onto my lap, and we pause a minute to pat her, to give her all our attention.

"You and your daughter have such beautiful skin," Yula says to Miranda. "Did you grow up here?"

"On the mainland."

I look at Miranda. I barely know anything about her life before I came into it.

And then it's Yula's turn to speak.

"Just sit with me a while," she says to me, Miranda, and Lydia-Rose. "I'll tell you everything."

26

It is my seventeenth birthday, and in some ways, this is where the story—at least this part of it—ends. Yula says we should spend the afternoon exploring the property while she cooks. If we want to wander over to Joel and Edwin's, she'll call ahead so they don't shoot. She laughs when she says this, but I can tell she's at least partly serious. She says it's really something to see all the rusted-out cars, tractors, bicycle parts, tires, old porcelain sinks, toilets, and stained-glass windows they've collected over the years. It's like an outdoor junk museum.

Winkie will likely have a few ticks on her by the time we return; Yula says she'll help me comb over her body, and if we find any, we'll burn them off with a match. She assures me that Winkie won't mind this, that it's a painless experience. The tick will retreat when it feels the match on its backside, and we'll pull it out with a pair of tweezers, flush it down the drain.

If we cross the street, we can visit a rescue farm. There are eight horses there right now, Yula says, two llamas, three goats, three pigs, and a bunch of chickens. Donkeys, too. No one will mind if we wander over and pet the animals.

Beyond that, the forest is always worth exploring. Some of the trees are over six hundred years old. Douglas fir, Western red cedar, hemlock. Bigleaf maples, arbutus, black cottonwood. Yula tells us all their names, points out the window. "Stand next to one of them and look up the trunk," she says. "But make sure someone is standing behind you. You'll fall over, you'll just tumble back and fall."

This is a rainforest. This is sacred land. "Go out into the woods," Yula says.

We leave her in the kitchen and say goodbye to Quinn, half-drunk, slumped on the porch in a rocking chair. No one is wearing proper shoes for a hike, and we gingerly make our way through the ferns and fallen needles and over the felled trees. Vaughn holds Winkie because my arms are tired. She takes in all the smells around her, her head over his shoulder, nose twitching. It's so much colder, damper, in the shade of the forest. Something I managed to pick up in school: the human eye is more sensitive to green than to any other colour. We see almost every shade of it.

We walk single-file. There is only a narrow, tamped-down path; the rest of the forest is thick with trees, and we would be easily separated. Vaughn makes a little trumpeting sound, and we trumpet back. This is what we'll do if we get lost: we'll trumpet at one another until we're all found.

He leads us, Miranda next in line, the back of her denim shirt already wet with sweat. Lydia-Rose walks behind me, the slowest of us all in her heeled gladiator sandals. She has to stop and readjust the straps because the heat makes her feet swell. My jeans are too long and slip under my shoes and I have to keep yanking them up. But we press on anyway, peculiar party that we are, and every once in a while Vaughn reminds us to stop and look around. The path is so gnarly with roots that I realize this whole time I've only been looking down. Lydia-Rose steadies herself against me and looks up the trunk of a Douglas fir. Yula was right. She stumbles into me, then doubles over, suddenly dizzy. We all do this; we all get vertigo.

The forest floor crunches under our feet and the trees are loud with birds. There are banana slugs on the path, and Vaughn dares us to lick the underside of one. He says it will make our tongues go numb, but we have no interest.

Miranda and Vaughn walk ahead of us for a while, comparing their lives. They seem relaxed around each other, and I'm relieved. Then the forest thins out a bit and we find ourselves in a sea of rusty automobiles, tall grass poking out the windows, tires sunk into the earth. Miranda and Lydia-Rose refuse to walk through it for fear of getting tetanus.

"You two go ahead," Miranda calls out. "Meet us across the street. We're going to go see the animals."

We wave to them, and Vaughn makes the trumpet sound. We stop and admire an old tractor, so old it looks like part of the forest—its rusty sides are the colour of cedar. Farther along is a drop tank from World War II. It's been here so long it doesn't smell of fuel. I put my hand on it, gingerly, as if it might explode.

A helicopter flies overhead, so loud I hold my ears. It looks like a giant silver dragonfly. There are all kinds of dangerous and sharp-looking things on the ground: anchors, chains, that sort of thing. The drop tank has rusted, but it still shines in the light. It looks like a big bullet and it's warm from the sun. Winkie runs up to it and nudges it with her snout. Some water trickles out, and she furtively laps it up and then bucks a few times.

Another helicopter appears, its shadow hovering over me, Vaughn, and Winkie. It's a relief from the white of the sun, and I wish it would stay. I look up. I count to three and hold my breath. Winkie cowers. The sound of the rotors is so loud it feels like my ears might melt. And then, just like that, it's gone.

A trailer is up ahead and we figure this is where Joel and Edwin live.

"You want to see if they're home?" says Vaughn. I shrug. I'm not sure that I want to meet these guys. Vaughn taps on the door, and we wait but nothing happens, no one comes. He tries again, presses his ear against the door, but there is no sound, save for a squirrel chittering at us in a nearby tree.

"All right," Vaughn says. "Let's go see those animals."

We push through the junkyard, past the trailer, until we reach a narrow street, the little farm across from us.

"You okay?" Vaughn says.

"I think so. I like it out here."

I can see Lydia-Rose and Miranda in front of a grey

barn, talking to a woman who is feeding a donkey. There are sheep here, too. They look alarmed. They look as though they haven't seen a person in years.

"I mean, is your mind okay." He puts his hands on his hips and stares at me.

I stare back. "Did you recognize her? Could you tell it was her?"

Vaughn looks at his cowboy boots, then back at me. He takes a while to respond. "I can't really. No. I mean, I can tell she's your mom. But if I saw her on the street, I'm not sure. I'm not sure anything would happen in my head."

"She seems kind of stunned. Shell-shocked or something."

"Yeah. Look, you call the shots here. We can stay for dinner or not. This is all completely up to you."

"Okay," I say. "I think I'd like to stay."

We cross the street, and Lydia-Rose bugs out her eyes when she sees me.

"This donkey is over forty years old," she says. His fur is as thick and dense as a Brillo pad. "He likes it if you scratch the insides of his ears."

So I do. I rub the donkey's ears and, sure enough, he puts his head down, like Winkie does when she's trying to get the most out of something. The ground is muddy and my Vans are soaked through, the bottoms of my jeans wet. Lydia-Rose's feet are black, and Miranda's espadrilles are mud-caked, probably ruined. We're all sweaty and shiny-faced, except for Vaughn, who breathes in deeply and evenly, oblivious to the heat. Three horses are nuzzling the ground in a paddock behind the barn, eating grass. I look around for the llamas but don't see them. Winkie sniffs at the donkey, and the two animals consider each other, each a little astounded.

Back at the big house, Quinn is drunk. Yula has coaxed him into his bed, tucked him under the sheets. He drifts in and out of sleep, his fingers clawing the air periodically, like an overturned bug.

"Hi, Papa," Yula says and drums her fingers on the edge of the bed, *People* magazine wedged in the space between the mattress and bed frame. The smell of Vicks VapoRub and yellow spit-up fills the room like sour milk and mint.

"Yula." Quinn looks at her with damp eyes. "What time is it?"

"About four-thirty."

"Hm?"

"Four-thirty. Time to put in the chicken." She takes his hand and massages the loose brown skin of his bad arm, works up the forearm, draws little circles on his shoulder with her fingertips. His skin looks like scales. She pick up a black comb and rakes a few strands of his long white hair, scuffs at the dandruff on his scalp, and holds her hand against his forehead to keep the flakes out of his eyes. His skin is so dry it crisps.

She folds down the sheet, squeezes a washcloth into a bowl of ice water by his bed, and presses the cold fabric to his skin.

Her father lies there, parched and shrunken, half rotten apple, half man. Paper thin in the narrow green bed. He falls asleep, finally, and his bad arm sinks heavy in Yula's hand.

Every time he falls asleep, she places her hand on the back of his head, hoping to finally feel his spirit lift out and away. She imagines the weight of being an orphan— suddenly, unexpectedly. She looks around the room. Someday she wants to be the only one here.

She notices me then, watching them both in the doorway.

"He's getting so old," she says.

I walk toward her. I'm hot from being outside. Vaughn, Lydia-Rose, and Miranda are still at the rescue farm, patting the horses. My clothes smell of the earth, my shoes rimmed in mud. I look down, suddenly aware that I'm wearing them still, that I've tracked mud into this perfect, spotless house.

But Yula is looking at her father. "We deserve each other, he and I." She tucks his arm under the sheets, smoothes them over his chest. "*Where you go, I will go*. Ruth 1:16."

I wrinkle my nose. It hadn't occurred to me that my mother might be religious. I feel a kind of sliminess in my stomach, a cold shiver. Suddenly, more than anything, I just want to go home. I want it to be nighttime, and I want to be in Vaughn's bright blue rental car, driving through the blackness, past the forest and the beasts and back into the city, with the hobos and the villains and all the weird people of the night.

Instead, we walk into the kitchen together, her arm lightly on my back. I feel a little bolt of electricity run down my spine when she touches me. I've noticed this before; some people's touch is charged. Others—they make no impact.

The kitchen smells delicious and sweet, the cake baking in the oven, a bowl of freshly whipped chocolate icing on the counter, covered with Saran Wrap. She tests the cake with a toothpick, puts it back in for a few minutes. It is round and golden, and I can't wait to eat a gigantic piece.

She tells me she has wondered about my father. He moved to Montreal years ago, she says—and I startle, wondering whether I should tell her that he isn't in Montreal, that he has two sons, a wife, a home somewhere in Ontario. I decide not to. She says when she closes her eyes she can see him driving an old car down the cobblestone streets, in the video store, pausing for the doors of the city bus, practising French with a store clerk. "*Je pense que ce lait est aigre, monsieur,*" he says, handing back the big jug with distaste. In her mind, my father, or an actor hired to play him expertly, pays for a new jug with a crisp five-dollar bill, his big square hands unmistakable as he fumbles with his wallet in the pocket of his coat.

She looks at me, staring at her. "You have your father's hair. He had curls just like this, like—"

"A tumbleweed. I know, I've heard it all my life."

Yula clicks her tongue. "It's not that we didn't want you." She tilts her head and looks at me. "Your father was a troubled man," she says, and we don't speak of him further.

I sit at the kitchen table and watch her cook. She takes two whole chickens out of the fridge, washes them, fills their cold cavities with water and dumps it out, and pats them dry with paper towels. She places them gently, side by side, in a roasting pan, heats up a cup of butter in the microwave and tips it over the skin, crushes rock salt between her fingers and stuffs the cavities with slices of lemon and sprigs of thyme. Every time her hand moves from salt to chicken to lemon to thyme, she wipes it with a paper towel. No contamination. I watch her quarter the potatoes, halve the parsnips and carrots, slice the fennel. She slices it all slowly and deliberately, as if it's important to her that the pieces look just right. She pours sunflower oil over all of it, then sprinkles more rock salt. She goes outside and emerges moments later with a bunch of rosemary in her hand. She moves with the efficiency of someone who has cooked all her life, but her hands are trembling and she keeps pausing, rearranging things in the roasting pan, adding a little more salt, a squeeze of lemon. She looks at me to see if I'm watching her.

"Lydia-Rose is an artist," I tell Yula and point at Quinn's drawings on the wall.

"He just draws whatever's lying around," Yula says.

I move to the window and look outside. It's a desolate place out here. Yula's cottage stands alone. Stumps and roots poke out from the long grass, which sways gently in the warm wind. I'm not afraid exactly, but I do find it kind of creepy.

"What happened to Luella?" I ask her. "Are you still in touch?"

Yula stands beside me at the window. "We were for a while. She's fine. She got married."

"Oh." I look at her, unsure of what to say next or how far to go.

"I'm so sorry," she says. Her eyes are angry, as though

she's simultaneously furious at herself and at me for suddenly being here, dredging up all the demons of the past. I see what a broken, fragile person she is. I see she isn't fit to be anybody's mom, despite what Harrison told me about her limitless capacity for love. But being loved so desperately isn't good for a person either, and it's Miranda's evenness that I crave, especially in this moment, when my mother is looking to me for comfort, and I need it to be the other way around.

"It's okay," I tell her. I need her to stop looking at me with those dead grey eyes.

"It's okay," I tell her again. There are swallows in the trees, so many swallows suddenly, and we watch them move in a great black swarm.

I try to imagine having grown up in the little moss-covered cottage across from us, in this field, in this isolated place halfway up a mountain. I try to imagine Yula as my mother, calling her Mom, my cheek against her bony little shoulder, walking hand in hand through the grass.

"I know it looks deserted, but there are a lot of us living out here," Yula says. "Might be a hundred or more."

What has my mother been up to all this time? I think of Harrison's letter, how he has moved on, begun a new life. Thousands of miles away. A wife. Children. My mother has not let herself experience a single moment of happiness since Eugene's death. She walked through the doors of the hospital after she was discharged, and the only person waiting for her was Quinn. *We deserve each other, he and I.*

I think hard and fast about what my life would have been like out here. What I would say, what she would say. I can't picture any of it. I can't imagine having lived anywhere but with Miranda, having had anyone else's life but my own.

"Sometimes I see a little smoke beyond those trees over there," Yula says and points to the edge of the forest. "There's a little cabin, like mine."

"Who lives there?"

"A woman and her children. She has two of them, a boy and a girl."

"Oh."

"I run into them sometimes when I'm out walking. The little boy loves marshmallows more than anything in the world. Do you like marshmallows?"

"I don't know. I guess they're all right."

"Huh. Yes, I'm never sure whether the little girl likes them or not." She laughs. Her eyes close, and I watch her, lost somewhere in the shadows of her mind. She pinches a crease in her loose jeans, by her hipbone, worrying the fabric between her forefinger and thumb. "Sometimes I stand by the window all day," she says, "hoping the boy will come and visit me."

When the timer goes off, Yula opens the oven door and the room fills with steam and the smell of chicken and thyme. The cake is iced and waiting to be eaten on the counter, a pack of birthday candles by its side. She puts on two big red oven mitts and takes the chicken out carefully, the muscles of her arms flexing as she sets it on top of the stove.

Vaughn, Miranda, Lydia-Rose, and I are seated at the

table, paper napkins in our laps. We have each spent a long time washing up, all the way to our elbows, and I've combed over Winkie's skin for ticks, which, thankfully, haven't latched onto her. All of us are in our stocking feet, our muddy shoes in a row outside. Vaughn keeps one foot over the other to hide a hole in the toe of his sock.

Winkie is served first and eats little bits of chicken out of a bowl, her tail wagging. Quinn emerges from the bedroom, sobered up from sleep, and takes his seat, a little dopey-eyed. Yula takes her time arranging the chickens and roasted vegetables on a large bright blue platter. "Just a second, just another second," she says. She brings the platter to the table and it is beautiful, the chickens in the middle surrounded by carrots, little browned wedges of red potato, and thin slices of fennel. She apologizes that she has nothing for a salad, but she's made green peas and puts those on the table, too, in a big glass bowl, steam rising into the air, a pat of butter melting in the centre. She trembles a bit, standing there watching us, and Quinn finally tells her to please sit down.

We don't talk. We chow down. We eat. We eat like we've never eaten before, like we haven't eaten in years. When our plates are empty, we fill them again. Yula cuts us each thick slices of sourdough bread, and we drag them through the chicken grease, mopping up the oil and the lemon and the salt.

She smiles at me while she eats, the corners of her mouth shiny. Her moon-grey eyes sparkle, and the story of the children in the forest rings in my ears.

We finish the loaf of bread and Yula slices the cake,

setting huge pieces in front of us on delicate blue-and-white plates. Each piece is decorated with a single bright red raspberry and fresh mint leaf, and mine has a pink-and-blue-striped birthday candle in the centre. The cake is warm and golden-white and tastes faintly of almonds. The chocolate icing stands up in soft little peaks and melts on my tongue when I taste it. We finish the cake and I trace my fingers along the plate, through the last bits of icing.

I'll visit my mother once a month for the next six months, take the bus all the way out here on a Saturday afternoon, or meet her every once in a while for breakfast in town. We'll get to know each other bit by bit, and each time we meet she'll tell me a little more about the circumstances of her life, and on and on we'll continue to probe, in an effort, I suppose, to reach the end of each other. Yet if we did—if we knew everything there was to know—we would become the most predictable, boring people in the world. If I have learned anything, it's that mystery is inherent to being interesting, especially when it comes to whom we decide to love. And so one day I'll call and say I can't make it this time, and for the next few years it will continue this way: some visits kept, others not.

After we exchange a few more letters, my father will take a road trip out to see me, unannounced, and we'll meet for lunch in a noisy café. He will be so soft-spoken that I'll struggle to hear what he is saying. He will tell me how broke he is, that his bad habits have taken hold of him again. When we part, he will hand me an envelope with a couple of twenty-dollar bills, and I will decide it is best to lose touch, to let him slip away. Miranda and Lydia-Rose will resume their rightful places in my heart, and Winkie and I will dream of owning a little apartment by the ocean one day.

When Quinn dies, Yula will decide to sell the land and move away—and on that day, the life she was meant to have will finally begin. Gradually, she and I will become strangers again, the spaces between our visits farther and farther apart. Because once the mystery is gone, she's just another person staring back at you from across the dinner table—someone who left you out in the cold, on a bare stretch of concrete one morning at five-fifteen. What do you say to a person like that? What do you say to them over the years? Knowing the story doesn't make it any better. We get what we're given, nothing more, nothing less. In the end, I do not get to have Yula as a mom.

There is no sound here except the calls of birds. The sun is setting, and the room fills with a deep orange light. Miranda rests her hand on her stomach and we all sit back, plates pushed toward the centre of the table. We let the sun go down and the room grow dark. And just when we can hardly see anymore, Vaughn plucks the wishbone from what's left of the chicken and holds it out for me to reach. It's the one thing in life he can't predict: who will get the lucky break.

Acknowledgments

For their generous support, thank you to the Canada Council for the Arts, Colgate University, Hawthornden Castle, the Iowa Writers' Workshop, the John C. Schupes Fellowship, the English department at the University of Cincinnati, and the remarkable people behind these institutions—Peter Balakian, Jennifer Brice, Ethan Canin, Lan Samantha Chang, Michael Griffith, Drue Heinz, Patrick O'Keeffe, and Jane Pinchin.

Thank you to my formidable agent, Claudia Ballard, and magnificent editors, Millicent Bennett, Sarah Savitt, and Nicole Winstanley. Thanks, too, to Karen Alliston, Mary Ann Blair, Meg Cassidy, Kathryn Higuchi, Beth Lockley, Chloe Perkins, and to everyone at Penguin Canada, Simon & Schuster, and Faber.

For helping me with my research, thanks to Carol Alexander, Lisa Cowan, Karen Dean, Roger Denley, Peter Hancock, Angela Hatch, Kate Schenck, and the book Nobody's Child by Kate Adie.

A special thank-you to Lorna Jackson, without whom none of this would have happened.

Lastly, love and gratitude to my mother, Jeanne Shoemaker, and to my family and friends, Shane Boudreaux, Alexis Celona, John Celona, John Connor, Jason England, Dama Hanks, Brian Hendricks, Tania Hershman, Sara Peters, Kate Soles, Mark Stern, Sarah Taggart, Brian Trapp, and Deborah Willis. In big ways and small ways, each of you helped me to write this book.